Child Finder

Special Limited Edition

First Edition

TotalRecall Publication, Inc.

Houston
London
Toronto

Child

Finder

Mike Angley

TotalRecallPress.com

1103 Middlecreek Friendswood, Texas 77546 281-992-3131 281-482-5390 Fax
6 Precedent Drive Rooksley, Milton Keynes MK13 8PR, UK
1385 Woodroffe Av Ottawa, ON K2G 1V8

Copyright © 2009 by Mike Angley

Hard Cover		Paper Back	
ISBN:	978-1-59095-827-8	ISBN:	978-1-59095-825-4
UPC	6-43977-87825-0	UPC	6-43977-87825-0
eBook: Adobe Acrobat		Audio Book	
ISBN	978-1-59095-826-1	ISBN	978-1-59095-828-5
UPC	6-43977-68268-0	UPC	6-43977-68268-0

The sponsoring editor is Bruce Moran and production supervisor is Corby R. Tate.
Book editor Barbara Weingartner
Jacket Design by Bruce Moran
Photo Illustration by Jaquelynn Tramble

This is a work of fiction. The characters, events, views, and subject matter of this book are either the author's imagination or are used fictitiously. Any similarity or resemblance to any real people, real situations or actual events is purely coincidental and not intended to portray any person, place, or event in a false, disparaging or negative light.

Printed in the United States of America with
simultaneously printings in Canada, and England.

1 2 3 4 5 6 7 8 9 10

First Edition

This book is dedicated to my father, William Michael Angley I.

Dad, no matter how often life threw you its worst, you always fired back with your best. Thank you for teaching me love of God, love of life, and love of family.

"I know God will not give me anything I can't handle.
I just wish that He didn't trust me so much."

Mother Teresa

The Author

Colonel Michael "Mike" Angley retired from the United States Air Force in September 2007 following a rewarding 25 year career as a Special Agent with the Air Force Office of Special Investigations (OSI). He held thirteen different assignments throughout the world, among which were five tours as a Commander of various units, to include two Air Force OSI Squadrons and a Region, the equivalent of a Wing.

Mike is a seasoned criminal investigator and a counterintelligence and counterterrorism specialist. Following the 1996 Khobar Towers terrorist attack in Saudi Arabia, he was dispatched to command all OSI units throughout the Middle East, with responsibility for 23 countries. During his tenure, he and his teams effectively neutralized numerous terrorist threats to U.S. forces in the region, to include an imminent threat to senior Department of Defense officials. Earlier in his career, while commanding an OSI unit in northern Japan, Mike conducted an operation that effectively blocked a KGB agent's efforts to steal critical U.S. technology, and thereby stymied Soviet military advances for years. In 1999 he was Chief of Counterintelligence within the Directorate of Intelligence, U.S. Strategic Command. His office competed for the prestigious Killian Award, a White House level honor that annually recognizes the very best intelligence unit in the entire U.S. government. His unit came in as first runner-up for this significant honor.

Mike has an M.A. in National Security Affairs from the U.S. Naval Postgraduate School, Monterey, CA, and a B.A. (summa cum laude) in Criminal Justice and Psychology from King's College, Wilkes-Barre, PA. He is a former National Defense Fellow and Adjunct Professor of International Relations at Florida International University, Miami, FL, and is an Honor Graduate of the Defense Language Institute's Korean language program.

Mike and Evelyn, his wife of 23 years, make their home in Colorado Springs, CO. They have three children, and they recently adopted a beagle puppy named Brynn.

Acknowledgments

There are so many people to whom I am grateful for making this dream a reality. My wonderful wife, Evelyn, thanks for not just being by my side, but for serving as my biggest cheerleader, as well. To our children, Kiernan Matthew, Kyle Patrick, and Meghan Nichole Marguerite...thanks for putting up with all those moves around the world, dad's crazy job, and for encouraging me in my writing project.

I want to thank my critique partner and editor, Barbara Weingartner. It seems like we talked about my writing project many years ago, and thanks to your sharp eyes and keen insight, you helped make this a reality.

Finally, I wish to thank Jaquelynn Tramble for designing the cover art for Child Finder...you keenly put into art form what I strived to capture in words.

Forward

The Child Finder suspense novel trilogy follows the paranormal adventures of Air Force Special Agent Patrick O'Donnell. After discovering he has a unique psychic gift the government eagerly exploits his abilities. He finds himself caught up in a TOP SECRET Special Access Program designed to rescue abducted children.

But such noble pursuits come at great cost! He must battle dark, murderous forces within his own trusted inner circle, as well as unimaginable evil that threatens his family. Before his journey ends Agent O'Donnell will learn explosive government information that will rock his understanding of life, the universe, and his own faith.

Perhaps some secrets are best kept hidden . . .

~ 1 ~

Patrick O'Donnell was transfixed. Glued in place. Even the ferocious sting of thorny briar thicket against his bare arms failed to stir him. He glanced down at his left forearm. Dried blood formed strange black lines and dots, the thorns having given him an unwelcome greeting. He was in his bed clothes, long blue sleep pants moist at the ankles with scattered shreds of leaves and pine needles clinging to the bottom edges. His white undershirt was flecked with dirt. Confused and shivering, he wondered if he had sleepwalked to this place.

The cold, damp, and dark woods surrounded and enveloped him in a misty moist blanket of autumn air. Strange sounds and scents filled the night. Branches and brush crackled as unseen nocturnal creatures foraged about. All around him were towering pines mixed with oak, ash, hickory, and poplar. Their fall leaves, bright and colorful by day, were now white and bluish in the moon's glow.

Pat was crouched down, the strain from this position making his feet and ankles numb. He had no idea how long he had been there, but his fingers, arms, and feet were icy stiff from the cold air. He stared through the brush and exhaled a dense frosty mist that obscured his vision. He paused a moment, and held his breath long enough to see through to a small clearing about twenty yards in front of him. Although he had no idea how he had come to be in this place, or even *where* this place was, he knew he had to stay perfectly still. And wait. Then, as if on some strange cue, the low clouds overhead parted, and a bright moon cast an eerie beam of light down through the mist. The moonbeam traced across the trees and brush and speeded toward the clearing Pat strained to see.

A spotlight from heaven, he thought. He did not want to look but was compelled to watch as if some force well beyond his understanding was controlling him. The scene was both familiar and strange. Pat had seen it many times before, yet never before. It was simultaneously distant and near. Real and surreal.

The spotlight from heaven moved about as if searching purposefully for something. Then it appeared. At the same moment as a screeching owl swooped down past him from behind, crying loudly with its claws outstretched, Pat saw it. The moonbeam centered ever so perfectly on the site in the clearing. The owl's trajectory helped aim his gaze as if intentionally leading him to the point where the moonbeam seemed to stop. There was the boy. He was lying in the small clearing, face down, cold, stiff from rigor long since settled in. Somehow Pat already knew he was dead. In some way he knew the boy had been dead for several days. Without moving, his gaze zoomed in on the corpse like a telephoto lens.

He was about seven years old. His red pajama top was torn open, barely covering his back. Nearby was a single light blue colored slipper with a Pokémon logo. A bright, cheerful looking Pikachu character was on top, but the creature's normal yellow countenance was mangled with a dark stain. The contrast in images was haunting, sickening.

"Blood," Pat whispered softly, as if he feared whoever perpetrated this horrific crime might be nearby.

But somehow in his heart Pat knew he was alone in the woods that night. Alone with the body of this lost soul. The boy had been beaten and strangled. He could see ligature marks on the side of his neck that he knew wrapped around to the front of his throat. The markings were neat and clean, and cut deeply into the boy's neck. He agonized over it all...no burial, no closure for his parents who surely grieved over his disappearance. He clumsily made the sign of the cross, his fingers shaking from the cold. In his mind he prayed a Hail Mary for the boy, his brain even stuttering out the words as he shivered in place.

Pat lifted his arms as if trying to fly, wanting somehow in this bizarre scene to be released from earth, to take the boy to heaven and deliver him. Personally. To God. The sensation at first was almost imperceptible, but then he began to feel it build. First in his head, and then his shoulders. Then his whole body moved up, slowly at first, as if being lifted by an invisible force. Up, up and above the skyscraping pines, safely away from the briar patch that had been tearing his skin. The moonbeam split into two and provided coverage of both Pat as he ascended and the boy who remained on the ground. He rose to a point above the clearing directly over the child. The moonbeams warmed and thawed him, providing a peaceful state of grace and giving him the confidence he needed to complete this task. He felt an incredible sense of joy in his heart as he hovered in the forest; his eyes began to well with tears as the excitement grew within him.

Would this time be the right time? The moment I've longed for night after night?

He clasped his hands together as if in prayer and moved his gaze from the boy to the heavens. In a flash, and at the moment in his mind when he believed he was going to lift the boy up to God, Pat sat up in his bed gasping for air.

"Honey! Honey what is it?" Sara cried as she shook Pat to wake him from his nightmare.

"I'm okay, Baby," he responded, regaining his composure, shaking his head to remove the image of the boy that still lingered.

"It was another dream about the little boy, wasn't it?" she asked rhetorically, propping herself up on her right elbow and squinting at him sideways.

"Yeah. God, I wish they would stop! These dreams have been torturing me all week. I wish I knew why I've been having them over and over."

"You need to see someone, Pat. You've been under a lot of stress at work, and I think you need to see a, well, you know..."

"A shrink?" he asked sarcastically, cutting her off.

"No!" Sara stammered, brushing her hair from her face. "Not necessarily a psychiatrist--maybe just one of the mental health counselors at the Pentagon, or maybe a priest."

"Sara, we've been over this before. I don't want to jeopardize my security clearance. If I see someone from mental health the Air Force will pull my clearances." Pat knew he had genuine reason to worry. As an Air Force Special Agent with a TOP SECRET clearance, seeing a mental health professional could cost him his badge, his gun, his career!

"Look, Pat--you've told me that you can talk with a priest and it's protected somehow--what did you call it?" Sara asked as she took his left hand in both of hers, snuggling up next to him in the cool silk sheets. Her hands were warm and soft and made him relax somewhat.

"Privileged communication," he answered, sounding slightly more resigned. He knew she was right. In the military whatever he told a doctor was a matter of official record. But what he told his priest was forever protected.

"Okay, Sorcha, I'll talk with Father Reynolds this week."

He sometimes affectionately called her Sorcha, an archaic Gaelic variant of her name. She was as Irish and Catholic as Pat with long waves of red hair, bright, clear green eyes, and no freckles...not a single one.

"Why don't you see Father Reynolds today? Take a day off from work and call him," Sara implored. "Colonel Lyons will give you the day off. He's such a good boss, and you know he won't even ask you why you need the time off," she continued, squeezing his hand even tighter.

"I don't know Sara, I took a day off last week because Sean got hurt at school, and I had to go and take him to the clinic."

She stared at him for a moment. "Pat. Look. You're just making excuses. Call the office and leave a message for Colonel Lyons. Say you are not feeling well today."

"All right, Sorcha, I will," he said, giving in to her insistence.

He also knew it was the right thing to do. He had to talk with someone after a week of these haunting dreams. He pulled Sara close to him, embraced her, and squeezed her tight for a moment. Then he kissed her softly on the lips.

"You know, I love you more than life, and I thank God every day for you and the two cherubs He has given us."

She nuzzled in close to him, her head on his chest. "And speaking of angels, angel number one is right over there," she whispered out a smile, pointing toward the bedroom door.

Pat turned to look, and sure enough, Sean was standing there in his bright green pajamas clutching a stuffed Superman action figure, his "absolute favorite," as he was fond of saying.

"What's going on, Buddy?" he greeted Sean who rubbed his sleepy blue eyes, as bright blue as his dad's, his light brown hair all in a mop, mussed up. "Get over here!" Pat insisted with a broad smile, beckoning him with both hands.

That was the signal Sean was waiting for. The skinny lad instantly jumped onto the bed's downy soft quilt and gave his mom and dad big hugs, giggling incessantly.

"Come on Sean," Pat said as he left the bed and stepped onto the cool oak hardwood floor. He picked him up over his head. "Let's let Mom get some rest, and you can help me find out what's going on in the world."

"Okay, Dad! I'll go get the newspaper."

Sean's little feet began to tread air as his six-foot-one-inch father started to lower him to the floor. As soon as he had some traction, he bolted and headed for the front door, never once letting go of Superman. When Pat entered the kitchen, the small Tiffany glass hanging light over the eat-in table was on brightly, and Sean was there holding the Washington Observer in his hands. Pat took it from him with a big grin.

"Why don't you go to the family room and watch some cartoons before Mom gets up."

"All right, Dad, I will. Love you," Sean blurted out, and then he was gone in an instant.

Pat picked up the paper, glancing at the date--October 4th 2001--as he unfolded it on the table and looked at the headline, *President's War on Terror Begins!* He skimmed the top story. It was about events the previous month when radical Islamic terrorists hijacked a handful of commercial aircraft in the United States and crashed them into New York City's World Trade Center Twin Towers as well as the Pentagon where Pat worked.   Because of his job, he already knew about the ramp-up in military operations in the area. Reconnaissance flights were intense, satellites repositioned, forward operating bases hastily prepared. There was no real secret to the buildup. The Intelligence Community wanted the bad guys to know America was coming. The Pentagon detected their reaction to the escalation, measured their likely response, and pinpointed target sets accordingly.   The Washington Observer article outlined a series of terrorist captures throughout Afghanistan. But the man most wanted by the United States, Usama bin Laden, the mastermind of the terror attacks, was still at large.

"Your day is coming you fookin' bastard!" Pat said aloud with an Irish brogue, with both anger and a hint of delight in his voice.

After all, this was his business, his world. As a Special Agent with the Air Force Office of Special Investigations, the OSI as it was known, and one who specialized in counterintelligence and counterterrorism, he had spent his career hunting down and capturing spies and terrorists. He was in the thick of it all at the Pentagon, though he longed for the chance to get back in the field and do operational work. That was another reason he hated missing a day of work. He called his office and left a voice message.

"Boss, this is Pat. I don't think I can come in today. My stomach is really sick, and I think I just need to lie in bed for awhile and let this pass. I'll call you later to see how things are going."

He hung up, thinking to himself how lame and transparent his little deception had been. Pat hated to lie, and he was not particularly good at it. His faith and heritage had taught him better. And after all, the Air Force's number one Core Value was Integrity. But it was more than a faith and integrity issue for him. He really liked and respected his boss on a personal level. He also knew Colonel Lyons well enough to know that he would never question why Pat needed the time off because it had to be a good reason, which made the deception all the more troubling to him.

He looked at the wall clock above the kitchen table. It was 0630, still early, so he went about the business of making a pot of coffee before even daring to wake Sara. He sipped slowly as he read through the newspaper, savoring the rare opportunity of time he had this day to peruse it at home instead of at the office.

His reading was suddenly interrupted by a chorus of, "Daddy! Daddy!"

He looked up and saw his two children bounding noisily into the kitchen.

"Hey guys! Get over here and give your daddy some hugs!" Sean and his younger sister, Erin Kathleen, rushed to him beaming broadly. Sean was the first to speak.

"What's new in the world? Have we captured that terrorist dude yet? What's his name?" he asked, shifting his eyes upward and to the left as if searching for a word.

"Usama bin Knucklehead," Pat replied with a smirk, generating giggles from both his children. "And what are you laughing at young lady?" he asked as he grabbed Erin and placed her on his right knee while he held Sean on his left.

Erin was just five years old, a kindergartner, and light as a feather. She had auburn colored hair, a mix of her mom's red and her dad's brown. Her light hazel eyes looked like two large freckles on her fair-skinned face.

"I love you, Daddy," she said placing about a dozen butterfly kisses on her father's cheeks.

She and her brother jumped off their dad's knees, into their seats, and gulped down a quick meal of breakfast bars and cold cereal seconds before their mom entered the kitchen.

"Let's get you guys moving and ready for school," she prodded as she began herding them from the table.

Sara was a stay-at-home mother, determined to raise their children in a solid Catholic home and not to leave them to be cared for by others. Pat appreciated their situation. Although he made good money as an Air Force major, they lived on a tight budget. Northern Virginia was an expensive place to reside, but for Pat and Sara, if raising their children right meant Sara took time off from being an interior decorator, it was an investment well worth the cost.

"I have a lot of errands to run today," Sara said as she finished putting the last few plates into the dishwasher. They clanked as she set them inside. The sound startled Pat who had been engrossed in reading the newspaper.

"Oh? What? Oh sorry, Sorcha. So you'll be out for awhile?" he asked, looking over the top of the paper.

"Yes, Baby. I'll drop the kids off at school and be gone most of the morning. Why don't you rest, and then go see Father Reynolds later this afternoon."

"I will. Just as soon as I finish the paper," he replied, mouthing a kiss to her as he finished his sentence.

She blew one back, and at once was surrounded by Sean and Erin bundled up in their winter coats, ready to go out to the minivan for the ride to school. "Kiss Daddy goodbye," she instructed both children.

They needed no prodding. Erin was the first to rush him with kisses and hugs, her fluffy pink coat making her seem twice her normal size. Pat gave Sean a bear hug, their usual goodbye ritual. And within a few moments, after the front door made a crunch sound upon closing, the house fell silent.

Pat continued reading the paper, sipping his coffee and enjoying the uncommon solitude he had this morning. A storyline just below the fold in the metro section caught his eye: *North Carolina Child Murder Has Local Ties.* The dateline was Mount Airy, North Carolina.

State police have joined the Mount Airy Sheriff's Department in the search for clues into the abduction, assault, and brutal murder of an eight year old Mount Airy boy. His battered and strangled body was found yesterday by hikers in a wooded area of Piedmont State Park, some 45 miles from his home. His parents reported him missing two weeks ago when he was apparently abducted from his home during the night. Authorities have few clues to go on at this point, and are appealing to the public to report anything suspicious they may have seen in the State Park or the boy's neighborhood over the past fourteen days.

Pat read the article with great interest. The boy's name was Josh Branford. There was a picture of his parents in front of news cameras from a week back appealing for their son's safe return. They had just moved to North Carolina from Northern Virginia two months earlier. Josh had attended the same school as Sean and Erin. The story continued on a different page. Pat fumbled with the newspaper until he reached it, and with it came an immense shock--a picture of the crime scene.

Pat knew this scene well. It was as clear in the light of day as it had been in his dreams night after night. There was the briar thicket and the clearing where the boy's body rested. A police blanket now covered the body, but the child's left foot was visible, turned in exactly the same direction as Pat had seen each night. His slipper was situated nearby with a dark stain on Pikachu's face that Pat knew to be yellow, despite the paper's black and white print. It was identical, except for the cordon of police tape that read, *Crime Scene Do Not Cross.*

Pat suddenly felt sick. He didn't know how to react, or even how to begin to make sense of this news in light of his dreams. He wasn't sure yet if he wanted to show the article to Sara. *How would she react? What did all this mean? Why am I connected to this crime through my dreams?*

He had a lot of questions, but no answers. Not yet, but that was to come in due time.

~ 2 ~

The light oak Howard Miller grandfather clock in the foyer chimed at the top of the hour, its deep bellowing sound resonating throughout the house. *BONG! BONG! BONG!* The last three strikes pulled Pat away from his trance as he sat in the kitchen with the paper on his lap, Josh Branford's crime scene photo square in the middle of the page. He looked at the kitchen clock. It was 0900. Nearly two hours had gone by since Sara left. He thought it was a good time to call Father Reynolds as he grabbed his cell phone, located the number to Our Lady of La Salette from an old church bulletin, and hit send.

Pat and Sara loved this parish, and they particularly loved Father Mike Reynolds who always humbly called himself "a simple parish priest." Our Lady of La Salette was much older and much smaller than any of the other Catholic churches in the surrounding communities. It was built in 1840 shortly after Burke, Virginia was founded and was one of the few original structures in the town to have survived the Civil War.

"Hello, Rachel, this is Pat O'Donnell calling for Father Reynolds. Is he available to talk with me for a moment?"

"Hold on please, Pat," the receptionist replied. "Let me see if he's in his office."

The next thing Pat heard was Father Reynolds's voice, imitating an Irish accent.

"Paddy O'Donnell! How are you? How's my favorite secret agent? Busy these days, I bet!"

"Hi, Father, I'm doing well. It's great to hear your voice."

"How can I help you? You're not volunteering to be an altar boy are you? You're a wee bit old for that!"

"Ha! Ha! Father Reynolds. A priest AND a stand-up comic!" Pat said returning the banter. "But seriously, Father, I would like to come see you today about something pretty serious--do you have time?"

"Of course, Pat, always time for you. Can you stop by after the noon mass? I'm free the rest of the day."

"I sure will, Father. I'll be there for the mass as well. Ciao Padre! See 'ya soon."

Pat hung up and began to think about the process he had set in motion. He had second thoughts about it all, unsure if he wanted to spill his guts openly to Father Reynolds. *How would he react to the dreams? Will he think I'm crazy and recommend counseling?*

He readied himself for the meeting by taking some time to sit quietly and go over the dreams he had been having. He experienced them every night for a solid week, growing in intensity each time. With each dream new details emerged, the images gaining a higher degree of clarity, fidelity. Last night's addition was the owl that seemed to guide him to Josh Branford as it swooped overhead.

It was just about 1130 when Pat entered the cold garage and hopped into his white Subaru Outback sedan. As he backed out of the driveway he looked at his house like he did everyday on his way to work. It was a beautiful light brown brick colonial with a big cherry tree in the front yard. Black shutters accented it perfectly, giving it the look of traditional colonial homes that once dotted the northern Virginia landscape going back to the days of the Founding Fathers.

He arrived at the church and easily found a parking space right in the front near the walkway. Weekday mass was sparsely attended, unlike the weekends and major Catholic holidays. Pat took a seat in a pew on the left side of the church, about halfway down. He knelt, blessed himself, and began to recite a series of prayers he held dearly in his heart ever since he could remember. It was just about time for mass to start, so he hurried along and finished blessing himself once again just before the procession began.   As Father Reynolds approached Pat's pew, he glanced to his side and looked at him.   The two made eye contact, and the priest winked in recognition.

At every mass Pat tried to find the meaning in the readings.   Not just the general meaning which the priest would help interpret during the Homily, but the deeper, personal meaning it had for him.   In some respects he even looked to Scripture to give him a sign of something, a guidepost, affirmation, or direction.   At this mass, the Old Testament reading was from the book of Ecclesiastes, Chapter 5:

Guard your steps when you go to the house of God; to draw near to listen is better than to offer the sacrifice of fools; for they do not know that they are doing evil. Be not rash with your mouth, nor let your heart be hasty to utter a word before God, for God is in heaven, and you upon earth; therefore let your words be few. For a dream comes with much business, and a fool's voice with many words.

He wasn't sure what to make of the reading, but it was the only one at this mass that mentioned dreams.   *Dreams come with much business*-sounded almost like a fortune cookie saying to him.   He wondered if it meant his dreams had something to do with his work, or if his dreams were going to create more work for him.

Before long, it was time for Communion.   Pat always looked forward to the Sacrament of Holy Communion.   To him, the whole process of the physical transformation of the bread and wine was something very special.   At each mass a miracle was performed.   What he ate and drank no longer were bread and wine, but the actual physical body and blood of Christ.   It was a special gift.   A privilege he felt completely unworthy to receive.   He approached Father Reynolds at the altar.

"This is the Body of Christ, Pat," the old, white-haired priest said as he held the Host out for him to receive.

"Amen," Pat replied as he stuck out his tongue signaling Father Reynolds to place the host there instead of his hand.

His reverence for the Eucharist meant that he should never touch it with his hands, even though the Church had allowed celebrants to touch the Host for many years. Pat was raised a Roman Catholic in the most traditional sense...a young boy who attended St. Lucy's church in Scranton, in a predominantly Italian neighborhood. The images of his experiences there burned forever in his mind. Old women in scarves kneeling at the altar before mass praying the Rosary in soft Italian voices. Faces in prayer looking upward at the domed murals on the ceiling as if it were heaven itself, almost within reach. Mass spoken in Latin. Fragrances of incense and candles burning. Colorful mosaic windows all around with scenes of stories from the Bible. Sunbeams would burst through these windows and cast colorful rays of light that danced off dozens of alabaster statues of saints lining the church. Faith filled all his senses. Pat was so lost in his memory of St. Lucy's church that he was a bit startled when the priest spoke next.

"The mass is ended, go in peace to love and serve the Lord."

His heart began to race as he realized he was now mere minutes away from baring his soul to him. As he shook hands with Father Reynolds at the back of the church the priest told him to wait in his office. Rachel closed the heavy, dark brown wooden door to the office with Pat in it, so he had no way of knowing exactly when Father Reynolds would walk in. That only added to his sense of unease. After a few eternal moments, the door suddenly burst open, and an exuberant Father Reynolds came rushing in, closing the door behind him with a loud THUD! Pat began to get up instinctively, out of respect, but Father Reynolds motioned for him to sit in a soft leather chair right next to his ornate wooden desk that was as old as the church itself.

"Relax, Pat. Have a seat! Tell me, how are Sara and the kids?"

"They are all fine, Father, and thanks for asking. Home is great, always is."

"And what about work--what's going on there? It has to be a nightmare at the Pentagon after the terror attacks!"

"It has been insane. I never could have imagined the state we're in right now."

"It's indeed a crazy world we live in. I'm just thankful to God that you were not hurt during the Pentagon attack."

He could see Father Reynolds was studying him closely as he spoke, clearly sensing Pat was worried about something.

"Tell me, Pat, what's troubling you?"

"Father, before discussing this, I want to make sure that what we talk about is kept confidential. I don't want anyone ever to know about this, okay?"

Father Reynolds gave him a peculiar look, seemingly affronted at the suggestion that anyone would question the implicit privilege of confidentiality he held so dear, so sacred. "Of course Pat. Of course. No one will ever know," he reassured him.

"Okay Father, I appreciate that, but bear with me as I insist on one more layer of protection. It has to do with how the military views this type of confidentiality. We have to establish a clear 'clergy-penitent' relationship to distinguish what I say today from all other forms of communication."

"You want to make a confession, Pat?" Father Reynolds asked with a look on his face suggesting he still didn't understand where Pat was going with all this.

"Well, yes and no. Look, Father, it's like this. I want to begin with my confession, discuss the matter I came here to see you about, then conclude with the absolution so that everything I discuss, EVERYTHING, is clearly within the bounds of the privilege as the military sees it."

"Pat, that's fine, and we can certainly do it that way, but I want you to know I don't care how the military sees it. I would never divulge anything we discuss to anyone. PERIOD! Let's begin first in the name of the Father, and of the Son, and of the Holy Spirit."

As Father Reynolds spoke he blessed himself with the sign of the cross. Pat did the same along with him. The old priest looked at him, and with a twinkle in his eye said, "Okay, Pat. It's your dime."

He began with the opening of the Sacrament of Reconciliation he had learned as a young boy in Catechism many years ago. "Bless me Father, for I have sinned. It has been about two months since my last confession."

He looked around the priest's office for a few seconds, glancing at the large crucifix on the wall next to where they sat, then at Father Reynolds's wooden rosary on the desk. Slowly, with obvious hesitation, he began to speak again.

"Father, I've been troubled by a series of dreams for the past seven days. They haunt me every night. I think I'm losing my mind, and I'm worried about losing my security clearance and job!" He proceeded to outline each dream in the series, providing details with tremendous precision.

"I can't help but feel they are leading me to something. A purpose. It's like someone is communicating with me through the dreams. I'm afraid to go to sleep at night!"

It was obvious the priest was genuinely struck by what Pat said, not just the content or potential meaning of the dreams, but the quality of the dream process itself.

"Pat, let me ask you a question. You described so many sensory aspects to these dreams. There's colors, sounds, smells, taste, touch. Is this unique to just these dreams, or do you have dreams like this from time to time?"

"I dream like that *all* the time, Father. Every dream, every night, since childhood."

Pat gave him a puzzled look, but he knew deep down he was unique. He was aware that most people dreamt in black and white, and rarely, if ever, had other sensory qualities to their dreams.

"That's amazing.   You have a tremendous gift, a way of experiencing the world that few could ever imagine. In your line of work have you had the occasion to investigate child assaults and murders? Perhaps you are troubled by a case from long ago that you had worked?"

"No, Father, I don't think that's it. Sure, I've investigated such crimes, but never one where a child's body lay in the woods for several days."

"Do you know who the boy is?" Father Reynolds prodded.

Pat stood up and walked silently to the window. He looked out and watched a handful of autumn leaves glide gracefully to the earth. Biting his lip, he turned and looked Father Reynolds in the eye and slowly said, "I do now."

He told the priest about the newspaper article about Josh Branford and his connection to the Northern Virginia. Father Reynolds let him speak without interrupting. There was a long pause in the room as the priest looked down at the dark green blotter on his desk and his old wrinkled hands clasped together on it.

"Pat, I'm not a psychiatrist, and I don't think you even need one, truthfully. I deal in matters of the soul, not necessarily the mind. But if I had to stick my neck out, I'd say you are fine. I suspect you, like everyone else in America right now, are feeling vulnerable after the terror attacks last month. You are also a loving father of two children who understandably fears for their safety. Let's face it, being a parent these days has never been tougher. What, with all the pedophiles and stalkers out there. Now terrorists? You have spent a career catching the bad guys, the dregs of society. I'm sure you're feeling the weight of a lot of old stress that probably has stayed hidden all these years bearing down on you so heavily now, along with the added strain over the terror attacks."

Pat began to nod as the old priest spoke. What he said *sounded* right. It probably was a series of old and new events coming together and gaining synergy, growing in strength and putting strain on him.

"But Pat," Father Reynolds continued, his tone becoming slightly more serious. "I don't know what to make of the fact that you had dreams about a boy--who used to go to Sean and Erin's school-- dreams about him before he was found dead. Perhaps the memory of your dreams is less clear than you think, and it was only this morning you put it all together when you read the article about the Branford boy. Perhaps your mind connected dots that weren't meant to be connected at all."

Pat didn't buy it. His memory of the dreams was incredibly clear. And he knew Father Reynolds didn't buy it, either. He was just trying to make an awkward situation easier to talk about. He could also sense the priest's genuine concern for him.

"I recommend you take a few days off from work--if you can--and do something with your family. Take Sara and the children to the zoo, or to a movie, or a park. Get out and enjoy some quality family time. If not time off during the week, then for sure this weekend."

"Padre, you're right!" Pat said nodding his head in agreement.

He reflected back at how long it had been since he had done any of the things Father Reynolds mentioned. He had worked twenty-two of the last twenty-three days since the terrorist attacks. And those were nearly sixteen hour days. He was tired and had little quality time with the family. He reached for Father Reynolds's hand, as if to shake goodbye.

"Thanks, Father, I--"

Father Reynolds interrupted. "Sit down Pat, aren't we forgetting something?"

"What's that?"

"Your absolution! Don't you want closure to this Sacrament of Reconciliation? The *extended warranty* on the confidentiality you were concerned about?" Father Reynolds smiled as he reminded him of the special request Pat had made for the meeting.

Embarrassed, and a bit red around the neck, he sat back down. "I'm sorry Padre! I'm just feeling so good now having had a chance to chat with you."

With his right hand raised, Father Reynolds recited the prayer of absolution, and concluded it by making the sign of the cross over him. When they stood up, Pat thanked him profusely and hugged him very tightly.

"You take care of yourself, Special Agent Patrick O'Donnell!" the priest gently admonished him, his old hands giving Pat a firm shake.

It was almost as if Father Reynolds didn't want to let go. Pat sensed the priest was more than concerned, perhaps even fearful for him. They walked together from the rectory to the church entrance.

"I will pray for you, Patrick!"

"Goodbye, Father!" he said as he walked away. He turned around one more time before opening his car door and saw Father Reynolds waving at him from the front of the church.

Pat probably would not have left so quickly, and he probably would have hugged him more tightly, had he known at that moment Father Reynolds would be dead within weeks.

~ **3** ~

When he returned home, there was a message on his answering machine from Colonel Lyons, inquiring about how he was feeling. With a tinge of guilt for having lied to his boss, he picked up the receiver and phoned in.

"Hey Boss, it's me," he began as Colonel Lyons picked up. "Sorry about missing work today."

"Not a problem. How's the stomach? Did you go see a doc?"

"No, Sir. Actually I stayed in bed, but I unhooked the phone in my bedroom so I could get some rest. Sorry I missed your call."

He hated having to expand upon the basic lie he started with his first call to the office that morning, but he was stuck having to explain why he did not answer the colonel's telephone call earlier in the day.

Sounding a bit more businesslike, Colonel Lyons continued. "You didn't miss much today. There have been some interesting developments on the CT side which we'll need to discuss on the STU. Are you ready?"

"Just a minute, Sir, let me switch phones and get out my key."

Pat headed to the den where he maintained an office. On his desk was a STU, or, Secure Telephone Unit, an encrypted system for communicating TOP SECRET information. He also had a small safe with an electronic keypad. He pressed the combination and heard a CHIRP! Then a green light flashed indicating he could open it. He extracted a special key made of black plastic with metal contact terminals instead of teeth like a regular key. At its heart was a microchip that contained current encryption codes developed by the

National Security Agency. After inserting it into the STU on his desk and turning it ninety degrees clockwise, he picked up the receiver.

"Ok, Sir. I'll go ahead and push here."

"Copy," the colonel replied acknowledging he was initiating the secure call.

Pat instinctively pulled the phone away from his ear because he knew that once he pushed the button at his end marked Secure Voice, he'd get an ear piercing screech as the two units "shook hands" and verified common encryption.

"I've got you TOP SECRET here," Pat informed his boss as he watched the digital display first flash USAF Inspector General, then PENTAGON, then TOP SECRET.

"Same here. Listen, nothing to come in on, and it can wait until tomorrow, but I wanted you to know CIA is reporting a fix on bin Laden's hideout, and NSA came in right after with a FLASH message confirming the same via cell phone intercepts. It looks like the clearest lead we've had in some time."

"Hot stuff, Boss!" he exclaimed loudly. "I assume the boys from MacDill will be moving in soon to snatch his sorry butt?"

"Don't know just yet, but I plan to pulse some friends in J3 in the morning. Take care, get some rest, and we'll see you tomorrow—and don't come in if you're still sick. We don't need a stomach bug at the Pentagon right now!"

"Understand, Sir. Chat with you soon."

He thought about the significance of the intelligence. He knew the NSA rarely transmitted FLASH messages—they carry a higher priority than IMMEDIATE ones and go directly to the White House Situation Room. He was confident Colonel Lyons would find out from some buddies in the Joint Staff's Operations Directorate, the J3, if the Special Operations Forces from MacDill Air Force Base in Florida would rock and roll on the news.

Bedtime this night was different from most. Pat was pumped up, excited about having had a chance to chat with Father Reynolds, and excited over the intelligence information his boss relayed to him. He and Sara went about the house and put out the lights, checked all the door locks, and retreated to their bedroom to get ready for sleep. While brushing his teeth, he began to tell her about his visit with the priest. Sara could barely understand him as he tried to talk with a mouthful of warm minty toothpaste.

"Well, Father Reynolds thinks I've been under a lot of stress with the terror attacks and long hours and all," Pat mumbled almost unintelligibly. "He wants us to take some time out and do family stuff. How about Kings Dominion down south? Is it still open?" he asked, thinking about the giant amusement park the family loved to visit. He spit out the toothpaste and rinsed his mouth.

"I doubt it. It's getting colder every day. How about we leave it to the kids to decide--we'll do something this weekend."

"That's a great idea, Sweetie. And I have my own idea." Pat had a sly smile on his face as he approached the bed.

"And what would that idea be?" Sara asked with a smirk, knowing all too well what he had on his mind.

He turned the nightstand lamp off and dove under the covers at his suddenly coy wife. He muttered something in her ear.

"You naughty Irishman!" was all Sara managed to get out, as he wrapped his arms around her and pulled her close. They tussled about in the bed, and he made love to her with a fervor he hadn't felt in many years. He was burning off stress, putting the events of the day out of his mind, and finding comfort and solace in her arms. After their lovemaking, he drew in a deep breath and thought about what Father Reynolds had told him. He *had* been under a great deal of stress, and he realized now that he hadn't made love to Sara in the three weeks since the 9/11 terror attacks. A peaceful, comforting feeling began to take hold of him, and he drifted off to sleep.

But once again, Pat was visited in his dreams. Just like the previous seven nights, he found himself alone in the cold, damp woods with the Branford boy. Suddenly, the owl appeared again. This time it didn't swoop down, rather, it fluttered about gracefully, gently landing near the boy. Pat stared intently as the feathered creature approached Josh, sniffing the air for signs of danger, closer and closer with small creeping steps. The owl stopped as if to look at something near the boy. Pat squinted hard, trying to make it out, until it became clear. A piece of thin, silver-colored picture frame wire was underneath the boy's torso, sticking out about two inches. *That's what the bastard used to strangle the boy!* Pat thought to himself.

The owl had completed its mission...it took him back to the crime scene and made sure he knew exactly how Josh was murdered. Before he woke, Pat tried once again to fly. As he reached the point above the trees, above the clearing, he looked up to the heavens. But when he looked down, he saw the boy was gone. Deep inside Pat knew he, like the owl, had completed his mission that night. He brought Josh to God.

He woke slowly this time. No gasping for air, no pounding heart. No shirt drenched in sweat. He woke with a peaceful feeling that he had come to grips with the nightmares, and he knew that his cathartic talk with the priest was the reason. Looking at the clock, which read 0513, he realized he wouldn't sleep any more, indeed, didn't *want* to sleep any more. He moved slowly down the hallway to the family den, tiptoeing in his bare feet on the cool hardwood floor so as not to wake anyone. An occasional *CREAK!* from a loose floorboard defied his best efforts to keep quiet. He stood for a moment in the doorway to admire the many plaques and certificates of his Air Force career adorning the walls. The soft, reddish Persian rug warmed his bare feet when he stepped inside. The glow of the computer screen lit the room dimly, adding an almost stately touch to the elegant cherry wood office furniture throughout.

This was Pat's sanctuary, his own space in a home otherwise occupied by the noises and messes of his children as they played. He settled in to the soft black leather high-back chair and logged-on to his computer. He headed straight for the news sites. The first one he opened had a *Breaking News* banner and a headline that read, *CIA and NSA Have Located Bin Laden.* As he read the article, he noted how it was remarkably accurate based upon what he knew from his phone call the day before with Colonel Lyons. He shook his head, muttering to himself about how it was impossible to keep a secret in this town.

He headed to the kitchen to make coffee and get ready for work, all the while thinking about how or what he would tell Sara about the last dream, about the news from North Carolina. He quickly developed a plan. A simple one made in haste. He would lie. Just then Sara entered the kitchen quietly and unexpectedly, given her typical pattern of trying to sleep in.

"Is everything okay, Baby? I was restless and worried about you," she said greeting him.

"Everything's fine, Honey. No more dreams last night at all. Father Reynolds's pep talk was all I needed."

He studied her face to see if she bought it. Pat had an innate ability to read people, and he honed those skills when he joined the Office of Special Investigations and quickly became one of the organization's best interrogators. Sara's expression spoke volumes. Pat knew she didn't believe him, but he also knew she would not press him. After thirteen years of being the wife of an Air Force OSI agent, she knew not to ask too many questions.

"That's great, Sweetie, and remember, you can always talk with me or Father Reynolds again if you feel the need." She kissed him on the cheek, pulled him close and whispered in his ear, "And you were an absolute animal last night!"

"It helps that you're Irish, too, my little Sorcha," he said with a wry smile.

Pat spied his two youngsters who had crept in for breakfast having heard their parents talking. "Okay gang, here's the mission," he began imitating a military general prepping his troops for a dangerous journey. "In one day, the weekend will be upon us. And this weekend, Daddy, er, I mean, General O'Donnell won't be going to the office--"

The children let out a loud cheer that interrupted him mid-sentence.

"Er, hum," he continued with a steely-eyed expression. "Your mission is to decide what we, the O'Donnell Squadron, will do with our family time. Report back tonight at the supper table, and have a great day in school!"

Erin was the first to grab her dad, hugging him excitedly and prematurely providing her thoughts for the weekend. "Let's go to Disneyland!" she exclaimed. "Or the Disney cruise boat I saw on TV!"

"Well, I'm not sure we can pull that off in just one day, Lieutenant O'Donnell--why don't you think about it at school today and come up with a few other ideas," Pat suggested, caressing her soft hair.

"Ok, Dad, I will." Erin sealed her promise with a big kiss.

Pat's Metro bus would be there soon, so he hurried about getting ready for work. As he stood in front of the bedroom mirror the tall, athletic major combed back his dark brown hair with flecks of gray, and checked his short-sleeved, blue uniform one more time. Grabbing his briefcase and blue Air Force windbreaker, Sara and the kids long since gone, he headed out the door to the bus stop just one block from his home.

He used the solitude of the commute to reflect on the newspaper article. He began to wonder if perhaps he had seen earlier reporting about the missing boy, *before* he was found. Perhaps he had read about it on the web over the last two weeks, and his dreams were the *result* of knowing the boy was missing. After all, he and his family occasionally traveled to that part of North Carolina to enjoy the outdoors. He was familiar with the pines and the typical forests down there. Cognitive dissonance was beginning to set in. Pat rationalized that his dream became complete when he saw the news story. The photo really didn't represent his *exact* dream. He filled in the missing dream detail with the photo's detail until the two became one in the same in his mind. He started to feel much better now, if not a bit silly for having started to believe some kind of "spooky" or "psychic" reason was behind his nightmares.

The bus jostled to a stop at the Pentagon's Metro drop off point near a large escalator that descended to the subway lines. Pat stepped off to the WHOOSH sound of the bus's hydraulic brakes, accompanied by a small gust of black smoke and diesel fumes permeating the air as he walked to the entrance. He made it through the long, slow line of people gaining access to the building. The pungent smoky stench of burnt jet fuel and charred bodies still lingered in the halls of the Pentagon three weeks after the attack. He knew he would never get used to the smell and wondered if it would ever really go away.

"Well, look who it is!" he heard his boss say as he walked in. "Morning, Pat--I see the bug you had has passed, er, *so to speak?*"

"Hi, Colonel Lyons. Yes, Sir. Feeling much better today."

Pat appreciated the minor chiding. It gave him the sense his boss wasn't upset with him at all, even if he had seen through the white lie he told to miss work yesterday. Colonel Lyons was a short, slender man in his early fifties. His prematurely gray hair and gentle demeanor always made Pat feel like he was chatting with a kindly grandfather, not a senior Air Force officer. Let alone his boss!

"Good, 'cause you're in for a doozy of a morning. We've had another leak, and the President is furious. Heads are gonna roll!" Colonel Lyons exclaimed, eyes wide and shaking his head.

Pat nodded. "You mean the NSA and CIA traffic you briefed me on yesterday? I saw an article about it on the Internet this morning."

Colonel Lyons handed him a folder marked, TOP SECRET. "Here, a little light reading before your nine o'clock with the XOI and his staff. They'll want to know what, if anything, OSI can do to find out if any Air Force people were behind the leak. I suggest you get on the bat phone with OSI's XOQ."

He quickly read the reports at his desk, in a tiny, depressing cubicle comprised of drab gray modular office furniture and matching fabric chairs. He grabbed the STU and called his buddy, Lee Cook, a civilian who ran OSI's Directorate of Counterintelligence--the XOQ as it was known. They chatted a bit *in the clear* before connecting via a secure link.

"Lee, have you seen the two FLASH reports from yesterday? The Agency's Date Time Group is 041932 Zulu, and the NSA's DTG is 041950 Zulu."

"Got 'em right here, and I've heard the RUMINT the President is upset about the leak. We've already sent a tasking out to our field units to determine which SSOs got the reports and what further distro was made, if any."

Pat always got a chuckle when people in the Intelligence Community used the term RUMINT. It was an informal acronym that meant *Rumor Intelligence*--basically gossip.

"Thanks. I knew I could count on you. I've got to see the XOI and his folks this morning at nine. They'll probably want a formal leak investigation, but I'll hold them off 'cause we don't know who to investigate yet, or even if someone in the Air Force was the culprit. I'll bet you a beer it was some flaming liberal State Department weenie analyst, but you know these things are almost impossible to nail down," Pat added as he tapped his pen on top of his desk.

"You're on! Let me know how it goes because the OSI Commander will want to know if he has to gin up a special team to go after this one."

"You got it, Buddy! I'll let you know if this thing grows legs!" Pat teased before the two old friends hung up.

He looked at his watch and realized it was nearly 0900. He grabbed a notepad and the classified reports and shoved them into a courier pouch and flew out the door to the Air Force XOI's conference room. The XOI was the Director of Intelligence for the entire Air Force. A major general, he was responsible for all Air Force intelligence activities worldwide, but not for counterintelligence. That was the business the OSI had exclusive authority over--a source of friction sometimes for professionals in the Intelligence Community. Even though Pat worked for the Inspector General, the Air Staff principal responsible for the OSI worldwide, he was still viewed as the token OSI representative at such meetings. He rushed into the conference room seconds before the general arrived. Everyone came to attention as Major General Robert D. Swank walked in and stated gruffly, "Seats, please."

General Swank was an intimidating man, not just because he was a two-star general and meaner than a pit bull. He was a big bald man, standing about six feet and five inches tall. He typically wore his Class B uniform combination: short-sleeved open collar blue shirt. But unlike any other general at the Pentagon, General Swank wore his ribbons on his shirt as well as his service dress jacket. He had a huge "rack" as the military called it, with thirty separate ribbons in ten rows of three each. He was a prior NCO and proud of it, making sure everyone saw all his enlisted medals.

A nervous Air Force captain at the podium picked up a remote control and dimmed the lights as he began his formal briefing to the general on the leak incident. Pat felt sorry for this briefer. Indeed, he felt sorry for all the intelligence briefers. They tended to be raw meat to General Swank. This one was young, slight, and frail in appearance, and he did not appear to have a command of the information. Pat knew what was coming. General Swank tore into him like a hungry lion. The general hated the way he carried himself--and told him this. He hated his appearance--and told him this. And he hated the "unpolished, unprofessional, sorry attempt at a briefing," as he called it. After his blood stopped flowing out onto the carpet, the poor kid tried to regain his composure and walk away with a little bit of dignity, but he tripped on a power cable and fell down. Pat thought he even saw him cry slightly as he hurried out of the room. Pat hated Swank for having done this.

The general began to speak to the attendees, some fifteen or so from within the Intelligence Directorate, the Staff Judge Advocate's office, and a handful of others Pat didn't recognize. As the general spoke, he reminded Pat of the Peanuts cartoon--specifically the Charlie Brown movies and the kids' teacher. She never said real words; it was always a muffled spattering of, "Wah wah wah wah wah wah wah wah wah." Pat secretly smiled inside as he pictured General Swank in Charlie Brown's classroom talking this way. The general's voice, muttered as it was in Pat's mind, began to fade out as Pat's daydream faded in. And with the daydream came a new assault.

Although his body remained in place in the conference room chair, eyes open and staring at the general, his mind was transported away in a flash to some unknown place. His senses were bombarded all at once with an image, a scent, a taste, a touch, a sound. Pat saw a young boy--not Josh Branford--but another small boy about his age, hanging by his neck in what appeared to be a large warehouse. He was pale and lifeless, eyes wide with a look of sheer terror. There were cuts and abrasions about his chest and arms. At the same moment the image seared in his mind, Pat had the sudden sensation of sweet cherry flavor in his mouth. It lasted but a second and was gone. Simultaneously, he smelled garlic. It was subtle and quick, yet unmistakable. Pat heard music playing--nearby, but not in the warehouse. He felt his throat constrict with the sharp pain of something being wrapped and tightened around his neck. Pat knew this boy had been strangled with a metal wire like Josh, and then hanged with what looked like a clothesline cord from the dusty, dry wooden warehouse rafters. He was hardly aware as he experienced this package of sensations, that he began to make an audible gasp that suddenly riveted the attention of the entire room upon him.

"Major O'Donnell--are you okay?" he heard General Swank ask

roughly. "Is there something you care to share with the rest of us?" he asked sarcastically.

As quickly as he had been abducted mentally, and taken to this place of horror to experience this gruesome scene, Pat was returned in time and space to the conference room. With everyone staring at him. Embarrassed, he could only muster a muted apology.

"Sorry, General. I had the stomach bug yesterday, and now my throat feels a bit dry."

A colonel passed Pat a glass of water, which he gulped down.

"As I was saying," the general continued, keeping a glaring eye on Pat, unconcerned for his welfare, and clearly incensed that he had broken his stride. "I want us all engaged on this leak incident. Major O'Donnell--is OSI prepared to run a leak investigation?"

"Sir, yes it is, as soon as sufficient information is developed to suggest Air Force culpability. The OSI has already sent leads out worldwide to try to determine who had access to the intelligence reports, and to whom they may have disseminated it further," Pat replied as confidently as he could sound.

"What? Just leads? Isn't that why we run investigations--to determine the facts?" the general stammered.

Pat began to speak, to try to clarify what he meant, when the Air Force Judge Advocate General interrupted and came to his aid. "Bob, I agree with Major O'Donnell. Let's let OSI shake the bushes a bit. After all, how can they even know who to investigate unless they establish a clear Air Force nexus to the leak?"

"All right. Keep me posted!" Swank boomed at Pat.

The general continued his bullying meeting for another hour, repeating himself several times, making the same points over and over again to the roomful of hostages. When it was finished, Pat started to walk toward his office, but he wasn't really ready to go back to work just yet. He needed to clear his head. He proceeded down the Tenth

Corridor to the A-Ring and Concourse. He walked among the shops for five or ten minutes, then went into the bookstore. He couldn't rid his mind of the image of the boy in the warehouse. He was worried this was all going to be repetitive like his dreams. Just as he thought he had put the dreams to bed, he now had renewed doubts. Maybe my dreams were, in fact, prophetic!

He was particularly concerned because this new experience invaded his daytime, his work time, and had interfered with his official duties. What Pat didn't know at the moment was that this instantaneous flash of multiple senses that attacked his conscious mind would never repeat itself. The image of the boy in the warehouse, and all the attendant sensory experiences, was a one-time event, but its meaning would have a profound effect on him. A meaning that would forever change his life.

~ 4 ~

Pat wandered around the Concourse a few minutes more before returning to his office. He needed some answers. And he needed them right away. Like the Branford murder that found its way into the local newspaper, he wondered if there may be some news out there related to the image that had just assaulted him in General Swank's conference room.

He logged onto his UNCLASSIFIED computer system and brought up the Google search website. He entered the keywords: *boy, murder, warehouse, hanging, and assault.* There were no significant hits. He found a few articles about various crimes against children, but none that seemed to come close to the frightening image he experienced this morning. He tried another search engine, and then another. Nothing.

"Hmmmmmph," he stammered out loud as he banged away at the keyboard, steadfastly trying to come up with something to validate the vision he had had, but to no avail.

There was one more thing Pat wanted to do--part of the overall new strategy he thought about moments before as he strolled through the Concourse. He would call the OSI detachment at Pope Air Force Base in North Carolina and ask if the agents there knew anything about the Branford murder. Maybe there were some details of the crime the press did not report that would lend weight in one direction or the other in his confusion over dreams and facts.

He knew the OSI detachment commander at Pope Air Force Base was an Air Force captain named Jack "Rusty" Baker. He didn't know Baker personally, but knew of him, his reputation over the years. He was well thought of in OSI circles, a "fast burner" as the leadership called him, meaning he was likely to get promoted early in his career because of his outstanding performance. The thing Pat found most amusing about Baker was how he got the "Rusty" moniker. Apparently when Baker was an OSI agent trainee, he couldn't shoot straight to save his life. When a range official berated him one morning about his poor scores, Baker claimed his handgun was rusty, always jamming, and never quite right. Everyone at the OSI Academy was in stitches, and the name stuck ever since. Pat smiled slightly as he called his direct line.

"OSI, this is Special Agent Baker, may I help you?"

"Rusty! This is Pat O'Donnell in the Air Force IG shop. How are you doing today?" He greeted Agent Baker enthusiastically and informally, something he liked to do with junior officers because he knew it put them more at ease.

"Hi, Major O'Donnell," Baker began, obviously knowing who Pat was even though the two had never met. "What can I do for you today, Sir?"

"Well, just calling to check up on you. The IG told me to, 'Call that guy at Pope and see if he's hard at work today,'" Pat joked, making him believe for a moment that the Inspector General--an Air Force three-star general--had for some reason taken a personal interest in him.

"Very funny, Sir! Now I know you didn't call here just to bust my chops. What's going on that the IG's office is calling me?"

"Relax, Rusty, not really even IG business. Are you familiar with the investigation of the little Mount Airy boy who was found dead in the woods yesterday?"

"Oh, my God yes, that's obviously big news down here. There's a local Task Force set up to work it right now. The Bureau, State Police, sheriff's offices, and even OSI has been asked to take part, just in case the killer is military."

"Wow! That's a huge effort. What's..." Pat started ask, but Baker cut him off.

"Well, it's because they are concerned about a possible serial child killer. You see, two weeks ago there were reports of a man trying to lure boys into his minivan here in the Fayetteville area, as well as Mount Airy. Lucky for those kids they got away. So the police want to stop this guy before he abducts and kills again."

"I see. Listen I was wondering about the crime scene itself; it really caught my attention when I read about it in the paper. Were the police able to do anything with the murder weapon--assume it was some kind of metal wire? Any potential forensic evidence like DNA of the bad guy?"

"Sir, I really don't know any detail yet. We're having our first Task Force meeting this afternoon--in a few hours, and I plan to be there. Maybe I'll find out more about the evidence at the meeting. I'll give you a call if I do."

"Thanks. Appreciate any insight you can give me."

When they hung up Pat checked his watch. It was lunchtime. His morning was so consumed with the leak incident and his dreams that he lost track of time. He made a beeline for his boss's office.

"Colonel Lyons, I was going to head out to the POAC unless you had something you need me to do?"

"No, Pat, go ahead and have a good work out. What'll it be today? A run or Nautilus?"

"I think I'm going to run. The weather has been great, and I want to take advantage of it before the cold settles in here."

"Well, enjoy!" Colonel Lyons said smiling as Pat headed out the door.

He meandered through the maze of rings and corridors to the POAC--the Pentagon Officers Athletic Club. It was situated outside the Pentagon proper, near the entrance to North Parking, making it an ideal place to change clothes and jog. He put on his blue nylon running suit and shoes in a flash and headed out the door to the jogging trails that would take him to the Memorial Bridge and over to the Capitol Mall area. Pat wasn't a fast runner. He averaged eight-minute-miles, but it was enough to give him a decent aerobic workout as he ran a circuit that took him around the Washington Monument and back to the Pentagon, right about three miles in just under thirty minutes.

The sun was warm, but the air was a bit crisp. He loved the contrast. He could feel his whole body warming to the touch of the sun's rays, while every breath he took brought cool, refreshing air into his lungs. For the next half hour, Pat forgot all about his haunting dreams and the frightening image of the morning. He enjoyed the brightly colored autumn leaves that had been falling for the past week, building up in small piles off to the sides of the trail. He liked the sound the dried ones made, crisply crackling under his feet with every step. If he tuned out all the sound around him, he could hear his own steady breathing, his own heart beating.

While slender and athletic, he enjoyed running not just for the physical workout he received. Running was also almost spiritual. Usually he felt God's presence jogging along with him. Today he contemplated a series of *truisms* he held dearly in his heart all his life--things he grew up mysteriously knowing would happen to him. As a child he knew that someday he would marry a red-haired woman. Perhaps this was a product of his heritage, knowing that Irish men oftentimes marry red-headed Irish women. Strangely, he also knew he would have just two children. As the youngest of seven children, he only knew one type of family...large! But his greatest truism was also the most elusive one. He sensed he was born to complete some profound and pre-ordained mission. Something yet to be revealed. As he jogged, he wondered if the recent events, the nightmares and visions, were somehow connected to this supreme truism.

He approached the Lincoln Memorial and kept his radar up, subtly scanning the area around him--360-degree coverage. As an Air Force

OSI special agent, and a counterintelligence and counterterrorism expert, he always maintained his vigilance. He was trained to do so and had been doing so his entire career--mostly out of necessity. Pat had considerable experience chasing terrorists around the Middle East, and his fair share of close calls, too. Following the 1996 terrorist truck bombing of the al Khobar Towers in Dhahran, Saudi Arabia, Pat was sent in to set up CT operations to protect Air Force members and resources. Nineteen airmen were killed in the June attack, and two hundred more injured. He thought about the many scrapes he had with terrorists while devising new operational programs to combat the growing threat in that region. He had been in numerous gun battles, mortar attacks, and even one knife fight that ended when his partner shot and killed the al Qaeda terrorist Pat had tackled. He returned home with a Bronze Star and a Purple Heart, both with highly classified citations he would never be able to display in the open.

As the reveries faded from his mind, he found himself on the final stretch of his refreshing run, barely one hundred yards from the Pentagon. He headed back to the POAC for a fresh shower, and then back into his uniform. Colonel Lyons was waiting for him with some good news--the Air Staff Crisis Action Team was modifying its schedule, and would only be active during weekdays. Someone would be on call on the weekends to come in as needed, but it didn't involve Pat. He was elated. He had planned to approach Colonel Lyons about getting the weekend off to have some quality family time, but now he didn't have to worry about it. The weekend work was over.

"Pat, you need to know what's really going on," Colonel Lyons cautioned in a half whisper, looking around down the center of the gray cubicle graveyard. He took Pat into his office and closed the door. "My friends in J3 told me the air campaign will kick off this weekend. On Sunday. They have a pretty good fix on UBL's current location and plan to bomb him back to the Stone Age."

Pat was puzzled. "But why stand down the CAT when we're about to spank the Taliban and al Qaeda?" he asked scratching his head.

Colonel Lyons smiled. "The deception guys in J3 say that intercepts of the Taliban's crude comm nodes suggest they are keeping an eye on current news reports about Pentagon planning. They believe we won't act, and proof of that will be standing down our CATs, the National Military Command Center, and so on. Of course, we're really not standing them down, but minimal manning will give it that appearance."

Pat smiled broadly. "Hmmm, so we lull them into letting down their guard and then smack them hard. I like it, Boss!"

The colonel's phone rang. "Colonel Lyons," he simply said as he picked it up. He looked at Pat as he listened, "Yeah, he's right here. Okay, I'll let him know. Thanks." He hung up.

"The secretary said Rusty Baker from Pope is on line two. Tell him I said hello. I recruited him into OSI many years ago. He's a good kid."

"Will do, Boss. And thanks for the insight into the attack plan."

Pat went back to his desk, paused, and took a deep breath before picking up the telephone.

"Hi, Rusty! How's the IG's favorite OSI agent?" he teased.

"You tell me, assume it's you since you work up there in the inner sanctum!" Baker shot back with a laugh. "Listen, Major O'Donnell, not much news for you on the Branford case. The Task Force meeting went well. The FBI profiler thought the killer likely was a white male in his late thirties or early forties, based largely on the reports of the other boys who had been approached over the previous few weeks. Apparently most of the evidence in the case has already leaked to the press, so you pretty much know what we all do at this point in time."

"Thanks. I appreciate the insight. Well, have a great weekend," Pat said as he hung up, looking at his watch.

It was a Friday afternoon before the first weekend that the Pentagon was going to stand down following the terrorist attacks. He knew that outside in the hallways throngs of people would be flooding the corridors on their way home. And he needed to be one of them.

When Pat stepped into his house, the smell hit him at once. Thick, dense, and heavy. His salivary glands responded before his brain could make sense of it. *Corned beef and cabbage!* he thought. *God I love that woman!*

Sara didn't make traditional Irish meals often, but when she did, it was usually because she knew Pat needed a treat to help take his mind off work or some other form of stress.

He set his briefcase down in the foyer and unzipped his dark blue windbreaker as he rushed into the kitchen to give Sara a kiss and tell her the good news about the weekend. He popped open an Irish ale, savoring the first bit of foam to hit his lips, as he sat down for dinner with the family. He was anxious to learn what the children had thought about doing as a family that weekend. Sean wanted to go to the zoo since he had been studying pandas at school, and he knew the National Zoo had America's most famous panda pair.

But little Erin--who in the morning wanted to go on some kind of elaborate Disney vacation--simply said, "Let's go visit Gramma."

Pat was intensely proud of her unselfish choice and broke out in a huge smile. He was equally proud of Sean who vigorously piped in his agreement.

"Then it's settled!" he said, proudly giving Erin a big hug. "We'll head out for Grandma's house early tomorrow morning."

Pat's mom, a silver-haired, short woman in her late sixties, still lived in Pennsylvania's Wyoming Valley, in a small town called Kingston, on the west side of the Susquehanna River. It was about a five hour drive from northern Virginia, but Pat didn't mind the journey. Her home was big, and the yard was large, and there was always a sense of peace being away from the hustle and bustle of the

Washington, DC area. Pat needed the time away from policies and politics. Time away from traffic and terrorists. It would be good to see Mom again.

The excitement was building in him like a child on Christmas Eve, waiting for the morning to come. He called his mother that night, and she was elated to hear the family would visit. It had been many months since they made the trip up north, and Grandma was always eager to see her grandchildren.

When they went to bed that night all Pat could talk about was the next day's trip. There were so many other things he knew he probably should share with Sara, but he just didn't know how. He didn't tell her about the new image he had that day of the boy hanging in the warehouse. Or about how he called the OSI at Pope Air Force Base, seeking more information about Josh Branford. Or that Josh Branford was the boy he had been having nightmares about. He didn't want to burden her any more than he already had.

He slept like a baby that night. Just pure, surrendering slumber. No sense of premonition, or vision, or prophetic warning. And no awareness of the dark sedan parked a block from the O'Donnell home with two men in the front seats. Binoculars and cameras in their laps. One with a .357 magnum revolver, the other with a .40 caliber Glock semi-automatic pistol, strapped in holsters on their hips.

~ 5 ~

Pat was already awake when the alarm clock screamed at 0600. He jumped from bed to get ready for the trip, but this morning he didn't make coffee. Before anyone else had even begun to stir, he slipped quietly out of his house, into the minivan, and headed for the Springfield-Franconia Parkway and the Springfield Mall. Across from the mall was a Starbucks coffee shop where he intended to buy a giant, venti-size coffee to get the road trip off to a great start.

It was beginning to dawn as he fired up the engine, but still dark enough to require headlights. He carefully backed out of his driveway and onto his street, turning east on the main boulevard in the town of Burke. As he straightened out the wheel to aim the van up the hill, he caught a glimpse in his side mirror of a dark blue sedan parked at the end of his street. He didn't recognize the car, and knew he had never seen it before. But he didn't think too much of it as he slowly drove up the hill to the stop sign. He let a few cars on the busy road pass by to his right and left before making his turn.

It was when he turned that he spotted the dark sedan again, coming over the top of the hill behind him with its lights off, moving slowly. *Flag on the field!* he thought, mocking what was an obvious amateurish attempt at surveillance. Rookie cops and new federal agents sometimes made that mistake--driving with headlights off while everyone else had theirs on. Not sure if he was the target of the surveillance--the rabbit as agents referred to it, Pat decided to dry some dry cleaning techniques. He busted a light at an intersection just before the on-ramp to the parkway, and the sedan kept pace with him busting it as well. When he entered the parkway, he slowly made his way to the far left lane, even though he intended to exit to the right only a few miles ahead. The sedan continued to follow his pattern, staying about a quarter mile behind him. Pat kept his left turn signal on the entire time, wanting to add to the confusion he was creating for his surveillants.

He wondered who they were. He doubted they were terrorists, but he didn't completely dismiss the idea since he knew he was well known in those circles as one of the Air Force's most aggressive CT agents. He also knew some of the people he rounded up in the Middle East, and their families, had a few scores to settle. No. This car had cop written all over it. It was dark blue with black wall tires, tinted windows, and a large antenna decorating the trunk. He was unable to see inside the dark windows well enough to discern even the number of occupants. *Why are they following me?* he wondered as he suddenly veered to the right and took his exit. The sedan had no time to react and continued straight on the parkway, managing to cross over only one lane to the right before overshooting the exit.

Happy that he had shaken the tail, Pat was also deeply concerned about being followed in the first place. He pulled into the Starbucks lot, intentionally parking behind the shop and out of view of the major roads that ran nearby. It was busy inside with many people like him looking for a hot, fresh cup of coffee to warm them up on this chilly fall morning. He studied their faces, looking at who might make eye contact and tell him in a mere glance if they were part of a surveillance team. But there was no one who piqued his interest or concern.

The ride back home was uneventful. He took a direct route so as not to tip off any would-be surveillance team that he was on to them. He was tempted to take a circuitous route back, which would be the prudent thing to do for safety reasons, but Pat knew these people--whoever they were--were not hostile. He was convinced they were the police or FBI or CIA or somebody interested in him suddenly.

The children were up and ready when he arrived home. Sara was showering as Pat fixed the kids breakfast and got their clothes ready for the road. He walked through the house with his coffee in hand as if it were a priceless piece of jewelry he didn't want to lose sight of.

"Oh, Starbucks I see!" Sara exclaimed as he walked in their bedroom while she was dressing. "I thought I heard the car start up earlier."

"Yes!" he said with a smile as he half-embraced her, holding the cup away so as not to spill any.

"Are the kids ready?"

"Sure are. Eating right now, and their clothes are laid out, so they'll be ready to go in a few minutes. I'll go check on them."

Pat headed for the kitchen, but stopped along the way and stood in the home's main hallway, lost in thought for a moment about the obvious surveillance he had just been under. He detoured to his den and popped open the safe where he kept his STU key. He reached into the back and pulled out his OSI sidearm, a 9 mm Beretta. He grabbed three loaded black magazines, opened the slide on the semi-automatic pistol, and inserted a magazine in the stock. He pressed the release. With a loud *CLANK*, the slide bolted forward, placing a round in the chamber. Pat de-cocked the pistol and placed it inside a canvas fanny pack, a specially designed pouch with Velcro compartments and straps to hold the gun and the magazines. As he was fastening the fanny pack to his waist, he turned to see Sara standing in the doorway watching him.

"Pat, is that necessary?" she asked with a look of worry across her face. "What's going on?"

"Everything's fine, Sara. This is my first weekend away from work, and with the recent terrorist attacks you know I can't be too careful. I mean, I could always get a call that I need to head out somewhere, so I should be armed and ready even while on leave."

He locked the safe and walked over to embrace her. "I hate that thing, Pat, especially around the kids. Be extra safe with it, okay?" she admonished him gently, then gave him a kiss.

"Let's go, gang!" he called as he grabbed his jacket and the suitcase Sara had packed for them, and headed for the van.

He discretely scanned the neighborhood as his family piled in, seatbelts snapping, and a little bit of early morning quarreling between the kids. No dark sedan in sight. Off they went, back up the same hill Pat had gone over earlier. But as he made his left turn, it was back. The same car was parked on a side road this time, and it pulled into traffic behind them as they headed for the parkway. Pat did not tell Sara what was going on. He didn't want to alarm her, especially in the heightened state of security following the 9/11 terrorist attacks.

The vehicle kept up with the O'Donnells as they made their way north. Pat took a route that brought him out west a bit to Route 15, then up to Interstate 81. While it was not the most direct route to his mother's house, it was much more scenic. There were lots of old farmhouses with cows and horses in pastures along the way, especially in Maryland and southern Pennsylvania. Although his family managed to enjoy the countryside beauty that surrounded them as they drove, Pat did not. He was too preoccupied with what was going on behind them.

He maintained a keen eye in his rearview mirror of the car following them. He knew the type of surveillance being conducted--a loose surveillance--meant to ascertain his general habits, to see where he was going without getting into the finer details of whom he may meet, or what he may specifically do if he left his vehicle. Somewhere just south of Pennsylvania, he lost sight of the sedan, and never saw it again for the rest of the journey. He surmised they might have gotten tired or bored. Perhaps they were called back by whoever sent them. It didn't matter. They were gone.

Before long, they were driving over the many crests in the Appalachian Mountain chain that formed the hundreds of valleys of northeastern Pennsylvania, one of which was the Wyoming Valley. The towns there had unique names, many of which reflected the colorful early heritage of the region. Miner's Mills. Forty-Fort.

Parsons. Sugar Notch. The dozens of cities, towns, boroughs, and hollows formed a patchwork quilt of communities linked by small roads and rail lines. Pat knew most of the thoroughfares since he grew up in that region. The mountains were at their prettiest this time of year. The leaves had started turning colors and falling down about a week before the leaves changed color in northern Virginia, and when the family reached the summit of one of the mountains of Appalachia, it was breathtaking. A rich carpet of gold, red, orange, green, and brown everywhere.

Grandma was waiting at her family room window, peering out when the van pulled up. She and son made eye contact and broke out into mutual smiles. She flew out the door and into the front yard to greet them all. When she hugged Pat, she held him a little tighter, and a little longer. He knew she worried about him because of his counterterrorism work, especially in light of the attacks in September.

"I missed ya, sonny!" she grinned.

When she spoke, she still had a touch of an Irish accent that Pat found so endearing, especially at this moment. Even Pat, a third-generation Irish-American, on occasion would find himself spitting out his words in a bit of the brogue, particularly after a pint or two of ale. He grew up virtually in an Irish clan environment. His father and grandfather had been coal miners in northeastern Pennsylvania and oftentimes spun tales of running with the Molly Maguires when they were younger.

The kids ran off ahead of their parents to explore their grandmother's big home. Pat hauled the family's travel bags upstairs to a guest bedroom, the rickety wooden steps in the old home creaking as he climbed. On his way back to join the ladies in the family room, he stopped for a peek inside his mother's refrigerator for a cold beer, but found none.

"Well, Mom, maybe in a bit I'll head out and buy some beer. You know how much I love Rolling Rock, and it's so hard to find in Virginia," he said with a slight grimace, gently chiding his mother for forgetting to buy some of his favorite locally brewed beer that came in its distinctive green glass bottles with horse logo.

The three of them chatted for some time, catching up on family news and discussing current events. Sara and Grandma wandered off in conversation while Pat looked around the family room, bringing back memories of where he lived as a young boy after the family moved from Scranton. His mom hadn't changed the room very much. The furniture was new, but the paintings and green window dressings were the same. It still gave him a warm feeling inside being back there, as it did every time he visited her. His mom's brown leather recliner was the same, though a bit worn over the years. Next to it was a small end table with a white-shaded lamp and Mom's essentials: a novel, reading glasses, and the television remote. Pat smiled to himself, finding some comfort in this one constant about his boyhood home. He looked at her wall clock and realized it was now 1600.

"Yikes, ladies! I'd better head out and buy some beer before it gets too close to dinner. Mom, is Tony Nardone's pizza joint still open on Kingston Corners? I just want a six-pack, and that is about the only place around here you can get one."

"It sure is. You remember how to get there?"

"Yes, Mom. I'll be back soon," Pat promised as he grabbed his car keys and bolted for the door.

It was nearly 1730 when Pat returned with a six-pack of ice cold Rolling Rock beer in one hand and a bag in his other from a "dollar-rama" type store.

"Well, it's about time!" his mother and Sara said in unison.

"We thought you got lost!" his mom teasingly reproached him. "Where did you go for beer? China?"

"Real funny, Mom!" Pat responded, his face and neck a bit red.

He was somewhat anxious but the ladies didn't key in on it.

"What's this from the dollar store?" Sara asked quizzically, taking the bag from him. "Of course, toys for the kids. I should have known," she smirked.

"Hey, I can't pass up a bargain--and everything for a dollar! What a deal!"

After a wonderful dinner of baked chicken, fresh hot buttered green beans, and Grandma's signature potato salad, followed by some homemade chocolate cake which the children devoured, it was time for bed. Pat's mom had fixed the bed in the guest bedroom, where he and Sara slept, while the kids camped out in the family room. Erin was on the sofa, while Sean curled up in a sleeping bag on the soft carpeted floor beneath her. To them it was a mini-adventure, and they talked and giggled for hours before falling asleep.

Morning came without alarm clocks or telephone calls from the boss saying to get to work fast because of some crisis. Instead, a peaceful dawn arrived with a near frosty chill that failed to deter a few brave birds. They chirped loudly outside the guest bedroom window. But despite the noise and rays of sun that filtered through the mini-blinds directly on his face, Pat did something this morning he rarely ever did. He slept in. Sara dared not wake him as she tiptoed downstairs in her pink robe, surprised to see the kids up and watching television with Grandma in the family room.

Nearly two hours later, Pat shuffled downstairs, groggy-eyed with hair unkempt, searching for and finding a pot of hot coffee waiting for him. After fixing himself a cup in his old favorite green and white mug from the Pennsylvania State Fair from many years back, he joined the family. Sean and Erin broke out into loud snickers seeing their father so tired and disheveled standing in the doorway slowly sipping the hot liquid.

"Well, look at you!   Mr. Sleepyhead!" Sara laughed.   "It's about time you got up!"

Pat's mother told them there was some breaking news coming up, but she didn't catch what it was about because they went right to a commercial.

"Great!" Pat said aloud as he stood in the doorway.   "I hope there's not been another terrorist attack."

He fully surmised the news must have been about the air campaign his boss told him would begin today.   The commercials ended, and the local news was on the air.   Behind the anchor and to her right was a banner that read, *Breaking News. Missing Child.*   She spoke:

"Police throughout Luzerne County are investigating the possible abduction of a seven year old Kingston boy.   He was last seen yesterday afternoon around four o'clock when his parents said he was on his way to this nearby store to buy some candy."

As the anchor spoke, the news station played a video segment showing the store...it was the same dollar-rama store Pat had been to the day before.   He felt a huge lump in his throat as the anchor continued to read her story.

"The parents of Ryan Russell are asking the public for any information they may have concerning the whereabouts of their missing son."

At the moment she said the boy's name, the news station put his picture on the screen.   And at precisely that same moment, Pat felt the blood drain from his body.   His knees became weak.   His heart pounded furiously.   His hand loosened up, instantly sending his favorite coffee cup crashing and shattering, almost as if in slow motion, to the floor.   Hot coffee and sharp ceramic shards sprayed everywhere.   Pat didn't move his eyes from the television.   He was riveted on the boy's photograph. He knew Ryan Russell.   He had seen him before.   He was the little boy who appeared in Pat's mind for a brief moment just two days before as he sat in General Swank's conference room.   He was the little boy Pat saw hanging in a warehouse--the image that flashed in his mind along with the full frontal assault on all his senses.

"Pat!" Sara screamed as she rushed toward him, grabbing his arm to steady him. "What happened? Are you okay? Why did you drop your cup? What a mess!"

"I'm okay, Baby. I just felt a little faint. That story of the missing boy scared me I guess. It happened so close to here. Our own kids. Same age."

Pat muttered a nearly incoherent string of thoughts as he continued to watch the television in a daze.

"You had better sit down Pat," his mom cautioned as she headed to the kitchen for some paper towels and cleaning solution.

"You were at that dollar store around the same time. Do you recognize that boy? Did you see him there? Maybe you saw something that you can tell the police. Something that might help find him." Sara was nearly pleading with him.

Pat turned his gaze away from the television and to Sara once the story about Ryan Russell ended. "No, I didn't see him there. I didn't see anything out of the ordinary," he told her as reassuringly as he could.

But judging from the look on her face, he knew she was as deeply concerned as he was. First the dreams about a murdered boy. Now a missing boy in Pennsylvania whom Pat most likely came near the afternoon before. It was obvious she couldn't make sense of it, and was afraid to press it. Afraid of what she might find out.

"Sara, we had better get our things together and head back to Virginia. It's going to be late when we get home if we don't leave soon."

It was about 1000 when they were ready to depart. Grandma tried her best to get them to stay for lunch, but gave up when Pat insisted they leave immediately to get ahead of any beltway traffic. The departure took less than fifteen minutes and had every appearance of being an evacuation, rushed and harried.

It was a long, quiet ride back to Virginia. Sara and Pat barely spoke, each busy in deep thought. Pat was confused about the entire series of events. Dreams. Images. Real boys murdered or missing. But there was something very unique about the image of Ryan Russell that made it stand apart from the dreams Pat had of Josh Branford, and it was not lost on him. When Pat dreamt about Josh it was after he had been abducted and murdered. But his image of Ryan—that vision came to him two full days before the boy even disappeared. If his dreams had been a connection to the past, then his image of two days back was an apparition of the future.

~ 6 ~

The ride back from Pennsylvania gave Pat time to think not only about the significance of the image of Ryan Russell, but also time to think about what he wanted to do next. He felt an intense need to talk with Father Reynolds again. He had to let him know about the new image. And the experience in Pennsylvania. And the new missing boy--Ryan.

The O'Donnells arrived in Burke around 1500 in the afternoon. For the first time in the last five hours, Pat attempted to talk with Sara. He grabbed her by the arm as she was walking in from the garage. She jerked her arm back with a gasp, signaling a fear he was uncertain existed, but now was confirmed.

"Sara, we need to talk. It's important," he practically pleaded with her.

She wouldn't look him in the eye. "Pat, I'm so scared. I don't know what to think about what has been going on. If you are going to tell me something that will cause me to take our kids and run from here tonight, then maybe I don't want to know."

She was almost tearful and her hands shook. It was clear to him that she feared he was some sort of depraved child murderer.

"Let's go into the bedroom and talk," Pat offered, once again trying unsuccessfully to take her by the hand. But at least this time she cautiously followed him.

Pat sat on the edge of the bed while Sara stood near the door. "Come here. Please. Sit with me. Hold my hand."

Sara slowly walked over and sat down. To Pat it seemed a widerthan-expected distance, but she held her hand out to hold his. He proceeded to tell her everything. Everything except about being followed Saturday morning by the apparent police car. He told her about Josh and the news story in the Washington Observer. About the phone call to the OSI detachment at Pope Air Force Base. About the vision he had in General Swank's conference room--the vision of Ryan before his abduction.

She stared silently at the throw rug as he spoke. She seemed to be examining its small patterns formed from strands of fabric that chaotically twisted and looped and swirled together.

"Is Ryan alive?" she asked sobbing slightly, looking at her hands now.

"I don't know, Sara. I hope so, but I am so worried about him because in my vision he was dead."

She turned her head and faced him with a look that suggested an ultimatum. "Pat. I will only ask this once, and I want you to be truthful. Did you have anything at all to do with these children and their murders or abductions?"

Tears streamed from her face as she asked this question, the answer to which might change her life forever.

He looked at her, and with all the conviction he could raise within him...Pat, the man unable to tell believable lies, simply said, "No. I had nothing to do with those boys and their abductions or Josh's murder."

With those words Sara slid closer, propped her head on his shoulder, and wept for a few moments. She seemed to believe him. He put his arm around her and held her close. He needed her support right now more than anything.

"What does all this mean? Why the dreams and why the image, Pat?"

"I don't know, but I want to go see Father Reynolds and talk with him like we've just talked--tell him everything, too. Maybe he can help me."

They sat in silence, Pat holding her close, for another half hour. When she seemed to regain some semblance of composure, he kissed her forehead softly, and left to visit Father Reynolds.

He took his Subaru once again over to the Our Lady of La Salette. The drive was a blur. He drove incredibly fast, and was almost caught by a speed trap the Fairfax County Police had set up on one of the main roads, close to the public library. If there were any sedans following him, Pat didn't notice. He temporarily suspended his CT training...eyes focused straight ahead, without scanning his surroundings. Just a determination to see the priest and try to get some answers.

He found Father Reynolds outside on the grounds raking some leaves from around the walkway that led to the church entrance. He seemed to be waging an uphill battle with the late afternoon breeze. Each time he made a pile of leaves, the wind would pick them up in small, spiteful protest and scatter them back about the walkway. A white stone statue of the Virgin Mary stood as if in sentry, with a smile that at this moment almost seemed to be a snicker at the priest for his war of attrition with the leaves.

"Hi, Father!" Pat called out as he hastily parked his car, rather crookedly, in front.

"Pat? What's going on? Is everything all right?"

"Well, no, Father. It's not all right. Things are very scary right now. Do you have time to talk?"

"Of course. Of course. Come in, Patrick," the old priest said putting an arm around him and escorting him into his office. "I wasn't getting anywhere with those leaves, so maybe it's time for me to quit anyway!"

Pat was breathing a bit hard as they entered the office. The scent of church rushed his head, adding more solemnity to the visit. It was a coalescing of incense, novena candles, and cherry wood. Father Reynolds asked him to sit and calm down a few minutes while he went to get a couple cans of Coke to drink. He came back and shut the door, handing Pat a cold soda can and a couple of white tissues to sop up the condensation that had already begun to form.

"I suppose we need to chat again within the safe confines of a confession?" Father Reynolds asked, recalling the session they had just a few days earlier in which Pat insisted on a confession to protect his privilege of confidentiality from military prying.

"Yes, Father. Please indulge me once again."

"It's my pleasure," he began as he made the sign of the cross and blessed him.

As he did earlier for Sara, Pat related all the details to Father Reynolds of the strange events he had been experiencing. The priest said nothing the entire time, listening intently as Pat opened up. He was unsurprised when Father Reynolds asked him the same series of questions Sara asked about his involvement in these crimes. And just as he reassured Sara, he also reassured Father Reynolds he was innocent. When Pat finished, Father Reynolds said nothing at all for at least five minutes. He stared at his hands, deep in thought. He ran his fingers over the gold band on his left hand, the symbol of his marriage to the church. Finally, the priest spoke.

"Assuming you have been truthful with me--and I have no reason to doubt you--after all, you appear to be deeply troubled by all this. Assuming you are not crazy--which I have never believed you were. I want to find some deeper spiritual reason for all this."

Pat interrupted him. "What do you mean, spiritual?"

"Well, the Bible is riddled with stories and references to dreams and visions. To deny them as real, and possibly significant in some non-earthly way, is to deny the early prophets were messengers of God. What I mean Pat, and I'm not suggesting you are a prophet, but perhaps you have been chosen by God for some purpose He has yet to reveal fully to you."

"I'm afraid I don't understand, Padre," Pat said with a look of skepticism on his face. But deep inside, Pat really did understand. *Perhaps there is a connection between these recent events and my one supreme truism, that I have some pre-programmed mission to accomplish in my lifetime. Something profound.*

"There are many things about our world and about our God we don't understand. The church is not quick to jump on strange events and declare them either miracles or the work of the devil," Father Reynolds continued, staring intently at him. "Look. When you told me about the deep sensory quality of your dreams, I was amazed. I told you how unique you were. I suspect you have had a gift laying dormant all your life which God has now chosen to unleash for some purpose."

"Father, pardon my language, but you're scaring the hell out of me!" Pat exclaimed. "What do you mean, a *gift*?"

"Look at it this way--the second boy about whom you had the vision--Ryan. Perhaps he's still alive and you have the clues that can help save him. Maybe you can help find this child!"

"If I go to the police and report my dreams and visions, they'll immediately suspect I had something to do with these children. Just like Sara did. Only, I don't think they'll be so quick to believe me when I deny it!"

"Isn't there anyone in your line of work you can talk with? I mean--isn't there an Ex-Files-like department where psychic or paranormal phenomena are explored?"

Pat silently studied the wall, staring at one of the portraits, as he thought about what Father Reynolds had said. It was one of his favorite images from childhood, a depiction of the Archangel Michael driving Satan down from heaven into hell. Michael had the devil pinned to the ground with a sharp spear in his hand, the flames from hell lapping upward all around. Pat first saw this depiction in St. Lucy's church, on one of the brightly colored window murals. Sometimes as a child he would pretend he was Michael and go on an imaginary glorious quest to drive away evil. As a federal agent, he wore a Saint Michael medallion on a chain around his neck, like many cops did. He sub-consciously touched his shirt right over the spot where Michael rested at this moment.

But there was more. There was always a spiritual component to his one *supreme truism*, though the connection was always unclear. Suddenly, he began to draw up from deep within his memory the thoughts and images he held in his mind as a child of only four or five years—when he first began to sense his purpose or mission. As he stared at the portrait, and touched his Saint Michael medallion, the same feelings began to flood back in his mind.

He didn't want to talk about it with the priest, but there *was* an office he believed had something to do with the unexplained. Pat wasn't cleared for the things that went on inside the mysterious vaults of this office within the Pentagon, but if it did anything at all remotely related to the paranormal, he was about to find out. He would go see an old friend in the morning.

"I don't know, Father. I'll have to do some scratching around on this. I just hope I've seen the end of all this craziness. I want my life back. My normal life!"

Father Reynolds wanted Pat to recite the Lord's Prayer out loud along with him. In particular, he asked him to pause and reflect on the words, *Thy Kingdom come, Thy will be done on earth as it is in heaven.* He told him this was important because it signified acknowledgment that sometimes God wants the business of heaven to be performed on earth. The priest was convinced God was tapping on Pat's shoulder rather forcefully with his dreams and the image, and that Pat needed to open himself up to hear God's voice for further direction.

They stepped outside together, leaving the peaceful scents of the church behind them, out to the brisk fall air. Pat could smell the homey aroma of fireplaces burning in the subdivisions nearby. The breeziness was gone, and the autumn leaves were ready for taming. Father Reynolds grabbed his rake once again as they said their good-byes.

This time Pat drove a bit slower. This time he noticed the sedan parked on the side road near the church as he drove away. *You bastards were there at my house again and followed me here!* he thought as he drove off, again taking a straightforward, and direct path home.

The fact these people followed him to his church enraged him. He felt tremendously violated--a line had been crossed that to Pat, because of his deep Catholic faith, was meant to be inviolable. The sedan was in tow maintaining the same kind of loose surveillance as it had the day before. He kept a check on it in his rearview mirror. Headlights off just like the day before, even though it had started getting dark outside. One thing was for certain. Whoever they were, there was no doubt in Pat's mind they were connected to what had been going on with him lately. Somehow, someone had connected him to Josh and Ryan, and now they were watching him closely.

~ 7 ~

When he arrived home he found Sara already in bed, but wide awake still. He told her everything about his discussion with Father Reynolds. She was stunned, to say the least, and unsure of the priest's advice.

"I dunno, Pat. That all seems kinda weird."

"That's what I told Father Reynolds, but he seems awfully sure about this. I figure I have no other real alternatives at this point. I'm going to try hard to open my heart and mind to God. If He's talking to me, I want Him to know I'm listening."

He tried to snuggle up with Sara in bed. He really wasn't trying to arouse her to the point of lovemaking. It was more like a subconscious test. She pulled away slightly, only allowing Pat to kiss her goodnight.

"Let's just get some sleep tonight. We've had a busy weekend, so let's just rest now," she said softly, looking the other way.

Pat rolled over without protest. He wanted to believe Sara was completely convinced he had nothing to do with the two boys, but he knew in his heart she had doubts. It sickened him to think she might actually harbor thoughts that he had something to do with their tragic disappearances. He wasn't quite ready for sleep so he flipped the television on and began to surf channels. Virtually every major station had breaking news about the air campaign that had begun in earnest in Afghanistan. *Just like Colonel Lyons told me*, Pat thought, smiling to himself. He left the television on, setting the sleep timer for an hour. But he was more tired than he realized. The clock radio's red glow mixed with the dim light of the moon as it trickled in through the sheer drapes. Red, and white, and sleep. They both drifted off in silence, talking no more that night.

The next day at work Pat approached Colonel Lyons as soon as he walked into his office.

"Boss, can I have a moment with you...closed-door, if you don't mind?"

"Sure, come in. What's on your mind?" he asked as Pat carefully shut the large oak door to keep it from slamming on its own weight.

"Sir, I want to go see Colonel Helmsley this morning. I believe I may have stumbled onto something of his recently that I need to talk with him about. Do you have any problems if I give him a call?"

"I know I can't pry into what this is about, but understand that Colonel Helmsley is not likely to be able to confirm anything for you. I guess what I'm saying is, if you think you have run across something in his bailiwick, there probably won't be any closure for you."

Colonel Lyons wanted Pat to understand that he would probably get a mere "Thanks" from Colonel Helmsley, without ever knowing where his information went. But Pat knew better. What Colonel Lyons didn't understand was that what Pat stumbled upon was *himself*. If what he had to tell Colonel Helmsley were to go anywhere or nowhere, Pat would have his closure.

"Roger that, Sir. I understand. I just want him to hear what I have to say, and then I can move on. As you may recall, I worked for him when I was doing my desert counterterrorism stuff. I feel very comfortable talking with him."

"I know, Pat. Well, good luck. Keep me in the loop to the extent you can."

Pat was incredibly fond of Colonel John Helmsley, also a career Air

Force OSI special agent, and his region commander at Langley Air Force Base in Virginia when Pat took control of all CT operations in the Middle East from his home station at Shaw Air Force Base in Sumter, South Carolina. Before calling him, he sat and thought for a moment about how he and Colonel Helmsley left their respective assignments in South Carolina and Virginia to work at the Pentagon together, but because their current jobs were so unrelated, they rarely saw each other these days.

While he fished his Air Staff directory from his desk drawer, he thought about the special job Colonel Helmsley now had. He was the Director of Security and Investigative Programs for the Secretary of the Air Force. The office was more commonly known as SAF/AAZ. Both names were fairly vanilla sounding on the surface, but hidden beneath was a complex family of Special Access Programs--SAPs as they were known--involving things only imaginable in science fiction movies. About all Pat really knew was that Colonel Helmsley was responsible for the security of classified Air Force acquisition programs--all the emerging high-tech weapon systems. He also knew, albeit unofficially, that his office was the focal point within the Pentagon for managing all the spooky things that went on at "Area 51" in Nevada. Open speculation within the Air Force, by those not privy to AAZ operations, suggested this was the place that held all the cards to extraterrestrial--alien--information.

Although he dialed Colonel Helmsley's direct line, he knew someone else would answer and screen the call. The staff there was suspicious to near paranoid.

"AAZ," was all the person at the other end stated when he picked up the telephone. Following this brief and somewhat cold greeting, Pat heard a click sound on the line. He knew this meant they had telephone handsets with buttons on them that one had to hold to transmit one's voice. It would go mute when released. It was a security feature to ensure that if a phone was set down on a desk, no one could inadvertently transmit background conversations that, most assuredly, would be classified.

"Hi, this is Major O'Donnell in SAF IG, calling for Colonel Helmsley. Is he available?"

CLICK! "Stand by, Sir, let me see if he's in."

Pat heard another click, then the familiar voice of his former boss. "Pat? Is this Patrick Sean O'Donnell?"

"Hey, Sir, how are you these days?" Pat asked with obvious excitement in his voice, beaming a broad smile in his tiny cubicle.

"Fine, Buddy. What's going on at your end? You're not calling to tell me OSI is investigating me, are you?"

"No, Sir. Not today anyway. Actually, I was calling to see if I could come up to your cone of silence to chat about something. I don't want to discuss it on a STU. Do you have some time?"

"Let me see," Colonel Helmsley began, as he pulled his day planner open. "Well, I'll be free from ten to noon--assume that will give us enough time?"

"That should be more than enough! I'll see you then."

"Bye, Pat." Colonel Helmsley hung up with one last click of his handset button.

Great! Pat thought. He busied himself until 1000 by checking all his emails and surfing the intelligence traffic on his TOP SECRET computer system. The daily intelligence was voluminous because of the massive strikes the United States leveled against the Taliban. He read with almost giddy delight the reporting on the initial air campaign...it was spectacular! The element of surprise was superbly achieved, in part attributed to the Pentagon's deception in "appearing" to stand down the CAT and NMCC. There were even reports that as the cruise missiles were en route, Taliban and al Qaeda forces were celebrating in the streets over the *cowardice* of the United States. Then all hell broke loose as a rain of fire came down from the heavens and from all other directions. Bunkers and buildings were obliterated. Thousands of Taliban and al Qaeda fighters were vaporized in the first few seconds of the campaign when the Air Force dropped huge air-fuel bombs over wide areas that detonated with nearly as much force as atomic weapons. He read each report with great fascination, occasionally snickering out loud.

The appointed hour came, and Pat headed for the door, somewhat nervous and unsure how Colonel Helmsley would react. Snaking his way through the Pentagon, he was almost run over by an old woman driving one of the Public Affair's electric golf carts. She honked a little horn when she was about three feet behind him, causing him to jump out of the way. He walked up to the door to the AAZ office--really a huge vault with a safe dial and a large chrome lever handle. He picked up the phone on the wall. It was merely a handset and cradle, without a dial. It connected automatically. The voice he heard answer was the same as the voice who answered the telephone when he called Colonel Helmsley earlier.

"Hi, this is Major O'Donnell, outside your door for a meeting with Colonel Helmsley."

CLICK. "Stand by, Sir."

About two minutes later Pat heard some muffled noises on the other side of the vault door, and then it opened. Colonel Helmsley stepped halfway out, propping the half ton battleship-gray painted steel door open with his left hand while shaking Pat's hand with the other. He looked up and down the hallway checking to see who was walking nearby. Pat grinned, knowing that Colonel Helmsley was reflexively exercising his counterterrorism training in the Pentagon halls.

"Come on in!" he said enthusiastically. "It's good to see you."

"Good to see you too, Sir!"

Pat thought about it for a moment--it had been at least six months or so since they last got together. The colonel still looked the same. A jolly, stocky man with thick gold-rimmed glasses. He parted his light brown hair in the middle--an almost unheard of practice for an Air

Force officer. It was his signal, an in-your-face expression of being a rebel of sorts. He also was a man with significant power in the Air Force and Department of Defense. The programs he worked were so sensitive, that it was nothing for him to waltz past the chain of command to see the Secretary of the Air Force or even the Secretary of Defense directly.

As they stepped into the office area, he understood the reason behind the muffled noises he had heard. There were two more doors to go through beyond the vault. He could see the alarm panel as he stepped through the second one. Motion sensors. Laser. Infrared. They had it all. He also took note of coverings over some of the wall hangings, and little screens over computer monitors as he walked through the area to the conference room. They had *sanitized* the place since he was not cleared, covering anything that might reveal their work. A flashing red light on the ceiling in the center of the office area was a last reminder to all who worked there that an *uncleared* person was in the area, so they had to be mindful of what they said in his presence.

Pat glanced around the Spartan conference room as Colonel Helmsley led the way. There were some pictures of stealth aircraft on the dark paneled walls. F-117 fighters. B-2 bombers. These were programs Colonel Helmsley worked when they were still in the *black*-- a term people in the military and the Intelligence Community used to refer to Special Access Programs, activities funded by deep-pocket budgets hidden from Congress and the public. In the center of the huge wooden conference table, he spied a large marble globe, supported by a shiny brass frame. It must have been fourteen or sixteen inches in diameter, and was solid black with the continents etched into the marble itself. This was the *black world* symbol of the people in this secret community--a kind of *wink and nod* way of recognizing each other informally.

"What's on your mind, Pat? What brings you to my world today?"

"Sir, I have to chat with you about something I have been

experiencing. Something very personal. I don't know if any of this falls in your area, or if you can point me to someone who can help me, but I figured you're a good start since you work all the spooky stuff in the Air Force."

Pat was savvy enough to know that he was bringing Colonel Helmsley an issue that had no Air Force connection. He was aware the FBI had lead in child abductions, so he was counting on Colonel Helmsley to point him to a trusted agent within the FBI with whom he could talk. Helmsley maintained a good poker face as Pat gave his opening soliloquy, occasionally taking notes. It was a *neither confirm nor deny* stare as Pat went on to describe the dreams and the image, and his suspicion that he was having some kind of psychic experience. He went over every step he took in Pennsylvania when he visited his mother, the dollar-rama, the pizza parlor for beer, everything. One point Pat emphasized was that he wasn't sure if Ryan Russell was still alive.

"That's some pretty weird stuff," Colonel Helmsley said removing his glasses and rubbing his eyes as he wrapped things up. Pat found this a bit odd coming from a man who was deeply connected to weirdness every day.

"As you know from your years in OSI, we've used psychics to help solve some tough cases. That's not a big secret. I'm personally not sure about psychics and their so-called powers, mainly because I think the bulk of those who claim such power are scam artists. But I know you, Pat, and you're no con man."

"So where do I go from here? Do you know anyone who can help me? Maybe use this information to help find Ryan Russell and maybe Josh's killer?"

"Well, I have some contacts in the Bureau with whom I work my programs. Let me call them and see if I can set something up. I have to be honest with you, if what you are telling me is the real deal, we'll have to move fast. If this kid in Pennsylvania is alive, then time is of the essence."

"Understand, Sir. The faster the better for me."

"One question. Other than me--who else have you had any conversations with about these kids?"

Pat paused and bit his lip before replying. He was determined to keep his contacts with Father Reynolds private. "I've told Sara everything, and I did call Rusty Baker at Pope last week to ask about the Branford murder. I didn't tell him anything about the dreams I had."

"Okay, good--" Colonel Helmsley began, but Pat cut him off before he could continue.

"There's something else going on, Sir. I don't know if it's related, and my wife doesn't know about this. I'm being followed--started Saturday morning."

He proceeded to tell the colonel all about the sedan and its actions, and his suspicions it was a law enforcement vehicle. He chuckled a bit when he talked about the headlights being off the first time he spotted the car.

"You taught me well, Sir. I would never make that mistake myself!"

"No I should say you wouldn't, Pat!" Colonel Helmsley said with a hearty laugh. "Okay, let me get on the horn, and I'll call you at your office. Do you need me to deconflict this with your boss?"

"That would help. He knows I came to see you, but if you could touch base with him and let him know you need to *borrow* me for the day, I'd appreciate it."

"It's done!" the colonel said as he stood to shake Pat's hand.

He escorted him back out to the hall, outside the vault door. Before Pat departed, the colonel looked him in the eye intently, as if what he was about to say was so important that he wanted to drill it deeply into Pat's mind, well below the surface.

In a low voice he said, "Pat, I don't know where this will go, but as an old friend and former boss, I want you to always watch your back."

"Thanks, Colonel. I will. And, can I make one request of you?" he asked with a sheepish look.

"Fire away!"

Pat looked up and down the corridor for people. He waited until after an Army NCO walked past before continuing. "Whatever happens with this, would you ensure you remain in the loop? I mean, even if you have to concoct some reason to keep Air Force relevant—would you do so? I don't want to be turned over to the FBI and see the ties to you cut."

"I wouldn't have it any other way, Pat. I'll be there with you as this unfolds."

Pat headed back to his office. He loved walking through the Pentagon. There were so many beautiful paintings and exhibits to see adorning the walls. He especially loved the area around the Chief of Naval Operations office, and oftentimes he'd take a longer-than-necessary route just to walk past it. Paintings of ocean battles. Old ships firing volleys. Flame and smoke. The paintings were so real, he felt they almost pulled him into the scene. But the beauty and majesty of these portraits were destroyed during the September 11th terror attack on the Pentagon. The "wedge" where they were proudly displayed took the most direct hit from the aircraft that crashed into the building. Pat got as close as he could to the area as he journeyed back to the IG's office, stopping in front of the construction barricade. He closed his eyes and imagined the Pentagon was whole again, as before, and through his memories of the past he enjoyed the paintings once more.

Colonel Lyons was waiting for him as he entered the office. "Come in, son! Let's chat," the colonel said, ever fatherly-like, swinging the heavy wooden door shut with a loud *THUNK!*

Pat knew what was coming. He could only guess Colonel

Helmsley's call beat him to the office. He was right.

"John Helmsley told me he will need you up in his office today at one o'clock. He didn't tell me what this was about but said it was important and asked for my indulgence. Of course, I am always willing to support John."

"Thanks, Sir," Pat said with a look of gratitude for his boss's understanding. "Well, any objection if I get in a run before I go back up to AAZ?"

"Nah--go ahead. Sounds like your day is shot anyway, at least with regard to work here."

Pat made one last check of his emails before leaving the office. He thought about the implication of Colonel Helmsley's call to Colonel Lyons. Since he called Colonel Lyons with a specific time for the meeting, then he most likely made a call to his FBI friends first. He knew the FBI was very busy these days due to the terrorist threat, so the agents there must have felt the issue was important enough to drop their pick and come over.

Following his run around the Capitol Mall area and a quick shower at the POAC, Pat was running a few minutes late for his appointment. In his rush, he failed to comb his hair properly, so a large calic tuft stuck up in the back like Alfalfa from the Little Rascals. The colonel came right out to greet him when he arrived at the vault door and announced himself. Apologizing profusely for being late, Pat stepped in to the familiar sight. The sanitized spaces. The flashing red light. When he walked into the conference room, however, he was surprised to see four people there. He didn't know any of them but thought one man looked familiar. He walked over to him, pointing at him with his right hand.

"You're Rusty Baker, aren't you?"

"Yes, Sir. Nice to meet you finally after hearing about you over the years and chatting with you on the phone last week."

There was no way Baker could have driven up from Pope Air Force Base that fast. He had to have been in the area for some other reason. Maybe he was already in town visiting OSI Headquarters.

"Listen, folks," Colonel Helmsley started. "Before we make the rounds, let me introduce you to Major Patrick O'Donnell from the IG's office."

They all nodded as they looked at Pat, who felt for a moment like a bug under a microscope. Rusty Baker was the first to introduce himself, not so much to Pat, but to the rest of the group. Next was a tall black man, perhaps in his late thirties or early forties. He was clean cut, with an athletic build, and dressed casually. He had a fanny pack on his waist that Pat knew contained a handgun.

"I'm Detective Ron Parsons of the North Carolina State Police," he said giving Pat a hearty handshake.

The next man to greet him was dressed like Detective Parsons...casual clothes with a fanny pack. He was younger than Parsons, perhaps about twenty-five years or so, but not as physically fit. Soft and a bit overweight. Pat mistook him as another state trooper in the split second between meeting the detective and him.

"And I'm Special Agent Dick Williams of the Raleigh-Durham FBI Field Office. Nice to meet you, major," he said giving him a soft and loose handshake, with a fluffy pale-skin hand.

Pat was beginning to piece some things together. *Rusty must have come up with these two guys from North Carolina over the weekend. But why?*

Finally, Pat was introduced to Colonel Helmsley's counterpart from HQ's FBI, Special Agent Vicky Desantis. As she extended her hand for Pat to shake, she gave him a sultry smile. Her hand was warm; her shake was firm, and it lasted a second or two longer than Pat had expected. He instinctively glanced down at her left hand as they shook in greeting. No rings. When she spoke, her deep voice magnetically commanded his attention. In a matter of a few seconds, he assessed her--very sexy, a bit flirtatious, and stunningly beautiful. At thirty-two years of age, she might as well have been twenty-one.

Long blond curls, clear blue eyes, about five feet eleven inches tall, and slender. She wore a dark blue business suit, a jacket and blouse that matched her skirt. Her long legs were perfect and graceful. Pat was conflicted--a happily married Catholic man--he found himself attracted to her.

"It's my pleasure to meet you, Vicky," Pat muttered, suddenly becoming self-conscious of his unkempt hair. He tried to pat it down, but it was nearly dry and wouldn't give up the fight to stick up a bit.

The colonel asked them to sit down, and was about to give an overview of why they were there, when Pat interrupted. He had given up looking at Vicky for a few moments to look again at the two men from North Carolina. *They're dressed for surveillance work!*

"I take it you were the team following me this weekend?"

"I told you he burned us!" Detective Parsons said scowling at FBI agent Williams. "You should have let me drive."

Rusty Baker jumped in sounding somewhat apologetic. "Sir, look, I was not part of the surveillance, but I knew about it. I came up here on my own to meet with the OSI IG because of the Bureau and state police interest in you."

For a moment, Pat was in charge. The grousing between the men made them vulnerable. "Is someone going to clue me in as to why you were surveilling me?" he asked with more than a hint of irritation in his voice.

Baker spoke. "When you called me and asked about the crime scene--"

Agent Dick Williams interrupted him in mid-sentence. "Rusty, let's not get into that until after the rights advisement."

"Rights advisement!" Pat stammered, face red with anger. "What the hell?" he asked in near rage.

Williams was about to launch into the Miranda warning when Desantis suddenly gave him a look and a wave of her hand that suggested he should suspend with his textbook requirements. Up to that point she had been silent, taking in every word, every gesture, every facial expression, as if she were tallying things up in some mental analysis of everyone in the room, not just Pat. He sized them all up a notch based on this. A clearer gradation appeared. Williams was obviously fresh from the FBI Academy in Quantico. That explained driving the car with the headlights off during the surveillance. The more seasoned and street-smart Detective Parsons knew better, but the young FBI agent played his "federal jurisdiction" card to the detriment of the investigation. And Desantis--she was clearly more experienced and was an out-of-the-box thinker, not compliance-oriented. She bent the rules a tad if she needed, probably something that was critical in the mysterious SAP world of the FBI. It was also clear that Williams wasn't going to buck her; she apparently had some level of authority over him. Before anyone could speak next, Pat threw a simple demand on the table.

"I want you all to know that I will answer your questions so long as you act professionally. I believe time is of the essence in finding the Pennsylvania boy, so I'll waive counsel for now. I want you to annotate that in your interview log," he said looking sternly at Agent Williams.

Williams nodded in agreement and hurriedly wrote down what he said. Parsons and Baker appeared to be disappointed. But Desantis and Colonel Helmsley both smiled at him--they knew exactly what he was doing, and he felt it. The statement he made about waiving counsel was brilliant. Pat had bought some insurance--he established a possible defense for himself in the event the government decided to go after him. *But what do Desantis and the colonel really want in this? What are their equities?* Pat thought, sensing there was more to this meeting than a criminal investigation.

"So, is anyone going to explain to me why you guys followed me this weekend?" he snapped at them.

"Let me explain things," Baker began. "Sir, when you called me last week to talk about the Branford murder, you asked about the crime scene. I didn't know it at the time because I hadn't been to the Task Force meeting, but there were things about the crime the police were keeping quiet about. Things not mentioned in the press."

Pat's mind was racing now, searching back over what he had said like a movie in fast reverse.

"It was the metal wire, wasn't it?" he asked, already knowing the answer. He was disappointed in himself for mentioning this level of detail on the phone with Baker last week--it was rare for him to slip up like that.

"Yes, it was," interrupted Williams. "We want to know how you knew about the murder weapon. We kind of figure only the killer would know what was used. That's why we set up the surveillance once Agent Baker told us about the phone call with you."

"Gentlemen, let me state up front, clearly and unequivocally, I had nothing to do with either the Branford murder or the disappearance of Ryan Russell. I do not know anyone who was involved with either crime. I believe Ryan Russell is still alive, and time is running out to find him!"

"Then how do you explain knowing the precise murder weapon that was used, and how can you explain being near Ryan Russell before he disappeared? That's an awful lot of coincidences, don't you agree?" Detective Parsons boomed forcefully.

Pat immediately liked Parsons. He liked his interview style and determination, which was much like his own. He looked at Colonel Helmsley and Vicky as if to ask for guidance. He wasn't sure how much of the *spooky* aspects of his dreams and vision he was free to tell these men. They both nodded their heads in approval.

"Okay, gentlemen, I'll tell you everything I know. I don't care if you believe me or not, but it's all true."

Pat gave the interviewers a full rundown of every detail of every dream and the image. He outlined the trip to his mother's house, and the pizza parlor beer run, and the dollar-rama where Ryan apparently met his fate. They were stunned and clearly not ready to accept the explanation. Parsons in particular was not buying it.

"So you expect us to believe you are some kind of psychic?"

"I'm not a psychic, never claimed to be. I'm simply telling you what I know about both crimes based on my dreams and this, this--image thing," Pat stammered.

Williams chimed in. "We know you have an airtight alibi for the Branford murder because you have been working nearly every day at the Pentagon for the last month, and we confirmed you were at work when the abduction occurred, as well as the other attempted abductions. But you sure look guilty of the Russell boy's disappearance--I mean, you were right there when he disappeared. Maybe you are part of some kind of weird psycho pedophile ring that abducts and murders boys!"

"Screw you!" Pat shouted at him, pounding his fists on the table. He stood up momentarily, towering over the seated Williams who flinched in obvious fear.

Williams started to regain some composure and was about to drill into Pat a bit harder, when Vicky interrupted, reached over, and took Pat's hand for a moment. It was warm and comforting, and he immediately sat down again.

"Patrick, let's take each crime apart separately. Tell me more about the sensory aspects of your dreams about the Branford boy. I'm interested in what is beyond the range of vision of a normal crime scene."

He began to describe the dreams again, but Vicky stopped him abruptly and asked him to focus on what was going on around *him* in the immediate area.

"Well, again, I'm crouching down by the briar patch. My arms are getting scratched up pretty fierce, but I can't move despite the pain. I'm forced to stare at Josh."

Vicky looked at Detective Parsons and Agent Williams. "Guys, did you search the area of the briar patch? How far did you extend the crime scene?"

"Look, Agent Desantis, we covered the whole area. Every inch," Parsons insisted.

"Look again. Take a forensics team to the park and use luminal on the briar patch. I suspect you'll find some blood on the brush. Hell, light up the whole area! I believe our killer crouched and watched the body for some time after he assaulted and murdered Josh. Check for signs of someone standing in or around the briar patch. Look for shoe prints, cigarette butts, hair, fibers, anything at all."

"Okay, Vicky," said Agent Williams. "Let me make a call now and get some folks on it. Anything's worth a try."

Williams grabbed a phone in the conference room and dialed his office in Raleigh-Durham. "Hello, this is Agent Williams calling from the Pentagon for--"

He suddenly appeared flustered, as if the person who had answered couldn't hear him and cut him off.

"This is Agent Dick Williams!" he stammered loudly.

Colonel Helmsley walked over to him and politely pointed to the button on the handset. "You have to hold this down or they can't hear you." Everyone in the room broke out in muffled laughter while Williams redialed his office.

Agent Desantis seemed to take charge of things, now that Williams was neutered by having made a fool of himself.

"Patrick, there are some serious discrepancies in the Russell boy's disappearance and what you've told us of your trips to buy beer and the dollar store."

"Like what?" Pat asked somewhat nervously.

He had a sinking feeling in his stomach. He could read her well enough to know that Vicky had a card she was about to play. A card he didn't see coming.

"I've got a report from the Kingston Police Department that details the dollar store's video surveillance system. Again, what time did you say you were at the store?"

Pat had a troubled look on his face. He knew he was about to fall victim to his own weakness--an inability to tell effective lies. He harbored a secret about that day in Kingston when he went out to buy beer and stop by the dollar store. A secret he didn't want anyone to discover.

~ 8 ~

"I need to take a break," Pat said suddenly, with every intention of breaking Vicky's momentum. "I need to go to the bathroom, so make sure you annotate that in your interview logs," he told Agent Dick Williams. Desantis glared at him slightly. He could tell she didn't like having her interview stride broken, but he suspected she also liked the challenge--the sport of one master interrogator against another.

"I'll escort him," proclaimed Williams in a half-assed attempt to regain some dignity after the incident with the telephone.

"Uh, I think I can manage fine on my own, Dick!" Pat announced sarcastically, intentionally stressing the pronunciation of his name in obvious mockery. Detective Parsons had to turn his head away in snorts of laughter.

Pat went to the restroom to clear his head. He washed his hands twice, three times. He slowly combed his hair in the mirror, even wetting the part that stood up to try to tame it. But finally he knew he couldn't delay the inevitable any longer. He solemnly walked back into the conference room and noticed Williams was gone, probably out of embarrassment. It was just as well. He could barely stand him after that squishy handshake. Vicky gave him a long stare as he sat down again next to her.

"You said you left your mother's home at four o'clock, arrived at the pizza joint at about four-ten, bought the beer and left around four-twenty. You walked over to the neighboring dollar store immediately and stayed there looking around the aisles until about five-twenty when you realized how late it was and quickly paid for your items and left. You returned to your mom's at about half past five."

"That is what I told you," he replied with an obvious tinge of equivocation.

"But here's the problem," Desantis said as she opened a folder containing faxed grainy images of Pat from the dollar store's video surveillance system. One photo showed Pat entering the store at 5:15 pm. Another photograph showed him paying for his purchases at 5:17 pm.

"Obviously you were in a hurry and bought a handful of items at the register as soon as you walked in. There's more. It seems you went to buy your beer *after* the dollar store, and you were in a real hurry there, too."

He listened intently as she expertly laid out the facts. Obviously there had been a great deal of urgent gumshoe work put into this investigation in the three hours since his meeting with Colonel Helmsley in the morning. Desantis pulled another fax from her folder, a witness statement from a clerk at Tony Nardone's pizza parlor.

"Patrick, this man remembered you. He said you flew in the door, threw a ten dollar bill on the counter, grabbed a six-pack of beer, and told him to keep the change. You were on the road in less than two minutes and back to your mom's house by about five-thirty."

Pat sat silently. He felt the weight of the entire room crushing him at that moment. All eyes trained on him as everyone searched for what he was hiding.

"What happened *before* you arrived at the dollar store Patrick? Where were you from four o'clock when you left your mom's house, and five-fifteen when you entered the dollar store? Ryan Russell left his home at four o'clock for the dollar store. Did something happen between you and Ryan before he ever made it to that store?"

Desantis had delivered the fatal blow, confronting him with facts he couldn't deny. Pat looked around the room at each of those present. Slowly, and with obvious reservation, he began to explain what happened that afternoon.

"I went to visit an old girlfriend. Amanda Pikalski. I grew up in that area, don't forget. She was my girlfriend in high school."

There was a strange look on Vicky's face as he spoke. It conveyed mild skepticism, but more so relief at the explanation he had laid on the table. She slid closer to him.

"Go ahead, Patrick."

"Amanda works at an ice cream shop on Wyoming Avenue in Kingston, about three blocks from my mom's house. A place called Good Scoops. We keep in touch by email, and whenever I get a chance to visit my mom I try to see her, too. She's a single mom now, having gone through a rough marriage and a rougher divorce. We get together from time to time to talk and catch up on our lives. I kept it a secret because I don't think my wife would ever understand why I was visiting an old girlfriend. Amanda needs my support. She was my best friend in high school, and since her divorce last year, she's needed a friend like me to help her cope."

"So you are telling us you never saw Ryan Russell that afternoon? You rushed over to the dollar store and quickly bought a few things as soon as you left Miss Pikalski, then beer, then home?" Vicky asked. "You know we'll have to interview her to confirm all this, right?"

"Of course. But do me one favor. Don't let her know the real reason you are asking her to confirm my time with her. Tell her you are updating my security clearance and want to find out the last time we had contact."

"It's a deal," Vicky promised. "But Patrick, there's one more thing we need to do. Even if your story checks out, we'll need to give you a polygraph examination. Tomorrow morning, please."

Pat rolled his eyes when she requested the lie detector test. "Polygraph is nothing but electronic voodoo. Look, I'll take it--but you get to run one chart on me, that's it. And no pre-test or post-test interrogation. Take it or leave it." Pat's offer was on the table.

"That's fine," Vicky replied. She turned to Rusty Baker. "Can we arrange for an interview room at Bolling Air Force Base tomorrow morning?"

"That shouldn't be a problem. I'll make the arrangements."

"Great then, nine in the morning at the OSI detachment at Bolling. I think we're done here for the day gentlemen," she announced.

Everyone shook hands as they departed, with Colonel Helmsley giving Pat an extra hearty shake and a pat on the back as he got ready to leave. Pat checked his watch and saw it was already almost 5:00. He hurried from the room and headed for the Metro station so he could board an earlier bus and arrive home sooner than he typically did.

Sara seemed more relaxed when Pat walked in the door than she was the night before, or even in the morning before work. She greeted him with a tight hug and a kiss, and a gentle expression of support. She told him she had thought all day long about his situation, resolving to believe in him, to support him, to see the family through whatever was to be. Although Vicky Desantis had been on Pat's mind since he met her, for a moment he forgot all about her, lost in Sara's warm embrace. He told her all about his day. Sara laughed so hard she nearly choked when he described Agent Williams and his antics. He also told her how certain he was that both Helmsley and Desantis seemed to believe him, seemed to have a higher purpose in mind, seemed merely to be going through the formal motions of the interview to appease the others in the room. But one thing he never mentioned to Sara was the fact that Agent Desantis was a woman.

He did tell her about Amanda Pikalski, believing that after all the recent events, white lies, and mistrust, he had to come clean with her about everything. Full disclosure. She was visibly upset to learn that Pat had been seeing an old girlfriend.

"Do you love her, Pat?" she asked, her eyes welling with tears.

He realized then that of all the things he had ever withheld from her, this had the greatest potential threat for Sara. She feared he had fallen out of love with her and back in love with an old flame.

He took her hand and softly said, "No, Sorcha, not like that. I love her as an old dear friend, but I'm not *in love* with her. No one could ever come between us. You are mine, and I am yours, for eternity."

Pat was visited in his dreams that night. This time it was not Josh or Ryan, but a creation in his mind...a succubus of sorts. It was not a vision of what was to be, but perhaps of what Pat would *want* it to be in his dream world. He dreamt of Vicky. Like a teenage boy with sexually charged hormones surging freely through his blood, he found himself making love to her. And like every one of his dreams, this one permitted him to use all his senses to explore the sensual desire he had for her. There was full color sight, lustful sound, and warm erotic touch. There was the subliminal scent of pheromones, and, of course, there was taste...the taste of Vicky's warm flesh and the taste of her hot and hungry mouth as they kissed. But unlike most of his past dreams, this one possessed an even rarer quality--Pat *knew* he was dreaming, so at some strange level of consciousness, he was free to romp with her, to be as lewd as he wanted to be without consequence.

But then just at the moment Pat was ready to push the dream to an even more dangerous sexual level and plunge himself inside her, he felt a gentle tapping on his shoulder. He was being pulled away from this dream, from this place where he had been free to explore what he could never do in reality. Sara was shaking him, calling his name. He had been thrashing about in the bed.

"Pat! Pat! Wake up!" she whispered insistently.

He woke with the sudden worry that he may have called out Vicky's name during his imaginary carnal encounter with her. The dream had subsided in waves but, the hormonal surge remained. It was inchoate. Selfishly, he felt cheated out of finishing his torrid sex with Vicky, almost angry with his wife for the interruption. He wanted to grab Sara, imagine her to be Vicky, and ravage her with ferocious intensity in their bed, to bring to completion the passionate dream he had started. His heart pounded rapidly.

His mind slowly began to regain some semblance of rational control. He despised himself suddenly at that moment. Although just a dream, profound guilt overcame him. As a Catholic with strong family values, and as a man deeply in love with his wife, Pat had essentially committed adultery by proxy, by dream. Never once before, in their thirteen years of marriage, did the thirty-five year old Patrick O'Donnell even think of cheating on Sara. Not until now.

"I'm okay," he said nearly out of breath. "It was a nightmare is all, not about the boys this time, just a nightmare."

Sara kissed his forehead and snuggled in close so Pat could hold her. She was asleep in no time, but Pat stayed awake for hours. His guilt was a wicked tormentor.

~ 9 ~

As he drove to Bolling Air Force Base, Pat mentally prepared himself for the polygraph. He was terribly unsettled and restless, having had only fits and starts of sleep because of his haunting, guilt-ridden dream of making love to Vicky. *I hope I get through this stupid test,* he thought as he bobbed and weaved in and out of the busy traffic on approach to the Woodrow Wilson Bridge. Once he made the slow trek over the Wilson, which seemed to sway precariously from the heavy traffic and wind, he was on his way up I-295 to the base. Bolling was the only Air Force base in the District and one of only a handful of Air Force bases in the world with no runway. Old, dark brown and reddish brick colonials, where many generals lived, dotted the perimeter of the installation along the Interstate Highway. Generals' Row, as it was known. Bolling was the former home of OSI headquarters which sat for many years in a series of buildings just below Generals' Row. The old buildings were long since condemned, and the running joke in OSI was that if the termites ever stopped holding hands the buildings would fall down.

Pat drove up to the OSI detachment office, inside the 11th Wing's headquarters building, just inside the main gate. It was a long, dark brown brick building that could easily blend in on any Ivy League college campus in America. He rang the bell at the detachment's main door and was buzzed in after apparently being recognized by whoever was at the other end of a video monitoring system that kept watch on the lobby. When he walked in, he discovered it was Colonel Helmsley who allowed him entrance.

"Morning, Boss!" Pat said excitedly, regressing back to what he used to call him in his former assignment in the desert when he worked directly for Helmsley.

"Morning, Pat, come on in. I hope you slept well. I'm sure you are ready to just get this over."

If you only knew! Pat thought as the colonel escorted him to the polygraph room. It was small but bright inside with a large two-way mirror, the other side of which was the rest of the group from yesterday's interview. Pat greeted the polygrapher, an older, gray-haired FBI agent who apparently had been briefed well. He didn't attempt any kind of pre-test interrogation, just as Pat demanded. They went over all the control and test questions, and before long, Pat was strapped in. There was a blood pressure cuff on his arm, a fingertip device to measure galvanic skin response, and convoluted tubes around his chest to measure respirations. Then the real test began.

Polygrapher: "Did you cause the death of Josh Branford?"

Pat: "No."

Polygrapher: "Do you know who caused the death of Josh Branford?"

Pat: "No."

Polygrapher: "Did you have anything to do with the abduction of Ryan Russell?"

Pat: "No."

Polygrapher: "Do you know where Ryan Russell is right now?"

Pat: "No."

Polygrapher: "Do you know who abducted Ryan Russell?"

Pat: "No."

The whole session lasted about forty-five minutes, and as he requested, the FBI only ran one test. When Pat left the room, the polygrapher busied himself examining the charts. Colonel Helmsley escorted Pat to a break room, then walked out, leaving him alone for a moment. Within seconds Vicky walked in and came right up to him, mere inches away. It almost seemed to Pat she had been waiting for a chance to be alone with him.

"Good morning, Patrick," she said in that sexy voice that did nothing but arouse him.

"Ah, good morning Agent Desantis," he replied without looking at her.

He was almost afraid she might be able to discover his secret dream if he looked at her the wrong way or said the wrong thing. But his change of tone betrayed him.

"My, my, why so formal today? Yesterday you called me Vicky, which I prefer, Patrick," she said smiling, inching slightly closer.

He could smell her breath and her perfume, and it was all sweet and inviting.

"Oh, nothing really, I guess it's just this formal step we're taking today--I mean the polygraph and all."

Just then Colonel Helmsley stuck his head in. "Okay, kids, let's wrap up the break and get back to the interview room. We've got the polygrapher's results."

As Pat and Vicky walked back together, she told him the FBI in Wilkes-Barre had interviewed Amanda Pikalski, and the story checked out. Apparently they faxed Vicky a report along with a Xerox of Amanda's driver's license for ID purposes.

"Pretty thing, this Amanda," she commented. "If she's this cute in a driver's license photo, then she must be a hottie in person. Explains why you'd want to spend time with her and keep it a secret from Sara," Vicky said with a twisted grin, as if she intentionally wanted to make him uneasy.

When they entered an interview room, he saw the same bevy of law enforcement officials from the day before. Sniveling Agent

Williams.   Seasoned Detective Parsons.   Capable Agent Baker. Colonel Helmsley closed the door before passing the polygrapher's handwritten summary to Vicky. She studied it for a moment.

"Well, Patrick, it seems you have been a good boy after all. No deception indicated to any of the test questions. Congratulations," she said with a warm, wide smile.

Pat glanced at Williams and Parsons who actually seemed pissed, but Baker breathed a very audible sigh of relief. Colonel Helmsley informed him he had some good news and some bad news that they withheld intentionally until he had completed his polygraph. They didn't want it to be a factor at all in his test. He looked at Agent Williams and asked him to brief Pat up.

"Well, we sent some agents back to the North Carolina crime scene yesterday and combed the area again, widening the search to twice what we had considered before. In the briar patch we found a piece of cellophane that looked like it came from a pack of cigarettes. There were no butts in the area, but the cellophane looked pretty fresh, not dirty, so we thought it might have been in the brush for only a short time. At night we also luminesced the briar brush and some of the leaves had trace blood specks that lit up."

"Shit," Pat whispered aloud. "Did you find any fingerprints on the cellophane?"

Williams nodded. "Yes, there was a partial print on the wrapper that AFIS matched to a convicted pedophile. A thirty-seven year old white male. Victor Ralston. He was last known to be living in Tucson, having registered there in 1998 under Arizona's sex offender registry laws once he was released from a New York prison. Agents went to his apartment last night, but the landlord said he moved without paying rent about a month ago. We think he's just drifting around right now looking for victims."

"Does this guy's MO match these recent abductions?" Pat asked.

"Yes, except he's never murdered his victims before now--at least the ones we know about."

Colonel Helmsley broke into the conversation again. "I'm afraid that was the good news."

Pat feared what he was about to say. *Ryan Russell was found dead. We all had acted too late.* Tears welled in Pat's eyes as Colonel Helmsley told him where Ryan was found.

"A restaurant owner in Wilkes-Barre found him last night in a warehouse he also owns right next to his restaurant. An Italian restaurant on East Market Street. He was hanging just like in your vision. His injuries were exactly as you described. And Pat, in one of his pants pockets was an open pack of cherry flavored candies."

Pat was trembling now as the significance of his vision hit home. The Italian restaurant explained the garlic smell; the cherry flavor no doubt was in Ryan's mouth--Pat experienced it along with him.

"But what about the music I heard, the elevator music?" Pat asked the colonel.

"Well, the restaurant has an outdoor café area where folks can eat their meals. It sits next to the warehouse. They have outdoor speakers that pump out that kind of music for the guests to enjoy while they dine."

"Have they been able to determine how long he was dead?" Pat asked as he wiped tears from his eyes.

Vicky chimed in, handing him a tissue. "The restaurant owner said he discovered Ryan around eleven o'clock pm around the time they were closing the restaurant. He last checked the warehouse around two o'clock that afternoon to get some supplies for the dinner meal, and Ryan was not there. That gives us a timeframe for when Ryan was hanged."

Williams interrupted. "The restaurant owner also ID'd Victor Ralston from a mug shot," he said shoving a fax copy of Ralston's old booking photograph in front of Pat. "He said Ralston came into the restaurant that night looking for directions to the Interstate. The owner walked out of the restaurant with him to point out the directions. He said Ralston got into a beat-up, older model Chevy minivan with Arizona plates. He's undergoing hypnosis this morning to try to recall the license plate number."

Pat was about to speak when Colonel Helmsley and Agent Desantis suddenly and rather abruptly stood up and told Parsons, Williams, and Baker to leave the room. They said that since it was now clear Pat had nothing to do with either crime, there was no more need to bother him. The trio gave Helmsley and Desantis a shocked look but stood up begrudgingly, and left.

Once the room was empty, Vicky closed the door. She and Colonel Helmsley sat silently across from Pat for a few moments. He was beginning to get nervous from their stares. After an eternal pause, Vicky looked deeply at him with her compelling, crystal blue eyes and asked, "Well, Patrick, how would you like to go on an adventure?"

~ 10 ~

Pat's heart raced when Agent Desantis asked him that question. *An adventure?* he thought while studying his wedding band closely, twisting its gold brilliance around his finger. *What could that mean?*

Neither Colonel Helmsley nor Vicky said anything more for a few moments. He knew the pair was studying him, trying to gauge his reaction to Vicky's vague offer.

"What do you need me to do?" Pat asked, finally breaking the silence.

"Don't be alarmed," Colonel Helmsley began. "There are some people we need to introduce to you, some things we need to check out before we proceed any further down the road. We can't discuss it any more in this room. Let's go back to my office, to my SCIF."

This has to be a big deal if we must discuss it in a Sensitive Compartmented Information Facility!

Vicky gave him a long, thoughtful look. Suddenly she became more businesslike than before.

"Patrick, meet us in the colonel's office at two o'clock. We'll grease it with your boss before then, and we'll let him know you'll be pulled off your regular duties for at least the next week. Tell no one about this meeting. Okay?"

"Yeah, I guess," Pat mumbled as he shook his head still somewhat stunned by the morning's chain of events. "I'll be there."

As he left the OSI detachment he checked his watch. It was just before noon, so he decided to drive out to the Pentagon City Mall for lunch in the food court before his 1400 Pentagon meeting. He reasoned he could at least park his car there and walk to the Pentagon to avoid the hassle of trying to park in one of the visitor's lots, which always seemed to be a hundred miles from any entrance.

Pat enjoyed the mall this time of year. Halloween was just three weeks away, but the mall already was decked out in a Christmas theme. It was sprinkled throughout in decorations of red, green, gold, and silver. Everywhere he looked he saw reindeer, elves, trees, and candy canes. In the center of the food court, the mall was wide open with three floors of space terminating at the top in a ceiling of glass that allowed the sun's warm, golden rays to light up all the glittering decorations. There were two wooden soldiers bracing the center court structure that must have been at least twenty feet high. Made of thousands of shiny, colorful plastic ribbons, they stood sentry. Glistening. In the background Pat could hear piped-in mall music. Christmas carols without words, just melodies that reminded him of the warmth he felt every year at this time. The peaceful place of the mall was an amazing sanctuary for Pat considering how close it was to the Pentagon. How just a quarter mile away, a five minute walk from there, terrorists flew a plane into the five-sided landmark and symbol of America's military might.

Never again! Pat thought. *Never again will those bastards get a chance to do this to my country!*

He finished his lunch and gathered his trash for the wastebasket. He looked up at the glass ceiling once more and noted the sky had begun to flurry. Smiling to himself, he zipped his blue Air Force windbreaker tight, and headed for the exit. The flurries picked up speed and volume and cruelly stung his face and hands as he walked back to the Pentagon, finding some temporary cover in a short tunnel that burrowed underneath the busy I-395 overhead. He arrived at SAF/AAZ right on time to find Colonel Helmsley and Agent Desantis waiting by the door finishing off ice cream cones.

"Hey! That's not fair!" Pat cried out teasingly. "Where's my ice cream?"

"Wanna lick mine?" Vicky asked with no effort to hide the obvious double meaning. She followed the offer by giving Pat a sexy smile while licking the cone's vanilla treat slowly, from base to tip, never once breaking eye contact with him.

This only served to conjure up for a moment in Pat's mind the steamy dream he had of her the night before. His eyes widened. "I can't believe you just said that! If I said that to a female in the Air Force I'd get fired!"

"Shall we go in gentlemen? We've got a lot of work to do in the next couple of hours," Desantis said with a wink and a slight giggle.

Once inside, Colonel Helmsley disappeared for a moment to retrieve a file folder. He returned and placed it on the conference table in front of his seat. Pat could see the cover. It was marked, TOP SECRET, SPECIAL ACCESS REQUIRED, PROJECT CRYSTAL ROUNDUP, in bold red block letters.

"We are going to give you an indoc into a SAP that exists between the Department of Defense and Justice Department. Over the next few days we'll send you to a medical facility in North Carolina to have some tests run," Colonel Helmsley said as he opened the folder.

His words sent shivers down Pat's spine. "Okay. But why? What's this all about and what does it have to do with me and my dreams?"

"This is an empty Special Access Program. It was set up years ago on the chance that someday the government would find someone with true...well, psychic ability. You see, we've had our fair share of charlatans over the years. We've been waiting for someone--perhaps you--to come along who is the real deal. There are three levels to the SAP. You will be briefed on Level One today," the colonel explained.

"Well, let's say I'm cautiously interested, but I'm not sure I'm the right guy for this," he said nodding his head hesitantly.

While he found the discussion intriguing, it was apparent both Colonel Helmsley and Vicky were genuinely excited, though they tried hard to conceal it. As he spoke, Vicky reached into her briefcase and retrieved a VHS tape box marked TOP SECRET. She cued up the tape on a television with a built-in VCR at one end of the room.

Pat leaned in to watch and listen. As a narrator spoke, a large red banner popped up on the screen which read, TOP SECRET, CRYSTAL ROUNDUP LEVEL ONE. Pat was struck by the narrator's appearance once his image emerged after the banner dissolved. Short, retro hairstyle. Plain suit with thin gray tie. Thick black plastic frame glasses. It was evident the video was copied from a movie made in the late 1960s or early 1970s. The narrator alluded to the program's history during the Vietnam era and how the FBI and DoD had searched for some connection between war protestors at home and enemy collaborators in Southeast Asia. Pat learned the SAP used a focal point system for contact between trusted agents. He was familiar with them--key people within agencies like the CIA, National Security Agency, and National Reconnaissance Office who were briefed-in and used to facilitate the SAP's operational success in their respective agencies.

"For now we will be the only points of contact in the focal point system for this SAP. If things pan out down south, we'll have to bring new trusted agents into the fold in some of the beltway agencies as necessary," his former boss cautioned him.

"Understand, Sir. I'll do my best--but I have to admit that I don't know how much I believe in this psychic mumbo jumbo stuff myself. I'm still very much a skeptic!"

"We need you to go to Pope Air Force Base tomorrow morning. Plan to arrive by one o'clock. Wait at the billeting office lobby, but don't check in. You'll be met by this man," the colonel said as he handed Pat a photograph of a handsome, gray-haired black man. "This is Dr. Woodrow Davis. He's CRYSTAL ROUNDUP Level One cleared. He will take you to the location for testing."

"Okay, so how long will I be there--I mean, how much clothing do I need to pack?"

"Plan for about a week," Vicky replied. "It shouldn't take any longer than that."

It was nearly 1700 when they finished the program indoctrination. As he turned toward the door to leave, Vicky tugged on his jacket sleeve.

"Patrick, remember no one can know about this. NO ONE at all. Okay?"

"I know Vicky. I've been around the block," he reassured her, chuckling slightly at her overly dramatic cloak-and-dagger warning.

Pat found Sara eager to hear all about his day when he arrived home, tired and somewhat bewildered by the barrage of events he had undergone.

"Okay Pat, tell me all about it. I assume you passed the lie detector test since they didn't arrest you!"

"Well, Sorcha, it's not all good news," Pat responded with a sullen look. He took her by the hand and led her to the bedroom for privacy. "They found Ryan Russell. Too late, though. He was found hanged like in my vision. They have a suspect, but he's not caught yet. I have to go TDY tomorrow for about a week. To Pope. The Task Force down there wants my help--I guess my insight--into these cases to help track down the killer."

It was a white lie, but he had to come up with something to explain his Temporary Duty, or TDY, assignment. Pat learned early on in his career never to play the, *I've got a secret,* game with anyone. He knew if he told Sara he needed to go to Pope for some TOP SECRET mission, it would have only invoked her curiosity needlessly. An innocuous cover story should be sufficient. Sara seemed to accept it all without question, but deep inside Pat worried that if the testing in North Carolina proved fruitful, he'd be in for many more TOP SECRET missions and TDYs. At some point, Sara would stop buying into the cover stories and begin to probe him for the truth.

~ 11 ~

Major O'Donnell woke early the next morning to get ready for his road trip down south. A quick cup of piping hot coffee brought his senses back to life as he hastily packed a suitcase. He woke Sara long enough to announce his departure. He could barely make out her silhouette in the sheets in the darkness of their room, lit dimly by the clock radio's red glow. Caressing her shoulders gently, rousing her long enough for a kiss, and a promise to call with a hotel phone number. And gone.

The shortcut down Route 123, the Old Ox Road in Fairfax County, took him to I-95, which Pat happily found had little traffic southbound this morning. It promised to be an enjoyable ride as the sun began to rise, making the fog in the low areas swirl and scamper about as if running away, fearful of the warm rays. There was a slight touch of frost to the long-since fallen, brown leaves littering the grassy banks of the Interstate. All around the highway, a micro-thin layer of frost glistened briefly with the touch of the sun, then turned moist, and glistened no more.

He eventually arrived at Pope Air Force Base, thankful to leave I-95 after counting no fewer than twenty billboards inviting travelers to visit the *South of the Border* attraction. *Ad nauseam--literally,* he mused as he pulled into the billeting office parking lot at 1235. He was feeling slightly jittery about his impending medical exam. A swarm of angry butterflies filled his stomach. He opted to sit and listen to music while waiting for Dr. Davis, not hungry enough to eat any lunch. After finding a classic rock station amidst dozens of country and western venues, he tilted the seat back, closed his eyes, and cleared his mind. Led Zeppelin. Boston. The Band. The melodies poured from the speakers, and gently lulled him into a power nap.

The transition to sleep was so subtle, so transparent, that Pat literally jumped forward when awakened by a tapping sound on his window. Groggy-eyed, he squinted past the sunlight at the figure of an elderly black man motioning for him to roll down his window. He fumbled simultaneously for the power window button and the radio volume control. The man reached into the car, seeking to shake hands with him.

"You must be Major O'Donnell," the man said with a broad smile of perfectly-aligned, pearl white teeth.

"Yes, Sir. Hi--you're Dr. Davis, right?"

"Woodrow Wilson Davis, but please call me Woody," he insisted, exuding an almost grandfatherly kindliness that immediately put Pat at ease. "My parents seemed to think if I had a famous name that I, too, would become famous," he chuckled.

Dr. Davis was neatly dressed in tan dress slacks, a dark blue sport coat, and white dress shirt without tie. He was a tall, slender man--in his late sixties, Pat surmised, distinguished and confident in how he carried himself. Pat liked him instantly.

"Great. And I'm Pat. Nice to meet you, Woody." Pat opened his car door and stepped out. "By the way, how did you know who I was?"

"Same way you recognized me," Woody said with a wink.

Pat smiled, amused by the obvious efficiency of Colonel Helmsley and Agent Desantis in setting up the meeting. Dr. Davis drove a brand new silver Lexus sedan with North Carolina plates. As Pat loaded the trunk with his bags, he noticed a sticker on the rear bumper for Drake University faculty parking.

"Say, Woody, how did you get on base? We're all in a high threat condition ever since the terrorist attacks."

"Oh, that's easy," he said pointing to a blue, military base decal on the front windshield, next to which was an eagle sticker.

"Ah, so you're a colonel--retired?"

"For a few years now. Actually, I was a reserve Army officer. Medical Corps, attached to several Ranger units. I did five years active duty as an MD during Vietnam, then left to go back to medical school to specialize in psychiatry. Was in the reserves forever, finally able to retire six years ago."

"Did you serve in Vietnam?"

"Just one tour in a MASH unit near Saigon. After that, off to Walter Reed for four more years. You sure have a lot of questions, Pat! But that's okay; we're going to get to know each other very well over the next several days."

With that they were off, back onto I-95 but headed north this time.

"I assume we're going to Raleigh-Durham?"

"You saw the parking sticker I take it?" Woody asked smiling. "Listen, I know it's no secret that Drake University has a long history of studying parapsychology. Actually, most of the former research has been moved to a new center, the Richmond Research Center, near campus. I spend most of my time at the Richmond, been studying these phenomena for many years."

"Dr. Davis, I mean, Woody--I have to tell you I am a huge skeptic. I studied psychology in college and absolutely hated this stuff. One of my profs forced us to read lots of nutty garbage about altered states of consciousness and the like. I always felt more comfortable with the science end of psychology. The experimental--"

Woody cut him off. "I understand, and I'm sorry you had some initial bad impressions of parapsychology--or *psi* as we call it. But I hope you will have an open mind, so I can *open* your mind!"

Dr. Davis erupted into a hearty laugh at his own spontaneous corny joke.

"You know, Pat, I'm glad you're a skeptic. I wish I had a dime for every wannabe I've seen over the years. People with zero psi ability who think they possess some kind of magic power. *Psi-groupies* as we call them in our business. A doubter like you comes in with a greater sense of objectivity--you don't cling to one set of beliefs or the other with any degree of forcefulness."

"Well, I must admit you guys will have your work cut out for you, but I'm open to anything at this point. I assume Colonel Helmsley told you all about my dreams and the vision thing?" Pat asked, somewhat timid about the level of detail he ought to offer up in the first encounter. He trusted Woody, but wasn't sure yet on the lanes in the road for the Special Access Program.

"Yes, he did. And John and I go way, way back in this business. Good friends."

The two men talked for the next few hours on the road to Durham about everything and anything. The ride helped Woody make an initial assessment of Pat, a kind of clinical interview done with extraordinary subtlety that even Pat, an expert interrogator, didn't pick up on it. They pulled into a local hotel in Durham.

"I already have you checked in, so you can go right to your room. Get some rest tonight. I'll pick you up in the lobby tomorrow morning at six, sharp. Oh, and no food or drink--after six o'clock tonight--okay?"

"Got it, Woody. And thanks for everything, especially the pep talk on the way up," Pat said, taking the room key Woody pulled from his jacket pocket and handed to him.

After unpacking his meager wardrobe of casual slacks, polo shirts, and boxer shorts, Pat was ready for a quick bite. He placed a quick call home and gave Sara the hotel number, then headed downstairs to the hotel's family style restaurant for a quick meal before bed.

"Morning, Pat--how did you sleep?" Dr. Davis asked with a huge grin, greeting Pat in the hotel lobby precisely on time the next day.

"Just great, Woody. Like a baby all night," he replied with a slight yawn. "I guess there's no way I could talk you into letting me have some of the hotel's free breakfast buffet, is there?" he coyly asked, already knowing the response.

"Sorry, but no food until after the exams this morning. Don't worry, we'll have something for you to eat after we get the necessary labs done. Let's go!" he said slapping Pat's back like an old friend.

During the drive to the Richmond Research Center, Dr. Davis explained the history of the center and its historical significance to Drake University.

"The Center gets its name from the founders, Dr. Arnold Richmond and his wife who began their work in the paranormal field in the Psychology Department in the late 1920s."

"I see, and how long have you been affiliated with the Center? I mean, did you work there far back enough to know Dr. Richmond personally?"

"Oh yes, my goodness. I've been with the Center for a very long time, and I was Dr. Richmond's assistant for many years before his death."

"I have to tell you, that's pretty cool to know. Even as a skeptic of this stuff, I am genuinely impressed by your experience and the sense of history you have about the place."

"And here's *that* place," Woody said pointing to a large, white two-story colonial home with dark green shutters on a residential street near the campus. If Pat had driven by it a hundred times on his own, he never would have guessed the quaint-looking place housed the world-renowned center for ESP research. He had assumed all along the Richmond Center was on Drake University's campus proper, behind concrete and glass in a sterile, office-like environment. He felt a sense of warmth flowing from the house even at the street. It was an older looking structure that, at some point in its history, likely had been home to a large family of Raleigh-Durham's high society.

"Wow! I must admit this is a big surprise for me!"

Woody chuckled. "I know, Pat. Most people have that reaction. Listen, before we go in, you have to know that no one else in the Center is CRYSTAL ROUNDUP cleared at any level. Okay? They know I do work for the government, and they know you are here in that capacity, but that's as far as it goes."

"Got it! Mum's the word here."

When they walked into the Center's foyer, Pat's senses were overtaken with a rush that complemented his initial impression of the home's warmth. There was a musky scent to the old house that immediately flooded his nostrils. He stopped for a moment to take it all in...musk from the hardwood floors and musk from the intricate dark wood staircase and open banister that twirled up to the second floor. The ceilings had a detailed pattern to them, old fashioned panels long since covered over with many coats of white paint. Sometimes Pat thought places, especially old homes, had their own personalities, if not their own souls as if living beings. This one spoke to Pat, telling him it was open and friendly, and the memories people had of living in it were good ones.

"What a great home!" Pat exclaimed out loud.

"Glad you like it...well, let's get started with a quick tour. We'll finish up in the lab where we'll take all the bodily fluid samples so we can get you something to eat."

Dr. Davis showed him around the entire facility, introducing him to the staff along the way. Everyone was very pleasant and seemed interested in helping Dr. Davis with his new subject. There were rooms for sleep and dream research, rooms with two-way mirrors that reminded Pat of interrogation rooms, still other rooms full of hospital-like equipment Pat was sure he'd soon be connected to. At the end of the tour, Woody led him to what was arguably the most sterile looking room in the Center. The lab.

"Becky, this is Pat O'Donnell. He needs the full blood and urine work-up I mentioned yesterday. Pat, this is our resident nurse, Becky Winters."

She extended her hand. "Hi Pat, nice to meet you."

"My pleasure," he replied with a shake.

Dr. Davis cut in. "Listen, I'm going to catch up on some emails. Take care of Pat, and I'll come back in about an hour. If you get done before then, please take him back to the kitchen for a bite to eat."

Becky was extremely pleasant, if not a bit of a chatter box. She had a touch of a southern accent that Pat found appealing, although she hardly took time to catch her breath in between sentences. Indeed, in between words. He guessed the short, fair-skinned brunette, with deep green eyes, was in her mid-twenties. Married, as evidenced by the wedding band and large diamond engagement ring. There was a framed photograph of her with a handsome young man in tuxedo on her desk, she in a gown.

"Is that your husband?"

"Yes, that's my sweetheart," she stated in her subtle southern twang. "Would you believe it's our high school prom picture? I like that picture the most so I keep it here, not like a lot of the other pictures we have at home. I mean, there's so many of them in boxes." Becky caught herself running off on a tangent. "Listen to me rattle on!" she exclaimed. "We'd better get started!"

Pat just smiled, adoring her charm.

She put him through a standard battery of physical examinations. Height. Weight. Blood pressure. Temperature. He hardly felt the needle when she retrieved five vials of blood from his left arm. When all the poking and probing was done, she took him to the kitchen where he helped himself to some fresh fruit and coffee and waited for Dr. Davis to retrieve him.

"Well, how'd I do, Woody?" Pat asked when Dr. Davis walked in mere moments later.

"We should know this afternoon when the results come in. We've got a rush on it at the University's main lab. Next stop is to check out your brain activity."

Dr. Davis led him to one of the rooms he had peeked into on their tour.   It was the clinical looking one with a bevy of hospital equipment all around. Everything was steel and sterile. There were large electronic instruments on tall metal stands with wheels, and there were blue-green curtains affixed to curved ceiling tracks that formed makeshift cubicles when drawn around. After asking Pat to switch into a gown, he had him hop up onto a cushioned table draped with cold, crinkly white paper.

"EEG time. This will take a bit of time, maybe more than an hour. So just lie back and relax while Becky takes some head measurements and applies the electrodes to your scalp. It won't hurt at all," Dr. Davis assured him.

He closed his eyes while Becky prepared him, and within moments the test was underway. For the first twenty minutes or so, Dr. Davis seemed content to let the machine record his brain's electrical patterns to establish a baseline. Then he darkened the room's lights, brought a strobe overhead, and asked Pat to open his eyes and watch the flashing light. He manipulated the strobe's speed and intensity, carefully recording on the charts the points at which he made changes.

But suddenly a peculiar pattern emerged on the charts. At first Dr. Davis thought there was a loose connection on the sensors because Pat's brain pattern began to flatten somewhat. Fidgeting with the connectors didn't seem to remedy it. He stopped the strobe and told Becky to flip on the room lights. When she did, they both noticed

Pat's eyes were wide open, and he had a distant stare as if he were in a trance.

"Oh, my God, Dr. Davis!" Becky exclaimed with alarm. "Is he having a seizure?"

"No, Becky, quite the contrary. I think he's fallen asleep. Here, look at the charts. These are characteristic patterns we see in deep sleep stages. But no one does this with their eyes open. Hand me a penlight."

Dr. Davis shined it into Pat's eyes one at a time. "Hmmmm. Non-responsive pupils. See how widely dilated they are? Just like they probably were when we darkened the room. Frozen now. They haven't begun to respond to the light in the room or to this penlight. We'll have to order up a CAT scan to rule out a brain tumor, but I don't suspect that is a strong likelihood."

What neither Dr. Davis nor Becky Winters knew at the moment was that Pat had left the room. Of course, he was there physically, but his mind was not. Once again, just as he had departed the confines of General Swank's conference room at the Pentagon when he had his vision of Ryan Russell hanging in the warehouse, at this moment, Pat's mind had taken leave of the Richmond Center. He found himself witnessing another horrifying crime. He saw the scene clearly. A small boy in a van. His hands and feet were bound together with gray duct tape. His mouth was covered with the same tape to keep him silenced. He was terrified but alive...at least for now.

~ 12 ~

Pat was helpless, unable to do anything but watch the horrific scene play itself out. The boy's dark red jacket was torn slightly, white down stuffing popping out from the spot where his abductor first grabbed him as he walked to school, yanking him into his van. His face was panic-stricken; salty tears streamed from bright blue eyes and stung his nostrils. Pat felt the burning in his own nose and a nauseating sensation he had along with the boy who was getting car sick from being unable to see out of the van. It was moving at a high rate of speed, bouncing the little boy about, bumping his head against the harsh metal interior. It was a minivan without rear seats, made dark from covered windows. Rubbish was strewn about the floor. Empty beer bottles rolled around. Filthy rags and fast-food paper bags everywhere.

Pat could see and hear the driver now as his vision allowed him to pan the scene of this abduction. He was a white man, balding slightly, overweight, in his late thirties or early forties. Pat instantly recognized Victor Ralston from his mug shot, the man believed to be responsible for the Branford and Russell murders. Ralston was taunting the boy without mercy.

"You ain't never gonna see your mom or pop again you know!" he growled with a sickening laugh.

The little boy cried harder, obviously fearing his life was about to end soon. Ralston kept up his torment. The boy's whimpers seemed to arouse the man who delighted in knowing he was terrorizing him.

Pat looked about the van, through the windshield, and saw something familiar. It was one of those obnoxious *South of the Border* signs that riddled I-95 in the Carolinas. This one read, *Pedro Sez You Only Have 50 Miles to Go to See the Donkey!* A trace of outside air reached Pat's senses as Ralston switched on the vent fan. It was familiar, too. Pat was certain this abduction had taken place close in time to the present, or would occur in the very near future. The signature of the scent was all too *current* to him. He smelled it yesterday morning on the drive down from Virginia.

Dr. Davis noticed Pat's pupils begin to contract slowly, finally responding to the room's light.

"Pat, Pat," he whispered, gently pulling him from his trance. "Can you hear me?"

He sat up quickly. Three electrodes popped off his scalp.

"Oh God, it happened again, Woody."

His face turned red, and he broke out into a cold sweat in an instant. He blinked rapidly, trying to moisten his searing eyes that had become dry after being open so long.

He heard Dr. Davis asked Becky to leave the room immediately, leaving the EEG running to record everything as he hastily refastened the remaining connectors.

"Hang on a minute," Dr. Davis cautioned him as he retrieved a small cassette recorder from his lab coat pocket. "I wasn't sure if you were going to have any of these experiences while you were down here, but I wanted to be ready just in case. I never expected it to happen so soon."

He switched on the recorder and asked him to relate everything that happened. Pat recounted the entire vision for him. Every detail, every nuance.

"Pat, I have my own suspicions this is a real-time event, I mean, happening right now. Let's just call it an old man's intuition.

We have to at least assume so and act fast!"

Major O'Donnell was startled at his words and watched with amazement as Dr. Davis pulled a peculiar looking cell phone from his lab coat along with a small plastic and metal card that resembled a media card used in digital cameras. Woody inserted it in the phone and placed a call to Colonel Helmsley.

"It's a STE cell phone with Fortezza card," Woody whispered to him with a smile.

Pat had only heard about them, but never saw one before. He knew Secured Terminal Equipment devices were being beta-tested at the time by only a few select government officials, principally in the black SAP world.

"John, Woody here. Listen, I think we need to move on something right now. Let me play a tape to you of Pat recalling a vision he had down here moments ago. I think this is an abduction in progress."

Pat sat on the edge of the examination table, arms crossed over his lap, wondering what to do next while the tape played out. Dr. Davis held the phone to his ear once the recording stopped.

"Uh huh, yes John. Sure, he's right here." He looked at Pat. "Colonel Helmsley wants to chat with you," he said handing the STE to him.

"Pat you are amazing! Is there any way you can tell if the van was traveling north or south?" Helmsley asked, concerned about trying to narrow the scope of the search for the van.

He took a breath and thought about the moment in the vision when he peered out the window. He was searching for directional clues. Then it struck him...the position of the sun.

"The sun was on my left--my left! That would mean they were heading south if the vision was a real time event," Pat said nearly jumping off the table. "I think they are in North Carolina, about fifty miles north of the border. That was about ten minutes ago," Pat added, mentally analyzing the facts.

"Thanks, Pat. I'll get right on this and let you know what happens. You take it easy, and God bless!" Colonel Helmsley hung up abruptly.

Pat was completely unaware of what he had just touched off, the series of behind-the-scenes events for which he was the catalyst.

Helmsley reached Desantis on her STE and gave her a quick rundown of what he learned from Pat. She immediately contacted Agent Dick Williams and told him to get the North and South Carolina State Police to increase patrols of I-95 along the corridor 50 miles north and south of the border.

"What makes you think Ralston is driving on the Interstate with another abducted boy?" Williams asked, intoning that he didn't appreciate Desantis having developed significant leads on *his* investigation.

She had to think fast, obviously not wanting to alert him to Pat's vision or his involvement at all in the new lead.

"Let's just say word got to me that Ralston was seen pulling another boy into his van and heading south on the Interstate. You have the van's description, now move it Dick! We may be able to save this boy!" she shouted at him, hoping to snap him out of his stubbornness.

Williams called Detective Parsons right away, grumbling somewhat about the information probably being a false lead, but reporting it out of a sense of duty, nonetheless. Fortunately, Parsons sensed the lead had some teeth. He immediately issued a BOLO to all law enforcement agencies in the two Carolinas. Within minutes, I-95, north and south of Pedro's village, was swarming with state police vehicles like honeybees on a hive.

Meanwhile, Desantis placed a secure call back to Helmsley.

"John, I think we're going to have to develop a Level Three scenario pretty fast!"

"I know, let's wait and see what happens here in the next few hours, and then let's plan to meet for lunch at my office. I have a few ideas already."

Trooper Reginald Warner was a recent graduate of the North Carolina State Police Academy. Still a rookie, he was patrolling solo for the very first time this morning when the BOLO came across the radio.

Trooper Warner had passed a van matching this description a few miles back. He was performing a routine patrol of I-95 in a section that stretched from Fayetteville in the north to Lumberton in the south. He noted the van because it had Arizona plates and wondered why the driver was so far from home. He decided to slow down and pull over to the shoulder to see if the van would pass him by in the next few minutes. It did. Warner's adrenaline surged with a rush as he pulled away from the shoulder and radioed dispatch that he had a fix on the van and was in pursuit. Then, the six foot, three inch, ruddy-faced blond trooper and former high school linebacker switched on his lights and siren and gave chase. Drivers all around pulled off to the sides to let Warner pass by, but not Ralston. He saw the lights in his mirror and heard the siren. He hit the gas. Trooper Warner grabbed his microphone.

"Suspect is picking up speed in the left lane. We just passed Exit Twenty-Two, the junction with State Road Three-Zero-One."

The dispatcher relayed his location to all units, and before Warner knew it, there was a throng of fellow state troopers and sheriff's vehicles rushing in to assist. Warner sped ahead of the van, which was clanking along as fast as Ralston could make it go. But it was no match for the high performance state police vehicle. He pulled into a position in front of the van and began to slow as several other police cars fell into place, surrounding Ralston, gradually reducing their speed to force him to slow down. But Ralston was undeterred. He screamed obscenities out his window to the state police, giving them the finger. Next he hit his gas pedal hard and struck Trooper Warner's vehicle from behind, but this only caused Ralston to lose control. His van swerved, sideswiping two other police cars until it careened to the left into an open space between two trooper's sedans. It struck the concrete median at an oblique angle. Screeching metal against concrete, sparks and smoke and glass headlights shattering. In a sputter, the van came to a noisy stop.

Unable to exit through the driver's side, Ralston made a desperate attempt to jump from the passenger's door. Trooper Warner was there to greet him. He grabbed the flabby Ralston by his right arm, slammed him against the van, and quickly handcuffed him. He forced Ralston to lie on the ground as other police cars came to a halt at the scene. Tires squealing, doors slamming all around them. Twenty or so state troopers and sheriff's deputies surrounded Ralston, shouting at him not to move. Several guns were drawn and black chrome retractable ASP batons were at the ready. With his face down on the cold asphalt of the highway, Ralston dared not make a move.

Warner rushed to the back of the van and popped open the rear doors. Inside was a terrified, but unharmed little boy. He was crying uncontrollably. Warner gently removed the tape from the boy's face, hands, and ankles, and told him everything was going to be all right.

"We've got the bad man, son. You are a very brave little boy. What's your name?"

"Mi, Mi, Mi, Mike," he said sobbing in spasms so hard he could barely catch his breath. "Mike Dris, Dris, Driscoll. Thank you, thank, thank you," he cried as he thrust his arms around the trooper's neck.

"It's gonna be okay, Mike. We'll let your parents know you are all right, and you'll be back home before you know it. How old are you? Where do you live?"

"Hope Mills. I'm eight. That man grabbed me when I was walking to school today!" Mike Driscoll whimpered in response, slowly regaining some control over his breathing, the heavy crying spasms gradually retreating.

As Trooper Warner was comforting Mike, another state trooper approached them and pulled Warner aside.

"Is this kid named Michael Driscoll?"

"Yes. Has he been reported missing?"

"Yeah. Just about twenty minutes ago. Apparently the school called his mom when he didn't show up for class. She went back home and frantically started searching for him, and then called Nine-One-One. It all just came together right now. You're a hero Warner!" he proclaimed, congratulating Trooper Warner with a hearty slap on the back.

"Thanks man, but it was pure luck I happened to be near this guy at the right time. We need to get this kid to the hospital for a good checkup--not sure if this jerk had a chance to hurt him."

"There's an EMT team on the way. They'll take him in. Why don't you hook up your collar and bring him to the barracks. The FBI is en route. This guy's got two felony kidnapping and murder charges out on him."

"Okay, Buddy. Pleasure's all mine."

Trooper Warner and a sheriff's deputy hoisted Ralston up from the cold, filthy roadway and placed him in Warner's vehicle. With a whirl of sirens and flashing blue lights, Warner sped away down the Interstate in his slightly battered cruiser.

———————————————

Pat was startled when Dr. Davis's STE phone suddenly and melodiously rang. It was Colonel Helmsley calling to report the good news. He wanted to speak with Pat.

"Pat. You are incredible! Great job!"

The colonel went on to explain to Pat in detail how his vision led to Ralston's arrest and, most importantly, saved Mike Driscoll from certain death.

"Boss. I, I, I guess I just don't know what to say," he stammered nervously, his mind in a fog over the events that had just played out.

"Agent Desantis and I are coming your way in a few days. There are some aspects to the SAP we need to brief you and Dr. Davis into. In the meantime, tell no one about your connection to today's events," Helmsley cautioned.

"Okay, Sir. Will do."

He handed the phone back to Dr. Davis, hands trembling slightly. "Woody, can I take a break? I'm a bit flustered by all that's gone on here."

"Of course, Pat, take your time. I'll track you down in a bit."

He walked back to the kitchen and found Becky taking a break. She was watching a local television station's coverage of breaking news. It was, of course, a story about the rescue of Mike Driscoll. A live news team was at the state police barracks as Trooper Warner arrived, escorting the handcuffed and belligerent Ralston inside. Reporters rushed to try to get live comments from Warner, but he wouldn't respond to their questions. Suddenly, Ralston began shouting and making obscene gestures with his shackled hands.

"Oh, my Lord!" Becky exclaimed. "Can you believe this guy? While you were in the exam room, this story came on the news. They caught this guy after he kidnapped a little Hope Mills boy. That trooper is a real hero!"

"Wow!" Pat gasped. "That's awesome they got that guy!" he practically gushed as the impact of his vision and its results firmly hit home.

Following his break, Dr. Davis escorted him to one of the rooms in the Richmond Center with a two way mirror. Pat walked in and immediately went right up to the two-way mirror, pressed his face against the cold glass, and tried to see through it in reverse. He knew sometimes it was possible to see into the other room if the lighting was just right. But this time it was not.

"Pat, this is Dr. Fred Johansen. He's the Center's director of psi-related testing," Woody said introducing the frail, middle-aged man with wavy black hair and gold-rimmed glasses.

His appearance was quintessential *nerd* in Pat's mind. His lab coat was opened just enough to display the obligatory pocket protector.

"Hi, Pat. Nice to meet you," Dr. Johansen said extending his hand and giving him one of those soft and squishy handshakes that made him cringe.

"Hi, Doctor. Are those playing cards you have there?" he asked eyeing up what appeared to be a small deck affixed to the clipboard.

"Oh, no. Have you ever heard of Zener cards?" Johansen asked, turning them over to show him five cards bearing different shapes: a star, a square, a plus sign, a circle, and three wavy lines like a ripple in a lake.

"I'm familiar with them. I've seen them in my undergrad days in psych class. You use them to try to test for ESP, right?"

"Right. Here's how we'll do it. Have a seat here and face the mirror. Every time you see a small red light appear at the base of the mirror it means I have selected a new card. Say out loud what you think it is. It will all be done randomly in sets of twenty-five. We'll do about three tests for starters to see how you do. Any questions?"

"Nope. I think I can handle that."

Woody departed and left the two alone to conduct the tests. Major O'Donnell took his seat as Dr. Johansen exited the room, shutting the door. When he did, Pat realized the room was well-soundproofed. The outside noises came to a halt, and the white noise of silence quickly filled the void. The incandescent lights in the room dimmed somewhat, allowing Pat to see with ease the red indicator light below the mirror. Over a loudspeaker he heard Dr. Johansen's voice. "Okay, Pat. We'll begin in a few seconds. I won't give you any feedback on guesses until we're all done."

The red light appeared. He closed his eyes and immediately developed an image in his mind of a square. It was dark, and it had a sharp sound to it...a mental audio flash that often accompanied thoughts of shapes in his mind. It was black, metal, warm, and licorice-flavored all at once.

"Square," Pat responded as he opened his eyes, awaiting the next red light signal.

On the other side of the mirror, Dr. Johansen held the square Zener card and marked the score sheet accordingly. Upon the next signal, once again closing his eyes, Pat received a sensation of a brown, wooden creosote-soaked railroad trestle that smelled of oil and tar. He could almost feel it in his hands, a miniature version of a section of train track trestle that had jagged edges and splinters. It was cross-shaped.

"Plus sign."

Again, Dr. Johansen scored Pat's correct response on the other side of the mirror. For the next hour, he went through the three sets of Zener cards. He would see, feel, taste, hear, and smell things all at once that provided him the clues he needed to guess the cards' shapes. When it was over, he heard Dr. Johansen's voice come across the intercom. It was different this time. It was louder, more vibrant, tremendously excited.

"Okay. We're done for now. Why don't you make your way to the kitchen for a break while I go and confer with Dr. Davis," Johansen suggested.

Dr. Johansen flew out of the observation room with clipboard and score sheets in hand, nearly falling down the stairs as he rushed in to Dr. Davis's office on the first floor. Without knocking, he hurried in, practically out of breath.

"Dr. Davis!   Dr. Davis!" he cried with excitement. "You won't believe this! Look!" he said shoving the score sheets in front of his face.

"Oh, my! He scored twenty-one, twenty-three, and twenty-three in the three sets? Are you sure you marked these correctly?"

"Yes, I'm certain. And I have to tell you, he didn't take much time at all with his guesses, maybe one or two seconds each. You realize the implications of this, don't you?" Johansen asked.

"Yes, I do--what's the statistical probability with random guesses again, five correct out of twenty-five?"

Dr. Johansen nodded. "Yes--five is probability, and in actual testing, the baseline is seven correct out of twenty-five. Anything above that indicates potential for having true psi ability. But Pat's numbers are off the charts! I haven't crunched them yet, but statistically, I'm sure we're talking about an exponential potential of genuine psi abilities!"

Dr. Davis studied the score sheets for a moment. "Do me a favor. I know this is unorthodox, but go back in there with an ordinary deck of playing cards. But don't tell Pat that's what you have. Tell him you want to run two more sets. See what happens. Oh, and do audio and video recordings of the session."

"Do you think he's cheating somehow?"

"No, precisely the opposite. I think he's the real deal. I think there's no challenge for him with the Zener cards."

Pat heard Dr. Johansen summon him over the intercom, asking him to return to the room again for follow-up testing. He had been engrossed in watching the local news coverage of the Driscoll rescue and didn't want to leave. He was fascinated seeing how the van appeared at its crash site exactly as he had envisioned it. A second intercom prompt from Johansen finally got him moving. He returned and took his familiar seat in the soundproof room.

"Pat, we're going to run just two more sets," Johansen told him, the exhilaration in his voice still manifest.

Dr. Johansen switched on the recording equipment, shuffled the deck of fifty-two cards, and held up the top one. It was the ten of hearts. When he pressed the button for the red light signal, Pat closed his eyes as before. This time, the impressions Pat received were very different. All five senses fired away at the clues they were receiving, causing him to express a look of confusion that was picked up clearly by the video recording equipment.

"That's not a Zener card. I'm kind of getting dual images. There's a guy skiing downhill. It's cold. Wind is whipping up fast, but he's a pro. He's having fun. Then there's a number ten with a heart next to it, bright red, many of them. Cherry flavored. If I had to guess, I'd say a playing card, the ten of hearts."

Johansen gasped as Pat spoke, not only because he correctly guessed the particular card, but Pat also saw the back of the card--the theme. It was a deck from the 1972 Winter Olympics in Sapporo, Japan, featuring a Swiss downhill skier careening down the slopes. Dr. Johansen was so stunned by the correct guesses about the card, that he didn't focus on Pat's other sensory descriptions of the images. Card after card, Pat correctly guessed what Johansen was holding. He dismissed the downhill skier once he realized after the second card it was the same image on each. Out of fifty-two cards, Pat missed only two of them. But each time he gave an answer, he felt compelled to explain the multiple sensory qualities of the image he received. Johansen was so overwhelmed, he bolted from the room when they were done, asking Pat to stay put while he went to see Dr. Davis.

While Pat was undergoing his testing in North Carolina, Agent Desantis was at Colonel Helmsley's Pentagon conference room with two other FBI agents. They were both cleared for CRYSTAL ROUNDUP Level Three and were there for the meeting Desantis and Helmsley mutually agreed was necessary in light of the day's events.

"John, this is Special Agent Hank Ratner, and this is Agent Bill Kennedy of the WFO," she said making the introductions.

The Washington Field Office was where Vicky and her small team of CRYSTAL ROUNDUP-cleared FBI agents, Ratner and Kennedy among them, maintained offices, although the team worked directly for the Director of the FBI.

Colonel Helmsley studied the men carefully throughout the meeting. They were both tall and athletic, clearly black bag operators within the Bureau, the kind that probably grew up in the FBI chasing bank robbers, then moved on to do risky operations like installing eavesdropping devices in La Cosa Nostra homes, or even undercover work in organized crime families. Neither man spoke much. Both were in their early forties, conservatively dressed--Ratner in a dark blue business suit, Kennedy in dark gray pinstripes. Each wore the standard, FBI-issued starched white shirt and London Fog trench coat. Ratner's nose was a bit crooked, like he had been in a fight at some point in his life.

"You do any boxing?" Helmsley asked him.

"Yeah. Back in college, then I boxed for a few years in the Army," Ratner responded, casually rubbing his nose, clearly self-conscious of the reason Helmsley asked the question.

"Ah, hum," Desantis interrupted, clearing her throat. "Shall we get down to business men?" she asked, switching the subject abruptly. "As we all know, our CR asset developed information that led to the arrest of Ralston and the rescue of a North Carolina youngster today. Protection of this national asset, Major Patrick O'Donnell, is the primary concern at the moment."

Helmsley chimed in. "Right. It looks like we have a gold mine in Pat O'Donnell, and we need to develop a cover scenario for the arrest that provides him a cut out."

"We all know the parameters at Level Three of CRYSTAL ROUNDUP," Desantis began. "We have a TOP SECRET Presidential Finding that allows us to fabricate witnesses or evidence as necessary to protect the true source of the information. These witnesses or evidence must be able to withstand judicial scrutiny, otherwise, the government loses the case, and the suspect goes free. Worse yet, we risk exposing the SAP itself."

"Any ideas?" Colonel Helmsley asked looking at the three of them.

Kennedy jumped in. "Agent Ratner and I can travel to Hope Mills this afternoon and start interviewing neighbors who may have seen the boy abducted. If we find one, we will have to convince him or her that they also called the FBI right away."

"Do you really think if you find a witness they will go along with the lie that they called the Bureau?" Helmsley asked with a look of doubt. "And what if you don't find any witnesses? Do you plan to ask someone to outright lie about seeing the abduction?"

Desantis shot back abruptly. "Look, John, these gentlemen are good at what they do. The FBI has used them in this capacity for a long time even without a CR asset. We've literally, well, practiced for such an event many times in case we needed it for a genuine CR asset."

"Incredible. And have you actually had people testify falsely in--"

"No one has ever been convicted based upon our practice work!" she snapped harshly before he could finish his question.

The colonel knew she didn't really answer him, and she seemed to be getting irritated. He also knew the Bureau hated being second-guessed, so he shrugged off her mild grouchiness for the time being.

"Okay, so let's say you find a viable witness willing to go along with a slightly altered scenario. This witness will have to be able to testify that he saw at least the suspicious van in the neighborhood, maybe even saw the abduction, then called who? The FBI Hotline? How do we go from what the witness saw to your notification, Vicky?" the colonel asked.

"The FBI Hotline is a good idea, and it's something we've used in the past. We can backstop the Hotline records without any difficulty, indicating I was notified because of prior guidance I gave them about any leads in the Ralston abductions and murders."

"Then you called Dick Williams who phoned Parsons, and the rest is history," Colonel Helmsley concluded.

"Sounds like a plan," Agent Ratner beamed at them. "Bill and I will leave now for North Carolina. We'll have a witness tonight or tomorrow morning," he added with an abundance of confidence.

"Gentlemen, as a reminder this has been a CR Level Three discussion. I will brief the Attorney General tonight. I'm sure he'll phone the President. Congratulations on waking the sleeping giant--CRYSTAL ROUNDUP," Desantis exclaimed with glowing pride.

As the trio of FBI agents left his office, Colonel Helmsley had a gnawing sense of concern in his gut. There was something else going on that they were hiding from him--especially the two gentlemen who looked more like Mafia hit men than FBI agents.

~ 13 ~

Woody Davis had just finished reviewing the video tape of Major O'Donnell's last psi session, duly impressed over his chart-busting score of fifty correct cards out of the playing card deck. An added bonus was the depth of sensory quality to what Pat had to say during the session. He met up with him in one of the Richmond Center's reading rooms to discuss the findings.

Pat had been waiting there for about thirty minutes before Dr. Davis walked in. He admired the hominess of the room. It was like a den. Big and wide with built-in bookshelves displaying hundreds of books on various psychology subjects, as well as the paranormal. The white walls, adorned with waist-high beige wainscoting, stood in stark contrast to the rich red carpet in the center of the room that nearly covered the entire hundred-year-old honey oak floor. A fireplace at one end crackled and sparked as its log pile slowly burned, throwing a toasty warmth into the room. Nearby was a soft, tan microfiber psychiatric couch. *Just like in the movies*, Pat thought. It was next to a large, old cherry wood desk with a high-back leather chair. He entertained himself by lying down on the couch and pretending he was being interviewed by a psychiatrist.

"No! I don't hate my mother!" he exclaimed out loud to no one. "What's that? You think I love my mother a little too much in some sicko Freudian way? Why you, you--"

"Having fun, Pat?" he heard from behind him, unaware that Dr. Davis had opened the door and walked in.

"Yikes! I'm so embarrassed!" he said blushing, sitting up straight and alert now on the couch.

"That's okay, we all need to let our hair down once in awhile. Why don't you stay right where you are so we can talk."

Woody smoothed back his gray hair with his right hand and paused before he spoke. "Pat, let's talk about some sensory aspects. And I don't mean extra-sensory. For a moment, let's talk about the five basic senses we all know--seeing, hearing, smelling, et cetera. Let's try a little experiment." He suddenly smacked his hands together in a loud clap that startled Pat. "Tell me what you just experienced. Describe every detail."

"Well, you scared the crap out of me for starters," Pat laughed. "But seriously. I heard the clap--it was kind of a triangle clap, and bright white."

Woody approached him and held his right hand out close to his face.

"I just scrubbed my hands in the kitchen using scented hand soap. Tell me what you experience when you smell it."

"Hmmmmm," Pat said crinkling his nose slightly. "It's kind of a flowery scent, but it gives me a moving sensation--you know, like the feeling you get on the first big drop on a roller coaster. It's curved and fast."

"Remarkable!" Dr. Davis exclaimed. "Have you always experienced the blending of your senses like this?"

Pat looked at him as if he were crazy to even ask the question.

"Well, of course. Doesn't everyone do that?"

"No, my son, not at all. There is a condition called synesthesia which entails the merging of senses like you experience. Very, very few people experience it. Colors have sounds. Sounds have shapes. Shapes have flavors. One big orchestra in the mind."

"Wait, wait, wait. You mean to tell me that when you *hear* a sound, you don't also *taste* it?" Pat asked with a look of disbelief.

"That's right. I'd say you're probably one in a million. We're going to do many more tests over the next few days, and we're going to zero in on your synesthesia because I think there's a nexus there with your ESP as indicated by our work today."

The two men talked for hours about Pat's entire life. From his earliest childhood memories to the present. The gentle crackling in the fireplace, the warmth that flowed from the Richmond Center's creaky old hardwoods, and his fondness for Woody enabled Pat to open up to him on any and every subject imaginable. With one exception. Pat would never reveal his conversations with Father Reynolds. The confidentiality he came to enjoy with the old priest was sacrosanct.

––––––––––––––––––

Special Agents Ratner and Kennedy arrived in Hope Mills just after 7:00 in the evening and went to work right away going door-to-door along the route from the Driscoll home to his school. One-by-one, they found families at home enjoying dinner or watching television or just relaxing after a hard day at work or school. Most of Mike Driscoll's neighbors were a bit irritated by the late intrusion and because they had already spoken with the FBI and state police that afternoon. They could not understand why the FBI was coming around for a second interview when they told the first team to show up that they weren't even home at the time of the abduction. But Ratner and Kennedy were undeterred. They continued walking the suburban streets of mostly brick rambler and colonial homes in the middle-class neighborhood of Hope Mills. It was an older community with established trees like strong oaks covered in Spanish moss that hung down eerily in the crisp night's darkness. All about were Halloween decorations on lawns, trees, and doorways. Witches, pumpkins...orange and black everywhere.

"This place gives me the creeps," Kennedy announced.

"Aw, the big brave FBI agent is scared?" Ratner teased, knowing they both had nothing to fear given their physical size and since each was packing a Glock semi-automatic handgun with hollow point ammunition.

Suddenly Kennedy stopped in his tracks and pointed to a house as they rounded a corner on the walk to the school.

"You see what I see?" he asked with a smile.

"Sure do. This may be our break," Ratner responded.

The home they saw stood apart from the ones on the street they had started out on. It was older than the rest, a wood frame Victorian with light blue siding, and black shutters and accents. Next to it was a large tract of woods separating it from the next house on the street. Out front was an old lady sweeping leaves from her walkway. Adorned in a white housedress and pink slippers, she happily sang to herself as she labored away.

"If I were going to kidnap a kid in this neighborhood, I'd do it over there by the woods. Fewer homes means fewer witnesses," Ratner snickered.

"Right. And a little old lady probably stays home all day long."

Ratner looked at him with a devious smile. "And she probably lives alone, right?"

Kennedy nodded *yes* as they made their way over to her front porch.

"Excuse me, ma'am," Agent Ratner said holding his FBI credentials out and open. "I'm Special Agent Ratner, and this is Agent Kennedy of the FBI. Mind if we ask you some questions?"

The old woman was startled by their sudden appearance. She quickly set the brittle bristled broom aside, and crossed her arms over her chest, somewhat embarrassed by her appearance.

"Oh, my word!" she exclaimed in a deep southern accent. "Did you say FBI?" she asked examining each of their credentials carefully in the dim light of her front porch.

"Yes, ma'am. And we'd like to speak to you about the Driscoll boy who lives around the corner. I'm sure you heard about him on the news today," Kennedy said.

"I certainly did, and I was so pleased to hear of his rescue! I was wondering when the state police or some G-men would come by to talk with me about this."

Ratner realized this meant Williams and Parsons had not been by her place to do interviews. *Incompetent boobs!*

"Ma'am, may we come in?" he asked.

"Why certainly, but don't mind the mess. Let me fix some tea and we can chat in the living room," she stated with obvious excitement about having two federal agents in her home.

The men studied the room carefully as they entered. All around were framed photographs and portraits of people, most likely the woman's ancestors. It was a stereotypical spinster's home. There was a dark green side chair by the fireplace with a white lace doily...knitting needles and a ball of yarn on the seat. The heavy scent of wintergreen muscle cream filled the air. The home was immaculate and tidy with no hint that anyone else lived there but the woman.

"Here we go!" she announced as she walked into the room slowly with a silver tray upon which was an antique tea pot, a matching set of tea cups, and sugar and cream. "I always have some hot tea brewing in the evening, so no trouble at all fixing some for you gentlemen."

They all prepared their cups as the FBI agents interviewed her. She was Rose McAdams, a widow of ten years. At seventy-three years of age she no longer worked, having retired several years earlier as an elementary school teacher in the same school Mike Driscoll attended down the street. The home she lived in was 125 years old and had been in her family for more than four generations. She also owned the tract of wooded land next to the home and bragged about how her family fought City Hall to keep it from taking the land and her home under Eminent Domain laws. The city had tried to move her family long ago, wanting to sell the property to land developers, but her late husband had the home listed on the National Register of Historical Places which completely nixed the plan. He managed to dig up some old Revolutionary War records and discovered the wooded area was the scene of a battle, which meant both house and land stayed put. Agents Ratner and Kennedy were amused by her recounting of history and sat silently as she rattled on and on about it. Finally, Ratner decided it was time to get down to business. He asked her if she had been home all morning and if she had seen anything.

"Well, yes, of course," she replied matter-of-factly. "I remember looking out my front window at about seven o'clock because I heard some tires screeching. Or was it eight o'clock? I can't recall. It was just one of the teenagers who lives up the street. You boys ought to go and knock on his door and scare him!" she giggled with a wink at the thought of setting the boy up.

"But it was then that I noticed the van. I mean, I didn't think much of it until I heard the news today and saw that same van smashed up on the highway where they arrested that man."

"Go on, Mrs. McAdams. Did you see the man in the van, or did you see the Driscoll boy at any time this morning?" Kennedy asked.

"Well, no, I didn't. Like I said, I saw the van parked by itself near the woods. The street was empty at the time, other than the car that was flying by."

"Do you wear glasses, ma'am?" Kennedy asked.

"Never have in my life," she replied with confidence, rapping her fingers on the wooden coffee table. "Knock on wood I'll never lose my twenty-twenty vision!"

Ratner interrupted her for a moment. "May I use your telephone?"

"Why certainly, there's one right through there on the kitchen wall."

Ratner stood up and walked into the kitchen. He picked up the receiver and looked behind himself to ensure he was alone, then placed it back on the hook quietly. The tall FBI agent reached into his left breast pocket and retrieved a small black plastic box and opened it slowly. Ratner pretended to be having a telephone conversation with someone as he withdrew one of two syringes from the box.

He crept into the room while Kennedy kept Rose McAdams's attention focused on him. Ratner walked up behind Mrs. McAdams as she sat in her knitting chair, eyeing her white and wrinkled right arm, exposed by her short-sleeved housedress. In one swift maneuver, he deftly jabbed the syringe deep into her arm, plunging its burning liquid contents into the old woman's muscle. There was no time for Mrs. McAdams to react to the sharp pain from the needle or the searing concoction in her arm. She was out cold. Unconscious. Instinctively, Kennedy lunged forward to grab her so she wouldn't fall. It was a routine he and Ratner had down cold. Something they had practiced together many, many, many times before.

~ 14 ~

It was a quiet and lazy morning back in the town of Hope Mills. The brisk fall winds had blown nearly every leaf off the trees in Mike Driscoll's neighborhood. All the colors had disappeared from them, long turned brown, dry, and crisp. They made crunchy noises as Agent Dick Williams and Detective Ron Parsons walked along the sidewalks, continuing to canvass the neighborhood, looking for possible witnesses to the abduction from the day before.

The men turned the same corner that Agents Ratner and Kennedy had rounded the night before. And just like Ratner and Kennedy, the pair also stopped for a moment as they eyed the scene...the woods that could provide good cover for a kidnapping...and Rose McAdams's home that was in excellent position to see the woods.

"Good morning, ma'am," Williams greeted Rose after ringing the doorbell, introducing himself and Parsons.

"My word! Real G-men!" the spinster stated excitedly. She was decked out in a conservative blue dress, hair fixed up real nice, bright red lipstick, and eyeliner recreating long lost eyebrows. "I was wondering when you fellas might come knocking on my door," she said in her deep drawl.

Rose invited the men into her living room and offered tea just as she did the night before to her other callers, but gave no hint to Williams or Parsons of the former pair's visit. As she entered the room with the tea set, she commented, "You know I saw that nasty man grab that boy yesterday morning!"

Williams's and Parsons's sudden excitement became palpable.

"Er, you actually saw the abduction occur?" Parsons asked in stunned disbelief.

"Why, yes I did, and that's why I called the FBI Hotline right away!" she said proudly, displaying a refrigerator magnet bearing the hotline's number. "I was afraid to give my name yesterday, so I just hung up after calling. But now that you caught that man, I want to help any way I can!"

"Amazing," Williams said scratching his head. "What time did the abduction occur?"

Rose responded instantly, with no apparent need to think about it at all.

"It was right at seven thirty-five. And I called the FBI at seven thirty-six!"

Mrs. McAdams provided, in marvelous detail, everything she knew from having *witnessed* the crime. The tire screech of the teenager from up the street that prompted her to look out the window. The van she found to be suspicious near the woods. Its Arizona license plate that she jotted down on a slip of paper she handed Agent Williams and Detective Parsons. She described how she saw the Driscoll boy as he approached the van kicking stones, unaware of any danger ahead of him. She saw Ralston clear as day with her 20-20 vision and immediately identified him from a photo lineup Williams had at the ready in his briefcase. The men thanked her profusely and promised to be in touch.

"Un-freakin' believable!" Parsons exclaimed once they were safely out of range of Rose McAdams's home.

Williams shook his head in amazement. "You got that right! That's the break we needed since Ralston copped for a lawyer."

"Yeah. Between our new friend Rose, and Mike Driscoll's testimony, Ralston is going away for a long time. And with the DNA from the two murders and assaults, he'll probably get the death penalty in at least one state."

Their chat was broken by the sharp ringing of Williams's cell phone. It was Vicky Desantis.

"Williams, how is your case going? Is Ralston talking yet?"

"Look, not that it's any of your business, but Ralston has a lawyer. We found the eye witness who phoned the hotline yesterday, saw the whole thing!" he stated proudly.

"An eye witness who saw everything?" Vicky asked with a wry smile as she turned and looked at Ratner and Kennedy who were sitting in her office.

Both men were smirking, soaking in the vicarious praise for their black bag operation from the night before. Rose McAdams had performed her starring role magnificently.

When Pat arrived at the Center that morning, he was greeted by Dr. Johansen and a smaller group of staff. Since it was a Saturday, most of the Center's staff was off for the weekend. Pat learned that Woody had turned him over to Dr. Johansen for more testing so he could meet with Colonel Helmsley and Agent Desantis. Dr. Johansen practically led Pat by the hand for the next several hours while he underwent a full battery of psi exams. Stopping midday only for a short lunch break, they pressed on again for many more hours until Pat, Dr. Johansen, and the staff were all exhausted. By late afternoon, it was time for things to come together. Dr. Johansen led him to the Center's conference room where Woody, the colonel, and Vicky waited.

"Hey, Pat! Great to see you," Colonel Helmsley said, springing to his feet as Pat entered.

"Boss--real glad to see you. What a meat grinder today!"

Vicky sauntered over and extended her hand. "Well hello, Patrick," she said with a warm smile, and equally warm shake.

"Hi, Vicky."

"Sounds like the testing went very well, according to Woody," she commented.

"Well, I'm anxious to hear about it myself," Pat replied.

"It would be my pleasure to give you the details," Johansen said as he shuffled some papers on his clipboard, then cleared his throat. "Well, let me cover the negatives first," he began. "The PK tests showed no discernable ability to move objects. Zilch. However, we noted significant telepathic ability. He was able to correctly guess colors and numbers the examiner thought of."

Dr. Davis stopped him. "Give me some stats."

"Well, we ran three series of fifty events. Pat scored, let me see—" Johansen's voice trailed off as he flipped a few more pages. "Here it is! He scored forty-seven, forty-five, forty-two correct in the sets."

"Congratulations, Patrick," Vicky said. "We didn't expect you were a mind reader, as well."

Johansen continued rummaging through his report.

"He did amazingly well on the precog and retrocog tests, too. We used a random number generator on both. In the precog, he correctly guessed the next number the machine generated forty-one, forty-eight, and forty-three times in three sets of fifty."

Colonel Helmsley had a curious look. "How many digits were in these random numbers?"

"Oh, that's the remarkable part. Anywhere from one to six digit numbers were randomly generated. And Pat still performed this well. Have never seen anything like it before!"

"And the retrocog?" Woody asked.

"Ha! Even better than the precog. It was his best. Way off the charts with forty-eight, fifty, and fifty scores!"

Although Pat didn't grasp the significance of the results, it was clear the other four did. He could see there was an almost giddy sense of exhilaration among them.

"We also did some remote viewing testing, and it was apparent that the closer Pat was physically to an object, the better he did at discerning it," Johansen concluded. "There's a definite spatial component at work with Pat."

The room was silent for a few moments. Johansen began to ask a question, but Woody cut him off.

"Thank you and the staff for all you've done today, Dr. Johansen."

The nerdy psychologist took his cue and departed gracefully.

Helmsley stood up and walked to the window. Pat watched as the colonel peered out at the quiet and still residential street to a white minivan parked in front of the Center. It had a nondescript appearance, except for tinted side windows that darkened it so much no amount of peering through would yield what was inside. Pat watched him watching the van. Clearly there was something special about it.

"Shall we all go for a ride?" Colonel Helmsley asked with a boyish grin.

~ 15 ~

They departed the Richmond Center into the chilly fall air, tumbling into the van, one-by-one, with Colonel Helmsley at the wheel. Agent Desantis rode shotgun, with Woody and Pat side-by-side on the bench seat behind them.

"Nice wheels," Pat grinned. "Courtesy of Uncle Sam, I take it?" he asked, running his fingers across the cool, dark gray leather fabric of Colonel Helmsley's seatback.

The colonel smiled back in the rearview mirror. "Let's buckle up, and I'll show you what this baby's got!"

They took a circuitous route through Raleigh-Durham to I-95 northbound. Pat noted how silent it was in the vehicle. No outside noise at all. Colonel Helmsley reached down to a console that separated the two front seats, mounted on the floor, but high enough for either driver or passenger to manipulate. He pressed a small silver button that released a panel. When it popped open, a small plasma screen was on the other side. About nine inches diagonally, it was a small laptop type screen that flickered briefly, then brightened slowly to display a map.

"Lots of new cars have GPS map and trip planning capabilities," he said. "But not to government specs like this one."

He manipulated a small touchpad and two buttons below the screen. "There, that's us right there," he said pointing to a small crosshair symbol on a blue colored vein-like line that represented I-95.

Pat was trying hard not to appear unimpressed as the colonel spoke. He had seen this type of GPS display many times before.

Colonel Helmsley pressed a small button, and the image changed. Instead of simple computer-aided graphics, like a typical GPS navigation screen, Pat sat looking at a camera view of their van as it traveled along the highway. It was like watching a live television broadcast of a police car chase shot from a helicopter. He could see all objects around them in real time. Cars, trees, litter, and...them! Pat rolled his window down and stuck his hand out, and as clear as day on the minivan's plasma screen, he saw his hand waving.

"Christ! This is precise real-time coverage, I mean, no lag at all!" Pat exclaimed.

"At the TOP SECRET level, we are geo-fixed down to less than a quarter inch resolution," the colonel said.

He played with the controls some more, zooming out a few gradients until they all could see where they were on the map, out to about six miles.

"Cripes!" Woody exclaimed. "I assume this is overhead satellite imagery--not a recce bird sent up for our current amusement?" he asked, knowing full well there was no way a spy aircraft was launched for this purpose only.

"Yes, Woody," the colonel said. "Part of why we brought you all here today is to brief you in on some new technologies we want to leverage in the CRYSTAL ROUNDUP program."

"The van is a dedicated SCIF--fully shielded," Vicky added. "So no worries about what we say or do here. And that brings us to another reason we're here. We need to give you both a CR Level Two and Three briefing."

As they drove along she pulled two manila folders from her briefcase, each marked TOP SECRET. Pat and Woody skimmed along the contents as she talked.

"Think of Level One as the administrative and support level," she said. "It gives you knowledge of the program's existence and for some people, the ability to support it. Like you have over the years, Woody.

Level Two is the operational level. Every time the SAP is used to perform an action--like going after Victor Ralston, it becomes a Level Two activity," she explained.

"And Level Three is what?" Pat asked.

Vicky hesitated a moment. "At the third level, covert action is taken to protect the SAP," she finally said.

For the next twenty minutes, Agent Desantis outlined the TOP SECRET Presidential finding going back to the Vietnam era and endorsed by all Presidents since. She explained the importance of finding or fabricating evidence or witnesses who merely established a *white world* causal link between perpetrators and a crime, to supplant the *black world* SAP nexus that really existed. Agent Desantis talked about many things, to include finding Rose McAdams who saw Ralston's van that morning. But there was one thing Agent Desantis failed to mention--exactly how Rose McAdams became such a cooperative witness. She was the only person in the van to harbor the true secret of Ratner and Kennedy. The forced injection. The searing liquid. The drugged-up and now completely-perfect, albeit robotic-like, eye witness...Rose McAdams.

Pat was uncomfortable with the arrangement. As a career law enforcement agent, he was well-disciplined in legal matters. Rules of evidence. Search and seizure. All things founded in the Constitution he was sworn to protect. These were things that meant something dear to him. Above all, were his deep Christian morals and values. Fabricating evidence like this was an issue for him, and it was apparent the colonel sensed it.

"Pat, I know how you feel. And Vicky and I have had this discussion. As uncomfortable as it makes me, I know the greater good is being served. We are, after all, going after people who have committed real crimes."

Pat was silent for a moment. "But, Sir, what if I'm wrong about someone? What if I lead you to the wrong person--and your *created* witnesses or evidence convicts the wrong person?"

"We'll just have to be careful, won't we?" Vicky asked smugly.

"Who has been briefed on the Ralston operation so far?" Woody asked.

"I've briefed the FBI Director and the Attorney General," Vicky noted. "Oh, and the President was briefed as well--and he said, 'Congratulate that young man for me for a job well done!'" she added as she turned around and gave Pat a huge smile.

That last tidbit alone gave him some needed comfort to ease his worries. After all, if the President was satisfied with the program, why should he worry? This was the ultimate top cover. And it didn't hurt hearing the President sent a personal message to him.

There was much more to CRYSTAL ROUNDUP that Pat learned during the rest of their ride around North Carolina. The cover requirements for the SAP meant they had to minimize the amount of time any two or more of them would be seen together in public. There were codenames and safe houses, surveillance and countersurveillance requirements. There were cut outs, backstops, and focal points. Although they talked about all these things in generalities now, Pat would come to learn and live by them in the near future.

He spent the next several days at the Richmond Center with Dr. Davis as the two worked closely together discovering all they could about his unique abilities. By the time they were done, Pat was so tired that returning home this time was more special to him than any other trip he had been on before.

"Give me a hug, Sweetie," Sara said greeting him at the door. Pat's fanny pack pressed against her as they hugged, Beretta inside pushing hard against her, just above her groin. "Oh, my!" she exclaimed.

She looked down at the fanny pack and giggled, blushing. For a moment it served up in her mind a dirty thought or two. It didn't require Pat's psychic abilities to read them.

"Sorcha!" was all he said shaking his head as if to say, *naughty girl!*

They were interrupted by Sean and Erin's loud and busy arrival.

"Daddy! Daddy! Daddy's home!" they exclaimed in unison. One at a time he lifted them up for hugs and kisses. He was overdue--having been gone so long. Erin, especially, demanded extra catch-up kisses. He scooted them off, back to the family room, after they bombarded him in shotgun style with blasts of information about school, new toys, and cartoons.

Pat and Sara walked hand-in-hand to the kitchen so he could eat the special welcome home meal she had prepared. She had grilled a one and a half inch thick juicy rib eye steak, cooked medium, with side dishes of mashed potatoes and gravy and homemade vegetable medley. It was all densely-packed flavor that, to a synesthete like Pat, meant color, shape, and sound, as well. He amused himself as he ate, thinking about his synesthesia. He was so aware of it now, that he concentrated hard about the confluence of senses it created for him. Prior to the week in North Carolina, it was always so transparent, so subconscious, so automatic. But things were different now. Pat fully realized and appreciated the great gifts God had endowed him with.

"So, tell me all about the trip. Were you able to help the folks in North Carolina with these kidnappings? Were you involved with that guy they caught last week?" she asked.

"Yeah, Baby. Sort of. I mean they interviewed me. The Task Force people, and they located this guy. He's the one responsible for the other two murders."

She had a look of shock. "Wow, Pat! You mean you helped solve the other two and saved a new kid?"

"Well, I can't take any real credit. It was a lot of great police work," he said in between chewing mouthfuls of juicy steak and swallowing gulps of ice cold beer.

"Oh, before I forget, Father Reynolds called. Checking up on you. He asked that you call him when you get back," Sara said, suddenly remembering to give Pat the message.

"Okay, Baby. I will."

Pat hadn't even thought about Father Reynolds in the past week, ever since getting wrapped up in the bizarre chain of events that led to the discovery of his psychic abilities. He would call him soon but needed some time to think of what to tell him.

"Listen, Sara. I've been asked by the FBI to work with some of their headquarters people who do serial killer profiling. They want me to help revamp their profiling course at Quantico based on my experiences in these cases."

He lied again, but out of necessity. He needed some rationale for why he would not be going to work every day in his Air Force uniform. Instead, as Colonel Helmsley instructed him before he left Raleigh-Durham, he would be visiting a safe house in Arlington each day, and wearing casual clothes. The lies were starting to become more complex.

"That sounds exciting. When do you start?"

"In a few days. They worked out some time off for me to unwind after the stress of these recent cases."

She walked up behind him and kissed his cheek. "You deserve it, Baby. I'm going to get the kids ready for bed. Enjoy the meal."

"I want to tuck them in, too! And tell them I want to make up a story tonight. Have them think of the characters they want in the story, and I'll work my magic when I get there."

"I sure will."

When he finished his meal, he walked into Erin's room where he found her and Sean huddled on her pink canopy bed giggling in anticipation of dad's story. From the looks on their faces, they had some creative characters in mind.

"Well, why don't we start with you, young lady," he said, nestling in between the children on the covers.

"Okay, Daddy," Erin replied with pride at being first. "I want a young princess in the story."

"Sounds like a good one. And you, Sean?"

Pat's oldest seemed to be rethinking his original character in light of what Erin had blurted out. Finally, he said, "I want an evil man wearing a disguise who kidnaps the princess! Ha! Ha! Ha! Ha! Ha!" he finished with a twisted laugh.

Erin began crying and protesting Sean's choice. "Daddy! No! That scares me!"

"Knock it off, Sean! Pick something else or no story tonight at all!" Pat said sternly. Sean's choice of story character struck a sensitive chord with his dad more than it did with Erin. It reminded him of all he had been through lately. He felt a sense of having his own home violated, his own children threatened, merely by Sean's thoughts.

"Okaaaaay! Hmmmmph!" Sean protested. "A goat. A freakin' goat. That's my character," he droned in a monotone of protest.

"Wow! A princess and a goat. And I thought you kids could come up with something more difficult than that!" Pat said accepting the challenge.

For the next fifteen minutes he weaved a complex tale that masterfully incorporated these seemingly disparate elements. The children chortled with delight as their dad amazed them with his story telling abilities. With the youngsters both tucked in for the night, Pat went to his bedroom where he found Sara fast asleep. He kissed her cheek gently, daring not to disturb her slumber. And within minutes of changing clothes, the tired and travel-worn Patrick O'Donnell was fast asleep next to her, unaware that a block away a technical surveillance van was busy recording every word spoken that night in the O'Donnell home.

~ 16 ~

Sara and the children had long since left for school when Pat rose the next morning and got himself about. He retreated to his den sanctuary, to his computer. He needed to catch up on the more than one hundred emails that awaited him since his TDY to North Carolina. There was one from Father Reynolds that simply read, *PAT--CALL ME SOONEST--URGENT!* He picked up the phone next to the computer and dialed the rectory. Father Reynolds picked up the line on the very first ring.

"Patrick, my boy! How are you? I was worried about you, haven't spoken with you for over a week!"

"Hey, Padre, I'm fine. Had to go on a business trip."

"I see, well, we need to talk. Can you come by here in about an hour?" he asked, his voice sounding different, clearly distressed.

"Sure thing. I'll see you then, Father."

Pat didn't want to probe him on the phone about the subject since he had been so vague in his email. With the way things were going for him now, he knew he had better be extra careful about his communication.

The drive over to Our Lady of La Salette was quiet and peaceful. Although he could not see that he was being followed, this time he had a feeling he was. It troubled him. The clues were subtle. Fuzzy. There were no suspicious vehicles in sight, but his sense was there was a sedan with two men watching him. It could not have been Williams and Parsons--too sophisticated, too experienced to be them. He instinctively reached down to his fanny pack and caressed it with his right hand. It gave him a sense of security knowing his Beretta was there. Locked. Loaded. Ready.

He found Father Reynolds waiting for him just inside the church entrance. He was dressed in his priestly black cassock with white tab affixed to a black Nehru style collar shirt. He seemed nervous and agitated. As he hurried Pat inside, the priest looked beyond him to the parking lot as if searching for someone else who might have followed him.

"Pat, Pat, hurry! Come on in," he urged in excitement.

He took the cue and double-timed it inside, hearing the *WOOSH* of the door as it closed tightly behind them. Father Reynolds put his arm around him and handed him a note while pressing a forefinger to his own lips. Pat opened it and read, *Some CIA men visited me and asked me about you. Wanted to know what we discussed last time you were here. I think my office is bugged. Don't say a word!*

"So, Padre, I came by to the see if you need some help organizing the Fall Festival this year," Pat said, providing a cover topic they could discuss openly.

"Oh, yes, bless you, Patrick!" Father Reynolds said catching on immediately. "We can always use the volunteer help!"

As they entered the priest's office Father Reynolds continued talking about the Fall Festival while he showed Pat a curious device he found. There was a wall outlet behind the priest's desk. The cover plate was removed, and the receptacle was pulled out. The device was attached by small alligator clips and wire to the electrical connections inside the outlet. It was tiny and black, about the size of a sugar cube, with what appeared to be a circular shaped microphone on top, no larger than a pencil point. Pat's jaw tightened. He was angry. He didn't know who was behind this, but had been around the Intelligence Community long enough to know how agencies like the CIA and FBI oftentimes competed with each other. He hoped this wasn't the case. Violating the sanctity of his confession with Father

Reynolds was over the top.

"Say, Father, where do you keep the Fall Festival supplies? I'd like to see them."

"In the attic. I'll show you!"

He eagerly escorted him to the rectory's attic. Pat felt comfortable enough there to talk, believing the bug planters most likely had not placed devices in the attic. It was musty and dusty as they climbed the small, retractable wooden staircase that Father Reynolds pulled down from the ceiling. Pat looked around for a moment at the clutter of old boxes and trunks deftly balanced across wooden joists, surrounded by blown-in white insulation.

"What the hell is going on, Pat?" Father Reynolds asked, stunning him with his choice of words.

The two men delicately balanced themselves on ceiling joists, crouching down under the low roof.

"I'm not sure, Father, tell me about these CIA guys. When did they come here?"

"Four days ago. Two tall men, one of them real big and burly, like in the movies. No nonsense types, either," the priest said, clearly upset and disgusted.

"What did they want?"

"Well, after showing me their CIA identification, they said they were doing a background check on you for a security clearance and wanted to ask me some questions. It seemed harmless enough, but then they asked me specifically about the last time you came to visit. They wanted to know what we discussed!"

"I assume you told them to get lost?"

"Well, yes, much more diplomatically though. But they were persistent. They wanted to know if you told me anything about your job or projects you were working."

"And you told them...?"

"Nothing. I simply said that I could never reveal anything about our private discussion, not even the general topics we discussed. Nothing."

"Thanks, Father, for your confidentiality, so tell me about this bug device. Did you just find it hanging out of the wall like that?"

Father Reynolds laughed. "Oh my, no. That's another story. A couple of nights back--after these two men paid me a visit--I couldn't sleep well, so I came to the rectory to work on some reports for the Archdiocese. I heard some muffled commotion as I approached the door."

"Did you find these same guys in your office?"

"No. Actually, I was afraid to go in, so I called out, 'Rachel, is that you in there?' I hoped to scare them off, to make them think I believed the receptionist was in there."

"So, what happened?"

"Well, I called out her name a few more times, heard some scuffling, then it got quiet. So, I went in. I saw my window was shut, but it was now unlocked. Then I saw some white powder on the carpet by the wall, just below that outlet."

"Oh, like wallboard powder?"

"Precisely. And you know how immaculate I keep my office! I unscrewed the cover and pulled out the outlet and found that thing!"

Pat thought for a moment about how sloppy the operation seemed to be, shaking his head in disgust.

"Pat, what is going on? I don't have to tell you how illegal this all sounds to me."

He nodded in agreement. He was at an important mental crossroads at that moment. Part of him felt compelled to tell Father Reynolds something about the CRYSTAL ROUNDUP program. He believed he at least owed this to the priest considering how the CIA now was on to things and causing him trouble.

"Listen, Father, you were right about me the last time we talked. Apparently I do have some kind of psychic power. I've spent the last week in a giant Petri dish being examined and tested. I got myself wrapped up in the black world--a covert program with the FBI and Department of Defense. They want me to help solve child abductions and murders."

Father Reynolds stopped him for a moment. A look of concern came across his face.

"Pat, this all sounds noble and righteous, but be careful. It seems to me your black world has an even darker underbelly. Why would the CIA have to bug my office and try to strong arm me about you if this was all clean and above board?"

Pat didn't have a good answer for him. That unsettled feeling he first had when Vicky told him about fabricating witnesses came back again. He knew he'd have to be very careful. They headed back to Father Reynolds's office, continuing the same chat about the Fall Festival as they had done before. Pat took one more look at the open outlet and shook his head.

"Stay warm, Pat!" Father Reynolds said, giving him a hug as he prepared to depart.

"You too, Padre!" He could see the worry in Father Reynolds's eyes.

Pat drove home thinking about what had just transpired. His CT radar was up and running at full power as he scanned his surroundings. And just like before the sensation of being followed was there, but the evidence was absent.

It was late in the day when he decided he would at least call his boss and report in, to let him know he'd be out of the office indefinitely.

"Hey Colonel Lyons. How are you, Sir?" Pat asked cheerfully.

"My long lost major! O'Donnell, you'll come up with any excuse to get out of work, won't you?" Colonel Lyons teased.

"I take it Colonel Helmsley spoke with you about me helping him out for the foreseeable future?"

"Yeah, he sure did. Apparently you've really made an impression on him recently, not that he could tell me anything about it!"

Pat laughed. "You know how these programs work--they all sound sexy from the outside, but it's a big yawn when you get briefed-in!"

"I know, Pat. Well, whatever it is, you are invaluable to John Helmsley, so just keep doing good things and check in every now and then, okay?"

"Sure thing, bye for now."

Unbeknownst to him and the colonel while they talked, FBI agents Ratner and Kennedy sat parked two blocks from Pat's home in an FBI technical services surveillance van. On the outside it was a dark gray panel van with red lettering bearing the logo of Virginia Power, the electrical utility company that serviced Pat's neighborhood. It blended in so naturally to the area that it was virtually transparent to people who lived there. Inside, however, Ratner wore headphones and listened in to Pat and Colonel Lyons's conversation while Kennedy operated the digital recording equipment to capture all the words. They even had STU III intercept and decryption capability in the event Pat and his boss decided to go secure. No matter what Pat or anyone in his household said, secure or in the clear, the surveillance van would pick it up, sound and sight. The house was wired with video cameras and listening devices everywhere. Home phone, cell phones, computer, and open conversation. It was also a passive system that didn't need real-time monitoring. All the transmitters tied into a computer system that tracked conversations throughout the home. Ratner and Kennedy would move the van from time-to-time and sometimes exchange it for a different vehicle that blended in equally well. No expense was spared in following Agent Desantis's orders to make sure Pat could be trusted in this operation.

"Well that was harmless enough, I guess," Ratner commented as he removed his headphones.

"Yeah, I suppose. Hey--who do I sound like?" Kennedy asked. "A goat, a freakin' goat!" he said in a childlike voice, imitating what Sean had said the night before when Pat asked him to rethink his choice of bedtime story characters.

Ratner chuckled, thinking about the conversation they found on the equipment that morning when they arrived to check on the recording.

"I kinda liked the idea of the evil man in the mask," Ratner laughed. "But that Sean kid better leave Erin alone, I mean she's so cute and all."

Kennedy gave him a strange look.

Ratner shook his head, "Hey man, I don't mean it like that! She's like what, five?"

Kennedy quickly changed subjects in an effort to redirect the uncomfortable conversation they began having.

"What are we gonna do about the priest?"

"I think we'll have to pay him another visit tonight. I sure wish I knew what him and O'Donnell talked about today when they went to the attic. We may have to be more persuasive this time."

Ratner lifted up a brown leather briefcase. He opened it, displaying a collection of dozens of badges and credentials from many, many different agencies...FBI, CIA, NSA, LAPD, NYPD, Fairfax County PD, even a set from Scotland Yard. He lifted two CIA credentials.

"Let's get some chow and then go see Reynolds tonight."

"Okay, Boss," Kennedy smiled.

The church parking lot was empty when Ratner and Kennedy drove up and parked in the side lot, out of view from the nearby street. From their car they could see Father Reynolds's office light was turned on. They walked up and found the rectory main door was unlocked, and the door to his office was slightly ajar. Father Reynolds sat at his desk working on reports when the two men pushed his door open slowly. He looked up and saw the familiar faces of Ratner and Kennedy standing there.

"You two again?" he asked sternly. "I told you I have nothing to say to you. Unless you're here for spiritual reasons, I think you should leave now."

Father Reynolds's voice grew more forceful as he spoke. He was both angry and frightened by the intrusion. At that moment, he also realized he had left the wall outlet opened, the eavesdropping device hanging out. He stood and walked over to the men to keep them from coming close to his desk and seeing the bug exposed.

Ratner spoke, again displaying his phony CIA credentials. "Look, Father, this is a matter of national security. It's imperative you speak with us."

Kennedy walked over to one of the walls and began to admire the collection of framed certificates and memorabilia the priest had gathered over the last forty years serving as a pastor in many different parishes around the United States.

"Say, Father, is this your seminary degree?" he asked, squinting at a large, framed document.

Father Reynolds approached him, distracted for the moment from his initial conversation with Ratner. He addressed them both as he walked, "Gentlemen, it's late, and I have a lot of work to do, so you really will have to go now."

The momentary distraction was all Ratner needed as he deftly reached into his jacket pocket and retrieved a syringe from its black plastic case.

"Oh, let me see," he said as he walked up behind Father Reynolds and swiftly drove the syringe into his buttocks, jettisoning its burning liquid into the old priest.

The big and imposing Kennedy was ready to grab him as he fell, but Father Reynolds was not to be like most people the two agents had practiced the routine on over the years. He felt the sting, and although he quickly became weak in the knees, he managed to turn and with a full fist, drove a painful blow square into Ratner's face. It startled Ratner, who jumped back, syringe in hand. He felt his nose, then looked at his hand and the warm, dark red blood that now covered his palm.

"That sonabitch broke my nose!" he shrieked. "Nobody's done that since I boxed in college!"

Kennedy grabbed Father Reynolds whose knees immediately buckled, eyes closed, nearly hitting the floor. He struggled to hold him up because he was laughing uproariously at Ratner as the latter stood sulking over his wound.

"Hank, if this shit weren't so damn secret, everybody in the Bureau would hear about this tomorrow! About how tough Hank Ratner let a priest break his nose!" Kennedy boomed.

"Yeah, real funny!" he replied, wiping the blood from his nose with a white silk hanky.

"Let's lay him down on the couch and wait for him to come to," Kennedy suggested.

They carried the priest to the dark green fabric sofa and set him down in a comfortable position. They pulled two chairs up next to the sofa, in position to talk with him once he woke from the short-term nap they induced. Nearly ten minutes to the second after being injected with the hot serum, Father Reynolds began to move. At first it was slow and steady, his eyes taking time to focus, a slight queasiness in his stomach from the potion they had given him. For the next half hour he remained in a hypnotic-like trance.

The drug was a special mix originally developed by the CIA for use in covert Cold War operations in the 1960s...programs now defunct. When CRYSTAL ROUNDUP was first crafted its framers suggested use of the serum in its Level Three actions. But the then-Attorney General disapproved it because its side effects were unclear. It remained unauthorized ever since, but Ratner, Kennedy, and their boss, Desantis, were rogues, determined to make the program work at any cost. They obtained a stock of the serum from the bowels of the CIA and kept it ready in the event they would someday need it.

Once injected, a person was extraordinarily susceptible to hypnotic suggestion. Ratner and Kennedy were the antithesis of the *Men in Black* urban legend. Instead of erasing memories, they used the drug to make memories, memories of things that never occurred. It worked best when used to steer an existing real memory into a new direction, bending its reality to whatever Ratner and Kennedy suggested. And at the end of every memory making event, they included the suggestion that the witness would forget ever having met them. One false memory inserted to replace a true memory removed.

But tonight, as Father Reynolds was rousing from the deep sleep of the injection, Ratner and Kennedy were experimenting. They reasoned the drug would also act like a truth serum of sorts, allowing them to probe Father Reynolds's mind for information about his discussions with Pat O'Donnell.

"What's going on? What did you guys do to me?" Father Reynolds asked groggily as he began to make out their faces once again through the dopey haze.

"Relax, Father, we just want to ask you a few questions about Pat

O'Donnell," Ratner replied, still smarting over the punch to the nose the priest had given him.

"I've told you I can't disclose anything about our chats," he said as his eyes closed again, then opened slightly.

"Try to concentrate on your meeting with him today, Father, and you'll see things very clearly. Tell us what you talked about in the attic," Kennedy urged.

For twenty minutes the two men tried in vain to get Father Reynolds to cough up information he held in private about Pat's confession. The priest wearily fought off their pressure and approaches. His convictions and his vows as a priest were so strong, that no amount of prodding by Ratner and Kennedy would pry out the information they sought.

"Christ!" Ratner said. "He's tough, and we only have about ten more minutes before the serum wears off. Let me try one more injection."

"Hank! Are you sure that's a good idea?"

"You got any better suggestions?"

Ratner retrieved the last syringe he had in his case and gave Father Reynolds one more injection in his arm. The priest winced for a second, then dropped fast asleep. The double dose of serum caused him to sleep longer this time. It was almost twenty minutes before he began to stir again. He had double vision at first which made him dizzy, giving him the feeling he needed to vomit. But he couldn't move. The drug was so powerful, it made his body feel like dead weight. His defenses were weakened this time, and Ratner's theory about the drug acting like a truth serum at higher doses had some merit. They began to ask Father Reynolds some simple *yes* and *no* questions which he answered with little protest.

But just as they prepared to ask him more weighty questions about Pat, the telephone rang on Father Reynolds's desk. Its ring was sharp and loud, and it startled the men. They paused their questioning to listen as the answering machine kicked in with its greeting. The voice they heard was all too familiar. It was Pat O'Donnell.

"Hey, Father Reynolds. It's me Pat. I know you probably aren't in your office this late, but I wanted to see if you want to go run with me in the morning. It promises to be a nice Saturday, so I plan to be at the Springfield Park jogging trail at nine. Come by if you can. Later."

Pat's voice drilled down deeply into Father Reynolds's psyche, cutting right through the layers of mental control the powerful serum had over him. As Pat spoke, Father Reynolds grew more conscious and aware of what was happening to him. He tried calling out, but his voice was weak.

"Pat, Pat, please help me," was all he managed to get out.

Ratner shot him a threatening glare. It was all the old man could take. The drug had been busy at work on his heart as well as his brain. And when he heard Pat's voice, and when he realized how much danger he was in, and when he saw Ratner look so menacingly at him, his heart gave out. In an instant he was dead and being lifted to heaven by a chorus of angels before Ratner and Kennedy realized he was gone.

"Shut up!" he heard Ratner growl.

It was Father Reynolds's last image of earth as he looked down once more at his own body lying on the couch. Turning his eyes upward, angels all around him, he saw a glorious light that drew him in with consuming joy. And gone.

"Hey, Father, wake up!" Kennedy said frantically as he shook the priest's body.

Ratner felt his neck with two fingers. "Crap! No pulse! I think he's dead!"

"Great--how do we explain this to Vicky? She's gonna be steamed!"

"Here, help me get him to his desk. We'll sit him in his chair and slump him over like he had a heart attack working late at night," Ratner ordered.

They carried his body to the desk and posed him in his chair. Kennedy looked down after they finished the set up.

"Hey--you see this?" he said pointing to the open outlet with their listening device exposed.   "We'll have to remove this and put the outlet back together."

Ratner agreed and told Kennedy to take care of the bug removal while he set the rest of the room back up. Chairs back in place, door ajar as they departed, lights on as they were when they arrived.
The only new addition was the blinking light on the answering machine signaling a message had arrived...and microscopic specks of Ratner's blood, from his broken nose, that spattered some of the certificates on Father Reynolds's wall.

~ **17** ~

The next morning Pat drove over to Springfield Park, wondering if he'd see Father Reynolds there. He was sure the priest had received his message, since he knew he went to his office early on Saturday mornings to prepare for weekend mass. Pat was oblivious to the siren of the ambulance that screamed past him, going in the other direction toward the church.

He parked prominently in front of the main opening to the jogging trail, confident Father Reynolds would easily find his car that way. He killed some time by doing stretching exercises and warming up. It was about 0915 when he decided Father Reynolds probably wasn't going to make it, so he set out on a nice, steady jog.

As he trotted along the man-made path, through the park's low hills and curves, he began to get the same sensation he had the day before. The sensation of being watched by someone he couldn't see. He maintained his pace, continually panning his surroundings. Rounding a curve that split a row of evergreens, he had a chance to take a subtle look behind him. That's when he saw them. Two other joggers keeping steady pace about fifty yards back. They were both tall men with fanny packs like his. One in particular was large and intimidating, just as Father Reynolds described the two CIA thugs who visited him. *I bet these are the same jerks from the Agency that visited Father Reynolds the other day*, he thought.

But there was something else about the men that bothered Pat. It was one of those elusive clues that reached his senses psychically. He had the unmistakable awareness they were wearing disguises. Both had on jogging suits and knitted ski caps pulled down low over their brow and ears, covering as much of their faces as possible, without looking like bandits. And goggles to complete the look, which seemed a bit too much in Pat's mind. Too forced. He had reached his limit with all the nonsense he was enduring lately. First it was Williams and Parsons who followed him when he went for coffee a couple weeks before. Then Father Reynolds and the CIA visitors. Now Pat and the CIA joggers. He decided to confront them and get everything on the table.

He reached a point along the path where it curved sharply to the right and then declined down a slope that was nestled in a thicket of pine trees. When he reached the bottom of the hill, Pat made a U-turn and bolted back over the jogging trail in the opposite direction. He ran fast and hard as he rounded the curve and headed straight toward the men. Despite their crude disguises, Pat could tell they were stunned when they saw him running at breakneck speed toward them, less than twenty yards away. They instinctively split apart, one running toward the right, while the other bolted left, both departing the running path in favor now of woods, cold dirt, and dry leaves.

Pat decided to run after the larger of the two, who he would later learn was Kennedy. He reasoned he would be slower because of his size. He couldn't have been more incorrect. The big man ran incredibly fast. He was large and powerful and effortlessly cut through the trees of the wooded park, kicking up dry brown leaves like a dustbowl storm. Pat's adrenaline was surging fast as he gave chase, making slow progress in catching up with him. His heart was pumping hard, and he was nearly breathless. He was about twenty yards behind the man when he shouted out to him.

"Stop! Federal Agent!"

His screams sent a flock of pigeons to flight just to Pat's right, adding further to the commotion. The CIA *thug* looked back and smiled as if to taunt him. All Pat could make out was his grin, somewhat obscured by a stream of frosty condensation coming from his mouth. He hated the smile. It smacked of arrogance and hubris.

Pat continued the chase until they reached an opening that led to a playground area.   There were about a dozen children playing on colorful swings, jungle gyms, and slides.   When the man ran through the center of the play area he stumbled on the loose bed of wood chip cushioning scattered around the play equipment.   He went flying, sliding along the chips, tumbling over several times until he came to rest against a large steel climbing structure with foam pads at the base.   His head smacked the metal hard and loud like a gong.   The children laughed and pointed fingers at him, seeing this grown man take a flying leap.   Pat had nearly caught up with him when the man regained composure and was back on his feet.   Fifteen yards, then ten yards was all that separated them as Pat came running up and drew his Berretta from its canvas bag.   He screamed as loud as he could muster in between breaths.

"Halt NOW! Federal Agent! FREEZE!"

Suddenly the children's laughs turned to cries and screams of panic.   Red-faced, sniffling children in vibrantly colorful winter coats and hoodies ran to their mothers who tried to shield them.   Total chaos broke out.   Pat ran with gun drawn through the morass of kids and their parents who tried to cover them.   The man picked up his pace and entered the parking lot where he lost sight of him.   Pat slowed down in the lot, taking one row at a time, cautious and uncertain if the man he had chased had decided to stop and ambush him.   He was sure the man had a gun in his fanny pack, and he wasn't about to take chances.   He tried to control his breathing, but it was difficult after the long, fast run he had just endured.   His heart was beating so fast, he thought it would rip out of his chest.   The adrenaline rush from the chase was multiplied by a new surge as he faced the danger of trying to locate the man.

He crept along practically on hands and knees, being careful not to stand up and create too large a target for the man should he decide to shoot. He looked cautiously under cars, trucks, and vans, looking for movement and for the running shoes he had been chasing. He came across a minivan with its side door slightly askew. Pat inched his way up to it, slowly and warily, hoping for the element of surprise in his favor. He listened silently outside the van for a moment. He could hear the faint sounds of rapid breathing from inside. Instantly, Pat jumped up, slid the side door open as hard and as fast as he could, creating a loud bang when it reached the end of its track. He aimed his Beretta at the back bench seat where he was certain the man was hiding.

"Don't move!" he screamed, his finger on the trigger and just a half pound of pressure away from firing a round.

"Okay, man! It's cool!" the half-naked teenage boy said with a look of terror. "Take my wallet man, it's right here!" the scraggly, brunette-goatee and acne-faced punk said as he slowly reached with trembling hands toward his blue jeans slumped over the middle bench seat.

The teen's petite blond girlfriend began sobbing out loud, trying to cover her bare breasts with both arms. "Please don't hurt us!" she pleaded with Pat.

Pat took a deep sigh and reholstered his weapon. He knew the man he had been chasing was long gone. He wiped his brow and looked around the lot for any movement. There was nothing but stillness. He turned back to look at the two teens.

"How old are you?" Pat asked the girl whose mascara, wet from tears, formed long, hideous black streaks down her face.

"Sixteen."

"Don't lie to me!"

"Okay, okay. I'm fourteen," she sobbed, sniffling her red nose.

"And you?"

"Eighteen, man."

Pat glared at them. "Eighteen and fourteen. Let me tell you something young man, find a girl your own age. She's just a kid."

"Ye, ye, yes, Sir," he responded with a stutter.

"And you! Save it for marriage with a nice man who will love and respect you, not some scum punk like this guy," Pat admonished.

With that, Pat turned and bolted back through the lot to the jogging trail. He took a backwards route to avoid the roadway into the playground area where he was certain a dozen police cars would be converging any moment. He was right. As he melted into the woods, he heard the sirens and saw the flashing lights of a large contingent of Fairfax County Police vehicles responding to hysterical parents on cell phones. When Pat reached his car he was suddenly aware of a *BEEP!* sound from his fanny pack. He retrieved his cell phone and saw he had a missed call from Our Lady of La Salette. He wondered how long it had been beeping, trying to get his attention. He called back to the rectory and reached Rachel.

"Hi, Rachel. It's Pat O'Donnell. Did Father Reynolds try calling me?"

Rachel was crying uncontrollably as she spoke. "Pat, please come over right away. Father passed away last night. He had a heart attack."

"Oh God, no. I can't believe this. I'm on my way, Rachel. I'll be there in five minutes."

Pat climbed into his sedan and sat for a few minutes. He put his hands over his face, wiping the tears away slowly. He said a silent prayer for Father Reynolds, asking God to receive his soul in heaven. What Pat couldn't know at the time was Father Reynolds was looking down from Paradise at him at that moment, smiling contentedly, proud of his friend.

When he arrived at the church he found a cluster of police cars and an EMT van. Rachel stood at the entrance to greet him.

"I'm so sorry Rachel," he said as he gave her a tight hug.

Tears streamed down her face, which she dabbed with a damp, white tissue in her hands.

"They said he died peacefully last night, while working in his office," Rachel sniffled out.

At that moment the EMT team came out rolling a stretcher with the priest's body, covered in a soft blue blanket. Pat held his hand up for them to stop.

"May I see him?"

"Sure, go ahead," one of the paramedics said.

Pat slowly pulled the covering down until he could see Father Reynolds's face. His eyes were closed, and his expression was peaceful. He gently caressed his cheek before he and Rachel walked inside to the rectory and Father Reynolds's office. Crime scene investigators from the county were there processing the scene. It was standard procedure...treat all deaths as homicides until the evidence convinced otherwise. In this case, there was every reason to believe the priest died of natural causes.

"Hey! Hey! Who are you? You can't come in here!" he heard one of the homicide detectives shout as he entered.

Pat retrieved his badge and credentials. "I'm sorry. I'm Special Agent O'Donnell, with the OSI. Father Reynolds and I are old friends, and I was with him just yesterday."

Detective Rick Sanchez studied his credentials for a moment, never having seen an OSI badge before. He was a middle-aged man, with a dark complexion, and thick wavy black hair. He appeared to Pat to be of Mexican descent, and even had a slight Hispanic accent.

"Are you the guy who left a message on the answering machine last night?" the detective asked.

"Yes, yes that's right. I called about nine-thirty."

"That's too bad about Father Reynolds," he said walking toward his desk. "Died right here," he noted, pointing to his chair

Pat looked at the desk and chair solemnly for a moment, but then his attention was riveted to the wall behind it. The outlet that just yesterday was open with a bug device dangling out, was today covered again. Pat didn't say a word. He didn't hear the question Detective Sanchez had just asked him. He was in a fog as his mind raced. Trying to figure out if the priest covered the opening after Pat left him yesterday. *Or did the bug planters come back?*

"O'Donnell? O'Donnell? Yo--O'Donnell?" Sanchez prodded, raising his voice to pull Pat back from his obvious distraction.

"Huh? I'm sorry. What did you say?"

"I said, what time did you visit Father Reynolds yesterday?" he asked, speaking a little louder and a little slower than before.

"Um, morning. Maybe around ten."

"And for what purpose, what did you discuss with him?" Detective Sanchez asked, his stubby fingers making notes in a small notepad he held.

Pat snickered to himself. He was amazed at how many people lately were interested in his private conversations with his priest friend.

"We talked about the Fall Festival. I came over to see what I could do to help with it this year."

"I see," said Sanchez. "And how did he appear? How was his health?"

Pat told Sanchez that Father Reynolds was in excellent health yesterday, as always, and that he was an avid runner and tennis player.

"You know, I'm a bit surprised a man in his excellent shape would die from a heart attack," Pat said. "Will there be an autopsy? To include a full tox screen?"

"Probably, because of his age and the fact the death was unattended," Sanchez responded giving him a peculiar look.

"Good. Can't be too certain a heart attack caused it. I mean at his age anything is possible," Pat said, suddenly realizing from the detective's reaction he may have pushed the issue a bit hard.

"I'll make a note of it. Thanks O'Donnell," Sanchez said as he jotted down some more scribbles.

Pat stayed with Rachel in the rectory's main office for the next hour until the police were done processing the scene. When they left, he asked Rachel if she would mind if he spent some time alone in Father Reynolds's office to remember him and to pray. She agreed and held his hand as they walked to the office. One he was alone inside he got on his knees in front of a statue of the crucifixion of Christ and prayed silently for the next twenty minutes. When he was done he walked over to Father Reynolds's desk and sat down in his chair, reminiscing over his fondness for the priest.

He fished an old screwdriver from inside a desk drawer, knelt down, and removed the outlet cover from the receptacle behind the desk. He pulled it out and saw the bug was gone. Pat knew instantly that Father Reynolds had been murdered. Murdered by the same CIA agents whom he chased in the park that morning. Clenching his fists tightly, Major O'Donnell was now more determined than ever to find the killers and make them pay. He would ensure there would be justice for Father Reynolds's death.

~ 18 ~

The next morning Pat readied himself for his first day at the safe house Agent Desantis and Colonel Helmsley instructed him to visit. Its code name was *Al's Garage*, and it was located in Arlington, Virginia, not far from the Pentagon.

He robotically snaked his way through the streets and roads of northern Virginia. Although it was a Sunday morning, there never seemed to be any abatement to the traffic congestion in the area. As he inched closer to his destination, he found it was in a quiet townhome subdivision nestled womblike away from the harried streets filled with exhaust fume belching cars, trucks, and honking horns. The new subdivision was clean, bright, and surrounded by older communities of single-family tract homes built right after WW II. He slowed to find the number for the safe house. Although they all looked much the same, this particular townhome was a luxury compared to most others. An end unit of brown brick on the face and white siding on the end, its veranda roof was bright copper and shiny, and it cast the morning sun's rays about.

As instructed, he pulled into the driveway and flicked the button on the remote control key fob Vicky had given him. The single car garage door opened slowly to reveal a virtually empty interior. All that was there were a few spare tires and a snow shovel. He parked his car and cut the engine, listening for a moment for any sound before he got out. It was silent. He headed to the side door in the garage. When he entered through the kitchen, he smelled fresh coffee. A half-full pot sat on the counter. There was a teaspoon resting on a damp, stained napkin next to it, near a sugar bowl. Obviously he wasn't the first to come by the safe house that morning.

"Hello? Hello?" he called out.

"We're in here, Patrick," came Agent Desantis's familiar voice. "In the living room."

He walked over and found Agent Desantis, Colonel Helmsley, and Dr. Davis sitting comfortably, sipping coffee.

"We were wondering when you would show up!" Colonel Helmsley teased.

Pat had a gloomy look as he explained his lateness. "I'm sorry guys. I had a rough day yesterday. One of our family friends, our parish priest, died."

"Oh, I'm so sorry to hear that!" Vicky exclaimed.

Her false expression of sorrow was so genuine sounding that she fooled Pat and the others. Of course, she already knew about his death...his murder. Agents Ratner and Kennedy broke the news to her the night it happened. She was furious with them. Their bumbling created a signature, a ripple, a fingerprint that could potentially be detected. If the priest's death was viewed with any suspicion, it would mean the homicide detectives would pursue it with a vigor the Special Access Program could ill afford. She cared less about the priest's death than she did about the black world SAP program.

"It looks like he had a heart attack," Pat informed them.

He didn't want her or any of them to know that he had been there to see Father Reynolds that day or any day before. Not just for all his original reasons of seeking confidentiality with the priest, but also because of the apparent involvement of CIA thugs in his death. Right now, Pat didn't know whom he could trust. Colonel Helmsley and Dr. Davis stood up and walked over to him. The colonel wrapped an arm around Pat's shoulder, offering his condolences.

"Do you want to take some more time off?" Colonel Helmsley asked.

"No, I'm okay. Really. I want to get started. Maybe it will help take my mind off Father Reynolds," he said, looking down sadly. "Later this week I may need a few hours off to attend the service and burial."

Vicky embraced him tightly. "Whatever you need, Patrick. Just let us know."

"Thanks," he replied, his head pressed against the side of hers. Despite his grief, there was something about Vicky's erotic mix of perfume and pheromones that drew Pat in once again. He closed his eyes and for a moment felt slight arousal, moving his fingertips up and down her back in a gentle, subtle, yet guarded caress. Vicky had a way of arousing him at the worst of times. He released the hug, somewhat embarrassed.

Colonel Helmsley gave them a sideways, askew glance. He quickly broke in to give Pat a quick overview of the townhome's layout.

"You can tour the place at your leisure later, but just to let you know, there are three levels. On the top floor are three bedrooms and two baths. On this level we have the kitchen, dining room, and living room."

He led the group to the kitchen and to a door next to the one leading to the garage. Pat hadn't noticed it when he first walked in moments before. It led to a stairwell down to the lower level of the townhome. Colonel Helmsley spoke as he walked.

"The downstairs was designed to be a large family or rec room, but we've turned it into an office and conference room."

As they entered the darkened room, Vicky flipped on a light switch. It was big, about fifteen by twenty feet, taking up most of the area beneath the main level of the home. At one end was a large, flat screen monitor mounted on the wall. At the other end, was a sliding glass door with a walkout to the rear yard. On one exterior side wall, was a fireplace with gas insert, either side of which were two windows. The windows and the glass sliding door had heavy, room-darkening blinds and curtains that didn't permit any light to pass in either direction.   In the center of the room was a large wood conference table with ten black leather chairs surrounding it.   Pat looked around and admired it all.

"Nice place!" he said aloud, nodding his head in approval.

He noticed a small safe in one corner and some electronic gear on racks next to it.   There were four STU III instruments on the table, and a fifth on a side table near the fireplace with two easy chairs next to it.   On the other side of the fireplace was a long sofa that matched the chairs, all beige leather with dark brown legs.

"Well gentlemen, shall we get started?" Vicky asked as she placed a laptop computer on the conference table at the end farthest from the screen.   "Patrick, why don't you sit near the front with Dr. Davis, and John across from you both?"

Pat could tell she was in her element.   This program was the baby she wanted to rear ever since getting wrapped up in the FBI's black world several years earlier.   She was determined to make it work, and in order to do so, she had to be in charge.   The three took their seats as the large, wall mounted plasma monitor warmed up, flickering to life.   Agent Desantis walked over to the safe and expertly spun the dial on the digital lock mechanism until it popped open to reveal a file drawer stuffed with documents.   She retrieved three folders and gave one each to the men at the table.

"This is the first case we want Patrick to help solve," she began.   "It is a recent series of child abductions and murders in various parts of the country.   As you can see, multiple victims in multiple states."

"What's the connection with them?" Dr. Davis asked.

"The killer leaves his calling card.   Same each time.   He tattoos the victims' arms."

As Agent Desantis spoke she worked the laptop and brought up a presentation in PowerPoint on the monitor.   The title slide read, "Tattoo Killer."   Below the caption was a picture of a child, a young girl about twelve years old with a tattoo of a butterfly on her right arm, just above the inside of her wrist. Pat leaned in to get a closer look at the tattoo. He was familiar with its unique design where the wings were formed from heart shapes. He gasped when he saw the image.

"Christ--that's sick!" he said aloud. "That's the Child Lover Logo!"

Dr. Davis had a strange expression on his face that suggested he wasn't following. "Woody, it's a symbol used among pedophile rings to signify an adult's love for children in general, regardless of sex," Pat explained.

"You mean these people have their own symbol--like some kind of secret handshake?"

Pat nodded as he spoke, fumbling through the photos of the victim until he found a close-up of the pale red and blue butterfly tattoo.

"Here, look. The upper wings are formed by two large hearts--one pinkish and one blue. They represent the adult female and male. The lower parts of the wings are formed from two alternating pink and blue smaller hearts."

"And I suppose the smaller hearts symbolize young girls and boys?" Dr. Davis asked in shock.

"Exactly!" Vicky said clearing her throat, her voice sounding slightly irritated, and seemingly demanding deference to her.

Pat couldn't take his eyes off the little girl in the photograph. She had a strange, cold expression even in death. A distant stare that suggested she had long since given up hope of life.

"This guy keeps his victims alive for a few months at a time, doesn't he?" Pat asked.

"Correct," Vicky said. "We believe he tattoos them as soon as he abducts them. Then he waits for a few weeks, even months after the tattoo site has healed, before he murders his victims."

Dr. Davis had been skimming the dossier, half listening to Agent

Desantis. "This is quite an unusual pathology," he suggested. "I mean, oftentimes serial killers, especially sexual predators, *take* something from their victims as a trophy--but this guy *leaves* something behind."

"Precisely. He brands them as his own," Vicky added.

Agent Desantis provided them with a detailed briefing on the history of the killings, going back to the first one that occurred nearly two years earlier. Six abductions in all. Four girls between eight and fourteen years of age. Two boys, nine and eleven years old.

"The problem the FBI has had in these cases is that, other than the tattoos, there doesn't appear to be a pattern to them at all," she said. "Except that in each case the children lived within two miles of an entrance to an Interstate Highway."

Pat squinted at the dossier for a moment. "You mean no real pattern because they have started out in six states, and ended in six different states?"

"Yes," Vicky replied. "This guy's all over the place. The Bureau's profilers have suggested he may be a truck driver or a drifter, but they've been stumped all along on this one. We really need your help."

He shook his head. "I hope I don't disappoint you. I need some time to read everything you have on each case. Police reports, autopsy reports, crime scene photos, videos, and so forth."

"You've got it," Vicky said opening the bottom drawer to the small safe. "Everything you need is in here. One more thing. We believe he has struck again. A week back in Tulsa a nine year old girl, Tracey Adams, was reported missing when she failed to come home from a friend's birthday party near her home."

"I take it she lived near an Interstate Highway?" Colonel Helmsley asked.

"Yes, she did. And none of the prior Tattoo Killer cases have begun or ended in Oklahoma."

Pat and Woody pored over the files for the next several hours, taking only a few short breaks. Colonel Helmsley and Agent Desantis left them alone. Each had departed for their offices to catch up on routine paperwork, agreeing to come back later in the afternoon to check in on the pair.

"I don't know, Woody, I'm not getting anything here," Pat said when he had read almost all the documents.

"That's okay, Pat. We've just begun our work. Take your time. Maybe we can take a break soon, and you can lie back on the sofa and close your eyes. Focus on what you've read and see if it takes you anywhere."

"Okay. Let me finish this last report here--the one on the latest missing girl, Tracey, in Tulsa."

Once he finished reading every last minute detail of each case, concentrating on the most recent abduction, Pat strolled over to the sofa. He kicked off his loafers and unhooked his heavy fanny pack , placing it on the light tan carpet. He plopped down, closed his eyes, and thought about the information he had just absorbed. Woody took up position in one of the easy chairs by the fireplace. He propped his feet up on an ottoman.

"Relax, Pat, and think with your senses, not with your brain. Let your synesthesia guide you. Don't try to analyze, just try to receive impressions," Woody coached.

"That's the problem I'm having. The reports we've read are too flat and sterile. There's not enough dimension to them--no sound, no taste, no touch."

"Try this. Put yourself in the minds of the victims. See with their eyes. Maybe the rest will come."

Pat thought about the first abduction. The twelve year old San Diego girl, Jessica Lane, whose eerie eyes he saw on the title slide to Vicky Desantis's briefing. Her eyes troubled him. Dead eyes even when alive. Cold, fixed, without hope. Then it came to him.

"That's it!" Pat exclaimed. "She's blind--they are all blind. I mean *he* blinded them.   Soon after he kidnaps them, he blinds them somehow!   That's the problem I've had.   *I* can't see because *they* couldn't see!"

"Try to slide back in time to each abduction to when the children all could see," Woody suggested, obviously growing excited over Pat's keen insight.

He closed his eyes and concentrated on Jessica Lane. He began to drift into a state of consciousness somewhere between daydream and sleep as he thought about her crime scene--trying hard to let impressions come through.   He thought in terms of colors, shapes, sights, and sounds.   Until, at last, he was pulled away in a sensation that felt like slipping rapidly down a steep, giant water slide...a sensation that carried him to San Diego, to December 1999, when Jessica was abducted.

~ 19 ~

In his mind, Pat was present in Jessica's neighborhood. Like a transparent spirit, he walked along with her as she hurried home for dinner. It was already dark when she looked down at her watch. She was supposed to be home an hour ago. Her parents tracked her down at a girlfriend's house, chastising her for being late and demanding she return home right away. Her father offered to come pick her up, even though she was just three blocks away. Jessica protested, insisting she could walk home fast enough.

As Jessica strolled along, her long brown hair jostled about her shoulders. It was chilly outside, even for southern California. Pat could smell the scent of ocean spray and hear the surf from where he and Jessica walked. She was a pretty girl, wearing the latest glitter-studded denim pants with matching denim jacket. Her white, monogrammed blouse was pulled out and tied in a knot to expose her belly button. Many girls her age dressed that way. She hastened to undo the knot and tuck her shirt in before returning home, knowing her parents wouldn't approve. In her effort to get home quickly, she was unaware of the white sedan, with all four side windows open, cruising along behind her until it came to a stop a few feet in front of her. The driver's door opened, and a woman stepped out.

"Excuse me," she said to Jessica. "I'm lost! Can you show me where I am on this map?"

Pat was shocked as the scene unfolded. *A woman?* He peered into the vehicle, through the open passenger side window, for a male accomplice. But it was empty.

Jessica approached her with some hesitation, built upon many years of warnings from her parents and schoolteachers about *stranger danger*. But the appearance of a woman seemed to soften her sense of peril. In her mind, only strange men were to be distrusted.

"Well, I'm kinda in a hurry. Maybe I can help if it won't take long."

"Great!" the woman exclaimed.

Jessica walked up to her. The slender, fair-skinned woman was in her mid-thirties, conservatively dressed. Her auburn colored hair was shiny in the glow of a nearby street lamp. When Jessica was within a foot or two of the woman, the scent hit Pat like a fist against his face.

Ether!

It was the distinctive smell of old fashioned ether doctors used decades ago to knock out patients during surgery. Hidden underneath the map the woman held in her hands was a small, blue cloth soaked in the substance. And when Jessica was inches away, about to peer at the map, the woman smiled at her, then stuffed the cloth against her face. Pat tried to scream out, but no words came forth. Deep down he knew he had no way of revising history. He wasn't watching the scene in real time. He was receiving images of events long past, that somehow made their way to his senses at this moment in the future.

Jessica sank to her knees, and the woman struggled to keep her up. She opened the back door with one hand, while wrestling to control Jessica's weight with her other arm. She managed to push the girl into the back seat and drove off without being detected. Pat watched in horror as the car sped away. The vision began to dissolve in front of him, as he quickly returned to the sofa in *Al's Garage*. Dr. Davis was peering at his eyes, shining a penlight at them. The bright light made Pat wince and cover his eyes as he came to.

"Jesus! I wish you wouldn't do that!" Pat complained to Woody, blinking rapidly and rubbing his sore eyes.

"Sorry, but I find your lack of pupil response fascinating when you have these episodes."

"I witnessed Jessica Lane's abduction. And you're not going to believe this, Woody. She was abducted by a lone woman--no man was with her!"

"What?"

"Obviously there's a male accomplice somewhere because of the assaults. It fits in with the Child Lover Logo and all," Pat said.

"Maybe you can add what you now know from the first abduction to the body of evidence and build upon it."

"Huh?"

"Well, jump from the first case to the last one--the current one in Tulsa. Maybe the freshness of the recent one, combined with what you know about the woman, will provide some sensory clues for you."

"I need a break first," Pat said wiping his brow.

He had become somewhat dizzy from the experience, a reaction to having smelled the ether along with Jessica. He understood why the car's windows were down when he peered in. Ventilation. It kept the woman abductor from passing out as she scouted the neighborhood, looking for potential victims. Pat wandered back upstairs and explored the rest of the safe house. The bedrooms were beautiful and filled with expensive furniture and custom decorations. The rest of the house was equally exceptional--clearly a professional decorator had done the job for the government. It also suggested to Pat that the FBI and DoD placed a premium on this safe house, and some deep pockets had picked up the tab. He returned to the kitchen to find a refrigerator stocked with food. He was hungry for a sandwich, and called down to Woody and offered the same. He hummed to himself as he prepared their lunch, finding the remote control to a small television sitting on one of the granite countertops. He surfed until he found a cable news station and caught up on the latest on the War on Terror. Usama bin Laden still had not been captured, but the coalition forces had the Taliban and al Qaeda terror network on the run. The air campaign was superb, and it was decimating the enemy in scores.

Woody walked in as Pat put the finishing touches on his platter. A neatly cut turkey breast sandwich on toasted sourdough bread with chips and a pickle on the side.

"Thanks Pat! This looks great!" Woody exclaimed as Pat handed him the plate.

They sat in the elegant dining room and ate their lunch together, almost afraid to let even a crumb hit the floor and upset the pristine surroundings.

"Pat, I've been thinking. We can try another coach session focused on the Oklahoma case, but I have a hunch--"

"A hunch about what?" Pat asked, interrupting him with a puzzled look, a couple of crumbs falling from his lips.

"Well, it's that whole temporal and spatial component thing again. I mean, I think the more current an event is in time, the closer you need to be to it in space. The older the event is, the further away you can be because those pesky psychic teasers have had more time to travel--if time is even relative in all this."

"Are you suggesting we go to Oklahoma?"

"Er, well, yes I am."

"Funny. I was going to suggest the same thing. Something told me I would do better there than here."

Woody smiled, took a bite of his sandwich, and then gulped down some Coke.

"It's settled then. When John and Vicky return later, let's propose this to them."

Within an hour or so, Vicky and Colonel Helmsley arrived at *Al's Garage* and found Woody and Pat in the basement SCIF chatting. Pat briefed them on his latest vision, generating jaw dropping awe from them both, to say the least.

"While not unheard of, female pedophiles--especially the predator type--are very rare," Vicky offered. "But it all seems to make some sense now, what with the Child Lover Logo and all!"

"We have an idea about tackling this case," Woody began. "Pat, please tell them!"

He outlined the Tulsa trip recommendation, explaining the importance of being closer to the most recent abduction site.

Without blinking an eye, Vicky said, "Let's do it! John, can you get your SCIF van airlifted to Oklahoma tomorrow? I'll arrange airline transportation for us all."

Pat's mouth hung open as he watched the ensuing dialogue. *Airlift a van? This isn't the movies. No one can make that happen at the drop of a hat!*

"No problem, Vicky. I have Secretary of Defense direct authority for the CRYSTAL ROUNDUP program. I can make it happen tonight."

The colonel extracted his STE cell phone from his jacket pocket and scrolled to the telephone number for the Commander of the 89th Military Airlift Wing at Andrews Air Force Base in Maryland. This was the elite air wing responsible for Presidential support, to include flying and maintaining the Air Force One fleet.

"Clint? This is John Helmsley, how are you doing you old dog!?"

Pat knew who the Wing Commander was--Brigadier General Kurt "Clint" Baxter. Calling him by his first name was another sign of Helmsley's informal power within the Air Force--an ability to be on a first name basis with some generals.

"Listen, Clint, can we go secure?"

The conversation was one-sided to Pat and Woody. They watched as the colonel pulled the receiver away from his ear and pressed the secure button.

"He's an old friend," he whispered to them as he waited for the secure link to finalize.

"Yeah, we kind of gathered that," Pat said, shaking his head in amazement.

They were both so fascinated listening to Colonel Helmsley's conversation they did not hear Vicky Desantis as she placed a call back to her office.

She whispered to her secretary, "I need two sets of airline tickets-- all one way for now. Make the first set for Dulles Airport for me Helmsley, O'Donnell, and Davis, with a morning departure--say around nine-thirty."

Before she spoke again, she shot the men a glance and saw they were all huddled around Colonel Helmsley's cell phone. They paid no attention to her at all. Once again she whispered her next order to her secretary.

"And the other set needs to be for a departure this evening for Ratner and Kennedy. Call them when we hang up and tell them to get ready for the journey."

Colonel Helmsley had finished the usual chit-chat pleasantries with General Baxter before he got down to business.

"I need airlift support tonight. In the black. No manifest. A four ton minivan to Tinker Air Force Base."

Pat could tell the general squawked about the arrangements, because Colonel Helmsley had to calm him down.

"Clint, I know, I know it's a short notice requirement. And yes-- four tons, you heard it right. It's a special van. This is a SECDEF generated special mission with a Priority-Alpha cargo."

Pat knew what those words meant. Priority "A" was reserved for national security cargo--to include nuclear shipments. When they hung up Colonel Helmsley told them General Baxter guaranteed he'd have a C-141 transport aircraft ready at the flight line at Andrews Air Force Base by 2200 that evening. The arrangements were all made in less than ten minutes.

"Welcome to my world," Colonel Helmsley smiled.

Vicky was done with her call, as well. "Gentlemen, let's meet at Dulles Airport tomorrow morning. United Airlines will have e-tickets for you all, so just go to the counter no later than seven. Let's plan to meet at the gate, so we proceed through security separately. For added cover."

Pat headed home to Sara, all along thinking of a good ruse to justify his latest TDY adventure. When he arrived, he found her sitting in the living room looking at a photo album of Erin's christening pictures--not so much to reminisce about the baptism, but to remember Father Reynolds. Sara gave him a warm smile as he stepped into the room.

"Hi, Baby. How did it go today with the FBI?" she asked in a soft, sad voice.

"It went well, gave their profiler people my insights on the recent serial abductor case they solved." Pat wasn't about to bring up the next TDY just yet.

"Looking at Father Reynolds's photos?" he asked, sitting down next to her on the sofa and wrapping his arm around her shoulder. Comforting her.

"Yes. Still hard to believe he's gone."

"I know. It's tough. Have you heard anything about his funeral service?"

"No. Listen, Honey, I don't want to cook tonight. How about ordering pizza?"

"I'm on it!" Pat replied with a kiss to her forehead before heading to the kitchen to place the order.

The pizza arrived in no time, and the family sat around the kitchen table as plates with slices were passed around. Erin looked at her parents, clearly sensing their sadness over Father Reynolds's death.

"Mommy and Daddy, can I say the prayer tonight?" she asked in her adorably squeaky voice.

"Sure, Princess," Pat said.

Erin closed her eyes, and then began to make the sign of the cross. "In the name of the Father, and the Son," she said touching her forehead and chest. "And the Holy Spirit, Amen," she finished touching her left and right shoulders quickly. "God bless this pizza we are about to eat. And God bless Father Reynolds who is with Jesus in Heaven. Amen."

"That was beautiful, Honey," Pat whispered.

"Love you, Sweetie," Sara added, blowing Erin a kiss from across the table.

The family ate in relative silence until Pat finally found the courage to break the news about his next day's trip.

"Gang, I'm sorry to have to tell you this, but I have to go on another road trip tomorrow."

Sara dropped her head to the side with a look of dismay. "Again, Pat?" she protested. "You just got back a few days ago from North Carolina! What's it about this time?"

"Er, well, kinda the same thing. You see, the FBI profilers have a new case they want me to look at, but I have to travel to a field office out west. Can't say exactly where."

"I don't know, Pat. This side work you've been doing is awfully generous to the FBI, but what about us?" she asked, clearly unhappy with the new revelation.

"I hope it won't take but a few days because I plan to be back for Father Reynolds's funeral--hopefully it won't be held for a few more days."

"After this one, please tell the FBI you are done helping them. Surely they must have other people equally skilled in profiling."

"I'll do my best," was all he could say. He knew he never could tell her exactly *how* skilled he was and how alone he was in those skills.

The children chattered away as the family finished its meal, but Sara and Pat barely spoke. He knew she was still upset over the TDY. He was thinking he had to talk with Colonel Helmsley about Sara's concerns over his support to the black ops program. He wanted some type of compromise in this equation to balance his job and family a little more fairly.

During the night, while he and Sara slept together in their bed, Pat was taken away in his dreams to Oklahoma. He couldn't see a thing, but he could hear. And smell. And feel. He was either in a dark place, or he was blind, rather Tracey Adams was either in a dark place, or she was blind. Her right wrist stung as needles pricked and probed her flesh. *She's being tattooed!* Tracey whimpered and moaned, but no real sound came from her mouth. She had been gagged. Pat could smell the stench and filth of her confines. It was damp. Rotten garbage, or putrefied flesh, or something equally foul filled the place. The first voice he heard was the woman's. He had heard it before...when he had his vision of Jessica's abduction in San Diego.

"Hold the brat steady!" the woman shrieked. "She's messing up my artwork!"

A man responded in a voice that sounded fat to Pat. He took heavy breaths, seemingly struggling just to talk, his words mumbled and muffled, rolling like gelatinous globs from his lips.

"Well, hurry up. I can't stand her crying all the time!"

Pat could feel Tracey begin to cry. The terror was intense for the helpless little girl. Blinded. Bound. But other than the tattooing, he didn't sense she had been harmed in any way. Thankfully. Pat forced himself awake this time, tearing his senses away from this horrific vision. It wasn't that he wanted to avoid the scene, rather, he wanted to wake up and hurry the morning. He needed to get to Tulsa. He needed to find Tracey before it was too late!

~ 20 ~

The silver and blue taxi showed up in front of the O'Donnell home precisely at 0600 the next morning, right on time. Pat jumped inside and was hit immediately with a sudden blast of tobacco smoke scent. The Indian driver, who spoke little English, had been smoking something before he arrived--a cigarette, a pipe, a cigar.

Pat simply said to him, "Dulles Airport, United Airlines."

The turbaned driver nodded with a smile of yellow crooked teeth in the rearview mirror as he sped off. Pat rolled down his window half way to get fresh air. It was icy cold but refreshing and clean. He clutched his single piece of luggage tightly, a folded-over garment bag with three days' sets of casual clothes.

They arrived at the United Airlines departure terminal at Dulles a few minutes before 0700. Flying with a handgun after the September 11th terror attacks was incredibly difficult, even for federal agents. In the past, all Pat had to do was show his badge and credentials to the ticketing agent who would issue him a "pink" form that whisked him past security without incident. He fully expected a hassle this time but was surprised--delighted--when the ticketing agent had a pink form waiting for him.

"FBI headquarters faxed your authorization over to us this morning, Agent O'Donnell," she said, smiling as she handed the form to him along with his boarding passes. One for a layover flight to Denver, the other to Oklahoma City.

Pat proceeded to the security checkpoint, more aptly called a chokepoint, with the abundance-of-caution screening put in place following the previous month's attacks. He bypassed it all, his pink form and badge giving him immediate privilege. When he arrived at his gate, he found the other three already there waiting for him. They had plenty of time to kill before boarding their 0940 flight, so they decided to head to an airport café for some breakfast. In the space of an hour as they ate and drank, they discussed all manner of conceivable topics: politics, health, sports, current events...everything but the elephant in the room--the CRYSTAL ROUNDUP program. It was as disconnected to them at this moment, for operational security reasons, as if it did not exist at all. Pat felt compelled, however, to at least alert them to his vision from the night before. He chose an old Intelligence Community technique called, "talking around," the subject. Although it was unsanctioned, everyone in his line of work did it.

"I had a chance to review the *proposal* last night," he began as he eyed each one for signs they understood his hidden message.

They did. Woody seemed the most intrigued.

"Yes, Pat? And what did the proposal *tell* you?" he asked, rather unskilled in the art, but obviously delighting in the secret agent nature of the way things were happening to him lately.

"The proposal isn't dead yet, and there's a chance we could revive it when we get there, but we need to work fast. Our competitors are determined to kill the current plan," he finished with a sad look.

They all understood. Tracey was clinging to life, and time was running out. Just then the loudspeaker in the lounge area crackled, *United Flight 713 to Denver is now boarding at Gate 22.*

"We'd better hurry," Vicky urged, as they finished off the last remaining sips of hot coffee.

They hustled to the gate and hopped right in line as the plane's boarding was well underway. They sat in different sections of the plane to minimize direct public contact with each other. Pat was thrilled to find he had seats in first-class, knowing that Vicky must have arranged that for his comfort and to minimize the potential he would be fatigued and not perform well when they arrived at their destination. He closed his eyes and thought about the mission at hand. The plan was to pick up the van at Tinker Air Force Base and spend the night in town. They would drive to Tulsa the next morning to begin retracing the steps of the little girl abducted there the week before.

It was late afternoon when they finally arrived in Oklahoma. Snow delays in Denver forced a late departure from there, getting them in four hours later than scheduled. When they left the plane, Vicky wanted to huddle off in an isolated area of the concourse to plan the logistics of the evening and next morning.

"I've arranged for us all to stay at separate hotels. I'm a bit bothered that we all flew together, but it was unavoidable."

She reached into her bag and pulled out four envelopes containing hotel confirmation information for each of them. "Here we are," she said. "Let's take separate taxis from here and then regroup tomorrow morning at my hotel."

"What time?" Woody asked.

"John, when can you get the van from the base?"

"I was supposed to pick it up this afternoon. It was greased with the Tinker Wing Commander. I'll have to call him and let him know I'll be late. Bottom line is I should have it tonight."

"Good. In that case, let's meet at eight o'clock at my place."

They all nodded in agreement, departed, and slowly blended into the mass of travelers making their way from the gate to the main terminal.

After he checked in to his hotel, Pat called Sara to let her know he had arrived safely.

"How are the kids?" he asked.

"They're fine. Just missing their dad, like me," she said softly. "Listen, Pat, Rachel called and said Father Reynolds will be buried in three days, this Thursday, the twenty-fifth. Service at the chapel at noon. Viewing starts tomorrow."

"Yikes--that's cutting it close, but I'm pretty sure I will be home the night before the funeral. No, I *will* be there. Please let Rachel know."

"I will. Oh, by the way, a Detective Sanchez called. He said you know him. He wants to speak with you. I told him you were TDY, so he asked for a number he can reach you at. I didn't want to give out your cell phone, so I asked for his number."

"Okay, shoot," Pat said as he grabbed a hotel pen and pad from the nightstand.

"So, I'll see you in two days?" Sara asked.

"Keep praying, Baby!"

They hung up. Pat looked around the room as he thought about whether he should call Detective Sanchez that afternoon, or the next morning. It was late in the day, later still in Virginia. *Perhaps the detective isn't even in his office.* But he knew Sanchez wouldn't want to talk with him unless it was important. Pat was still seething with anger inside over the likelihood the two CIA thugs, as he called them, had murdered Father Reynolds. He flipped open his cell phone and dialed. He heard a female voice at the other end.

"Fairfax County Police Department, how may I direct your call?"

"Hi, Detective Sanchez, please. Extension three-two-seven." He heard another series of rings, five, six or more, then the familiar voice of Detective Sanchez.

"Hi, Detective, it's Pat O'Donnell. My wife says you called and needed to talk?"

"Yeah, when you coming back?"

"Not sure, maybe in two days. Why? What do you need?"

There was a pause. "Listen, O'Donnell. You pushed a little hard for us to run a full toxicology screen on the priest. Why the interest?"

"What did you find?" Pat asked without acknowledging his question.

"Someone gave him a nasty cocktail that caused his heart to stop."

Pat's worst fears were being confirmed. He stared at the wall for a moment, gritting his teeth.

"You still there?" Sanchez asked.

"Yes. What was it? What was in this cocktail?"

"The coroner said it was a combination of two types of hypnotic agents, as he called them. Both in the ben---zo---di---az---a---pine family of drugs," Sanchez said, pronouncing the drug name slowly.

"What the heck is that normally used for?"

"He says they are usually in pill form for sleeping disorders."

"And in Father Reynolds's case? Did you find he had a prescription for that?"

"Nooooo. Actually, the coroner found two puncture wounds on the priest. One in his arm, the other his butt. That's why I said he was given a nasty cocktail. O'Donnell, Father Reynolds was murdered," Sanchez bluntly said.

"Christ!"

"And that's not all. There was enough of these two drugs in his system to knock down a horse, but there was something else. Ever hear of Thiopental Sodium?" he asked.

"No."

"How about Sodium Pentothal?"

"Truth serum?" Pat asked disbelievingly.

"Yup. Smaller amounts of it than the hypnotic agents, but enough in combination to make someone pretty malleable."

"What do you mean?"

"The coroner said in reduced amounts this mix would make someone pretty open to suggestion, like being hypnotized. It would also lower their inhibitions and make them more willing to open up and talk."

"Do you have any suspects?"

"Not a clue yet. That's why I need to talk with you again. What are you holding back from me, O'Donnell? Why did you lead me to having the tox screen done?"

"Look, I don't know anything about this, really." Pat lied, but in typical fashion, his attempt to sound convincing fumbled.

"Bull!" Sanchez stammered. "When you get back I want to see you. You know more than you're telling me!"

His Hispanic accent thickened as he spat out the words, suggesting to Pat that when he was calm, Detective Sanchez actually consciously controlled his pronunciation.

"Well, I'll be happy to talk with you, but I don't know anything more. If I think of anything, I'll call you."

"Look, Pat. I really need your help. Let's not play the, *I gotta secret game*, okay?" Sanchez asked, this time a bit more calmly, his accent under control.

"I'll help in any way I can, Rick. Bye for now," Pat responded as he hung up, but he knew he could not tell the detective what he really knew. At least not right away.

He kicked off his shoes and closed the drapes, making the room nearly pitch black. He needed a nap and time to decompress his mind after the news he had just received. He also needed a plan of attack to get to the truth about Father Reynolds's murder. He closed his eyes and prayed silently to himself. Calm, peaceful prayers. He prayed for understanding and guidance, and he prayed for the peaceful repose of Father Reynolds's soul. Then sleep.

As Pat drifted off into the slumber of a power nap, his mind worked on two parallel paths simultaneously. On one path, he floated along receiving impressions of the past, ghosts of an abduction. On the other path, was an awareness level, a mode that allowed him to understand his senses for what they were. To process. To analyze. To actively search for new sensations and clues.

He found himself wandering a meadow in Tulsa, Oklahoma, a field that cut between the small wood and brick homes of two girls who had been friends since pre-school. Tracey Adams took a shortcut through the field, more like a well-worn path barely a foot wide, after spending the afternoon at her friend's birthday party. Although she lived just one block away from her, Tracey liked the shortcut because it cut diagonally to her home. She and her friend oftentimes would laugh about how they shared the field as one big backyard between them.

As Tracey skipped along the dirt path, goody bag of treats in hand, she sang a tune from one of the popular boy bands of the day. Her long blond hair, tied into two pony tails, bounced up and down on her shoulders, with light blue ribbons waving in the breeze. Pat could see her dark pink winter coat clearly. It didn't quite fit long enough to cover her yellow dress and her skinny bare legs with short white socks and black shoes sticking out. Crumbs of yellow birthday cake were on her cheeks. Pat could taste them as he read her thoughts of all the yummy treats she enjoyed that afternoon. Her carefree innocence was about to be taken as she headed for a small clump of trees several yards from her home. It was dusk now, getting harder to see, intensifying the cover and concealment the woman already enjoyed among the trees. Pat knew her...the auburn haired woman who had abducted Jessica Lane in San Diego two years ago. As Tracey approached the trees, the woman stepped out from her hiding place and startled her.

"I'm sorry, Sweetie. I didn't mean to scare you. I'm looking for my puppy. Have you seen him?" the woman asked.

She had a disarming charm about her, the same appeal that lured Jessica into a false sense of trust that fateful night in 1999 when she was abducted. Tracey took a step back instinctively.

"No, I haven't seen a puppy."

"Are you sure? I have her picture right here," the woman said, coaxing Tracey to come closer to see the Polaroid photograph she held in her hand.

Tracey slowly stepped forward to within two feet of the woman who handed her the photograph. Tracey squinted at the fuzzy picture of the dog, distracted long enough for the woman to retrieve a small cloth from her jacket pocket. And as she had done six times to children before, she clamped it tightly around Tracey's mouth and nostrils until the little girl collapsed. Limp. Unconscious.

Dusk had turned to darkness seemingly within seconds. In the cover of night, the woman was joined by a male accomplice who had been crouched behind some nearby trees. The two of them hurriedly carried Tracey off into the darkness to their sedan that was parked, ironically, in front of Tracey's house.

What struck Pat about the man was his size. He was of average height, maybe five feet ten, but obese. Pat surmised he was 300 to 350 pounds and about forty years of age, balding on the top. The man grunted and sweated as he carried Tracey's lithe body, even her small frame posing a struggle for him. In his mind Pat ran to catch up with them, and as they opened the car door to slide Tracey inside, Pat hopped in, too. The pair was panting from the rush of adrenaline they shared as they quickly drove off. Pat caressed Tracey's hair and face in his image in a vain attempt to comfort her.

"That was close!" the woman stated in between deep breaths.

"Yeah, taking a real chance this time parking in front of her house," the man added.

Pat realized they had stalked Tracey. Hers was not a random abduction, a clear sign the couple had become more sophisticated, if not more daring, in their crime spree. He watched the fat man wipe his brow at least four times with a filthy, stained hanky, removing the sweat from his forehead. The pair didn't speak much more as they drove away from the residential area of Tulsa onto a small highway. They pulled onto a side rode that was so dark from a lack of streetlight, Pat couldn't make out the street signs. The man began to slow as they approached the end of the road. Pat could hear the tires suddenly squeak and crunch on the familiar sound of gravel underneath. Ahead of him he saw rows of campers and recreational vehicles. *Christ*, he thought. *They have a camper of some kind!*

Sure enough, they approached a medium sized RV that had a car trailer hitch attached to the rear. It began making sense to Pat now. They were abducting children in the sedan and then cruising around with them in the RV, where they would assault and tattoo them. The fat man stopped the sedan behind the RV, and in the instant before he killed the headlights, Pat saw it...a butterfly painted on the back of the camper. It was pink and blue and large, perhaps twelve or fourteen inches across. But it was not the precise heart shape wings that characterized the Child Lover Logo Pat was all too familiar with, the logo the pair tattooed on their victims. Pat suspected they were just smart enough not to put the exact pedophile logo so prominently on their vehicle. Just below it was a map of the United States with a half dozen states filled in with solid color decals.

They are traveling the United States collecting children from each state like trophies!

The last image he had of the scene was when the man opened the door to pull Tracey Adams out into the darkness. Pat stepped out of the car, and woke.

The rush back to reality was intense. He felt as if he had been held under water the entire time and came back up gasping for air. He slowly came around, his breathing calming a bit. He looked at the clock. It was 1905. The need to help Tracey overwhelmed him, creating an almost physical, visceral reaction. He clutched his gut. Tight. Sore. He was nauseated. He grabbed his cell phone and called Colonel Helmsley, who was at Tinker Air Force Base trying to secure the van.

"Hey, Sir, is there any way we can roll on things tonight? I think we have little time left," Pat said nearly in tears, fumbling his way about on the unsecure line.

There was a loud whine in the background as Colonel Helmsley spoke. He was on the flight line, and all around him were engine noises and the steady din of hydraulics and machines. Electrical generators whirred about busily. Pat could almost smell the JP4 jet fuel and diesel exhaust mix over the phone as he tried to talk to his former boss.

"Pat, we need to wait until morning. I'm sorry, but the van is listed as frustrated cargo right now, some mix up with the Priority-Alpha designation. I'm waiting for clearance from the crew, but frankly, in a few minutes I'll have to call the local wing king if I can't get them to move faster," Colonel Helmsley shouted over the noise, his voice sounding exasperated.

"Okay, Sir, but please understand we are almost out of time!"

"I know, Pat. I know. And I suspect neither of us will sleep well tonight. I will see you tomorrow, hang in there."

The colonel was spot on. By the time he got the van off the plane and drove it to his hotel, it was almost 0500 the next morning. As for Pat, he stayed up all night staring at the walls in his hotel room worrying about the certain hell Tracey Adams was enduring. He paced about in his room, not even once dozing off again. By the time morning came, he would be exhausted and in less-than-optimum shape for the important mission ahead of him.

~ 21 ~

"I had two dreams about Tracey," Pat informed the rest of his team as soon as the last door to Colonel Helmsley's special van shut firmly. "One last night, and the first one was the night before we left. She doesn't have much time left, guys. We need to find her fast!"

He related the full details of the haunting nightmares. Woody was particularly impressed that in his second dream Pat had managed to maintain a separate awareness of events, a consciousness that allowed him to make mental notes of what was going on in the impressions he received.

"I believe your abilities are maturing. At least you are becoming better able to manage them. Keeping focus. Not just getting caught up in the rush of images," Woody said with a broad smile, amazed at how his pupil was progressing.

Pat half-smiled at the compliment, but suddenly became more interested in what Vicky was doing. She warmed up the van's hi-tech satellite system. Her long, red-painted nails deftly worked the controls until she had an Internet browser on the screen. She gave a quick turn look back at Woody and Pat.

"Oh, did we tell you we also have digital satellite Internet connectivity on this gadget, as well?"

"You looking for RV camps in the Tulsa area?" Colonel Helmsley asked as he turned the van onto I-44, the Turner Turnpike, east to Tulsa.

"Yes, I figure we can at least try to locate the camp where they took the girl and do some interviews. Maybe Patrick can update his senses by being at the site."

"I think that's a good idea. But I am dog tired right now--didn't sleep a wink last night. I'll do my best."

"Here we are. Looks like there are seven campgrounds in the Tulsa area that accept RVs, according to this one website," Vicky noted.

She read the names and locations off to Pat.

"Any of these strike you as familiar in any way?"

He shook his head. He was frustrated because nothing came through based merely on the names. Agent Desantis input the address information into the computer, then made a map overlay of the Tulsa area showing the camps in relation to Tracey Adams's home.

"These are all within twenty miles of her home. I guess we ought to start with the ones closest to her house and move outward," she suggested.

She next brought up the satellite system on the screen and directed its peering lens onto each park. In real time they all could look into the camps and examine each for signs of the RV camper with the butterfly logo Pat had seen. Nothing.

"I guess somehow I knew even last night they had left the area already," Pat said grimly.

Woody piped in. "That's okay, Pat. I still think if we visit each one, your physical closeness will facilitate new impressions coming through."

"Well, we've got about an hour before we get there," Colonel Helmsley said. "Let's just sit back and relax for now."

"Oh, I have some good news folks," Vicky suddenly blurted out. "Dick Williams called me last night. Seems our buddy Victor Ralston copped a plea."

"Wow! That's great news!" exclaimed Colonel Helmsley.

"Well, when his lawyers were confronted with the eyewitness

testimony of the little old lady in Mike Driscoll's neighborhood, along with the physical evidence linking him to the other two murders, he agreed to plead guilty. The deal they worked is he pleads guilty to the murder and abductions in North Carolina, gets life in state prison with no chance of parole, and Pennsylvania doesn't push extradition for the murder charge there. Also, the federal government drops interstate child abduction charges."

"So he never leaves prison?" Woody asked.

"Never."

Pat had no idea exactly how relieved Vicky was about the guilty plea. She knew this meant there was now no longer any need for Rose McAdams to testify. Although she was confident Rose would do a good job if called to the witness stand, Vicky had become uneasy about things with Ratner and Kennedy over Father Reynolds's death. She was worried about the SAP being exposed.

Time flew by as the group traveled along the turnpike in relative silence. Pat marveled at the flatness of things, a terrain that perfectly met the horizon, with only an occasional bump from a cluster of buildings in small towns along the way. Behind them, Oklahoma City looked like a clump of skyscrapers stuck together on a sheet of paper. The scent of cattle filled the air, and all along the Interstate were rusted-out oil derricks from a bygone industry that once made the area thrive.

"Okay, let's begin our journey at Tracey's house, then proceed to the first RV camp," Colonel Helmsley suggested.

"Yes, and I think it's a good idea that we return to her home each time we go to a new RV camp so that we travel the most likely route the kidnappers took," Vicky added.

Pat interrupted. "I think that's a good idea, but don't we run the risk of looking suspicious driving through her neighborhood so many times? I mean, after all, there was an abduction in that area just a week ago. People may become suspicious."

Woody nodded in agreement.

"Relax, guys," Colonel Helmsley offered. "There's another feature to this van that makes it ideal for surveillance work. Pat, you know how the Air Force has been experimenting with chameleon skin for aircraft, right?"

"Sure, you mean to change the paint color in flight--especially for stealth aircraft?"

"You've got to be kidding?" Woody asked.

The colonel smiled. "No, not at all. See, the dark black F-117s and B-2s are great for night flying, but you can see them in the daytime. Kinda defeats the notion of stealth. It's all still experimental, but our R&D facilities have devised special electrochromic polymers--paints that change color when differing electric charges are applied to painted metal panels."

"And this van has these panels?" Pat asked.

"Yup," the colonel said beaming. "I'll show you later, but we can change from blue to brown to gray to green to whatever in a matter of seconds. The Air Force wanted to test the technology on ground vehicles before applying it to aircraft. Flying is much more stressful to airframe skins than driving a car or van."

Colonel Helmsley turned the van onto the small, quiet suburban street where Tracey Adams's home was situated. He stopped a block away to check the map and get his bearings for the first RV camp. Being present there awakened Pat's senses to the images he received the night before. As they slowly rolled past her home to get a look, Pat's head was filled with the same scents, sounds, and tastes from his dream. He could smell the ether from the cloth used to knock out Tracey. Its scent lingered even a week later. He also could smell the reeking fatness of the man, the Tattoo Killer who had taken her from behind her home. The woman's cologne was in the air. A gentle, somewhat refreshing scent that belied her true, wicked spirit.

Pat's brain was busy processing all the bits and pieces of colors, shapes, textures, and tastes he received. Still, despite the extraordinary ability he had to receive and catalogue this sensory data, nothing new emerged to point the group in the right direction at that moment. His fatigue had weakened his abilities.

They headed out of the suburbs, slowly making their way along a county road to the first RV camp. It was called Eagle's Nest, and like most camps of its nature, was situated far and away from everything. It had a gravel road that coursed through it from the entrance to all points in the park, but then, so did all the others.

"This isn't it," Pat said as they cruised the entire park searching for the camper or any new clues that might materialize.

When they exited, Colonel Helmsley looked at Pat and Woody in the rearview mirror.

"We'll pull off to the side of the road up ahead. It's time for a minivan makeover," he said, referring to the color change they needed to make.

The colonel found a road cutout that had plenty of small trees along it to provide excellent cover. The three passengers hopped out to witness the color change first hand. The colonel called out from his rolled-down window, "What will it be? Green? Black? What?"

"Patrick, you have the honors," Vicky said.

"Let's make it gray, Boss!"

Colonel Helmsley pulled up a color palette panel on the plasma screen after a few button clicks and selected a light gray from the panorama. It was remarkable enough that the van could change color, but what Pat found difficult to believe was that the color possibilities were in the trillions.

"Dear God!" Woody exclaimed as he witnessed the van's color seemingly melt and morph from its original white to a medium gray within seconds.

"How do you like it?" the colonel asked. "Want it darker or lighter?"

"It's just fine!" Pat cried out excitedly.

They were on the road once again and headed for Tracey's house to try the next RV camp on the list.   For the next few hours they repeated the process three more times.   Back to Tracey's house and then off to a new campsite with no success. The van went from white to gray to brown to blue that morning.   Nothing triggered in Pat's mind as they made their journeys.   He was growing increasingly frustrated and worried.

"Shall we get a bite to eat, decompress, and then hit the next camp after lunch?" Vicky suggested as they left the fourth location.

"No!" Pat spat out harshly causing the others to tilt their heads back in shock. "Time is running out; we need to find Tracey now!"

The lack of sleep and the lack of success in finding Tracey were gnawing at him fiercely. Without saying a word, they nodded at him, made a quick color change to yellow, and headed for Tracey Adams's house and then to the fifth camp of the seven on their list. It was called the Buffalo Lodge and RV Campsite, and it was about fifteen miles north of Tracey's subdivision. As it was four times before, suburban roads turned to country roads that led to the RV camp. When they entered the Buffalo Lodge campground, the van's tires crunched the coarse gravel beneath them. It was at that precise moment Pat knew they had hit the right one. Hidden below the surface of his psyche was a special signature to the sound and feel of the gravel that he first felt the night before in his vision. The sound had texture like an icy snowball. It was round and frozen and gave him a sense in his mouth of eating snow as a child.

"We're here! This is the place. Boss, turn right at the next lane, then to the third camp stall."

As they rounded the corner, there was a large RV in the third stall, but it had no vehicle tow hitch for a sedan. They drove past it and saw the word *Explorer* stenciled on the back, but no butterfly logo. It wasn't the Tattoo Killer's RV, but at least now they had a solid lead to go with.

"Let's go to the manager's camper, and I'll talk with him," Vicky said. She was taking charge again of the situation as an FBI matter.

They walked over to the manager's RV, clear on the other side of the park. The ground beneath them crunched as leather soles disturbed the gravel bed, alternating with soft swishes as they passed through grassy areas between camper slots. The manager's motor home was old. Cobwebs connected the tires, long-since flat and cracked from dry-rot, to the metal frame. The sound of country music emanated from within. Vicky knocked on the door. No response. She rapped harder.

"Just a minute!" came the shout of an older woman's voice.

The door flung openly suddenly, country music instantly booming louder. A haggard woman in her seventies appeared. Scraggly. Curlers in her hair. Cigarette held in nicotine-stained fingers. The stench of booze hit them long before her words.

"Who the hell are you?" she asked with a raspy voice, taking one last drag before tossing the lit butt into the gravel in front of her RV.

Vicky extended her credentials, gold badge briefly flashing a bright reflection of sunlight on the woman's face.

"We're from the FBI, ma'am."

The woman was startled for a moment. She pulled her tattered bathrobe about her tightly.

"What does the FBI want with me?" she asked nervously.

"Relax ma'am, we just want to ask you a few questions about one of your recent guests," Vicky explained. "May we come in?"

Pat could tell the woman appeared uncomfortable with the request, but agreed reluctantly.

"Well, I suppose so. But excuse my place. It's a mess. Been meaning to clean it. Just been hard to find the time these days."

"That's no problem. We won't take much of your time," Agent Desantis assured her.

Vicky gave a quick glance backward at the other three, smiling almost mockingly about the old woman. They stepped up and inside, one-by-one. Pat surveyed the small messy living room area with just a small sofa and a side chair for sitting. The woman dragged a wooden chair from her kitchen area to the room so they all had seats. She lowered the volume on the radio just before sitting. The place was cluttered with all manner of collectibles. A veritable flea market of junk. In the center of the living room area was a small coffee table with a pile of tabloid newspapers. A glass ashtray rested precariously near the edge with a mound of ashes that had long-since spilled over the sides. The air was thick with a mix of grain alcohol, cigarettes, and pet urine. Pat glanced down by the sofa and saw a small box with a square hole cut out at its base. Two cat eyes peered out from the darkness within.

"Ma'am, we want to ask you about the people who stayed in space number eleven within the last two weeks," Vicky said.

"Them new people?" the woman asked. "They just got here last night, the Johnsons. Nice old couple."

"No, not them. Who was in the space last?"

"Oh, that fat guy and his good looking wife you mean."

"Yes, and their daughter."

"Nope. No kids. Just them two."

"You never saw a little girl there?"

"Nope. Never did. I thought it was just them. Besides, they never did much away from the camper. Quiet folks."

"Do you have a registration card for them?"

"Sure do, but I doubt they used their real name. A lot of people like to use fake names when they visit camps," she said as she shuffled over to her kitchen counter and retrieved a recipe-sized box from a cabinet. Inside were index cards separated by old and crinkled tab cards containing camp space numbers. She fumbled through the cards behind number eleven.

"Here we go. John and Jane Smith. Gives an address in North Dakota."

"Ah, the Smith family! That's original," Colonel Helmsley said sarcastically, shooting Vicky a disappointed glance.

"Oh, that's okay. I knew it was bogus. But I outsmarted them," the woman said with a wry smile.

"How so?" Vicky asked.

"Look on the back. I copied down their car and RV license plate numbers. I do that just in case people leave without paying or break something here. I can track 'em down!" she said proudly generating a whistle sound through her missing-teeth smile.

Sure enough, on the reverse side were two Washington state license plate numbers.

"May we keep this card?" Vicky asked.

"Oh sure. I don't need it now. They paid cash when they left."

"When did they leave?" Pat asked.

"About four, maybe five days back."

"Thank you ma'am. We appreciate your help," Vicky said.

Once they were safely inside the security of the magic van, Pat watched as Vicky got on her cell phone and telephoned her office. She told her secretary to have the license plates run and to cross check any hits with the National Crime Information Center system for arrest or prosecution history. She also wanted a list of credit cards owned by the registrants and an immediate credit card transaction history run on them. Vicky wanted to see if the pair was still in the area. If they made any recent credit card purchases, it would show.

About thirty minutes into the drive, Vicky's cell phone rang.

"Uh huh, uh huh. You're kidding me?" Vicky grabbed a note pad and pen from her purse. "Okay, go ahead," she said as she jotted down notes. Two pages of notes in all by the time she hung up.

"Well, what is it? Any promising leads?" Colonel Helmsley asked.

She nodded and grinned. "It seems our Mr. and Mrs. Smith are actually John and Jane Smith. He was born in North Dakota, but currently resides in Seattle."

"Amazing!" Woody snickered. "He didn't lie to the old lady after all. Guess it was good she thought he had."

"Listen, neither he nor the wife have any arrest record, but he was questioned two years ago by the FBI in Seattle after he was accused by a teen girl of soliciting her for sex on the Internet."

"What happened?" Colonel Helmsley asked.

"Well, there was not enough evidence to bring charges. Seems our Mr. Smith was working as a software engineer at one of those dot-coms in Seattle. He was fired over the incident because he allegedly used company computers to chat with girls online, on company time. Nobody would hire him after that, so it appears he may have gone off the deep end and started his crime spree as a result."

"Any credit card purchases?" Woody asked.

"Yes. He bought gasoline last night at a Jiffy-Mart center off the Indian Nation Turnpike just south of here, outside the town of McAlester. A lot of gas. Much more than the sedan could hold, so it appears they are on the move in the camper."

Colonel Helmsley pulled up his online map on the van's display. "McAlester's not far at all. I wonder if they had been staying at another RV camp in this general area since they left this one four or five days back?" he asked out loud.

Woody turned to Pat. "Do you think you can close those tired eyes of yours and try to get some kind of impressions about these folks? I wonder if the events of today will stimulate new images."

"I'll try," he replied with a yawn.

But it was difficult, at best. He was so tired, he thought he might just fall asleep without a vision and miss the opportunity to find Tracey. He knew he needed to stay awake, but drift just close enough to sleep without actually going there. He had to unearth that sweet spot. Five frustrating minutes went by. Then ten more minutes. Then, when he simply allowed his brain to go on autopilot, he became relaxed enough to find that mental center of gravity he sought.

A symphony of senses swirled around in his mind until they rested on the RV. It was parked behind a fast food restaurant, a place called Tasty Tom's, sedan fixed in tow. Jane Smith was inside the camper, dozing in the passenger seat. John Smith was inside the restaurant, slowly gorging himself with a huge breakfast platter.

Pat's gaze returned to the RV. As he visited each detail of each scene, he spoke out loud to the others. He was alert and present with them, while simultaneously alert and present with the Smiths and Tracey Adams. Tracey was alive, but barely, so it seemed. She was chained to the inside of the camper behind a curtained area that prevented someone from peering inside the windshield and seeing her. Her hands were shackled to the cold, faux-wood paneled walls in a makeshift dungeon. Her mouth was securely wrapped tight with tape. Her hair was matted and straggly. She was sleeping. Pat strained to see through her eyes but only saw darkness.

"I think she's already been blinded," he announced sadly. "A police car just pulled in. I don't know if this is real time or past or what. But I see a cop car in the lot now. It says Plano on the side."

But then suddenly the impressions stopped. Pat opened his eyes and blinked several times. The sunlight bothered him.

"Plano, Texas?" Colonel Helmsley wondered aloud. He adjusted the map settings to show northern Texas. "They could have driven there today. It may be real time."

He accessed the Internet browser and searched for all Tasty Tom's restaurants in Plano. There were three in all. Vicky took control so he could drive. She frantically ordered up satellite coverage of each restaurant in turn. When the image of the third one appeared on the screen, Pat cried out, "That's the one! That's the parking lot I saw. I recognize the landscaping."

But there was neither an RV nor a police car from Plano in the lot.

"Damn!" Vicky muttered aloud.

"Think we should phone in an anonymous tip to the Plano PD?" Woody asked.

Colonel Helmsley shook his head. "No, I'm not sure that's a good idea yet. See, you told us that sometimes Pat gets images from the future. If this is one of them, it would stand out as very odd that someone called in a sighting of the girl at the restaurant *before* she was even there."

Vicky nodded vigorously. "The colonel's right. We have to protect CRYSTAL ROUNDUP at all costs. Even our anonymous tips have to be credible!"

She seemed almost irritated with Woody for not considering operational security.

"So what do we do?" Pat asked, rubbing his eyes.

"For now, I'll program the satellite system to run scans in concentric circles from the restaurant in Plano, outward with an increasing radius upon each scan. If they had been there, or will go there, I hope we catch them from overhead," Vicky said as she opened the notepad on her lap and meticulously entered into the van's computer the Smiths' license plate information along with the address of the restaurant in Plano.

Pat watched in amazement as the screen display changed from a simple nondescript data entry template to one bearing the official symbol of the National Security Agency. At the top and bottom were banners   in   large   red   letters: TOP   SECRET SPARK//AVALANCHE//RHOMBUS.

Woody squinted through his spectacles, mouth open with a puzzled look. "What the hell is that all about?" he asked, confused.

"That's the NSA's code words for the program in which this particular satellite technology resides. I guess you don't recall your indoc from a few years back," Vicky chuckled.

Next she moved the cursor over a button that said: START UPLINK. When she pressed the touchpad key, a status bar appeared and began filling itself in, slowly displaying its progress.

High above them all, in low earth orbit, a class KH-12 satellite was speeding its way from a stationary position over the equator to a new position just above Colorado. It was from this new stationary point that the KH-12 had optimal video and infrared coverage of the western half of the United States. Once in place, it established connectivity with a host of GPS satellites around the globe. Then it began scanning as ordered, reading hundreds of license plates every second...every vehicle, on every road, on every highway, in every parking lot. It sent its data back, silently, in real time to Air Force Space Command computers located at Peterson Air Force Base in Colorado Springs. Trillions of data bytes were assembled and crunched and analyzed against the parameters in Vicky's order. The status bar reached 100% when the satellite had come to rest and the scanning began. A message appeared on the screen: SCAN IN PROGRESS.

Vicky looked back at Pat and Woody and smiled. She turned to Colonel Helmsley, "John, I think we ought to split up a bit on our way to Plano. How about dropping me off at a car rental place. I'll drive down myself while you gentlemen go together. I want to add some randomness to our travels."

"Er, I guess. Okay, Vicky, if that's what you want to do. You know it's about a five hour ride, you sure you wanna do that on your own?" the colonel asked, puzzled.

"I do, John, and really it's not a problem for me," she responded as she fidgeted with the computer while the scan proceeded in the background. "Here, I've located a car rental place a couple miles ahead."

The onboard GPS system navigated them to the rental agency. They dropped Vicky off, and she walked around to Colonel Helmsley's window before they pulled away.

"I'll call you when I arrive. But please call if you get a hit on the scan in the meantime. Bye!"

Pat did not notice, as the three men drove off, that Vicky pulled her cell phone out of her purse, approached the car rental office door, and hit a number on speed dial.

~ 22 ~

Agent Desantis stood just inside the rental agency's office and watched through the smudged glass door as the van sped off. Her call to Special Agent Ratner connected within seconds.

"Hank, you and Kennedy need to head to Plano, Texas ASAP!" she ordered. She yanked her notepad from her purse and read off the address of the Tasty Tom's restaurant. "Go to this location and set up surveillance of the parking lot, but stay far from it. You can't be seen anywhere near the place. I'll be coming down separately, probably a little bit behind you." She gave them the description of the RV and sedan. "If the RV arrives, stay on it. Loose surveillance, but don't lose them!"

"You want us to *find* a witness for anything, Vicky?" Ratner asked, clearly not understanding her specific instructions.

Vicky became annoyed with him. "NO! Just watch the place, spot the RV and follow loosely if it moves! Got it?!"

"Okay! Okay! Got it! See you there," he acknowledged as he hung up.

She shook her head in frustrated disbelief as she walked up to the counter.

"Give me something big and comfy."

The minivan moved along the highway at a fast clip as the three men sat in silence for awhile. Woody had hopped up front with the colonel at Pat's insistence. It was now late night, and although Pat was exhausted from a lack of sleep, he was too anxious to doze off. His mind was clouded with many thoughts. Tracey Adams. Sara and the kids. Father Reynolds. With Vicky gone, he felt it was a good time to discuss his growing angst over the operation with the two men.

"Gentlemen, I need to talk with you both about some concerns I have."

"Shoot, Pat. What's on your mind?" the colonel asked, looking at him in the rearview mirror.

"Well, two things. Sara is getting more and more concerned about my sudden travel and involvement with helping the FBI. I think it won't be long before she blows her top at me and makes it tough for me at home to keep supporting the program. She thinks I'm helping Quantico with its profiling school, but it's getting hard to justify trips. Like this one. She said when I left to tell the FBI this is the last one."

"Yikes. That is a problem," Dr. Davis said jumping in. "We need her support but she can't know why. Any ideas?"

Pat looked at the colonel in the mirror. "Sir, maybe you could call her sometime next week and talk with her about supporting me, like you did a few years back when we were chasing those Iraqi intelligence agents around South Carolina--the guys doing pre-op surveillance of Shaw Air Force Base. It really helped when you told her that I was supporting some sensitive ops."

Colonel Helmsley nodded as Pat spoke. "That's a great idea, Pat. I'll do that. Sara's a very supportive woman, and I'm sure once she understands this is one of those super sensitive ops, she'll give you the space you need. And what was the second thing you needed to talk with us about?"

"Well," he began hesitantly. "It's about Father Reynolds's death."

The colonel gave him a strange look. "What about his death?"

Once again Pat stared at the colonel's reflection in the mirror, directly and deeply into his eyes. He was looking for that sign of trust he needed to proceed. Of course he had known Colonel Helmsley since forever. The colonel was his mentor and his close friend, and once saved his life. In an instant flashback, he recalled how they had chased after two Hezbollah operatives in Kuwait four years earlier. They stumbled upon the pair as they were preparing mortars they planned to launch against a row of F-117 stealth fighters parked on the flight line at Ahmed al Jaber Air Base.   The terrorists had positioned themselves high up on a sand dune behind an abandoned gas station with a perfect line-of-sight to the multi-million dollar airframes. Pat and Colonel Helmsley were returning from Kuwait City when they saw the attack about to take place. Pat was driving and instinctively hit the gas pedal hard, departing the highway for a side road covered in slippery sand. The jeep slid and swerved. The tires kicked up sand sprays as the jeep made a menacing high speed approach to the pair. Once he regained control, Pat aimed straight for them. The two had little time to react. Pat struck the closest one as he stood up to see what the commotion was. The front end of the jeep hit him hard and direct. *THUMP!* In a loud crushing sound, the terrorist was thrown into the air and came crashing down headfirst into the sand, snapping his spinal column just below the neck. He was dead instantly.

The jeep continued forward and crushed the mortar tubes before stopping. The other Hezbollah terrorist had run down the hill toward the gas station. He was screaming in Arabic when Pat jumped from the jeep and gave chase. Colonel Helmsley yelled for him to stop and come back, but Pat disregarded his order. The colonel shook his head and screamed, "Pat, squeeze the trigger, don't pull, two shots, center mass!"

He was belting out the standard firearms training drill that all OSI agents had memorized from their earliest indoctrination at the OSI Academy. Agents were trained to aim off the front and rear sights of their Berettas until the target became fuzzy, then squeeze off two rounds in rapid succession.

The rush of adrenaline was powerful. When Pat was no more than ten yards from the abandoned structure, three terrorists came out, firing automatic weapons at him. Pat dove behind a rusted-out oil truck. Colonel Helmsley, taking cover behind the jeep, expertly took out two of the men with his MP-5 machine gun. The third terrorist ran back inside the gas station with Pat in pursuit. *BOOM! BOOM!* The explosion from his gun was magnified inside the metal structure, almost deafening Pat. He walked out, holstering his Beretta and grinning.

"All clear, Boss! Two rounds, neatly delivered center mass. I think these guys are in conference with Allah right now."

The memory of that day faded as fast as it had surfaced. Pat now looked at Woody. Although they had little history together, he felt a strong bond with him from the day they met at Pope Air Force Base. He concentrated for a moment that seemed forever suspended in time and read Woody's thoughts. Not words. Just feeling and affect. And trust.

He took a deep breath before continuing. But when he did, he opened up completely. He told them of the concerns Father Reynolds expressed to him before he was killed. The visit from the CIA thugs. The eavesdropping device in the rectory. The homicide investigation. He told them about chasing the two men in Springfield Park, men he was sure were the ones who killed the priest.

Colonel Helmsley stared straight ahead at the road for a moment. Then he shot Pat a glance in the rearview mirror. "This is huge. We have a focal point guy at the Agency, but I've not spoken with him. No one at CIA should even know about you yet. We planned to have an interagency meeting next week."

"Maybe Vicky told someone at Langley. Want to talk with her?" Woody asked.

"Not yet. Vicky is too intense. I'm not sure she would take this well. Let's let it lie for now. Pat, when we get back, see what you can get from that detective in Fairfax. I know you have the skills to turn the interview around."

"I will, Sir. And I want to cooperate with the murder investigation. I want these assholes to pay."

Colonel Helmsley stared at him for a moment. Pat could tell he had something else he wanted to say, but was uncertain if it was the right time or the right place. He bit his lip momentarily.

"Pat, there's something you need to know about Vicky that has to be kept close-hold."

The colonel looked at Woody who nodded his head. It was immediately clear to Pat that Woody already knew whatever it was Colonel Helmsley was about to reveal. Pat could sense his seriousness.

"Ssssure, Boss," he said slowly.

"And I mean, if you ever breathe a word of this, I'll beat your butt! Vicky didn't just stumble into the CRYSTAL ROUNDUP program by accident. She was recruited as a young FBI probationary agent ten years back. Fresh from Quantico in her first field assignment in San Francisco, she was working on a series of bank robberies. The so-called, *Gas Bandits*. They'd enter a bank and toss a couple of tear gas canisters, don masks, and rob all the tellers."

Pat nodded. "I remember seeing that in the news long ago. Didn't these guys do this for several years, and then suddenly stop? Never caught?"

"Yes and no. Vicky took over the case--it was cold by then. What she didn't tell her superiors was she believed she had some kind of psychic abilities, and wanted to use them to solve the case. Make a huge splash as a new FBI agent. Make a name for herself."

Dr. Davis interjected. "Well, truth is Vicky did, or I should say, does have some level of psychic abilities. They are very, very limited however--she's no Pat O'Donnell, let me put it that way."

Colonel Helmsley continued. "The Special Agent in Charge in San Francisco at the time was a mover and shaker in the Bureau--for a long time rumored to be in grooming for a Deputy Director stint or even the Director's job one day. But things took a turn south. For starters, Vicky didn't immediately tell any of her superiors how she developed her leads--the whole psychic thing. They all assumed it was based on solid detective work. Then the press caught wind that the *Gas Bandits* case was suddenly moved from the back burner to the front. They started to ask questions."

Pat's eyes widened. "Uh, oh. I think I see where this is headed."

Colonel Helmsley snickered. "Yeah. It got ugly. Vicky wanted her fifteen minutes of fame and agreed to speak with a reporter *off-the-record*. Instead, her remarks appeared in a front page San Francisco Chronicle story the next day, attributed to an *unnamed* FBI official."

"Did she talk about the psi stuff with the reporter?" Pat asked, grimacing.

"Oh, yeah. She didn't take credit for being a psychic, but she told the reporter the FBI had used a psychic and as a result were focusing on two Army guys. The Special Agent in Charge's phone began ringing off the hook. The media. The FBI Director. The Attorney General. It made the entire FBI look foolish. The Army guys got attorneys who threatened to file lawsuits. Even with some pretty good circumstantial evidence they were the *Gas Bandits*, the federal government was loathe to prosecute because key to obtaining that evidence was Vicky's self-proclaimed psychic powers. The suspects dropped the suit once the government declined to indict them. The SAIC was admonished by the Attorney General for not having a grip on his operations. He retired early. Vicky was called back to DC to undergo psychiatric testing," the colonel added.

Woody smiled and turned to face Pat. "I guess that's where I came in. The Bureau's mandate was simple and honest. They wanted her tested for psychic abilities, and when I reported back that she had indications of limited, but largely unremarkable, psychic abilities, they thanked me for my services, and that's the last I heard of her or from her until you came along, Pat."

"So they decided since she was briefed in deep enough to test her, that she should become the successor to the CRYSTAL ROUNDUP manager at that time?" Pat asked.

Colonel Helmsley nodded once more. "Right again. The guy she replaced was ready to retire, and the Bureau needed to deep six her for some time until memories could fade about the *Gas Bandit* fiasco. It was a perfect solution. She took over and has remained there since."

Pat rolled his eyes. "I suspect that a lot of what makes Vicky who she is has to do with redemption. She wants to be respected in the Bureau and have power and all. But what about her personal life, I mean a good looking young woman, and no husband?"

"She was married once. But it fell apart after she lost her baby about five years ago. She was to have a little girl, but it was a breeched birth which the surgeon botched up. Her baby died, and in the process the doc messed Vicky up so bad, she can never have children."

"Jesus, that's sad," Pat said.

"Yeah. It tore her and her husband up. They eventually drifted apart, and about four years ago they got divor--"

The colonel suddenly interrupted himself. He started tapping the plasma screen vigorously.

"Take a look at this! We've found the RV!"

He excitedly pointed to the camper onscreen, moving along a dark highway. At the top and bottom of the screen were the TOP SECRET SPARK//AVALANCHE//RHOMBUS security banners, along with a flashing red-lettered message: TARGET ACQUIRED. Colonel Helmsley worked the keyboard and pulled up the RV's geo-coordinate data.

"They are on Interstate Thirty-Five heading south," he announced. "It looks like they're just north of Denton. Pat, you realize what this means? It looks like your vision was indeed a future event. It sure looks like they're headed for Plano now! Let me call Vicky and let her know about the hit, and meanwhile this system will keep a lock on them. Now that we've found them, the satellites won't let go until we release them."

"I had planned to rack out for a few," Pat said as he sat forward in his seat, staring intently at the computer screen. He watched as the RV lumbered along the Interstate, knowing that Tracey Adams was inside, shackled and in terror.

"I think we'll hit Plano right around dawn. I just can't sleep now. We're so close. So very close!" Pat said, almost breathlessly.

~ **23** ~

"That's fantastic news, John!" Vicky exclaimed upon learning about the satellite lock on the RV.

She held her cell phone in her left hand while steering her rental car with the other, maniacally driving at a high rate of speed down I-35. She was passing cars hectically while her speedometer consistently broke eighty, ninety, sometimes even one hundred miles per hour. She was determined to get to Plano before the rest of her team. Vicky was already forty miles ahead of them, actually getting closer to Denton and to the RV than even she realized. She had reasons for wanting to arrive early. She wanted to have a chance to scope out Ratner and Kennedy, in whom she was losing confidence. They were beginning to become a liability to the CRYSTAL ROUNDUP operation. She had to make sure they didn't drop the ball again.

"I should arrive Plano maybe an hour before you guys. I'll call you when I get there. See you then, John."

Ratner and Kennedy had just gotten onto the President George Bush Turnpike, less than an hour outside of Plano when Vicky called them.

"Remember, set up a fixed surveillance," she cautioned after filling them in on the satellite's fix. "No need to worry about losing them now, so operational security is your first priority. When you arrive, locate a pay phone near the restaurant and discreetly get the phone number from it and call me back, okay?"

"Okay, Vicky, but why?" Ratner asked.

"Just do it! I'll explain later," she barked as she flipped her cell phone closed, disconnecting them.

She swerved to avoid a slow car in the left lane, rammed the accelerator, and honked her horn furiously as she passed on the right. While rushing at breakneck speed, Vicky thought about the entire series of events in the CRYSTAL ROUNDUP program since discovering Pat. She knew she was on the verge of catching another serial pedophile, which, when combined with the Ralston case from a week before, would surely put her in good graces with the Attorney General. She decided to give him a call even though it was very early in the morning on the east coast.

She reached him on his secure cell phone. At first he did not realize who she was, but once she mentioned CRYSTAL ROUNDUP, he remembered her. Although an honest slight for a busy man, it was huge in Vicky's mind. Irritating. She excitedly filled him in on the details of the Tattoo Killer and the couple's imminent arrest in Plano.

"Vicky, I am very impressed with this young man--O'Donnell, right?" he asked, without giving her event the slightest praise for her work as the director of the operation and the Special Access Program itself.

"Yassir, that's right," she replied, her jaws clenched. "Major Patrick O'Donnell, an Air Force OSI agent." Her voice was strained somewhat but the AG didn't pick up on it.

"Well, please pass along to Pat my appreciation for a job well done. Good-bye, Vicky!"

"YES SIR!" she screamed at the phone after she hung up.

She grated her teeth. Gripping the steering wheel tightly, she floored the accelerator and cruised at 120 miles per hour. When she was about ten miles outside of Plano, she slowed down, calmed down, and called Ratner again.

"Where are you?" she asked, her voice sounding irritable.

"We're at a local park. Haggard Park--or something like that. It's near East Sixteenth and J by some train tracks. We got visual on the fast food joint but no RV yet," he said, undoubtedly sensing she was not happy.

"Did you get a pay phone number for me?"

"Yeah, yeah, here goes. It's outside an electronics boutique about twenty yards from the restaurant."

Vicky jotted the number on her notepad on her right leg as she drove. "Sit tight, I'll be there soon."

The sun was just coming up in Plano when Vicky pulled into the park, spotting Ratner and Kennedy in their vehicle. They had actually set up a decent surveillance point, but she had to be sure and see for herself. When she parked next to them, they lowered windows simultaneously, letting a gust of cool Texas morning air blow in.

"Good morning, gentlemen," she cooed. "Good job on the fix point. I'm not sure we will need your services with witnesses if all goes the way I have it planned. So just sit tight and wait for further instructions."

Ratner and Kennedy were unaccustomed to compliments coming from her.

"Er, okay Vicky, but exactly what's the plan?" Kennedy asked.

"When the RV arrives, I'll make an anonymous call from the van, but it will appear to the emergency services folks to be coming from the pay phone number you gave me."

"Cool, you can do that?" Ratner asked.

She gave him an incredulous smirk. "You have the same technology in your surveillance van near the O'Donnell home. It's a black box inside the safe. Just in case you should ever need it," she informed him derisively.

She couldn't believe her two best operatives didn't know about all the special equipment at their disposal.

"And when I use it today, I'm sure that when they respond and find Tracey, they won't even try to find the caller, let alone check any surveillance cameras in the area of the pay phone," she added. "Well, I need to go and ditch this car. You guys wait for me to call and hang up. That will be my signal to break off and head home to DC."

"Got it, Vicky," Ratner said.

She drove past the front of the restaurant, finding a shopping center parking lot with an excellent vantage point, yet far enough away from Ratner and Kennedy so as to keep the two surveillance teams from seeing each other. She called Colonel Helmsley and told him where she could be found.

"Good, 'cause the RV is on the turnpike right now. We picked up our speed and passed them several miles back. Don't worry, we'll do a color change when we arrive just in case the Smiths eyeballed us for any reason," Colonel Helmsley assured her.

"You must be close to town right now, John. Hurry!"

Colonel Helmsley chuckled over her excitement. "Don't worry Vicky, almost there."

Within moments, Vicky saw the minivan approach and pass by the Tasty Tom's restaurant. The van was a light yellow color when it drew near. But it ducked behind the shopping center only to emerge from the other side a dark blue. When they pulled up to Vicky, she was standing outside her car, arms crossed, obviously upset about something. Colonel Helmsley parked the van and got out.

"What's wrong, Vicky?" he asked, puzzled by her apparent anger.

"John, you drove right in front of our target point! That's lousy OPSEC!" she admonished him.

Of course, despite doing the exact same thing mere moments before, it did not seem to register in her mind as a double standard.

The colonel tilted his head back in surprise. "Young lady, I was doing surveillance work back when you were in diapers, so don't lecture me on technique. The Smiths aren't even here yet. They're acting alone, so there's no concern about countersurveillance!"

She quickly lowered her hackles. "I'm sorry, John. You're right. I've just been so stressed over this whole operation and without much sleep," she lamented. "Come on, let's get ready for the Smiths' arrival."

Colonel Helmsley scowled as they walked to the van. Pat saw and heard the entire argument the two just had. It bothered him to see a crack in the foundation of their team. Woody jumped out of the front seat to allow Vicky to sit next to the colonel. They sat silently listening to the radio softly playing background music. Five minutes. Ten minutes. Twenty minutes went by. They watched the RV the entire time on the plasma screen, and as it arrived in Plano, the excitement level in the van increased exponentially.

"Vicky, are you going to call emergency services on your cell when we spot the camper?" Pat asked.

"Yes, Darling, I've got a special way of doing just that."

She proceeded to explain how the 911 call would work, to provide cover to the operation while ensuring a rapid police response. She connected a small computer cable to her cell phone, and then attached the other end to a port on the minivan's computer.

"And don't worry, Hun, they'll act on my call," she said with a perfect, native Texan accent.

"What's that I see down at that intersection?" the colonel suddenly asked, breaking into their conversation with a burst of excitement.

They looked in unison as the RV stopped at a red light. Suddenly the radio faded into the background as energy surged through the van. The excitement was thick and alive. The light changed green, and the RV slowly passed through the intersection. Its right blinker came on, and it slowed to turn in to the fast food restaurant parking lot. As it turned in, Pat could see the fat man, John Smith. He caught a mere glimpse of his wife in the passenger seat. Smith pulled over to the right of the lot as he entered, stopping in an open area near the back. His rig took up more than six or seven parking spaces. He shut off the engine and rolled out. He seemed to be talking with Jane Smith as he stood by the open door for a few moments.

"Probably taking the food order," Woody said.

Vicky interrupted. "Let's give fat boy about five minutes to order and take a seat. Then I'll call. I like the idea of dividing and conquering."

Time seemed to hang in the air as they sat watching. Pat nervously waited for Vicky to make the call, so he could witness the take down and arrest of this pair and the rescue of Tracey. Finally, Vicky picked up her cell phone. She pressed the buttons slowly as if to make sure she dialed right. Pat leaned in to listen as Vicky switched the phone to speaker mode.

It rang. "Nine-One-One, what's your emergency?" came a man's voice.

"Y'all need to hurry on down here!" Vicky replied in an impressive Texan twang.

"May I ask your name, ma'am, and what the problem is?"

"Oh, my Lord, no. I want to remain anonymous," she said giving the 911 operator the location of the restaurant.

"What's the problem, ma'am? What's going on there?" he asked.

"Well, I may be crazy, but I think I saw that little Tulsa girl there. You know, the one that's been missing like a week now, what's her name--Tracey, Tracey Adams?"

"Now slow down, ma'am. What makes you think it's her?"

"Well, her missing poster is everywhere. I'm sure it's her. She's in this big old RV camper with some kind of butterfly decal on the back. A big fat guy got out as I was getting in my car. When he opened the RV door, I saw her. She seemed to be tied up or something. The fat guy went inside the restaurant. He may still be in there. He's got on a red Polo shirt and tan pants. Can't miss him. He's a biggun!" she exclaimed.

"All right, ma'am, we're sending someone over right now. Please stay on the line with me." But instead of waiting as asked, Vicky abruptly hung up.

At that moment, a Plano PD patrol car pulled into the restaurant parking lot, just as Pat had seen in his image. Two officers stepped out and went inside for breakfast.

"Vicky, one question," Woody said. "We know from Pat's image there's a curtain in the RV that shields Tracey from anyone being able to see her. The story you just told the emergency folks doesn't seem to jibe with the facts. I mean, won't they get suspicious?"

She smiled. "I doubt it will matter much at this point since we know they will find Tracey in the RV. It will be a detail that will disappear into the fabric of the arrest, which will probably be the biggest thing to happen in Plano, Texas in twenty years."

As the patrolmen entered the restaurant, they instinctively looked around to see who was there. They looked for familiar faces. Troublemakers. Wanted persons. They saw Smith sitting down eating, but he did not register with them. As they stood in line deciding what to order, the call came over the radio. The dispatcher whispered into both their earpieces...suspected child abduction...description of suspects, vehicle. Both men looked around the dining area once more. Now Smith stood out. The senior patrolman keyed the microphone clipped to his epaulet and whispered into it.

"Unit Nineteen is on site inside the restaurant right now, we have a visual on the male."

"Roger that, stand by for back-up from Unit Twenty-Four, en route about three mike out," the dispatcher said in between soft static bursts.

"Copy. Unit Twenty-Four, Twenty-Four. Do you copy?" he asked.

"Twenty-Four here, go ahead."

"Roger. Once you arrive, secure the vehicle, and we'll take down the male inside."

"Unit Twenty-Four, copy, we're pulling in now."

The two patrolmen looked outside and saw the other Plano PD car come to a screeching stop in front of the RV, pinning it in. John Smith saw this at the same time and began to stand up to try to get away. The patrolmen jumped over the metal railing of the food order line. They ran to him, each grabbing one of Smith's flabby arms, shoving him face down onto the table. Under control now, the rookie handcuffed him as the senior patrolman stood a few feet away with gun drawn. Within a matter of seconds, more than a dozen Plano PD and Texas Ranger vehicles converged onto the restaurant lot. Sirens wailing. Blue and red lights flashing. Complete chaos, noise, and confusion. The Unit 24 patrolmen approached the RV with guns drawn and opened the passenger door, jumping to the side as they did so.

As the door swung open, Jane Smith tumbled out curled into a ball, hitting the pavement hard. She was motionless, her hands held tightly against her waist as the patrolmen shouted at her not to move or they would fire. One of the patrolmen holstered his gun while the other maintained a nervous finger on his trigger. The first officer removed a set of handcuffs from his belt, reached down, and grabbed one of Jane Smith's hands and pulled it around to her back. He recoiled in disgust and let go when he felt wet, warm blood. His own hand was now covered with it. He turned her over and found a small caliber revolver in her right hand, still clutched tightly against her belly where she had fired one round upward and into her vital organs.

No one heard the shot during the chaos of arriving response vehicles. Jane Smith was dead. A large pool of her blood now formed below her. It oozed out and created small rivulets that flowed gradually through the filth of the parking lot.

The other Unit 24 officer entered the RV with his gun drawn shouting, "Police, police. No one move."

He was uncertain how many suspects he had to deal with. He approached the curtain slowly, keeping as much of his body plastered to the side of the camper as possible, staying out of the center line of fire. He heard muffled sobs coming from behind the fabric partition. Drawing the curtain aside with his nightstick, he peered into the back.

Sunlight flooded into the back of the RV for the first time since Tracey had been abducted, although she could not see it. She was not blind; however, her eyes were covered in duct tape. The patrolman gently pried the tape off. Accustomed more now to darkness than light, she squinted and blinked as the rays burst through to her dungeon. She began to shake and sob uncontrollably, realizing her nightmare finally had come to an end.

Pat gasped and covered his eyes at the precise moment the patrolman removed the tape from Tracey's eyes. Although Pat could not see what was happening from the surveillance point, he was telepathically connected to her. And when she was suddenly able to see again, Pat experienced it right along with her.

"She wasn't blinded after all!" Pat exclaimed wiping tears from his face. "They had her eyes taped closed!"

Her rescue was an emotional drain on him; he shuddered in small spasms, trying desperately to regain control just like Tracey. The colonel, Vicky, and Woody erupted in a cheer they quickly suppressed so as not to draw any suspicion to themselves.

Woody placed an arm on his shoulder to comfort and congratulate him. "Good job Pat, good job."

The Plano PD officer let out an audible gasp at the sight and smell of it all. He slowly removed the tape from her mouth.

"Are there any others besides the man and woman?" he asked her.

She shook her head. "No, just them," she said, trying her best to get control of her composure.

It was hard to do. She was just nine years old and had been through a horrific, traumatic experience. And by the grace of God, she had not been assaulted.

"It's gonna be okay, Honey. We're gonna get you home to your mom and dad real soon. Your name is Tracey, right?"

"Yes. I wanna go home now!" she cried at his words.

He told her he'd be right back as he went to the front of the RV and called out to his partner to get a paramedic unit there just for Tracey. She was going to need medical attention right away. He rifled around the front of the van looking inside the glove compartment and then inside a small storage box underneath the passenger seat. In it he found a set of keys. He went through about a half dozen of them before finding one that fit the locks that secured Tracey to the wall. *POP!* And free. Tracey rubbed her wrists. They were sore from the shackles, almost like bed sores. The first police officer wrapped her in a blanket, readying her for removal from the camper. As he and his partner walked to the front of the camper, they began to hear the outside noise slowly getting louder. They stopped and looked around to assess things before bringing Tracey out into the madness. A virtual squadron of noisy news helicopters hovered overhead, while local media pressed against a police line on the sidewalk in front of Tasty Tom's. An ambulance was situated about fifteen feet from the camper, doors open, empty. An EMT crew stood by with a stretcher.

The patrolman shouted at them as loud as he could over the ruckus, "Put that back inside. I'll bring her to you!"

He wanted to minimize the amount of time Tracey would be visible to the reporters on the street and overhead. He wanted to secure as much dignity for this young girl as he possibly could. Having her walk to a gurney to be strapped down and rolled to the ambulance would take too much time. The scene most surely would be broadcast live on local news and possibly even national news. The EMT crew nodded and placed the stretcher back inside the ambulance. He looked about again and called for several patrolmen to clear a path for him to the ambulance to guarantee he would not have to bump or dodge anyone along the way. Like sentries, they formed two lines blocking the street reporters' view of the scene. The patrolman turned around to face Tracey who had been patiently and bravely waiting for him in the rear of the camper, bundled up in a blanket.

"You ready, Honey?" he asked.

She nodded, "Uh huh."

"K, let's go!"

He reached for her with two strong arms and picked her up. She held her face close to his chest as he carried her off in a hurry past the lines of policemen that seemed like a blue blur. Into the ambulance. The only thing visible to the helicopters above was a policeman carrying a bundle wrapped in an olive drab Army blanket. At one end was the back of Tracey's head with nothing but strands of blond hair visible. Her face was completely hidden. At the other end were a few toes of her right foot that dangled out of the wrapping.

Three police cars moved forward from the lot to J Avenue. The road had long-since been closed once the scene unfolded there. They each pulled into position, stopping side-by-side on the three lane road, lights flashing almost in unison. Next came the ambulance with Tracey, with three more patrol cars behind. Her Unit 24 rescuer stayed by her side. She insisted on it. He held her hand as the ambulance jostled upon entering the highway, its rear tires cutting the corner a bit too close and coming off the curb hard. She squeezed his hand--ever so tightly, afraid that if she let go she would find her rescue was only a dream. In a movement executed with the precision of a

Presidential motorcade, Tracey's ambulance and six car police escort rushed her to a local hospital.

Back at the restaurant the chaos continued. "Okay, big guy, up we go!" two policemen said, lifting Smith up.

His 350 pound frame was almost too much for the two patrolmen. Once on his feet, they walked him to the door. There was no rush with him, no need to worry about his dignity. No respect. Once in the parking lot they stopped. The senior patrolman from Unit 19 reached over to the back of Smith's head. He grabbed a handful of his hair and yanked back, forcing him to look up at a news helicopter hovering over them.

He whispered in his ear, "Smile, let the world see your sick face!"

Rubber-gloved investigators were inside the camper combing through everything and collecting all manner of hairs, fibers, latent prints, blood spatter, and rags stained with a host of bodily fluids from the two suspects and all their victims. There was tattoo making equipment and photographs of each victim. They were part of a nationwide pedophile ring that traded kids, and the evidence from this day would result in over thirty-five more arrests in the weeks ahead, and the rescue of a dozen more children.

"Nice job, Pat!" Colonel Helmsley said, beaming a proud smile to him in the rearview mirror.

"Great work, Patrick!" Vicky added.

His face was red in embarrassment over the rush of compliments. He really hated the fussing.

"Whew! I'm glad this is over. I really agonized about Tracey. It's remarkable to me how exactly I saw these people in my images. I mean even the fat guy down to the clothes he was wearing when he entered the food place! Kinda freaks me out a bit."

He didn't notice while he spoke that Vicky had secretly pulled her cell phone from her purse and dialed Ratner's phone. As soon as it indicated her call was connected, she hung up. They understood the signal. Their job there was done. Vicky's henchmen slowly pulled out of the park onto J Avenue and into the only lane police had re-opened to traffic, then south and away from the chaos.

"We need to get the van back to Oklahoma City. Back to Tinker," Colonel Helmsley said.

"Right. Let's head out now. We've got a long drive," Vicky added.

Pat thought a moment. "Hey! Wait. I have to attend Father Reynolds's funeral tomorrow. I'll never make it if we drive all day back to OKC. Can you just leave me here, and I'll catch a cab to Dallas and fly out this afternoon?"

They all nodded. Colonel Helmsley popped open the rear door latch with a press of a button. He jumped out of the van to come around and assist Pat.

"Here you go, Buddy!" he said as he yanked Pat's carry-on bag from the back.

Pat sensed there was something on the colonel's mind. Something he needed to tell him. Colonel Helmsley slammed the rear door shut with a thud, sealing all outside noise from those inside. He grabbed Pat and gave him a tight hug.

"Remember what I told you when you first came to see me about your dreams?"

He almost whispered his question out.

"Yes, Sir. You told me to watch my six."

"Right. Keep that in mind! You never know who you can trust" he said releasing Pat from his bear hug.

Pat nodded at the colonel, then slung the carry-on garment bag over his shoulder. He was relieved to be done with this latest adventure. And exhausted. He gave a slight wave of his hand as the van pulled away. He smiled, and as he did, Vicky gave him a wink. And then she blew him a secret kiss.

~ **24** ~

During their long, quiet ride back to Oklahoma City, Colonel Helmsley brought up the looming interagency meeting. "I mentioned it to Pat earlier, but didn't give him any details. I'll call him Sunday night and let him know."

He was testing Vicky. He was convinced she'd protest. Insist on calling Pat herself to maintain control of all aspects of the SAP. But surprisingly, she didn't.

"That's fine, John. You know the meeting will be at FBI headquarters, right?"

"Yup--and Woody, we want you there too, the whole team. It's gonna be a full house. This is Pat's introduction to the entire team of focal point system officers," Colonel Helmsley added. "And we'd like you to give a pitch--maybe ten minutes or so--on Pat's abilities."

"Can do easy. It would be my pleasure!" Woody replied with a yawn. He was fast asleep within minutes.

By sheer luck, Pat managed to get the last seat on an American Airlines flight that night from Dallas/Fort Worth International Airport to Dulles. Like his flight into Oklahoma City, it happened to be a first-class cabin seat, the comfort of which enabled him to sleep the entire flight home.

While he was en route, agents Ratner and Kennedy, who had arrived two hours before him, were busy in the surveillance van processing the digital recordings. It was an easy and automatic process. Kennedy's big stubby fingers worked the controls, sending digital input into a computer processor that scanned the ones and zeroes for key words and phrases. They had two hits in no time at all. First was the telephone conversation between Pat and Sara when he arrived in Oklahoma City. Then the call between Pat and Detective Sanchez. It was clear the Fairfax County PD now saw Father Reynolds's death as a homicide, and they wanted to talk with Pat more about it.

"Oh man!" Kennedy exclaimed as they both listened in. "Vicky's gonna be ticked about this. What do you think she'll want us to do?"

"I'm almost afraid to find out. Remember how upset she was with us after we accidentally killed the old priest."

"Well, I guess we'll have to be ready for anything the queen wants."

"You realize there's a lot of loose ends right now. I mean, not just the detective. There's the coroner, the autopsy report, the toxicology results," Ratner noted with a slight smile, as if he enjoyed the prospect of committing more crimes.

"Yup. It's gonna be tough to clean this up," Kennedy agreed, nodding.

"But it has to be done," Ratner smirked sarcastically.

Pat stepped out of the taxi that took him home from Dulles. He stood for a moment in front of his brick colonial home; two piles of leaves greeted him on the front lawn. He smiled, surmising his kids had been playing out front instead of properly raking the leaves and bagging them. He had called Sara from his cell phone during the taxi ride, so she was awake and excited to see him when he walked in the door.

"Hi, Baby!" she said, greeting him with a warm smile and a hug.

He held her tight. Then he kissed her face gently. "Love you, Baby. And let me say it is GREAT to be home!" he said, his voice getting a bit loud for a moment.

"Ssssshhh!" Sara cautioned, finger pressed against her lips. "I just got the rugrats to sleep."

Pat took her by the hand. "C'mon, walk with me while I give each angel a kiss goodnight," he said in a whisper.

They crept into Erin's room. She was sleeping soundly, facing the window. Pat leaned down to kiss her cheek. She stirred, moving her head 180 degrees to face him, but her eyes never opened. Strands of auburn hair clung to her face; lines from her pillow pressed into her warm, sleep-damp skin. He smiled at Sara.

"She's a deep sleeper!" he whispered.

Ratner and Kennedy watched in real time inside the van as Pat and Sara moved from room to room. Watched and listened.

"Good night Erin," Ratner whispered out loud, blowing a soft kiss at the screen at the precise moment Pat kissed her.

"Okay, you know what, you're creeping me out, man!" Kennedy growled giving his partner a strange look. "You know Hank, I think all those years you spent in the Innocent Images program warped your mind. Maybe you started to like looking at thousands of pictures of kiddy porn from those cases."

Ratner laughed, trying to dismiss him, "Lighten up, just having fun, okay? Chill out!"

Pat and Sara next slid into Sean's room. Pat gave him a goodnight kiss. He stirred more than Erin, opening his eyes briefly.

"Hi, Daddy," he said in a drowsy mumble. But he was fast asleep again in seconds.

Pat and Sara retired to the bedroom where he unpacked his carry-on bag, tossing rolled-up, dirty clothes into a large wicker hamper, and got ready for bed.

"Pat, there's something you need to know before the funeral tomorrow." Her voice had a serious, almost ominous tone.

"What is it, Baby?"

His mind raced. *Surely she wasn't aware of the CIA thugs or any of the things Detective Sanchez told me on the telephone?*

"Here, read this," she said, sliding the local section of the Washington Observer across the bed to him.

He stared at the headline. It sent chills down his spine. *Local Catholic Priest Dies Suspicious Death.* He read the article to himself quietly. The story related how the Fairfax County PD Homicide Division was expanding its investigation into Father Reynolds's death because of suspicious circumstances. The police weren't ready to rule it a natural death. The article was sparse on details, but the implications were inescapable. If the CIA had killed him, then it now was aware the police did not buy the natural death scenario.

"What's going on, Pat? Is that what that detective needed to call you about the other day?"

"Yes. He told me basically the same thing as you see in the paper. That Father Reynolds's death was suspicious. Since Rachel told them I had visited with Father the day he died, they wanted to talk with me about anything I may have seen that was out of the ordinary."

"And? Were you able to help?"

"I don't think I was much help at all. I mean, all I could tell them was that he seemed fine when I saw him earlier that day."

Sara's eyes welled up. "Pat, all this stuff lately has me so scared. Ever since these dreams 'started, you've been surrounded by death. The kids that were kidnapped, now Father Reynolds. And there's one more thing."

"What is it, Sorcha?"

"You need to have another talk with Sean about taunting Erin. He keeps getting a rise out of her about this evil man in a disguise thing. You know, the one who wants to kidnap the princess."

Pat shook his head as he turned off the nightstand light.

"That boy is trouble sometimes! Okay, I'll have a little one-on-one bonding time with him tomorrow."

~ 25 ~

Nearly fifteen hundred mourners showed up for Father Reynolds's viewing and funeral, swelling the pews to standing-room-only capacity. His open coffin was displayed in front of the altar where he served at Our Lady of La Salette, surrounded by dozens and dozens of flower arrangements. The O'Donnell family arrived early, all dressed in dark clothing. Sara and Erin had nearly matching black dresses with black lace veils. Pat had on a dark blue suit, while Sean wore a blue blazer, gray slacks, and red clip-on tie. His little boy white shirt was a bit too large, giving lots of open space around the collar, and it wrinkled fiercely as he fidgeted about in the pew.

Pat took some time, just a moment or two, to view his old friend once more. He stood in the long, slow procession of friends, family, and parishioners who had come to pay their last respects. He approached the coffin and gently touched Father Reynolds's cold right hand in which the priest clutched a dark brown wooden Rosary. The crucifix was well worn, Christ's features smoothed over from countless years of being handled by him. It was a gift from Father Reynolds's parents, given to him the day he was ordained a Roman Catholic priest many, many years before. Father Reynolds never parted with it, and now not even death could seize it from him.

"Good-bye old friend," Pat whispered as he released his touch of the priest's hand.

He turned to the left and approached the altar next to the coffin. He knelt down and prayed. *Jesus, give me the strength to do what is right to ensure those who killed Father Reynolds receive justice.*

He stood and headed back down the center aisle to join his family.

Off to his left, he saw Detective Sanchez kneeling in a pew. Hands clasped in prayer, Sanchez opened his eyes for a moment, as if knowing Pat was approaching. He made eye contact and smiled.

The Archbishop led the mass. He was a tall, thin man in his sixties, his pure white hair giving him a look of wisdom and experience. But Pat could not help but think that despite his appearance, he was most likely younger than Father Reynolds. Before the bishop began, he walked among the assembled devotees waving his censer to fill the church with sweet-smelling incense, then he retrieved holy water and once again walked through all the aisles, this time sprinkling everyone with it. A small spray hit Pat in the face while his eyes were closed. It sent shudders through his entire body as he felt a surge of power, no doubt from the Holy Ghost, enter and join with his own spirit.

The Archbishop delivered a fitting eulogy that outlined the tremendous service Father Reynolds performed for God in tending to His church. A Rosary was said. Pat loved the Rosary. He was devoted to Christ's mother, the Virgin Mary, and the Rosary was a perfect dedication to her. The O'Donnell kids hated the length of time it took to pray the Rosary; however, and they oftentimes squirmed in the pew while it was being said. But Pat had a way of tuning the distractions out. And although he had always felt a special sense of connectivity with the Blessed Virgin, it was incredibly intense during the Rosary, as if all sound and sight were erased for fifteen minutes while he communed with the Mother of God. And today, when Mary spoke to his heart, she told him to ensure justice was served, that she would be with him every step of the way so that he would not stumble or fail in his journey.

When the mass was over, the O'Donnells joined the long line of vehicles that quickly formed to escort the hearse to the cemetery. In the center of it all, in their minivan, lights on like all the others, they waited for the pall bearers to bring the coffin out. Two police motorcycles led the way with a patrol car in the rear to keep line crashers from disrupting the procession. It was a slow journey to the cemetery on the other side of Burke. Although it was just two miles from the chapel, it took twenty minutes or so to arrive. The Archbishop rode along in the hearse with Father Reynolds's body and was the first to get out at the gravesite. The pall bearers and cemetery workers handled the casket. Delicately, and with great reverence, they hoisted it up on the rig that later would lower it into the ground. The assembly gathered slowly once they all found places to park nearby the burial site. About half the original church service crowd showed up.

The Archbishop spoke, "Let us all bow our heads and say the Lord's Prayer. In the name of the Father, and of the Son, and of the Holy Spirit, Amen."

The gathering droned out the prayer while holding hands to form one unified body. Many mourners broke into tears as the casket was lowered into the cold earth following the prayer. The Archbishop picked up a shovel and ceremoniously scooped up a clump of cold, brown dirt and tossed it into the deep hole. It made a loud *THUD!* Then it scattered as the moist clump broke apart upon hitting the hard wood coffin. The Archbishop looked around, as if seeking volunteers. Pat's eyes lit up, and the Bishop nodded at him. He handed Pat the shovel.

"Thank you, Father," Pat said.

He scooped up some dirt and tossed it in, then turned and handed the shovel to another man waiting in a line that suddenly began to form on its own.

Pat stepped away from his family and off to the side of the large crowd where he saw Detective Sanchez standing.

"Morning, O'Donnell," Sanchez said shaking his hand.

"Hi, Detective Sanchez. Wish we could stop meeting under these circumstances."

"Me, too. Can you come by my office Monday morning? I have a few questions to ask you about this death. Say around nine o'clock?"

Pat thought for a moment. He didn't know of any plans to meet the team on Monday, so he agreed.

"Okay, that should be fine--where's your office located?"

Detective Sanchez pulled a business card from his leather police credentials case.

"Here. All the info is on the card."

"Great. Listen, do you know any more about the drugs found in his body? What was that stuff called again?"

"Crap, I can't pronounce it. It was some kind of hypnotic agent, according to the medical examiner. But it's what he told me after we talked on the phone the other night that I found very interesting," Sanchez said with a coy smile. "He did some research and found that the specific combination of these types of drugs was first put together by the CIA during the Vietnam War."

As he spoke, Pat could tell the detective was studying his face, searching for any indication at all that he knew something about this. He did his best to maintain a blank stare.

"What did the CIA use it for?" Pat asked.

"Well, the ME said he thought it was used during interrogations of captured Vietcong. To make them a little bit more pliable, so to speak. A little more willing to say what the CIA wanted to hear."

Pat thought about the connection to the Agency, and it all seemed to fit.

"Why would someone use some kind of vintage CIA drug on Father Reynolds?" Pat asked.

"That's what I'm hoping you can help me with on Monday."

Just then Sara and the O'Donnell children walked up from behind the men. The pair had gotten lost in their conversation and failed to notice the mourners had begun to disassemble.

"Well, there you are!" Sara said.

Sean and Erin flooded in around their dad, clinging to an arm and a pant leg. "Hi, Baby. This is Detective Sanchez. He called the house the other day. Detective, this is my wife, Sara."

She extended her hand for him to shake.

"Good morning, Mrs. O'Donnell!"

"Nice to meet you," Sara returned. "And this is the O'Donnell gang!"

One at a time, the kids introduced themselves politely.

"Well, listen, I've taken up enough of your time. It was nice meeting you all. And Pat, see you Monday!" he reminded him before he departed.

Pat hugged Sara then whispered in her ear, "Listen, why don't you go on ahead with Erin. I want to chat with Sean for a few minutes."

Sara eagerly agreed. She knew this was an important and necessary chat.

Pat grabbed Sean's hand. "Come on, Buddy. Let's have a talk."

The little boy's eyes widened in fear. He knew one-on-ones with his father were rarely opportunities for praise.

"What is it, Daddy? Am I in trouble?" he asked innocently.

"Hmmmm, well, sort of. Why do you keep telling Erin that some bad man in a disguise is going to kidnap a princess? You know that scares her."

"Because it's true, Daddy!" Sean stammered.

"What are you talking about?" Pat asked. He grew alarmed at Sean's sudden insistence this was real.

"I saw the bad man, Daddy!"

"What? Where?" Pat belted out turning his head from side to side, looking around the cemetery thinking Sean may have spotted one of the thugs who had been following him lately.

"In my head. I made it up."

Now Pat was confused. "What do you mean you saw him in your head, but you made it up?"

"I dunno, I guess I didn't really see anyone. I guess I just imagined it."

"Sean, look this is serious stuff. Did you or did you not see a bad man someplace?"

"No, I really didn't see one. I guess it was just my imagination. Hey look! A red bird on that rock!" he exclaimed suddenly, pointing to a headstone nearby upon which a cardinal had just landed.

"That little bird better find his friends and head south before it gets much colder!" Pat said with a chuckle. He realized he probably milked all he could out of Sean.

"Listen.   Keep your imagination to yourself--especially bad imaginations. I don't want to hear anymore about you teasing Erin. If I do, then it's no more video games for a week. Okay?"

"Okay, Dad, I won't tease her anymore."

"Shake?"

"Shake!" Sean said with a smile as he gave his dad's hand a firm squeeze. He continued holding it as they walked to the van together.

Neither of them noticed the florist delivery van parked at the far end of the cemetery.   FBI agents Ratner and Kennedy, under instruction from Vicky, surveilled Pat to the funeral. A long-range microphone had picked up his entire conversation with Detective Sanchez.

"This doesn't look good," Ratner said.

"Nope, and I don't think Vicky's gonna want Pat talking with Sanchez on Monday.

Isn't that when they're supposed to have that big meeting anyway?" Kennedy asked.

"Yup. It will buy us some time anyway. Not much, but maybe just enough," Ratner said with a smile.

When the O'Donnells arrived home, the answering machine light was flashing. It was a message from Colonel Helmsley asking Pat to call him. He reached him on his cell phone.

"Hey, Boss. I got your message."

"Hello, Pat, good to hear your voice. Glad you had a safe trip back home."

"Yes, Sir. Thanks. We were out at Father Reynolds's funeral this morning."

"Sorry again about your loss. I'm happy you were able to be there for him."

"Thanks. So what's up?"

"Well, I don't want to say much here, but you need to be at the Bureau headquarters at nine-thirty on Monday, third floor conference room. You have a building pass, don't you?"

"Yes, I do. No need for an escort. I'll see you then."

"Great. Take care!" he said hanging up.

Pat was so pre-occupied with his sadness over Father Reynolds's death and recent events that he failed to realize the schedule conflict he now had on his hands for Monday morning. There was no way he would be able to make both his appointment to speak with Detective Sanchez and his meeting at FBI headquarters.

Ratner and Kennedy smiled at each other later that day when they reviewed the recording of Pat's conversation with Colonel Helmsley.

"This is perfect. O'Donnell won't be able to make both appointments. You know he'll go for the Bureau meeting first—he'll call Sanchez to reschedule," Kennedy snickered.

"Couldn't be more perfect," Ratner agreed. "Gives us a window to take care of things."

~ 26 ~

Monday morning came quickly, and Pat needed to get ready for his meeting at FBI headquarters. He changed into a conservative dark blue pin-striped business suit and carried his Beretta in the OSI standard-issue leather belt holster, instead of his heavy bulging fanny pack. It was nearly 0830 when he bolted from the house to his sedan, security passes in hand. He carried a slew of them on a lanyard around his neck. One for the Pentagon. One for the Defense Intelligence Agency Center at Bolling Air Force Base. One for HQ OSI. One for the CIA in Langley, Virginia. And one for the FBI in downtown DC.

He planned to drive to the Springfield-Franconia Metro Station and take the Blue Line into the District, then walk the block or two to HQ FBI. He encountered virtually no traffic getting to the Metro station along the parkway near his home. But parking was a different matter. He circled and slinked through the maze of parking levels until he found one slot far from the escalator. He rushed to catch a train just as it was getting ready to depart the station. It was 0925 when he emerged from the Metro station in the District. Looking at his watch suddenly reminded him he had missed his appointment with Detective Sanchez. He pulled his cell phone from his jacket pocket and fumbled with the buttons. It rang three times before Pat heard the voice mail prompt.

"Detective Sanchez, this is Pat O'Donnell. Listen, I'm real sorry to have missed the appointment this morning, but I got pulled away to a meeting in DC. I'll call you later to reschedule at your convenience. Bye."

Pat practically ran as he spoke reaching HQ FBI at precisely 0930. He approached the security screener and flashed his gold OSI badge, along with his FBI building pass. The guard let him through quickly. The door to room A317 was closed when he arrived. There was a sign affixed to a standing, shiny chrome metal display that read, *Quiet Please, Conference in Session.* Pat slowly turned the door handle, just in case it was the kind that would make a loud, creaky noise. He figured there probably was someone standing in the front of the room talking, so he did not want to make a scene with his arrival. As he opened the door, he heard a familiar voice. It was Vicky. She was addressing the group, apparently giving some kind of opening remarks. Pat really was not sure what the meeting was about, but he had his suspicions. He believed this was at least going to be an introduction to some of the other focal point system officers in the CRYSTAL ROUNDUP program.

"And here is the star of our show now, everyone," he heard Vicky say as he slid into the room.

More than fifteen pairs of eyes riveted upon him. But he was shocked to see one pair he did not anticipate being there. In addition to Vicky, Colonel Helmsley, and Woody, was Major General Robert D. Swank, the Air Force Director of Intelligence. Pat's eyes widened seeing him, and a gut wrenching fear clutched him tightly. General Swank smirked at Pat, a look suggesting he was completely dumbfounded that Major O'Donnell could be at the center of such a secret program.

"Come up here, Patrick," Vicky said waving for him to come fully into the room. "Everyone, this is Major Patrick O'Donnell, our CRYSTAL ROUNDUP operative."

He looked around the room. Everyone was smiling at him. The air was charged as if electrical. He quickly realized he was there in celebrity status. This was his *coming out party* for the community at large. He had no idea that word about him in the black, Special Access Program world had spread like wildfire. He had achieved legendary status at the speed of heat. Pat nodded and smiled, trying to regain some composure for himself as he stepped forward next to Vicky. She was beaming from ear to ear with palpable excitement. She grabbed his hand and held it for a moment to calm him...and herself.

"Well, um hello. I take it this isn't the Foundation for a Better Internet meeting? I think I came to the wrong building!" he said joking with the crowd, playing upon the FBI acronym.

Everyone broke out into a roar. Pat looked at the gathering of people he had never seen before, all seated at a long, dark cherry conference table. Placards in front of each read like a can of alphabet soup. CIA. NSA. DIA. NRO. And so on. The focal point officers all looked senior. Older men and women. They were the gray beards of their agencies entrusted with the most secret SAPs in government. A voice came from the front of the table. A skinny, salt-and-pepper-haired man in his late fifties, sitting by the CIA placard, interrupted the laughter.

"Young man, I just want to say that on behalf of the DCI, a grateful nation thanks you for your service, and we look forward to any help you can give the Agency on any matter what-so-ever."

"Thank you, Sir," Pat said, embarrassed by the high praise.

He drilled a stare into the slightly wrinkled old man as he thanked him, wondering if he could pick up any clues about the two thugs who had killed Father Reynolds. It was hard for Pat not to pounce on him and demand answers. But the slate was blank.

Vicky asked them all to introduce themselves, typical of government conferences or meetings. But atypically, Pat decided to walk around the table and shake everyone's hand as they introduced themselves. He was hoping the physical touch would help him connect to any images he could assemble about Father Reynolds. But it was fruitless. Frustratingly, nothing at all flowed forth.

"Let me give you a formal briefing on the status of CRYSTAL

ROUNDUP to date and Patrick's wonderful work in the program. Patrick, please take a seat up front here. Feel free to add anything or answer questions as we go along," Vicky said.

She darkened the room and fired up a projector, then opened a formal presentation bearing a classified banner which read, TOP SECRET CRYSTAL ROUNDUP LEVEL Three. She expertly brought everyone up to speed on the entire program from the moment Pat first approached Colonel Helmsley, to Tracey Adams's rescue in Plano, Texas five days back. She covered every minute detail, pausing only once to ask Woody to discuss his findings from the Richmond Center. There was stunned silence as they listened to Dr. Davis's description of Pat's abilities as one in a hundred trillion or more. Then there was an awkward pause. Then robust applause. Pat's jaw dropped as he witnessed the entire room stand up--actually delivering him a standing ovation. General Swank rolled his eyes and begrudgingly stood up, slowly clapping his hands but twice.

Just then the commotion was broken by a loud knocking at the door...the persistent kind that suggested the knocker had been there for some time trying vainly to get someone in the noisy room to open the door. Vicky motioned for them to settle down as she scurried over. Everyone took their seats. She opened it but a crack, not wanting the intruder to see the *who's who* of the CRYSTAL ROUNDUP community. A visibly perturbed young rookie FBI agent stood there in his starched white shirt and conservative business suit. He handed Vicky a note.

"Oh, my!" she exclaimed as she read the note to herself. There was still a murmur of voices in the room. "Everyone, listen please. I've just been informed the FBI Director and the Attorney General will be here in..." She looked at her watch. "In two minutes!"

The room grew silent as everyone waited. Vicky motioned for Colonel Helmsley and Woody to come forward and stand with her and Pat when the gentlemen entered the room. Then, in a sudden gush of motion, the door flew open exactly two minutes later and in walked the FBI Director and the Attorney General.   Pat's eyes widened when they walked right up to him, as if they instantly recognized him.   He also noticed Vicky awkwardly strained for recognition and moved to intercept them so she could make the introductions.

"General Coppock, Director Markovitz, I'd like to--" she began but was cut off, ignored by the men.   She shrunk back a little from the sting of embarrassment.

"You must be Major O'Donnell," the Attorney General said extending his hand to Pat.   "I'm Ryan Coppock," he continued, giving Pat's hand a firm, almost painful squeeze.

"Nice to meet you, Sir," Pat replied with a slight wince.

Attorney General Coppock turned to the FBI Director.   "And I'm sure you've seen this chap on television a lot lately.   This is Director Markovitz."

The FBI Director shook Pat's hand as well.   "Rich Markovitz, nice to finally meet you Pat."

Vicky clumsily inserted herself back into the fray once more.

"General Coppock, I'd like to introduce you to the rest of our small team."

She started to introduce the men to Colonel Helmsley and Woody. But as soon as the Attorney General saw Colonel Helmsley, he shook his hand firmly and gave him a hug, the kind old friends share when they haven't seen each other in a long time.

"John, how are you?" the Attorney General asked with a big smile.

"I'm fine, Sir, just lending support to this new series of operations," Colonel Helmsley replied, causing Vicky to all but shrink away.

It was very apparent to everyone in the room that Colonel Helmsley and the Attorney General had history together.   Good history.

"We'll need to catch up on things soon. Give me a call John; my cell number is on this card."

The AG handed the colonel a business card before he turned to the rest of the room and motioned with both hands for them to sit. He stood at the center of the room with Pat on his left and Director Markovitz to his right. Then he addressed them.

"Ladies and gentlemen, I came over to visit with Director Markovitz today to get a tour of the new National Security Division where the FBI is running the search for al Qaeda cells in the U.S. When I learned this meeting was taking place, I just had to come meet Pat O'Donnell and his team."

Pat glanced over at Vicky, sensing she was growing angry. He tried to read her thoughts and managed to capture but a flash of them. It was enough! Vicky was furious because she received barely an ounce of the ton of recognition she craved, the recognition she felt entitled to receive. *HIS team?* she thought. The slight seared her. Her scorched thoughts reached Pat's psychic brain and singed it in the process. General Coppock put his arm around Pat's shoulder, pulling him back from his mind reading moment.

"Pat I want you to know that the President has been fully briefed on your work, and he is eternally grateful for your service. When I informed him of your recent efforts in Tulsa and Plano, his exact words were, 'That's incredible. This young man is a national treasure!'"

Pat turned red from the top of his forehead to well below his visible neckline. The attention and heaps of praise were terribly hard for him to process at that moment. He fumbled for words.

"Thanks, really. I, I just don't know what to say. I mean all this is very flattering. I'm just grateful I can help in some small way to solve some of these crimes."

The Attorney General chuckled slightly. "Well Pat, you've proven yourself to be very capable in solving these major crimes; perhaps it's time to broaden your worldview a little bit. I'm sure these fine folks in the room have some ideas of their own for how you can contribute to other projects."

Pat was confused. He turned to the Attorney General and was about to ask what he meant by this, when the FBI Director tapped his watch in a subtle reminder to General Coppock that they had a schedule to get back on track with.

The AG took the cue saying, "Well, we have to run along and make our next round. Pat, once again, thank you for your service. We look forward to bigger and better things down the road."

Once more the Attorney General and the FBI Director gave him vigorous handshakes, then rushed to exit the room. Vicky was right behind them like a puppy dog.

"Nice work, Veronica!" the FBI Director said as they turned, then briskly walked down the hall. And out of sight.

"It's VICKY! My name is VICKY, you ass!" she muttered to herself.

When she walked back in the room, she suggested a ten minute break. Pat grabbed her by the arm and motioned for Colonel Helmsley and Woody to come over for a huddle.

"Some nice kudos there, Pat!" Colonel Helmsley beamed.

"Okay guys, what's going on here? What bigger and better things does the AG have in mind for me?" He was steamed at being blindsided.

"Er, that's kinda what this meeting is about today, Pat," Colonel Helmsley said with some hesitation. "Look, remember your initial indoc into the program? When we told you this was a joint black world program between the Justice and Defense Departments?"

"Yes," Pat replied cautiously.

"Well so far you've just been focused on the justice side, finding missing children. We want to expand your scope a bit to some DoD interests."

"Like what? You know, to tell the truth, I kinda like finding children. I feel almost a sense of mission and purpose in this." He turned to Dr. Davis. "Woody, remember when we talked about your theory at the Richmond Center you told me that finding children through this psi stuff was all related to what interests me? Right?"

Woody nodded. "Pat's right. I'm not saying he can't do other things; it just may be more difficult unless his level of interest or focus is as intense as it is for saving lost children."

"What other kinds of things do you have in mind for me, specifically?"

Colonel Helmsley stared at him for a moment, then swallowed hard before speaking.

"We want you to find bin Laden. It's national security priority number one right now," he said with stone-cold seriousness.

"Christ! You want me to go from finding innocent children, victims of crimes, to finding this cave-dwelling, rock-eating, terrorist?"

"Precisely," Vicky said.

Just then the room began to fill back up with the focal point officers once again.

"I need a break," Pat said roughly as he trudged out of the room to wander the halls and collect his thoughts.

Internally, he hated the new proposition. It was not that he thought bin Laden was unworthy of his skills in hunting for him. It was that he feared abysmal failure in his pursuit. He had just begun to get up to speed in finding children--his certain, almost spiritual mission, what he believed was finally the one supreme truism revealed to him. But he also knew the political ramifications if he refused to try. *How could anyone at this moment in America's history fail to support the war on terror? Especially a federal agent sworn to protect the nation?* His thoughts raced. He knew he had to at least make an effort. He found a fountain and took a long drink of icy cold refreshing water.

When he returned, all eyes were upon him. It was as if Vicky had briefed them that he was hesitant to help out. He hoped she hadn't done that. He didn't need his loyalties to be called into question.

"Let's roll!" he announced to the crowd. "Where do we start?"

"Great, Patrick!" Vicky said with a smile. "First things first, we need to devise a CRYSTAL ROUNDUP Level Three plan as for cover of your activities." She turned to the room, "Do you all have notional plans to support this op?" she asked.

They all nodded enthusiastically, but Pat wasn't completely convinced it would be seamless.

"Who's in charge of all this? I mean, surely there needs to be a coordinating mechanism so that my information doesn't get duplicated into ten different reports by ten different agencies?"

"I'm going to be lead on that, Pat," Colonel Helmsley said.

It was clear when he spoke that this hadn't been worked out yet, but Colonel Helmsley's leadership in taking charge made Pat feel very comfortable.

"Glad to hear that, Boss."

The group met for the next few hours, hammering out the finer details of the coordination mechanism for the new operation. Pat sat through it all. After all, he had the most equity at stake. Indeed, the most risk to take. He and Colonel Helmsley ensured they crafted and carved the operation into a plan they both were comfortable with. But there was one vexing problem that seemed insurmountable no matter how they looked at it--Pat would have to travel to the theater to make it work. Woody and Pat were both convinced, based upon his success in the Tattoo Killer operation, that Pat needed to be physically close to UBL in order to find him.

About halfway through the afternoon, Vicky's cell phone rang. When she looked at the green glow on the display, she saw it was a call from Hank Ratner.

"Excuse me, folks. I have to take this call," she said as she left the room. "Yes, what is it?" she asked as she answered the call in the hallway.

"We need to go secure," Ratner said. "I'll punch from here."

"Listen, it's done," he said once they were sure their call was encrypted. "The detective has agreed not to pursue the investigation any further," Ratner informed her, talking around the subject even though they were having the discussion on a secure line.

He wanted Vicky to know he had taken care of the problem of Detective Sanchez in a very special way this time, a way Vicky would understand without having to hear the precise details.

"My, you are so persuasive!" Vicky said teasing him. "Good work Hank, and keep in mind, we may need to persuade others. This thing has the potential to become a runaway freight train."

"Roger that. Out here."

Vicky knew what he really meant. This time there was no use of drugs, no attempt to fabricate memories for Detective Sanchez. Sanchez received the ultimate persuasion. At the same moment they spoke, the detective's body was sprawled out on the floor of his apartment. A pool of rich, red blood had soaked into the carpet around his head. His service revolver rested nearby. The gunshot residue on his hand would later confirm the theory--suicide. Blood was spattered on the wall next to his sofa along with chunks of skull and brain matter. It all would be forensically analyzed and proven to have come from the proper direction and the proper angle to have been the result of a self-inflicted gunshot. There would be no doubt that Detective Sanchez sat on his sofa, distraught over mounting financial problems, and placed the barrel of his revolver against his head. And pulled the trigger. Bills and past due notices of many kind scattered on his coffee table would wrap the suicide theory up nicely. A single shot, then his lifeless body slumped forward, head striking the table on the way down to the carpet. Everyone would believe the suicide theory. Everyone that is, except for Pat.

~ **27** ~

When Vicky returned to the room, the group had finished the operational plan. Pat back-briefed her in detail, in particular on the need for him to go in-theater to increase the chance of success.

"Okay. How easily can we get airlift support, and where exactly shall we go out there?" Vicky asked.

"Airlift is not a problem--I'll just call my buddy at the Andrews wing. We probably have to set up operation at the U.S. Embassy in Pakistan. Afghanistan is too hot right now with the ongoing airstrikes," Colonel Helmsley said.

Vicky pursed her lips in thought. "All right, but keep in mind, the Ambassador is not cleared for CR. Our State Department focal point officer will have to devise a cover story for Pat. Maybe say he's a CIA officer. I'll let you work with State on that."

Pat smiled when she made the comment, finding it rather amusing. It wasn't exactly like Vicky had any say in what happened on the DoD side of things, but it apparently made her feel good thinking she was calling the shots.

"Don't worry, Vicky, we're big boys--I'll take care of all the coordination," the colonel said, affirming his central role in the hunt for bin Laden.

They all rode the elevator together to the lobby of the FBI building, where, one at a time for operational security purposes, they departed the building and went in different directions. Pat made a beeline for the Metro station. It was almost 1600 hours, and he knew if he played his cards right, he'd be home in time for dinner. He was about halfway down the steep escalator, when his cell phone rang. He looked at the display. *No Data Sent.*

"Patrick, it's Vicky. Something urgent has come up. Please meet us tonight at *Al's Garage*, say around six?"

"Yeah, okay. I guess you'll fill me in later rather than sooner?" he asked, already knowing the answer.

"Ha! Ha! Nice try. And yes, it will all be clear when you arrive."

He was puzzled that something popped up so suddenly and urgently, considering their meeting ended less than fifteen minutes earlier. He called home, but Sara was out with the kids picking up some groceries, so he left a message on their answering machine to have dinner without him.

Since there were no train stops anywhere near *Al's Garage*, he knew the only way he would make it to the Arlington safe house was to Metro back to his car and drive. And he had precious little time to do it. He reached the Springfield-Franconia station right at 1715 and drove like a maniac on the crowded parkway to try to get to Arlington as quickly as he could. Fortunately, at this time of day, he was headed away from most of the rush-hour traffic. He turned onto the dark street of the safe house, dusk having settled into night during the drive there. He attempted to park in the garage, but as the door crept slowly upward, he saw Vicky's BMW already parked in it. *So much for her insistence on OPSEC!* He slowed to a stop and parked in the street a couple of doors down.

He headed up the short curving walkway made of red and brown bricks to the front porch. When he stepped inside a fragrance hit him. It was a potpourri smell of wildflowers. He didn't see anyone, but he heard soft music coming from another room. He headed in that direction, calling out, "Hello? Anyone here? It's me, Pat."

"In here Patrick, in the dining room," came Vicky's voice.

He made his way there, and when he saw her, he stopped dead in his tracks. Vicky stood next to the dining room table in a tight black dinner dress. It was cut low to her breasts, ample cleavage greeting him. Spaghetti straps barely hung it on her shoulders. Her hair was down, bundles of blond curls no longer restrained as he had seen so many times in the past. Her lips were dark red and shiny with gloss, and her perfume gently wafted over to him. Her blue eyes sparkled as she smiled at him. And this time, it was no dream.

"Surprise, Patrick!" she said with wide-eyed excitement, stepping forward to within inches of him.

"Ah, where's the others?" he asked nervously, looking around the place.

"Relax, just us tonight, Patrick. I felt you deserved a little time off. A little treat," she said. "Look, everything's catered."

She pointed to the trays of gourmet French foods she apparently had delivered to the safe house. Fine china was laid on the table in two elegant place settings.

"Look, Vicky, I really appreciate all this, but I don't think this looks right. I mean, people might talk about--"

"Ssshhhh, don't worry about what others think," she said pressing her fingers to his lips. "Besides, this is a safe house, and no one will know who we are or why we're here."

She stood close to him. Her sexual energy was unmistakable, filling every one of Pat's senses. His synesthesia mixed and blended them together into an almost hypnotic sensation.

"Let's toast to our success in the past and certain success in the future," she said as she pulled a chilled bottle of 1999 Dom Perignon from a silver ice cooler and poured two crystal flutes.

Pat awkwardly took a sip. The champagne was indeed wonderful. Vicky walked over to the table and struck a match. She lit two tapered candles set on elegant silver holders. Pat thought about his situation. He didn't want to offend her, but the food smelled wonderfully good. The champagne was superb, after all. Vicky's seduction was powerful. He began to rationalize. He was determined that if he stayed, it would be just for dinner, small talk, and then out of there as fast as he could. No monkey business.

"Vicky, you really shouldn't have done all this. I mean, I've been flattered to the point today that I don't think I can take any more attention!" he stammered.

"I know, and you deserved it all. And you deserve this. Now come on, take a seat, and let me serve up this food."

"Okay, but I can't stay long tonight. I've spent so much time away from home my wife is going to put my face on a milk carton one of these days!"

Vicky laughed at his joke. "That's fine Patrick. Let's enjoy this wonderful food while it's still hot. Then maybe we can chat a little before you have to leave. Deal?"

"Okay. Deal," he said, reluctantly.

He sat down and watched Vicky move from covered tray to covered tray, deftly putting together a seven course meal of French foods, the names of which he couldn't even pronounce. They laughed and chatted away throughout the meal, finishing first the bottle of Dom Perignon, and then a vintage 1966 Bordeaux from the A. de Luze & Fils St. Julien vineyard in France.

"It's from the year you were born, Patrick," she said as she poured his glass and then caressed his hand as she set the bottle down.

Time slipped by on them as they became relaxed in their dinner and conversation together. They talked about their lives growing up in opposite ends of the country. School and college. Politics and romance. They occasionally flirted with each other. Subtle compliments. Soft smiles. Warm stares. They both pushed dangerously close to that hidden precipice that Pat only had dreamt about once before. Following dessert and coffee, Vicky stood up to put on more music. They had become so lost in talking and flirting, they both failed to notice all three CDs in the changer had played through.

"Vicky, I really should be heading home now. Let me help clean up, and I'll get out of here."

"Oh, don't worry about the clean up. Wait. Please. Just five more minutes. I want you to hear this next song."

The soft sounds of a saxophone came from the stereo, playing a slow, sexy jazz tune. Vicky kicked off her heels.

"Get over here, major! Just one dance, and I'll let you go."

He cautiously stepped forward. "Okay, just one, but then I *really* need to leave."

She slipped one arm around his waist, the other over his shoulder. He put both hands on her hips, intentionally trying to keep some space between them. Vicky would have none of that. She pulled him in close and tight as they began to move to the rhythm of the soft jazz, resting her head on his chest for a moment. Holding her was powerful and mesmerizing for Pat. He closed his eyes and thought about his lustful dream of her. When he opened them, she was staring at him, her mouth open and no more than a half inch from his. She leaned upward until their lips met. Vicky closed her eyes and kissed Pat's mouth, then slid her tongue inside. He was lost in the moment, seized in the grip of lust just like in his dream. He kissed her back, two hot and ravenous mouths and tongues probing one another.

They paused for a moment. Then Vicky smiled at him and began to lick his face and neck. She was like an untamed cat, wild and aroused. And she was driving Pat insane with excitement. Suddenly, in what seemed like one single fluid motion to him, she stepped back, slid the spaghetti straps off both shoulders, unzipped her dress from behind, and let it fall to the floor. His jaw dropped when he saw her nearly nude in front of him. No bra, just bare, firm breasts which she seemed eager to display, arching her back slightly. And the only stitch of clothing that remained was a pair of black lace thong panties.

"You know we both want this, Patrick," she said almost breathlessly.

She walked up to him again and began kissing his mouth. He felt her warm skin. She was on fire and ready. It was too dangerous. Too convenient. Yet, somehow, through the intense passion of the moment, through the lust and secret carnal desire he harbored for Vicky ever since meeting her, Pat O'Donnell managed to regain his conscience. He pushed her away.

"No! Vicky, stop! This isn't right. I can't. We can't. Oh, forget it. I have to leave," he said grabbing his jacket from the coat rack.

"No, Patrick, don't go. I need you now!" she was practically pleading with him as he threw it on.

"Look, Vicky, I like you. I really do. But I love my wife. I love my family. And nothing can come between us."

She managed to slip her dress back on clumsily as Pat headed out the front door. He walked briskly to his car while she stood on the front porch holding her dress against her breasts with one hand.

She called out to him, "Patrick, please. Come back. I'm sorry. We need to talk about this."

Pat didn't respond as he hit the car's remote unlock button on his key fob. All the interior lights came on when he did, casting an eerie glow in the dark suburban street. His wheels spun wildly as he floored the accelerator, kicking up dust and dirt and a puff of tire smoke as he sped off into the darkness.

~ 28 ~

"You're home late," Sara whispered when Pat slid under the cool, silk sheets next to her. "What was so important that kept you out so long?"

He closed his eyes before answering her. He was a bit drunk from his share of champagne and fine French red wine. He also was tremendously guilt-ridden about having flirted with Vicky.

"Oh, Baby. You know I can't talk about my work. I'm getting a little stressed by it all I guess." He tried to sound convincing, but it didn't seem Sara was buying it.

Although he kept his eyes closed, it was as if his eyelids were, at best, translucent. He could almost see her studying his face in the dim glow of the nightlight. He felt her move closer to him, his shameful heart pounding rapidly in fear. He knew he should embrace her...that's what she wanted, after all. When he didn't respond she put her arm over his chest and snuggled up to kiss him. It was too late. Pat knew deep down all the evidence from his infidelity crime scene was now exposed. Vicky's scent lingered. Sara could smell the subtle fragrance of her perfume; she even knew the exact brand from its distinct signature. She also could smell the wine on his breath.

"Tell me where you've really been tonight! Tell me who you've been with!" she demanded as her Irish ire grew.

She sat up abruptly in the bed; her face was so bright red it almost seemed to glow in the darkness when he opened his eyes.

"I really can't say. It was business," he insisted.

"Bullshit!" she stammered with tears forming in her eyes. "Tell me the truth! You've been with some woman! What the hell is going on?"

She began to beat on his chest with both fists, until he grabbed her wrists to stop her.

"Sorcha. I'll tell you what I can, but you must never let on that you know this, okay?"

"Go on," she said sternly, her face red and angry, still trying to flail her arms held tight in Pat's firm grip.

"One of the FBI agents on the team, Vicky Desantis, told me to--"

"*VICKY* Desantis? You mean *Agent* Desantis, as you always used to say, is a *woman*? Why did you leave out *that* important fact all these weeks?" Sara demanded cutting him off.

He didn't have a good answer. It really had been unintentional if not perhaps a subconscious avoidance.

"I, I guess I never realized I hadn't used her first name. Really. Nothing secret here."

Sara gritted her teeth and sneered loudly, showing her obvious disgust with him.

"So this Vicky told you to do what tonight?"

"She told me to meet her at a safe house. I thought it was going to be the whole team. But it turned out she was there alone. She had this whole big gourmet meal thing. I didn't want to stay, but she insisted, and I felt obligated since she went all out and everything."

"Hold on mister! What kind of nonsense is this? Some woman prepares a fancy meal for just the two of you and you just *have* to stay so you won't hurt her feelings? Pat, don't you know how this looks? I mean, first you sneak off from your mom's house to see your old flame, Amanda, now this?"

"I know, I know. It was stupid. I never should have stayed."

"So tell me Romeo, how did her perfume get on you? How much booze did she ply you with?"

Pat rubbed his tired eyes. He couldn't tell her the whole truth. She'd be furious to know he kissed Vicky's mouth hotly and held her nearly nude body in his arms.

"I got ready to leave after dinner, and she grabbed me, tried to dance with me. Look. She was drunk. She got a little carried away. But nothing happened, okay? Nothing!"

Sara pulled her arm away and lay on her back, staring at the ceiling. She clenched both fists. Tears welled in her eyes.

"I pushed her away, Sara. I told her that I love you and our children, and that nothing could come between us. Then I got the hell out of there as fast as I could!"

"Are you telling me the truth, Pat?"

"Yes, Baby. I'm embarrassed I got tricked into going there. I'm ashamed I was so stupid that I stayed once I arrived. But I'm proud because I resisted her, and that in the end my love for you overcame everything. And that's the truth!"

She turned to face him once more, searching for the truth, knowing Pat had no poker-face ability. He stared at her with saucer-wide eyes, and then bit his lower lip waiting for a sign that she believed him. Although he sensed that deep down Sara believed him, she was not about to let him off the hook so easily. She was still angry that he let himself get into this situation in the first place. She frowned, shook her head, and rolled over and went to sleep without saying another word.

Pat slept in the next morning. When he finally awoke, he shuffled into the kitchen in his long red, white, and blue sleep pants. Yawning. Stretching. He flipped on the small counter-top TV as he prepared some breakfast. He thought that if he didn't have any CRYSTAL ROUNDUP business to tend to, he might just head in to his Pentagon office to see Colonel Lyons and catch up on whatever needed tending.

He tuned to a local station hoping for morning traffic news. Commercials. He sat down at the kitchen table just as the local news began. The anchor, a pretty young Latina woman, spoke.

"Here are the top stories we're covering today. In the metro area, we're following the apparent suicide of a veteran Fairfax County homicide detective. Also, the latest fall fashions--glimmer, or dimmer?"

Pat was jolted in his chair. He held his face in both hands, hoping the story about the detective was not going to be about the only homicide detective he knew--Sanchez. The anchor continued.

"Fairfax County police are investigating the death of one of their own. Detective Richard Sanchez, a twenty-two year veteran of the department, was found dead yesterday afternoon in his apartment in Fairfax City. He died of a single gunshot wound to the head. According to a Fairfax County Police Department spokesperson, Sanchez may have been having severe financial problems following a divorce last year. No foul play is suspected, and the police are treating it as an apparent suicide."

Pat's heart sank. First Father Reynolds, and now the detective investigating the priest's murder was dead. *There's no way he killed himself!* Things were spinning way out of control. He sat and thought long and hard about the implications. One thing was clear--Pat was at the center of everything. Ever since discovering his psychic abilities and confiding in Father Reynolds, he had been surrounded by murder. Then suddenly something else hit him. *If they planted a transmitter in Father Reynolds's office, maybe they have my house wired, too!* The more he thought about the possibility, the more convinced he became he was right. After all, since he was indeed the center of all the intrigue, it seemed likely he would be the target of an electronic surveillance. Pat knew enough about the wiretapping world to know that unless the eavesdroppers had line-of-sight clearance for a microwave receiver, then they had to be in the local area with either UHF or VHF equipment. He doubted a microwave system would work in his neighborhood of densely-packed old tall trees that obscured any real possibility of an unobstructed link. That meant there was either a safe house conveniently located in Pat's neighborhood, or there was a technical services vehicle parked nearby with radio wave reception. The latter option seemed the most likely.

Not certain if he was being covered at the moment by video surveillance, he decided he would go about his business of getting around as normal. He would not tell Sara or the kids about his suspicions, lest they begin to act strangely and burn the surveillance. He knew the CIA thugs meant business. They had already murdered two people, and he didn't want his family to be next.

He went to the Pentagon in casual clothes this day, no uniform so he could carry his handgun in his trusty fanny pack. But he took a different route to work this time. Instead of the bus, he opted to drive his car so he could make a sweep through the neighborhoods around his home...concentric circles that started out small, then extended outward gradually until he had covered about one mile in radius. It took him nearly one hour to complete, and when he was done, he had recorded the license plates and description of every potential technical services vehicle...everything from minivans with curtains or dark windows to delivery vehicles and utility company trucks. There were nine in all when he was finished.

But there was one in particular that would later prove to be the key to unlock all the mystery. Squirreled away in a pest control van were Ratner and Kennedy. Safely tucked away behind a thick door that formed an inner compartment within the van, they weren't visible to passersby. Nor were they actively watching what was going on outside their van. So when Pat drove by, they never saw him. They had no idea that he had outfoxed them, and only time remained between this moment and when Pat would discover the truth.

When he arrived at the Pentagon, his boss rushed up to him.

"Patrick my boy! Come on in, let's have a chat!" The colonel pulled him into his office and shut the door. "So tell me, waddya been up to?"

Pat grinned and shook his head. "Boss, you just never would believe me if I told you. I can only say that Colonel Helmsley works in a pretty freaky world."

"Yes, he does. You know, he's kept me informed at an unclassified level. Tells me you are doing wonderful things, and that the President is personally aware of the name of Major Patrick O'Donnell!"

"So I'm told," Pat said somewhat embarrassed. "Boss, how are things going here? I feel so guilty about abandoning the office. Is there anything I can do today to catch up?"

"The gang has everything under control. So not to worry. And whatever you're doing, I'm awfully proud of you!"

Pat headed to his cubicle with his day planner in hand, the one he used to make notes about the suspicious vehicles he saw in and around his neighborhood that morning. He grabbed the STU III phone and hit the speed dial button for his old friend at Headquarters OSI--Lee Cook, the Director of Counterintelligence.

"Lee? This is Pat O'Donnell. How are you?"

"Hey Pat, it's been a long time. Where are you? Word has it you are deep undercover someplace ferreting out the Mafia or something," Lee teased.

"Might as well be, the way things have gotten crazy for me lately. Listen, I need a big favor from you, but we need to go secure," Pat said as he initiated the link. "Got you TOP SECRET at this end," Pat said once it was established. "Listen, Lee. Do you still have that contact at the FBI who does backstopping for undercover ops--you know, the guy that arranges for all the cover vehicles and state registrations?"

"Yeah--I talk with him a lot. You know he helps OSI from time to time with cover vehicles."

"Great. Here's what I need, and it has to be discreet. I've got nine vehicle descriptions to run through him. I think one or even more of them are CIA cover vehicles. Can he check them out and let you know if there are any hits?"

"He probably can. I don't know if he supports the Agency like he does us, but I bet his contacts at the state registration offices can tell him whether CIA has registered the vehicles through a cut out or some other arrangement," Lee said with confidence.

"I owe you one. I mean big time. This is real important and very close-hold, okay?"

Pat gave Agent Cook a verbal rundown of each vehicle, five with Virginia registrations, three with Maryland registrations, and one from the District.

"Got it. Now, keep in mind this can take a few days since my friend will probably have to go out to each state office and the District independently, okay?"

"That's fine--sooner is better, but I'll be happy knowing it was done whenever the results are ready."

After they hung up, Pat flew out his door and raced to Colonel Helmsley's office. The timing was perfect as the colonel stepped from around a corridor corner just as he arrived. Pat almost ran right into him but stopped quickly, huffing a bit, outside the heavy steel vault door.

"Jesus! What's going on, Pat? This must be serious!"

"Yes, Sir. We really need to talk. Can we go into your secure confines?"

The colonel rushed Pat in to the same conference room where his journey began three weeks before. Pat laid all his cards on the table. He told Colonel Helmsley about Detective Sanchez and his most certain murder-dubbed-suicide. About Vicky's attempt at seducing him. About his suspicions of his home phone being bugged. About having Lee Cook run the vehicle checks for him.

Colonel Helmsley's mouth was wide open as Pat spoke. He was clearly shocked and worried by it all. He pulled the gold wire frame glasses from his face and ran a hand over his eyes.

"Pat, I don't understand why the CIA would want to kill your friend and now this detective. That old guy from the Agency who was at our meeting yesterday. He didn't seem like he had a hidden agenda or anything. Maybe he's pissed I took control of all SAP coordination?"

"I don't think so. I tried scanning the guy's head when I shook his hand. Nothing."

"Hmmm. I don't get it. And Vicky's behavior is disturbing. I had a feeling..." he started to say. "Oh, never mind."

"What? Don't leave me hanging!"

"Well, I just knew that if we ever got the CRYSTAL ROUNDUP program fully operational like we have it now, that someone in the community would come along and try to destroy it. Our bureaucracy is a quagmire. Too many agencies. Too much overlap. And sometimes we put more energy into protecting our operations than we do into producing something meaningful from them!"

Pat nodded. "Everyone seemed to be getting along and cooperating yesterday. I mean, correct me if I'm wrong, but I felt a whole lot of love in that room! But seriously, where do we go from here?"

"Well, here's how I want to approach things. At home, go on with life as normal. In the meantime, let's see what Lee comes back with. I'm afraid we may have to approach the Attorney General with this information. If there's a couple of renegade CIA agents running around killing people, we need to stop them cold!"

"And what about CRYSTAL ROUNDUP? Should we press on with the UBL operation?"

The colonel nodded. "Yes, but with a twist. I'll ask Vicky to stay behind and run things from DC while you and Woody and I get on a plane."

"Think she'll go for that?"

"Actually, I think she will. I'll argue that since this is primarily a DoD operation, we'll surge forward and let her coordinate any Justice leads back here. She'll cherish the face time with the Director and the AG."

The colonel handed Pat a fax he received from the 89th MAW at Andrews.

"It's our manifest. We fly out to Pakistan Thursday morning. You're the first to know."

Pat studied the documents and noticed something puzzling. "Sir, Vicky's not on the manifest. You were planning to leave her off the trip all along, weren't you?"

The colonel chuckled and smiled. "Let's just say my own intuition suggested you probably needed a break from Vicky. There's something about the chemistry between you two that told me it would be prudent to keep her off this trip."

Pat broke the news of the trip to Sara Wednesday afternoon. Although he did not tell her he was going to Pakistan, it was clear he was leaving the country when she saw him packing his black diplomatic passport in his fanny pack along with his Beretta. She was not happy in the least, so he did his best to stay out of her way throughout the afternoon.

It was Halloween, and when his children came home from school they were eager for him to take them out trick-or-treating. Sean was dressed up as a mummy, clumsily wrapped in white papier-mâché material from head to toe, his eyes peering out through two slits.

"Hi, Daddy!" he mumbled in a muffled tone, the costume distorting his voice.

Erin had on a lengthy, multi-pastel colored gown and a long, pointed hat with lace that flowed downward to her back from the point. She was a princess. They insisted on a quick dinner, so as not to lose precious trick-or-treating time. Pat took them door-to-door throughout the many streets in his subdivision. For nearly two hours, they went about collecting all manner of candy and other treats until their bags were heavy and their little feet could take no more. It was nearing 2000 hours when Pat called it quits to get home. Sara had a strange look on her face when he walked inside carrying Erin in his arms, tired and ready for bed.

"Colonel Helmsley called tonight. He wanted to talk to me about your recent trips and late hours. He told me you are supporting some kind of sensitive project, and he appreciates my understanding and support to you."

"I'm glad he called. I know the long hours have been bothering you a lot," Pat said setting Erin back on her feet. He walked up to Sara and gave her a hug.

"Pat, I'm sorry if I've been stressing so much lately. It was good to hear John's voice again, reassuring me."

"I'm glad, Honey. And again, I'm sorry about the other night and Vicky and the whole thing. Like I said, she is not going on this next trip with me and the colonel. I think I need some time away from her!"

She kissed him softly on the lips and then hugged him tightly.

"I love you, Patrick Sean O'Donnell," was all she said.

Ratner and Kennedy were holed up in *Al's Garage* that night. Although not perfect for operational security reasons, Vicky allowed them to stay there knowing there was little chance Pat would come by because of Halloween time with his children and his preparation for the upcoming trip to Pakistan.

The two men sat in the living room drinking beer and eating a pizza as they watched television, relaxing with feet up on the coffee table, newspapers strewn about. Ratner's head rested comfortably back in the soft leather recliner. He had begun to get drowsy, his eyes fighting to stay open when Kennedy spoke.

"Hank, you think Vicky will let us have a few days off since O'Donnell is going to Pakistan tomorrow?"

"Huh? I think so. She mentioned something to me about completely pausing the surveillance at their home for a few days more since Pat would be gone."

"Cool. We need the break."

~ 29 ~

Colonel Helmsley's buddy--the "Wing King" at the 89th Military Airlift Wing at Andrews Air Force Base arranged for a C-20 to ferry the three men to Pakistan. The jet was a military version of the Gulfstream III. It was sleek, quiet, and comfortable. Its blue and white exterior made it look like Air Force One's little brother. Getting country clearances was murder for the State Department focal point officer, but he pulled it off after a late night telephone call from the Secretary of State to the Ambassador in Pakistan finally opened the door. There would be one refueling stop along the way, but it would entail only limited time on the ground en route. Still, it would take almost twenty-two hours to arrive in country once they departed.

The early morning takeoff was so smooth and subtle they hardly realized they were airborne. The flight attendant was a young Air Force airman with one stripe. *Skeeter wings*, as they were called. His crisp, blue service dress uniform was barren except for one single ribbon--an Air force Training Ribbon of blue, red, and yellow. He was nervous and overly respectful as he addressed the three of them. He brought them all coffee and a hot breakfast meal once they were up to cruising altitude. Otherwise, the crew left them alone in the luxurious first-class equivalent cabin except to occasionally check to see if they needed anything.

After breakfast and chatting a bit, they settled in to watch an in-flight movie. Pat found himself drifting off to sleep as the jet's hypnotic motion lulled him along. His synesthesia took control as if on autopilot. Images and senses of sweet, fruity tastes filled his mouth, toast smell in his nostrils. Sticky-sweet fingers held a cold glass of orange juice. It was Sean sitting at the breakfast table hurrying to finish up so Sara could take him to school. His half-eaten bowl of cereal in front of him, he watched as his mom jumped when the toast popped out of the toaster, startling her. Sean giggled. Pat smiled inside. He found his remote viewing gift amazing, enabling him to see his family in their home, to check up on their welfare and safety. It wasn't a complete scene for him. There were times when it seemed like the events he witnessed in his mind were incomplete. Choppy. Like a badly edited film.

Next he saw Sara backing out of the driveway in their minivan with both kids safely strapped in and headed to school. And for a brief moment, Pat found himself inside Sean's head. Through his young boy's eyes he witnessed the world around him like a child. It was a fascinating flashback to feelings and perceptions of his own youth, long ago faded. He marveled at how a single, curved branch on the front yard cherry tree looked amazingly like a large scimitar. Pat and Sean's thoughts converged and flashed a scene of derring-do...Lawrence of Arabia sword fighting with Turkish warriors. Swashbuckling and exciting.

Being able to see Sean's world gave Pat a warmth and bond with his son on a level he never could have imagined. As the minivan cruised along, Sean's peripheral vision picked up another image. Not of swashbuckling heroes. But a car. A sedan with a lone occupant. A man in a dark blue jogging suit with a winter ski cap pulled low over his brow, sunglasses and a scarf. *So overly disguised as to be obvious,* Pat thought, *and so much like the CIA thugs in Springfield Park a few weeks back!*

The man seemed to be watching the O'Donnell's minivan as he pulled away from the curb to follow them. Sean turned around to watch, then saw the sedan turn in the other direction at the next intersection and disappear. And in Sean's mind Pat heard the words he had found so troubling for several weeks, *Why won't anyone believe me when I tell them about the evil man in the disguise?*

Pat let out a loud gasp as he was riveted back from this vision. Woody and the colonel gave him a curious look, allowing him to catch his breath and composure.

"Please tell me you've already found UBL!" Woody asked, visibly excited.

Pat shook his head and rubbed his eyes. "No, but I'm worried about Sara and the kids. I had a vision I was watching them in real-time going to school."

They marveled at his description of sharing thoughts with his son. But there was this darker side to Pat's vision that was not lost on any of them.

"Boss, I guess I'm concerned about those two agency guys. I think they may be targeting my family now, you know, like Father Reynolds!"

The colonel nodded, his face clearly showing his anger over the threat to his protégé's family.

"Save my seat! I'll be right back," he growled as he briskly headed to the front of the plane.

"Do you think he's going to have them turn the plane around?" Woody asked.

"I don't know, in a way I hope so, but I also want to get this UBL thing over with."

The colonel was gone about five minutes, and when he returned he had a reassuring smile.

"Guys, I spoke with Vicky, and she's going to get some agents to do countersurveillance in the neighborhood. She said they'll keep an eye on the family for you while we're gone."

"Thanks," Pat replied with a look of genuine relief. He let out a long sigh and leaned back in his chair. He was all right for now, but still intensely worried.

Vicky was on her way to work when the colonel reached her via cell phone. She immediately called the FBI's Washington Field Office Special Agent in Charge, Jack Hannerty. They had worked together in San Francisco back when Vicky was a rookie. Hannerty always had a bit of a crush on her, and he was one of only a few agents from her earlier days who hadn't shunned her over the *Gas Bandits* fiasco.

"Good morning, Jack," she cooed when he picked up, knowing he was still somewhat smitten with her, and as such, she could get him to do anything for her.

"Hey, Vicky—good morning! What can I do for you?"

"I need a favor. I have an asset who is out of the country right now who has reason to believe his family is in danger. Can you spring a couple of agents to do some CS work in northern Virginia for the next three or four days?"

She knew she was asking for a huge favor. The FBI's CS teams in the Washington, DC area were overworked ever since 9/11, and to top it off she was asking for support over an entire weekend.

"Well, I might. Exactly what can you tell me?" he asked, somewhat intrigued that Vicky would invite him to support a black world operation into which he rarely had any insight.

"I'll have someone in my office bring his file over to you when we hang up. The asset seems to think his family is being followed to school and when the wife is out running errands."

"Okay. You just want us to pulse the neighborhood and see if we can detect surveillance?"

"Right. And if you detect any, make a stop and detain anyone suspicious. Just for today, tomorrow, and the weekend. Daytime hours only; the family rarely goes out at night. If there's nothing there, there's nothing there, and they can plan to break off Monday morning if nothing's going on" she responded as she slowed to a stop at a red light.

"All right. Our Russian team has a few agents off rotation right now. I'll get them to work this."

"Great, and thanks a million, Jack. I owe you one!"

Next she dialed Ratner at the safe house.

"I told you the other day to cease your tech coverage at O'Donnell's house--you did that, right?" she asked harshly, her tone suggesting they had once again let her down.

"Sure did. It's not been turned back on at all," Ratner assured her.

"Good. Keep it that way! And stay away from his neighborhood altogether. O'Donnell thinks his family is being followed. I've got some WFO guys going over to do CS. I don't need you being burned," she ordered.

"Okay, but you know you can count on me and Kennedy if you need help," Ratner said, seemingly pleading with her.

"Forget it! You both have been overexposed lately. You need to lay low, let the WFO folks do their thing. Got it?"

"Okay, okay. Got it," Ratner said rolling his eyes at Kennedy as he hung up the phone. "The bitch says we need to stay put!" he stammered looking at him.

"Good thing you ran out for a long jog and to get the paper earlier this morning. Now we're stuck in here." Kennedy said, somewhat resigned.

"The hell we are. I'm getting tired of Her Majesty's garbage. You can stay here, but I'm not taking her orders anymore," Ratner said defiantly. He walked out of the room in a huff.

The two WFO agents arrived in Pat's neighborhood within two hours of Vicky's call to Agent Hannerty. They were a middle-aged man and woman, a *husband-and-wife* team as they were called in the Bureau. They were dependable, proven experts from the Russian squad with many years of Cold War experience tracking KGB, GRU and SVR agents throughout the Washington, DC area.

"Kiddy patrol! Look at us, checking up on some Air Force guy's wife and kids while he's out of town. I mean, what's that about?" the woman asked, clearly perturbed.

He shrugged his shoulders. "Beats me, but if it's important to our SAIC, I guess it's important to us. Some kind of favor for an old friend of his. Supposedly top priority within the Bureau."

"And we have to do this until Monday!"

Pat's family would be safe for the next four days. Whenever Sara left her home the WFO agents--her invisible angels--would be nearby, watching her drive to pick up the kids, then home to make supper. And again the next day, and the next, and the next, wherever the O'Donnells went.

~ 30 ~

After a short refueling stop at Aviano Air Base in Italy, the C-20 aircraft was back in the air and on its way to Islamabad. Colonel Helmsley took advantage of the ground time and called Vicky in the evening as promised. She assured him the WFO team was in place, and Pat's family was safe. Pat was thankful when he heard the news...incredibly grateful, actually. So grateful, that he managed to get a few hours of uninterrupted sleep on the final leg of their journey into theater.

When the jet finally landed in Pakistan, everyone on board was relieved to be getting off and able to walk around. The morning air was cold and reeked of bittersweet smoke from burning wood and trash piles in the surrounding, slummy neighborhoods. Intermixed with the nauseating smoke stench were the collective smells of jet fuel from the airport and decaying vegetables wafting over from an outdoor market nearby.

There were two embassy vehicles waiting for them and a contingent of Pakistani security personnel who, along with the Embassy staff, were curious about the new visitors. While the Air Force crewmembers helped jockey all the bags from the C-20 into an embassy minivan, the Pakistani security people, along with the Deputy Chief of Missions, approached. Apparently, the Ambassador sent his Deputy as a way of saying he felt snubbed by their mysterious visit. The short, middle-aged man walked crookedly with a cane toward them, wearing a brown corduroy sport coat, complete with worn leather elbow patches. He looked like a nerdy college professor with frumpy wild brown hair.

"Gentlemen, I'm Pete Simpson, the DCM. On behalf of the Ambassador, welcome to Pakistan," he said, extending his hand to Woody who he surmised was the senior member of the party given his abundance of gray hair.

"These gentlemen from Pakistan's Interior Ministry will perform customs and immigrations processing. Can we have your passports, please?"

While an immigrations officer was examining the passports and placing entry stamps inside them, another American emerged from the other embassy vehicle, a large black Mercedes sedan--the hard car the State Department focal point officer promised. He was a slight man, short, and nearly bald except for two tufts of strawberry blond hair above either ear. Practically albino, his pale skin seemed perpetually sun-burnt with dry peeling flakes on the top of his head. The DCM introduced him.

"This is Gary Olson. He's our Political Affairs Officer. You'll be using his office during your stay."

Pat knew immediately this was the CIA Station Chief, operating loosely under the cover of being a political affairs officer. Olson gave Pat's fanny pack a stare that suggested he knew what it contained and didn't like it. He wanted to control any agents coming into country with weapons and enforce the concealed weapons prohibition. Pat knew his type all too well. Sniveling, wimpy CIA bureaucrats in operational assignments for which they were ill-equipped. Socially retarded at best.

At that moment, one of the other Pakistani officers, a tall, thin, dark man in an awkwardly large tan uniform, walked around the open van and gave the bags a cursory glance.

"Are any of you carrying narcotics, explosives, or weapons of any kind?"

They all replied they were not. He walked up to Pat and pointed to his fanny pack.

"What is in there? May I look?"

Pat didn't miss a beat. "Sorry--it's a diplomatic pouch. Off limits."

Olson glared at him. Pat suspected Olson had tipped off the Pakistani official to scrutinize the trio for possible concealed weapons. Perhaps he had hoped to get the visitors quickly bounced from the country and off his turf. The Pakistani official pursed his lips and stared at Pat. Each was waiting for the other to blink first. The Pakistani slowly nodded his head.

"Okay, welcome to Pakistan!"

With that, the immigrations officer handed them the batch of processed passports. Pat, the colonel, and Woody entered the hard car. Although the Mercedes was large, it was cramped with five people inside. The DCM rode up front with the driver, while the guests rode in the back. Simpson turned his head to talk with them as they drove away from the airport.

"Look, I don't need to tell you guys that your presence here hasn't gone over real well with the Ambassador. So I hope you can wrap up whatever you're doing quickly and head home."

"No problem," Colonel Helmsley replied. "We hope to spend only a couple of days here. Trust me, we don't want to stay any longer in Pakistan than is necessary!" he said with a chuckle.

They headed out to the embassy compound and straight to their quarters. They were given a single, two-story villa with four spacious upstairs bedrooms. On the main level were a large living room and a dining room, and off to one side was a huge kitchen. The marble-floored villa interior was professionally decorated with expensive furnishings and window treatments. They took some time to freshen up and change clothes before the driver came back for them. He said he would give them two hours, and he was on time to the minute.

The drive to the Station Chief's office inside the compound took a mere five minutes during which the driver proceeded to give the men his life story. He was a native Pakistani, thin and dark-skinned like the immigrations official with a thick, black moustache and beard. He was born in one of the small villages just outside the city of Islamabad proper, and although he was thirty-one years old, Pat thought he looked about fifty-five. He felt a little sorry for him and the hard life he most likely endured, but at the same time, he suspected he was one of Olson's snitches, so his pity only went so far.

"We're here," the driver said as he approached the gate shack in the center of the compound.

Olson's office was within the same facility that housed the Ambassador's office, an ornate sand-colored three-story building with two large marble pillars in the front. Once past the guard, they snaked around a series of concrete Jersey barricades designed to stop a vehicle from rushing the gate at high speed. Olson was in place and greeted them when they stepped from the car, seemingly eager to pick up whatever clues he could about their identities, purpose, and mission. Pat didn't trust him at all. It was partly because he believed Olson snitched on him about his handgun at the airport. But it was mostly because Pat believed the CIA had killed Father Reynolds and Detective Sanchez, and now was after his family. Despite the effort that went into their cover for the mission, Pat didn't want to assume Olson was completely clueless about their real purpose for being there. If Olson had tipped off the CIA's Thugocracy about his trip outside the U.S., it could explain why his family was being followed while he was gone.

They finally reached Olson's office. It was larger than any of them expected. There was a huge solid oak desk near a back wall with matching bookshelves behind it. A large, colorful CIA shield was on the wall behind his desk, where apparently cover for his identity no longer was necessary.

"Did your headquarters pass along to you the list of intelligence products we need access to on a real-time basis?" the colonel asked him.

"Yes, I got the list. That's quite a tall order. The first batch is in the box on my desk. Do you really need all NSA intercepts and Agency HUMINT reports about Hamas, Hezbollah, al Qaeda, and the Egyptian Islamic Jihad?"

The team had intentionally added the other three terrorist groups to the list to mask their real target--al Qaeda. It would also mean Olson would be kept busy trying to assemble the reams of technical and Human Intelligence data that flowed constantly on all these groups, giving him less time to pry into their activities.

"Uh huh. We do. Oh, one more thing, Gary," Woody said. "We need a large, comfortable sofa and two easy chairs. We will need them right away."

Olson glared at him.   "Anything else?" he asked, his words dripping with sarcasm.

"Nope, that should do it for now. Thanks for all your help," Woody replied.

"Well, shall we get started?" the colonel asked as he opened the box on Olson's desk.

"Roger that, Boss," Pat said, eagerly grabbing a stack of reports and sitting down to read.

About an hour into the effort, there came a knock on the door. The colonel opened it and saw three Pakistani maintenance personnel in the hall with the furniture Woody had requested. Olson was with them. They positioned the furniture in the center of the office and quietly departed. Pat skimmed all the printed reports, about 300 pages total, glancing for key words or phrases that seemingly leapt off the page at him. He'd drill into them if they caught his eye, reading and absorbing the report in detail. It was nearly 1600 hours when he finished browsing the last document. Then it was time to lie back on the couch and attempt to pick up psychic images of UBL.

Pat drifted into a gentle, steady state of consciousness that came close to being asleep. With his eyes closed, he began to concentrate on UBL, allowing the myriad of intelligence information he had read to settle in and melt in his mind among all his senses. The colonel and Woody sat silently in the two easy chairs across from him. Waiting.

A torrent of images began to fill Pat's mind...images of confusion and fear, false bravado and despair. He was inside a cave complex with UBL and his closest cadre of al Qaeda and Taliban officials. Although they spoke in Arabic, Pat understood their thoughts in a way that didn't require spoken words or translations. Their leader, America's most-wanted terrorist, was urging them to fight on despite the overwhelming force America had unleashed upon them. In the name of Allah and Islam, he encouraged them. Like the coach of a pee-wee football team about to go on the field with the New England Patriots, he was doing his best to maintain their spirits. But the faithful were fearful. Cut off from reliable supplies of food and water, and forced to use inadequate communication systems, they felt trapped and cornered.

Pat's synesthesia was hard at work in the shadows of this vision. He was connecting his thoughts with sights and sounds, shapes and colors, textures and smells. He began relating what he saw to the colonel and Woody who meticulously took notes. Pat could hear the roar of a fighter jet overhead. It had a distinct sound. An F-16 probably. The colonel marked the time. It would be a clue, perhaps, or a dead end. The colonel brought Pat a map of Afghanistan and asked if there was some way he at least could draw impressions about the location of the cave. Pat kept his eyes closed and traced across the map with two fingers of his right hand. His movement slowed as he crossed over one section of the map. He continued, only once more to come back to the same area that seemed to capture his tactile attention.

"What is it?" the colonel asked.

"Well, it kinda feels warmer here to me for some reason. It's the only part of the map that is different from the rest. I don't know if it means this is where UBL is or not, just that it is different."

The colonel and Woody looked at the spot to which Pat had been drawn.   It was the Tora Bora mountain region of northeastern Afghanistan.   Some of the Signals Intelligence reporting they read contained intercepts of radio transmissions from that region, possibly by al Qaeda leadership, but so far there was nothing else to corroborate it.

"There's one more thing to all this," Pat added.   "I got the impression that UBL and his gang won't stay put once the shooting starts near their present location. There seemed to be some talk about moving on to Peshawar--here in Pakistan if things get too dicey for them."

They studied the regional map. Peshawar was not far from the Afghanistan border, near the Tora Bora mountains, so it seemed to make sense.

"It just seemed like a contingency plan. I got the sense they have loyalists in the Pakistan Army who may help them cross the border when the time comes," Pat added.

"Is there any way you think we can add a finer degree of resolution to what you've seen so far?" Woody asked.

"Not unless you can get me closer to Tora Bora," he said jokingly, opening his eyes with a few blinks.

The colonel and Woody looked at each other for a moment. Pat could sense they took his suggestion seriously.

"Well, what if we could? I mean, how about a flyover as close as we can get?" the colonel asked.

Pat nodded enthusiastically. "I'm game if you are, Boss!"

He loved the idea of teaming once again with Colonel Helmsley on a dangerous CT operation, like the good old days in Kuwait. The colonel smiled and told him he had to make several telephone calls and wake a few people up back in the United States. Pat watched while he telephoned Vicky and passed along the information about Tora Bora. Her job was simple. She would relay it to the NSA focal point officer for CRYSTAL ROUNDUP. The FPO would generate an intercept report of radio transmissions from al Qaeda leadership that emanated from Tora Bora, including talk about moving on to Peshawar in the event of a strike on their cave complex. This NSA report would slip into the mix of daily intelligence reporting from genuine intercepts and become grist in the analytical mill. The colonel also called his deputy and told him he needed to gin up a special mission to fly them into the hot zone--the area between Peshawar and Tora Bora. He needed top cover--it had to come from the SECDEF directly. And he needed it approved for the next day in Pakistan. A tall order, indeed.

"Well, we should see some movement in the morning on all this," the colonel said when he finished his last call.

The men stayed in Olson's office for the next three hours, continuing to read through reams of reports in an effort to further refine the impressions Pat received. But there was nothing more Pat seemed to be able to do with the intelligence information. It would simply just have to wait. It was late by the time they finally returned to the villa. They were tired and hungry and ready to eat whatever was in the refrigerator, and then rack out for the night. There was a message on the answering machine. Colonel Helmsley hit the play button. It was his deputy. He sounded tired.

"John, you really owe me big time for this! Everything's greased. Be at the airport tomorrow morning at eleven o'clock local. There will be an Army helicopter there to shuttle you to another point. Dress warm. The mountains are frigid this time of year. By the way-- SECDEF had to call your Ambassador whose hair was on fire over this one. Just thought you'd like to know."

"That's fantastic!" Woody exclaimed. "Maybe we can wrap this up by the weekend."

~ 31 ~

Pat had a peculiar and disturbing dream that night. He was walking to his children's school to pick them up at the end of the day, when he spotted a strange man off in the distance. He was in a dark blue running suit with sunglasses and a scarf that covered most of his face. When he saw Pat, the man began walking briskly in the direction of the school. An empty yellow bus clanked by, spewing diesel exhaust that seemed to conceal the man for a moment in a puff of black smoke.

"Hey you! I want to talk with you!" Pat called out as he hurried to catch up with him.

The man turned his head around briefly to look at Pat, then picked up his pace and began to jog toward the school. Pat was in pursuit, but his legs seemed like molasses. The harder he tried to run, the slower his pace became. The man ran to the school and became lost in the crowd of children. As he blended into the chaotic mass of school kids, he shrunk to a height to match theirs. Pat rounded the corner in time to see him reduce in size, but he lost him in the confusion. He looked around to the front of the school for Sara's minivan, but it wasn't there. *She should be here by now! She's always here in time to pick up both kids.*

With his heart pounding, Pat rushed in to the school to look for Sean. He was sure the strange man--the "evil man in the disguise," as Sean called him, was after his son. His classroom was empty. He ran back outside. Sean was standing by the flagpole in the center of the curved drive in front of the school entrance. He was rubbing his eyes. Pat rushed to him and dipped to one knee in a swift movement. He flung his arms around him, struggling with the backpack on his back.

"Sean! I'm so happy to see you! Are you all right?"

"Yes, Daddy," he said through small whimpers. "But where's Mommy? She's always s'posed to be right here after school."

But in that instant, before he could answer his son, Pat was ripped from the dream and transported back to the embassy villa in his comfortable bed. He got up and went to the bathroom. Through sleepy eyes, he glimpsed at the clock in the bedroom through the doorway. It was 0233. When he went back to bed, he said silent prayers asking God to protect his family while he was gone. He also had a profound sense of frustration in trying to pick up clues about the man in the disguise. He was sure it was one of the two CIA agents who had killed the priest and detective. But the more Pat tried to focus on the figure's face, the fuzzier the details became. There was something in the way--something actively working to block him from seeing what should be so clear in front of him. As he thought and prayed, he drifted off again in sleep.

———————

"Morning, Boss. Morning, Woody," Pat mumbled as he shuffled into the dining room at 0800.

"Pat, see what the Ambassador sent over for us?" Woody said, pointing to a large breakfast spread in the dining room. There was a variety of hot items like scrambled eggs, pancakes, and sausages, kept warm in their trays by Sterno can burning underneath.

"Wow! That's nice of him. Maybe he wants us to stay longer," Pat said coyly.

"Not bloody likely," Woody responded in a British accent. "I have a feeling he got his ass chewed--I suspect he objected to today's helicopter ride and called the President personally."

While Pat ate, he told them about his dream of the man from the night before. "The problem is that I want so hard to see this guy's face, but every time I try it seems like a lens that goes out of focus."

"I'll get in touch with Vicky here later on when it's a decent hour in DC. She said she had the WFO on your family, so I'm sure all is fine back home," Colonel Helmsley assured him.

The driver was there at precisely 0930 to take them to the airport where the Army helicopter was waiting. It was a fast ride from the villa to the airfield. Traffic was scant. A UH-60 Blackhawk was sitting at a far end of the ramp, guarded by three heavily-armed Army Special Forces members...two Rangers and a Green Beret. The driver slowed down cautiously as he approached, not sure of the protocol. A husky Airborne Ranger NCO in his red beret approached the vehicle, putting his hand out to signal the driver to stop. His desert camouflage shirt off, he wore just a tan undershirt and dog tags around his neck. He had two huge arms with tattoos, and at least a size 52 inch chest of pure muscle. There was no way anyone would dare mess around with this guy! The other Ranger aimed an enormous M-60 machine gun at the car while the Green Beret kept watch of the perimeter around the helicopter. The driver rolled down the window.

"May I see your passports, gentlemen?" the NCO asked with resolute seriousness.

He compared their names to the TOP SECRET manifest his unit received via a FLASH message from the Office of the Secretary of Defense the night before.

"Please roll down all the windows gentlemen."

Pat watched as the Ranger walked around the vehicle and one-by-one matched the faces with the names on the passports. Satisfied, he directed them to exit the vehicle. His tone and demeanor softened once he verified they were the right passengers for this mission.

"Follow me, Sirs. And watch your heads when approaching the chopper."

As they neared the helicopter, the pilot cranked up the engines. A thunderous boom echoed across the flight line as they fired up, startling Pat for a moment. They hopped inside, all three sitting side-by-side in a bench seat in the back.

"Here, put these on," the NCO shouted over the noise.

He handed them helmets and flak vests. They did as told, finding it difficult to secure the shoulder and waist harnesses over the bulky gear. As soon as they managed to get strapped in, they lifted off gently. The NCO helped them lower the microphones attached to each helmet. A long, coiled black wire connected each helmet's voice mechanism to the helicopter's audio system so they all could talk with each other and with the crew. Once airborne, the noise abated somewhat. The NCO told them they were going to rendezvous with another helicopter in eastern Afghanistan. From there they were to fly in a grid pattern over a predetermined route based upon orders from the Pentagon. It was the area between Tora Bora and Peshawar that Pat had clued in to.

"When we get to Afghanistan, the LZ is going to be hot. You all will need to hustle from this chopper to the next. Keep the gear on," he shouted into his microphone.

After what seemed like an hour, they arrived. As promised, another Blackhawk was waiting for them. Sitting nearby were three Apache attack helicopters with blades running. Pat thought that from the air it looked eerily like a scene from a Desert Storm war movie.

"Your escorts," he said to Pat as they touched down on a marked section of the desert about twenty five yards from the second UH-60.

The rotary blades kicked up so much dust and sand Pat couldn't see more than ten feet in front of him. They hustled from the first helicopter as directed, shielding their eyes from the blowing sand and making a fast break for the second chopper as the Ranger ran ahead of them frantically yelling, "Let's go! Let's go!" to keep them running.

Woody and the colonel made sure Pat sat by one of the two open doors, so he had as many visual cues available to him as possible. They were up and away within minutes in a very efficient transition between airframes. As they rose, Pat could see the Apache helicopters take up their positions...two behind and one ahead as the formation began flying the route for this special mission. No one said a word as they flew for several hours, crisscrossing the mountainous terrain, sometimes flying low, sometimes at several thousand feet. The pilot threaded through the dangerous airspace corridors and alleys the intelligence people at U.S. Central Command recommended, to help minimize potential surface-to-air missile threats. In contrast, and almost anti-climatic in its execution, the journey was seemingly uneventful. Pat stared out the window at the rugged snow-covered terrain, occasionally spotting cave openings or puffs of smoke as enemy militants tried firing whatever small arms they had at their disposal. With both right and left Blackhawk doors wide open, freezing cold air whipped through the helicopter as they bobbed and weaved up and down along the mountain line. But it was over a region on the eastern slope of a very high mountain range in eastern Afghanistan that Pat picked up a scent.

"Can you head over there?" he asked the Ranger who sat across from him, tapping on his knee.

He pointed to a crevice about midway up a mountain, about two miles ahead. It seemed to have a path or small road leading up to it. The NCO spoke into his microphone and guided the pilot to the point, then he relayed to the Apache escorts the plan to check out the area Pat wanted to see. While his helicopter hovered in place, Pat watched the Apaches swoop down low and fast at first toward the crevice. Then they came back around and flew even lower, and this time slower. The lead Apache fired its 30 mm chain gun in the area of the crevice to ward off any would-be attackers and soften the area for Pat and his fellow passengers to approach. Its massive gun was like a giant jackhammer pummeling the rocky slopes and crevices, spewing shards of rock, ice, and earth up and out in all directions. Within minutes they were over the spot, hovering at about five hundred feet. There was no cave opening visible anywhere near it, but the existence of the path was suspicious. It seemed to stop at a point that made no sense. There was no place to go but down the mountain from that point.

Pat closed his eyes and the images oozed into his brain slowly. Musty, stale odors emanated forward. Scents of people holed up in a dark cave. Crude air vents pierced the rock and provided small relief. One brought in fresh air, and the other exhausted the air that built up inside. Rickety, rusty blower motors affixed to each vent helped push and pull the air in the proper direction. A single light bulb hung from exposed copper wire in the center of the cave. It was prayer time. Several men were in position on their prayer mats. Kneeling. Praying to Allah. From within the cave, Pat could hear the muffled sound of their helicopters overhead. He knew the cave was very close by, and he now had no doubt the opening was at the end of the path he had seen.

When the prayer session ended, all the men formed a circle in the center underneath the light. A figure appeared from out of the darkness and took a seat on the bare floor amidst the others. They all nodded their heads, almost bowing as the man sat. In the dim light, Pat could make his face out rather well. It was Usama bin Laden. He smiled and spoke to the men, motioning with his hands in a circle as he looked upward. He was telling them not to be afraid of the helicopters because they were well-concealed and Allah would protect them. This brought comfort to the others who Pat could sense were fearful of an imminent American attack. The chain gun fire the Apache sprayed earlier sent the scouts outside scampering for cover and down into secret openings into the cave.

Pat mentally stared at UBL, seeking any clues he could uncover, any secrets he might reveal inside his head that he would never share with his followers. As Pat concentrated on his thoughts, bin Laden's face began to change. It morphed slowly. His beard disappeared. His turban was replaced by a ski cap. Pat watched in horror as UBL changed into the disguised man who had taunted Pat in his dreams the night before. The man tilted his head upward in this vision as if to stare directly at him in the helicopter. Beneath the sunglasses and the scarf, Pat could tell he was smiling at him. As he tried to shift his focus onto the man, to connect with his thoughts, he once again experienced the image getting fuzzy. As it faded out into ever worsening granularity, Pat was shaken from his psychic reverie into the reality of the here and now of the freezing cold helicopter.

"You okay, Sir?" the NCO asked.

At the moment he asked the question, the Blackhawk's air defense systems lit up; piercing wails from multiple sirens erupted startling the crew into immediate action. The pilot banked hard left, exposing the open side of the chopper to the ground just as a Stinger missile left the earth below them. It ripped through the helicopter, entering the open left side and exiting directly across on the right through the other open door. Pat would later swear he saw the rocket in slow motion as it passed through the Blackhawk cabin in front of them all, mere inches from their faces, a deafening roar and blazing white heat that blinded them for a moment. The pilot then jerked the chopper hard right and made a rapid vertical climb while the Apaches swooped down and fired their chain guns at the spot, exposing a hidden defensive position that, in short order, they obliterated. Chunks of metal and bloody body parts splattered the rocky terrain once they finished taking out a dozen Taliban militants.

The jerky defensive motions left them all with little to hold onto except each other, their shoulder harnesses thankfully keeping them from falling out. Once they were safely away from the immediate threat, Pat turned to the NCO and asked him if he had marked the location of the site they hovered over.

"Yes, Sir," he said handing Pat a note paper with GPS coordinates for the spot.

"Can you call Vicky right now?" he asked the colonel, passing him the note. "I think she needs this info along with what I related to you about last night. I just want some assurance the WFO is on the case back home. Just before the rocket attack I got another one of those danger signs about home."

The colonel nodded as he pulled his secure cell phone out. The connection was bad, and it was awkward trying to hold the phone under his helmet, but he got through to Vicky at work.

"Let me pass along some GPS coordinates for you to give to whichever focal point folks you deem the best to generate the community report--probably NSA. And Vicky--make sure the information is characterized as highly reliable. Pat's pretty sure of this, and it's real-time sensitive," the colonel screamed so she could hear over the helicopter noise.

Pat watched him intensely, hoping for a morsel of good news from home.

"Good--glad to hear that because he is very concerned," Colonel Helmsley said turning to look at Pat. "He's been picking up continuing hints of some kind of imminent danger to them. By the way, I'm not sure when we'll be back. If I can swing the flight tomorrow, we'll be back probably late Sunday your time. Bye for now!"

Colonel Helmsley grabbed Pat's shoulder and told him Vicky had things covered. He was cautiously reassured by that, but a nagging sense of imminent danger still loomed in his complex mind. It was just too simple to say all was well.

When Vicky hung up the phone she immediately dialed Ratner.

"Yes, Vicky. I know--we promise not to leave *Al's Garage*," he said clearly exasperated with her.

"Make sure. I don't need you guys being spotted near the O'Donnell home at this stage of the game!"

"Don't worry, Vicky. We'll stay put," he retorted, smirking at Kennedy who stood across from him.

But it was clear to Kennedy that Ratner was not ready to listen to Vicky much longer.

~ **32** ~

As Pat and the others headed back to Pakistan, Vicky was hard at work. Within an hour of the phone call, the National Security Agency focal point officer had generated a TOP SECRET cable that went out to the entire Intelligence Community. It described a "conversation" that NSA's huge electronic ears intercepted between Usama bin Laden and al Qaeda operatives in Peshawar. Purportedly, UBL and one of his lieutenants discussed the need to move from the cave complex in Tora Bora to Peshawar. Of course, the conversation occurred over a cell phone—making its triangulation easy to do from space. The National Reconnaissance Office focal point officer received the NSA report and crafted his own intelligence product pinpointing the location of the cell phone call. Within minutes, he had the piercing eyes of imagery satellites trained on the spot. Digital images from space were taken that depicted the same footpath Pat and the other had seen from their helicopter. When the satellite snapped infrared shots of the site, heat patches became visible, as did the two vent shafts that were hidden from the naked eye.

A TOP SECRET report was delivered to the President and the Secretary of Defense within thirty minutes. It was complete with the NSA intercept, the satellite photos, and a notation at the top that read OPERATION CRYSTAL ROUNDUP. The President smiled when he saw the report knowing that the "young major," as he called Pat, had come through for his country. The President buzzed the intercom and told his secretary to get the SECDEF on a secure line right away. The Secretary of Defense had just finished reading the report when the President's call came in.

"Yes, Mr. President. I have read it. Looks like some good intel from our boy wonder."

"Indeed. I want that UBL sonabitch in U.S. custody! What course of action do you recommend?"

"Sir, I'll call CINCCENT and make sure he's seen the non-SAP intelligence reports and tell him to mount an operation to ensnare UBL in the cave and capture him and his cadre."

"Good, but do we have the ground forces in theater right now to do this?"

"Well, we've got a couple of battalions of the 10th Mountain boys out there now. This is well-suited for them. We also have several Special Forces companies. It's really the CINC's call on who to use and how to do it."

"Okay--make sure he takes action soon. From the sound of things, UBL is probably gonna move soon. And listen, if he can't reasonably and safely capture UBL, then I want him dead. I'd want the CINC to smoke his ass--you got that?" the President said sternly.

"Got it, Mr. President. Hell, he can obliterate the side of that mountain if he has to. We may need to use our stealth, satellite-based plasma weapons for the first time."

When the chopper landed at the Islamabad airport, the embassy driver was there to pick them up. Even though it was ice cold outside, all three were sweaty as they removed their helmets and flak vests for the first time. Pat's moist clothes had actually started to freeze slightly and were icy stiff as a result. They headed back to the villa quickly so the colonel could hunt down the C-20 crew to arrange their flight back. It was almost dark in Pakistan when they got back to their quarters. The colonel got on the telephone and rang the officers' rooms but found no one available. He left messages for them to call back ASAP at either at the villa or on his cell phone.

Pat was distraught. He paced the marble floor in the villa, his mind preoccupied with concerns for his family and their safety. He felt helpless being so far away and unable to protect them. His concentration was broken when the colonel's cell phone suddenly rang. His mind raced. He hoped it wasn't Vicky calling with bad news from home.

"Hello. Yes. Uh huh. Well, we need to depart as soon as possible. That's the best they can offer?"

Pat and Woody looked at each other. Pat's face was long and worried. It didn't sound like real promising news.

The colonel continued, "Well let's go with that plan for now, but I want you to keep trying. If I need to call the SECDEF for some leverage, I will. Let me know. Bye."

Colonel Helmsley looked at the others. "Our pilot says the earliest we can leave is late Monday afternoon. It seems the Pakistani President is due to fly out Monday morning, and they have a security quarantine in-place at the airport beginning now."

"Oh my, that's not good news," Woody said consolingly, walking up to put an arm around Pat's shoulder.

He nodded and attempted to smile, mouthing out the word, "Thanks," before walking to his bedroom to think and to pray. He felt so sure the danger to Sara and the children was near, that he wanted to be ready to protect them the moment he returned home. His preparation was to be a spiritual and psychic journey. The closeness he felt to God all his life carried him at this moment. He entered his bedroom in the stately villa, curled up on the bed in a fetal position, and prayed. His spiritual connection with God, the Blessed Virgin, and Saint Michael was incredibly intense, and he knew that if he continued to pray deeply he would drift off into sleep. And once he was asleep he hoped to become a silent psychic sentry standing guard with his family until he could return home to protect them in the flesh.

"Pat, Pat, wake up," the colonel said as he shook his shoulder.

Sunlight had begun filtering into the large bedroom where Pat slept, still curled into a fetal ball, tightly clutching his Saint Michael medallion. The spiritual and psychic workout the day before had drained him so much that Colonel Helmsley shook him for nearly three minutes before he began to stir.

"Huh? What time is it?" he asked, squinting at the clock.

"It's four o'clock in the afternoon. Sunday! Geez, you've been sleeping for almost twenty-four hours! We need to get around and leave here by six. The SECDEF weighed in, and we got clearance to leave at seven o'clock tonight. A lot earlier than we expected, but it will get us home by Monday afternoon."

"Oh, man. That's great news," Pat said as he sat up in the bed. "I'll be ready in no time at all!"

Like clockwork their driver was there at 1800 sharp. Outside were the minivan and hard car that brought them from the airport to the villa just a few days before. The aircrew was already at the plane going through its preflight checklist, enabling them to depart on time. Pat looked around one more time before entering the cabin. He took in one last sight, one last smell of Pakistan, and prayed he never would have to come back.

The three men played several hands of gentlemen's poker while they flew. In between cards and in-flight movies, they managed to rack out and sleep a few hours. During the refueling stop in Italy, Pat checked his watch and roughly calculated it was about 0600 in Virginia. He borrowed Colonel Helmsley's cell phone and called home.

"Hi, Honey, it's me!" he said when Sara picked up and answered in a groggy voice.

"Hey, Baby! When you comin' home?"

"This afternoon, Sorcha. I should be wheels down around two o'clock, so I should be home around the time the kids finish school."

"That's great. We all miss you so much and--"

Pat cut her off. "Sara, listen. This is important! Please be extra careful today. I think someone is following you guys, someone may be after you and the kids. Just be extra vigilant!"

Although he expected to hear her voice again, the last thing Pat heard were two sharp beeps from the phone. He looked at the display which read, *Low Battery*.

"Shit! I hope she got that!" he muttered as he watched the cell phone power itself off.

But unfortunately, back at home Sara was shouting into the phone, "Pat? Pat? What did you say? I didn't hear you. Pat?"

It was almost 1100 in the nation's capitol when FBI agent Bill Kennedy woke in the safe house. He had slept in long past any normal hour for him. He went downstairs only to find it empty. Hank Ratner wasn't there. Despite Vicky's orders, Ratner left the safe house without permission and without informing him.

Kennedy found a note from him on the refrigerator: *Bill, went jogging and to see my "new" girlfriend. Be back early evening. Don't tell Vicky! Ha! Ha! Hank.*

"Great!" Kennedy said out loud.

He thought back to the disturbing comments Ratner had made about Erin and the kiss he blew her on the surveillance monitor. But more unnerving to him was how Vicky would react knowing Ratner had left the safe house despite her orders.

"Well, I had nothing to do with it!" he grumbled as he crumpled the note and tossed it in the trash.

The WFO surveillance team looked at their watches at precisely the same moment as Kennedy found the note. The husband and wife team had been on the job for four full days per instructions. They had seen the O'Donnell children delivered safely to school that morning, and all was well. There was no hostile surveillance detected whatsoever during their watch.

"Well, shall we call it in as mission accomplished?" the female agent asked.

"Let's do it!" the man replied.

The pair radioed in to the WFO that they were off duty and returning to their homes for a mandatory break following the near-constant surveillance they had put in over the past four days, departing the Burke neighborhood as discreetly as they had arrived.

Woody, Pat, and the colonel were awakened by the C-20 communications specialist. "Excuse me, but I've got a secure call from OSI headquarters for Mr. O'Donnell."

She escorted Pat to the front cabin and handed a headset to him. He recognized the voice immediately. It was Lee Cook, his friend and Chief of OSI's Counterintelligence Directorate. Pat began to shake, assuming Lee had brought him bad news about his family.

"Hi, Lee, what's up?"

"You're a hard man to find! Colonel Helmsley's people told me how to call you. Listen, I finally got a hit on that list of cars you gave me to run by my backstop contact in the Bureau."

"Yes, yes, what did you find?" he asked eagerly.

"Well, it was a wild goose chase at first."

"What do you mean?"

"Looking for CIA vehicles! We need to send you back to the basic agent's course to learn the difference between the CIA and FBI!" Lee teased.

"What the hell are you talking about?" Pat asked, his concern growing rapidly.

"There was only one cover vehicle in the list you gave me. It tracked back to the FBI's WFO, not to the CIA. A special purpose surveillance rig of some kind. My contact tells me it was signed out by an agent named Bill Kennedy. He says this guy works in some special secret unit in DC. Maybe Colonel Helmsley will know who he is."

"Lee, are you sure about this? I mean can there be any mistake at all?"

"Sure as I'm sitting here. I hope this helps. Oh, hey, forgot to mention they found the idiot who leaked the reports about bin Laden, some low level State Department analyst! You must be psychic or something! Looks like I owe you a beer."

"Yeah, sure thing. Thanks Lee," Pat said in a monotone as he handed the headset back to the NCO.

He walked back to the colonel and Woody. His face was ashen. He had a distant stare as his mind tried hard to process this new information. *If it hadn't been the CIA that killed Father Reynolds and Detective Sanchez, could it have been the FBI? If it was the FBI, were these people--the two thugs--affiliated with Vicky somehow?*

"What's the matter? Everything all right back home?" Woody asked.

"I'm not sure. Boss, do you know an FBI agent named Bill Kennedy?"

"Kennedy, Kennedy. Sounds familiar. Why?"

"That was Lee Cook with feedback on the cover vehicles I had him run. It turns out the vehicle I spotted doing surveillance in my neighborhood belongs to some special unit in the Bureau. I was wondering if you knew this guy--maybe he works with Vicky."

"Wait a minute. Early on in the operation Vicky introduced me to two of her goons. One was Bill Kennedy, the other Hank Ratner. Black bag operators."

"Sir, I think these are the guys who killed my priest and the detective! It wasn't the CIA after all. No wonder I never got a reading from the Agency's focal point fellow I met at FBI headquarters."

Just then the flight attendant came back and informed them they were beginning their descent into Andrews Air Force Base. They would be on the ground in thirty minutes. He asked them all to buckle up and get ready for the landing.

"Pat, if this is true I need to alert the Justice Department ASAP. We need to round these guys up. Maybe it's them you keep seeing in the form of the disguised man."

"Maybe you're right. But what about Vicky? If these guys work for her, do you think she's authorized the killings?"

"I don't know about Vicky. Anything is possible. I won't alert her myself. I think we need to play this one close to the vest right now."

The colonel was nervous and excited as he pulled his cell phone out. The flight attendant spotted him and rushed back.

"Sir, I'm sorry, but you cannot use the cell phone now. It will interfere with the aircraft's navigation system."

"Screw your rules. This is a priority. Tell the crew to fly VFR," he said looking out the window at the crystal, clear blue sky of the nation's capitol.

The colonel looked at the display.

"Shit! Battery's dead!"

Pat's heart sank. He left his own cell phone in his car since it did not have international calling capability.

Woody reached into his pocket and pulled out a cell phone. "Try mine, John; it should be fully charged."

Colonel Helmsley could not recall the Attorney General's cell phone number since he kept it in his contact list on his dead cell phone. He did his best from memory, once, twice, three times. All wrong numbers. Pat was starting to shake he was so nervous. Finally he recalled he placed the AG's business card in his wallet after entering the information into his cell phone. He yanked it out and carefully dialed, leaving the phone in speaker mode so they all could hear.

"Hello, Ryan, this is John Helmsley, I need to speak with you on an urgent matter!"

"Hello, John, I hope this is a real emergency, I'm on my way to brief the President on the latest in the terror investigation," he said from the backseat of his hard car as his driver cruised along Pennsylvania Avenue toward the White House.

"Ryan, you know me. This is hot. I think we have a couple of rogue FBI agents running around committing murders. Two that I'm sure about, and they may be poised to conduct more."

"I'm listening," Coppock replied, his tone becoming very serious.

Colonel Helmsley related the nuts and bolts of the crimes. He gave the Attorney General information on their possible whereabouts to include Pat's neighborhood and the safe house in Arlington.

"I've got the Director here with me. I'll make sure we yank these guys in until we can sort this out."

"Thanks, Ryan, thanks so much," the colonel said as he hung up.

The ground rose to meet the plane as it dropped out of the sky on final approach. Pat's heart was pounding as he mentally traced his exact route home...how many traffic lights he'd have to get through...alternate routes to take if certain main roads were jammed up. But there was no getting around the Woodrow Wilson Bridge that spanned the Potomac between Maryland and Virginia. If there were to be a chokepoint, the Wilson Bridge would be it. It was a smooth landing. Pat was unbuckled as the plane taxied to the passenger terminal.

"Boss, can you get my bags? I'll get them from you later."

"Sure thing, Pat. And be careful," he said grabbing Pat's arm pulling him back for a final thought. "Remember Kuwait--squeeze the trigger, don't pull. Two rounds, center mass."

Pat smiled for the first time in hours.

"Let's hope I won't have to, but if I do, I'll drop him cold."

~ **33** ~

Pat flew out of the plane as soon as the door opened. He hit the cold tarmac running, frantically trying to recall exactly where he had parked. The lot wasn't large, but he didn't want to waste even a few seconds looking for his car.

His tires squealed as he pulled away. In his head he said some final, silent prayers as he headed home. The traffic was minimal, as he had hoped for.

"Thank you God!" he cried aloud, while racing at high speed along I-95 in Maryland. He looked at his watch. It was 1401. He hoped Sara would be home getting ready to pick up the kids from school at 1445. He powered up his cell phone from his glove box and dialed home. The phone rang and rang until the answering machine picked up.

"Crap!" he muttered loudly upon hearing his own voice announce that no one was home.

Next he dialed her cell phone. It rang several times.

"C'mon Sara, pick up!"

"Hi, Pat!" she said excitedly, pulling a cold set of keys from her purse as she walked through the Springfield Mall parking lot to the minivan.

Pat was relieved to hear her voice.

"Honey, I'm back in the area trying to get over the Wilson Bridge. Is everything okay?"

"I'm fine, what's wrong? Are you still worried about us?"

"Uh huh, and I think you and the kids are in imminent danger. Please go get them at school as soon as you can. Early if possible. Just get them and start driving--drive someplace, anyplace very public."

"Pat you're scaring me!"

"Please, just do it. I'll call you as soon as I get to Burke," he said as he gunned the engine on the Capitol Beltway, jerking in and out of traffic precariously.

"Okay, I will. Hey, I love you Pat," Sara said with a worried tone.

"Love you too, Sorcha. I'll be home soon. Bye."

He hung up and set the phone down on the passenger seat. He approached the two miles or so before the Wilson Bridge and ran into typical pre-rush hour traffic build up. He guided his car expertly to the left shoulder and drove it past honking cars, drivers furious with his boldness. A few even tried to out-position him by nosing their vehicles into the left shoulder as they saw him approach in their side mirrors. Pat honked his horn desperately, flashing his OSI badge as he passed them. He saw the bridge in the distance and began praying it would not raise up to let a passing ship slip by below in the icy Potomac.

Sara walked to her minivan in the frigid parking lot. She cleaned some light snow from the windshield with her gloved hand before opening the door and cranking up the engine. She thought about what Pat had told her, so she rushed back as fast as she could. She was about a mile from the school when her cell phone beeped. When she looked at the screen, she saw a text message from Pat, *Change plans. Meet me @ house b4 picking up kids.*

Unbeknownst to Pat or Sara, in an FBI surveillance sedan parked a block from their home, a black-gloved man had a small black box on his lap connected to a cell phone. And from the cell phone he had tapped out the text message to Sara using Pat's cell phone number as the decoy sender. The man smiled to himself, knowing it would divert her from going directly to the school.

Sara shook her head, confused. Pat rarely used text messages to communicate, but she shrugged it off. Also, given Pat's serious concern when they talked, she didn't want to question anything. She turned left two blocks before reaching the school and headed home. When she pulled into her garage, she saw Pat's sedan wasn't there, so she assumed he had text-messaged her from the road and would be there soon. She did not notice the dark sedan parked about four houses down the block. It was empty.

Sara lowered the garage door and carried a small shopping bag with her into the house. She set it down on the kitchen table. As she rifled through the bag, and pulled out a couple of smaller plastic bags from within, she was unaware of the figure slowly approaching her from behind. It was a tall man in a dark blue jogging suit with ski cap, sunglasses, and scarf. The man raised a large knife up slowly, and just as he was about to thrust it down into Sara's back, she sensed his presence and turned around abruptly.

Sara screamed in horror at the intrusion, instinctively raising both arms above her face to block the knife as it came down fast, slicing her left wrist deeply. She was in horrific pain but continued to block the thrusts as the attacker came at her again and again with the knife. She screamed as loud as she could, sustaining several defensive wounds to her wrists and hands as she painfully fought him off. Precious blood sprayed the kitchen, covering the walls, floor, counters, and table. Sara was getting weaker by the moment as her blood loss began to take its toll on her strength. Suddenly her cell phone rang. It was Pat calling, wanting to check up on her whereabouts, her progress in getting to the school. The ring startled the attacker for a moment. Sara seized the opportunity, and in what little strength she had left, lunged at the man and knocked the knife from his hands. They struggled on the floor, rolling over each other back and forth several times, her blood soaking his dark clothes. She reached the knife before he could get his hands on it again.

Sara held the knife in both hands, weak from lacerations and blood loss, and through the sheer force of gravity managed to drive it into her attacker's right shoulder. He winced in pain and stood up. Sara collapsed and slumped on the floor in a pool of blood. The man pulled the knife from his shoulder and dropped it next to her. He saw Sara's life blood slowly draining from her and left her for dead. His work had only just begun as he left the house and headed for his sedan.

Pat was frantic that he couldn't reach Sara on the telephone. Warm, moist, crimson images began to fill his mind. He tried with all his energy to focus on his family and received disturbing sensations that they were being threatened at that very moment. A sense of blood, lots of it, filled his thoughts. He grabbed his cell phone and called 911 and told the emergency services operator that his wife had been attacked in their home, that she had been stabbed and was dying. He was convinced his impressions were right about this.

He approached the Wilson Bridge where traffic seemed suddenly to be moving slightly faster, leaving nothing for a moment but fifty yards of open space ahead of him...he gunned his engine. At that precise moment, the loud drawbridge claxon began ringing in concert with the lane barriers as they slid inward to stop traffic ahead of the rising decks. Pat swerved hard left and floored the accelerator. The white and red arm with flashing red lights was halfway across his lane when Pat struck it with the front right bumper of his Subaru. He tore the old arm in half sending chunks of wood and metal flying all around, some crashing into the Potomac River below. He spun around several times before his car came to a stop, barely two feet from the deck seam that had begun to widen automatically. He rapidly backed his car up to the point of the arm, straightened the wheel, and was about to gun the engine when two bridge operators came running toward him waving their arms. Undeterred, Pat shot forward as fast as he could make his small car go up the deck, now at a fifteen degree angle, toward the open seam which measured five feet across. The open space threatened to swallow his car as he approached at nearly sixty miles per hour...then airborne. His front tires struck the other side of the bridge hard, making a loud crunch sound. His rear tires barely caught the back edge of the deck, but thankfully his all-wheel-drive system kicked in. His rear tires spun rapidly with a nasty burnt rubber smell and white smoke until they caught the edge, just enough to inch over. Once all four wheels were firmly on the west side of the bridge gap, Pat's car seemed to explode forward as if it had a turbo rocket attached. Onlookers on both sides of the Wilson Bridge stood outside their cars and cheered as if watching a stunt driver on a movie set.

He quickly made the sign of the cross, took a deep breath, and checked his watch. Ten more minutes and the kids would be leaving school. On a normal day it would take him another twenty minutes to get home. But this was anything but a normal day. He gunned the engine, praying to himself that the highway patrol had better places to be at that moment, though he fully expected a BOLO was now out for him. He didn't need a police pursuit to distract him from his mission. He sped along through the growing traffic, sometimes using the shoulder and risking road rage from other drivers. He took the Franconia exit. It meant more lights, but it gave him a straighter shot at the parkway near his home and near the school. He approached the red lights like they were stop signs. He'd coast, glance quickly, and then fly through them when it was safe. By pure luck, or by the presence of angels, Pat was never at risk of an accident, and no police cars were to be seen that afternoon.

As he approached the last block near the school, he saw buses making their treks back through the subdivisions to return children home for the day. He realized school had been out for about four minutes already. He raced up the circular driveway and came to a screeching halt in front of the flagpole. And just like in his dream, he saw Sean standing there, backpack in place, sobbing softly. Pat flew out the door, leaving it open. He rushed to his son, knelt down, and hugged him.

"Sean! I'm so happy you're okay. Where's Mommy?"

"She didn't come today, Daddy. She's never late. Where is she?"

"I'm not sure Buddy, but where's Erin?" Pat asked, suddenly realizing his daughter should be with Sean waiting for Sara.

"The evil man in the disguise took her, Daddy. Just like I told you he would."

"When? What kind of car? Where did they go?"

"A dark blue car. Same one like you used to drive to work in the last place we lived. They went that way," Sean said pointing toward the Parkway on-ramp.

"Sean, listen. This is very important. Run inside and stay with the principal or a teacher. Tell them there's been a family emergency, okay?"

"Okay, Daddy, please be careful," Sean said, giving Pat a big hug.

He jumped back into his sedan. He had a hunch they would head east on the Parkway, back toward the District or Maryland, but he needed more. He gathered together all the power he could and in his mind searched the Parkway for dark blue Chevy Lumina sedans...the exact kind of car he drove when he was the OSI commander in South Carolina. And then he found it. As clear in his mind as the overhead images Colonel Helmsley could produce on his magic van computer screen, there was a dark blue Lumina. It was heading east, nearing the Springfield Mall, about five minutes ahead of him.

Pat flew down the Parkway in hot pursuit. The sedan was moving surprisingly slowly. He surmised it meant the FBI thug--Ratner or Kennedy--was confident he had gotten away with it all. Pat was closing in on him as he drove like a madman, his speed sometimes reaching 90 miles per hour as he flew along. The distance was growing shorter and shorter now, and as he approached to within 100 yards of the sedan, his mental image faded away only to be replaced by the real image of the car in front of him. He came up behind it fast, directly behind it now. His first instinct was to ram it from behind, but he knew there was precious cargo on board...his baby girl Erin. Pat swung left and pulled up evenly with the driver, honking his horn. The man looked over, and through the disguise, Pat could tell the driver recognized him. They were approaching an area known as Kingstowne, where the Parkway ended, and where traffic was reduced down to two much slower lanes.

Pat saw his break. He hit the gas and forced himself in front of the sedan as traffic slowed for a light. The car was trapped now. He unleashed his Beretta from his fanny pack and jumped out of his vehicle, taking what little cover he could from his car parked at a slight angle. He aimed the gun at the driver's face.

"Get out of the car now! Keep your hands where I can see them," he ordered loudly.

The driver's door popped open slowly. He saw one sneakered foot step out, then another. As the driver stood up, coming out of the vehicle, Pat saw he was holding Erin in front of him as a shield. Erin's face had blood all over it, from her attacker's wound, but Pat didn't know that. He assumed Erin had been hurt in some way. His heart felt like it would explode. His mouth went dry like cotton.

"Put her down!" he commanded.

"Daddy! Daddy! Help me, Daddy!" Erin cried, tears streaming down her frightened, blood covered face.

Pat's aim was directly on Erin's face. Center mass on the kidnapper. He knew that if he set Erin down, he would have a clear shot should the attacker decide to come at him.

"Put her down now!" Pat screamed again.

The man began to lower Erin slowly, never taking his eyes off him. Pat held his aim perfectly. *Squeeze the trigger, don't pull. Two shots. Center mass*, he repeated in his head, recalling the words of his former boss. Pat's stance and his grip on the Beretta were textbook perfect. As Erin's feet were about to hit the ground, he caught a momentary glimpse of dark black metal. The man had been hiding a gun behind her. When Erin hit the asphalt, she bolted and ducked behind the Lumina. And when she bolted, the man seemed to turn the gun toward Pat.

In slow motion sequence Pat's aim became natural. The front and rear sights of his semiautomatic came into crystal-clear focus. As they did, the image of the attacker became fuzzy. In an instant it all made sense to him. Pat's psychic images of the attacker and his face becoming fuzzy were images he had of this moment when the attacker became his target...in total silence. The screeching tires of cars braking, and screaming drivers running from them, faded out along with the approaching wail of police car sirens racing to the scene.

As soon as the man was reduced to a fuzzy mass, Pat squeezed the trigger. A gentle, relaxed squeeze. The first round reached its target dead center mass before the man had a chance to fire his weapon. It was followed by a second round that struck the man's chest about a half inch to the right of the first entry point. The 9 mm copper ball rounds flattened perfectly as they pierced the man's chest, widening as they coursed through his vital organs. Then he fell backwards to the ground.

Pat approached him cautiously, never taking his aim from the man, ready to fire two more rounds if necessary. He kicked the man's gun underneath the Lumina. It was a .40 caliber Glock, standard FBI-issued handgun. The man wasn't dead yet. He was trying to speak. Pat leaned down.

"Why, Patrick? Why?"came the familiar voice.

Pat felt a sickening jolt run through his spine at that moment. He pulled off the ski cap and blond curls spilled all around the attacker's head. It was Vicky.

"I just wanted for us to be together. You, me, and Erin," she cried in slow painful spasms.

"Vicky, I don't understand. Why?"

"I love you, Patrick. I wanted a family I never could have. Pray with me, Patrick," she urged, her voice faltering, gloved hands trembling, blood oozing from a corner of her mouth.

Pat made the sign of the cross and together he and Vicky prayed a Hail Mary. She could barely get her words out, but she seemed to follow along with him.

He held her hand tightly as they prayed, and when he said aloud, "Holy Mary, mother of God, pray for us sinners, now and at the hour of our death," Vicky let out her last breath, and her soul departed the earth.

All the while the scene unfolded, the invisible Saint Michael stood sentry next to Pat, ready to assist if needed. And the Blessed Virgin's spirit was holding Erin in her arms, caressing her hair, comforting her, and making sure Pat succeeded in his mission. Just as she had promised.

~ **34** ~

"Say cheese!" Colonel Helmsley directed, holding a digital camera in his hands. Woody made sure to stay out of the picture, jumping behind him when he saw the camera come out of his jacket pocket.

Pat and the O'Donnell kids were in position, posing next to Sara's hospital bed. She tried her best to smile without giggling too hard. Her arms were bandaged tightly, and IVs still pumped fluids and antibiotics into her bloodstream even one week after she was rescued by the Fairfax County Police Department at her home. She had lost a lot of blood, and was near death when they found her, but they made it just in time. The room was full of flowers, cards, and balloons, and well wishers and visitors never stopped buzzing in and out. Pat practically hadn't left her side.

"Can I talk with you for a moment, Pat?" the colonel asked.

"I'll stay here with the kids and Sara," Woody said.

The two men took a walk down a quiet and empty hall in the Inova Fairfax Hospital.

"Well, it turns out Ratner and Kennedy did kill Father Reynolds and the detective," he informed him. "Those two knuckleheads left behind enough forensic evidence placing themselves at the crime scenes to ensure they will be locked up for a long time!"

"Amazing," Pat said. "And they did a good job of making everyone believe it was the CIA. Where are Ratner and Kennedy now?" Pat asked.

"In jail. Cooling their heels. The Attorney General is mulling a variety of prosecution options between the federal government and the State of Virginia. No matter what, those two idiots won't be getting out of jail any time soon."

Pat smiled. "I guess I just don't get Vicky. I mean, all along I thought this menacing force I picked up was part of some elaborate government conspiracy, like in the movies, or in a novel."

The colonel nodded. "I know. But in the end it was all about pure human emotion. Love. Jealousy. Her desire to be a mother following the loss of her own baby girl drove her to such an extreme. I told you Vicky was complex. I guess she was far more complex than any of us really knew."

Pat shook his head. "So what's going to happen to CRYSTAL ROUNDUP now that the Justice Department side of it seems wiped out?"

"Well, I never told you this Pat, but I put in my retirement papers six months ago. It usually takes a year to work the actual retirement date, but I've got a little pull you know," he said with a wink.

"What are you saying?"

"I'm saying the Attorney General has asked me to head up the program. I retire next month. And start at Justice a week later."

"That's fantastic, Boss!" Pat said excitedly.

"Well, the first order of business is to clean up the program. The President has weighed in heavily on some of the less-than-perfect ethical aspects of the way it was run. I've promised him and the AG a clean, above-board operation."

"That's encouraging after all that's happened."

"Listen, Pat. We need you. The info you gave on UBL panned out perfectly. Unfortunately, CENTCOM didn't have its act together and waited too long to mount a search and capture operation. We even fired up the plasma satellites and ripped through the mountain where you said he was holed up. You probably saw the news about the 'earthquake' in the Tora Bora region," the colonel said with a chuckle.

"UBL fled to Peshawar as predicted. Now he's even harder to find."

"I bet the President was pissed," Pat noted as they walked along the sterile hallway, their steps making small echoes off the marble floor.

"He sure was. His orders were clear, but the CENTCOM Commander was too cautious, and missed the window."

"Can I have some time to think about it? To be honest, finding UBL was fun and all, but I think my true calling is in finding children, the way this all began."

"We'll take it slow. We'll take it slow."

Just then they heard Sean's squeaky voice come up from behind. "Boo!" he shouted trying to startle the men.

Pat swooped him up and gave him a big hug. "Hey, Buddy, you know you're not supposed to sneak up on people, don't you?" he said, tickling his belly.

"I know. Sorry," he giggled.

"I'll leave you men alone. Let's go get a beer sometime soon, Pat. We both need it!" the colonel said with a wave as he headed back to Sara's room.

"What were you and the colonel talking about, Daddy?"

"Oh, nothing. Just boring work stuff. Listen Sean, let's play a little guessing game," Pat suggested.

"What, Daddy?"

"I'm going to think of a number in my head from one to a hundred. Can you tell me what it is?"

"Sure," Sean said, bubbling with confidence.

"Okay, here goes!"

But instead of thinking of a number, Pat conjured up in his head an image of a field of green shamrocks as far as the eye could see.

Sean closed his eyes tightly, obviously concentrating hard on the task at hand.

"You're tricking me, Daddy!" he cried in protest.

"What do you mean?"

"There's more than a hundred numbers. There's millions of them. Green and green and green numbers," he cried. "And they're soft and wet, and they taste like sour apple!"

"Pretty good," Pat said, nodding his head and beaming with pride.

"And, Daddy, I heard you tell the colonel about finding bin Laden. But if you want my advice, stick to finding kids. You're a good terrorist finder, but you're a great child finder."

Pat smiled as he walked along, holding his boy tighter than he could remember holding him in many, many, many months.